NIGHT SHADE & OAK

Something was seriously wrong. I slumped to the ground, unable to carry on. Belis, who had been plodding along behind me, caught up in a moment.

"What is it?" she asked, looming over me like a storm cloud.

"I think this body is dying," I said, clutching my chest. "The heart is beating so fast I think it's going to just explode. My lungs feel like they've been peeled raw but also somehow like there's a wasp nest inside my ribcage. My stomach hurts, my legs, my thighs, my calves are burning, literally. I think they might be on fire. You'd better go on without me. If my soul makes it to Annwn I'll tell the lord you're coming."

Belis bent down and took me by the arm. She pulled me to my feet with no discernible effort and brushed the chalk dust off my cloak.

"You're not dying," she said. "You're just a little out of breath."

By Molly O'Neill

Greenteeth

Nightshade and Oak

MOLLY O'NEILL

NIGHT SHADE & OAK

ORBIT

First published in Great Britain in 2026 by Orbit

1 3 5 7 9 10 8 6 4 2

Copyright © 2026 by Molly O'Neill

Excerpt from *Swordheart* by T. Kingfisher
Copyright © 2018 by Ursula Vernon

The moral right of the author has been asserted.

*All characters and events in this publication, other than those
clearly in the public domain, are fictitious and any resemblance
to real persons, living or dead, is purely coincidental.*

All rights reserved.
No part of this publication may be reproduced, stored in a
retrieval system, or transmitted, in any form or by any means, without
the prior permission in writing of the publisher, nor be otherwise circulated
in any form of binding or cover other than that in which it is published
and without a similar condition including this condition being
imposed on the subsequent purchaser.

A CIP catalogue record for this book
is available from the British Library.

ISBN 978-0-356-52263-0

Typeset in Apollo by M Rules
Printed and bound in Great Britain by Clays Ltd, Elcograf, S.p.A.

Papers used by Orbit are from well-managed forests
and other responsible sources.

Orbit
An imprint of
Little, Brown Book Group
Carmelite House
50 Victoria Embankment
London EC4Y 0DZ

The authorised representative
in the EEA is
Hachette Ireland
8 Castlecourt Centre
Dublin 15, D15 XTP3, Ireland
(email: info@hbgi.ie)

An Hachette UK Company
www.hachette.co.uk

orbit-books.co.uk

for Ally

Chapter 1

I had run a hundred leagues by the time the moon had risen. The night sky glittered above me as I paused at the eastern end of the Chalk, listening to the wind whistle along the escarpment. The dogs settled around me, flopping to the ground and panting loudly. I stretched, reaching up to the harvest moon so that all the vertebrae in my back seemed to pop apart. I dropped my arms and swung them around, bouncing on the balls of my bare feet.

The dogs formed a white fur carpet along the ground and the leader, Dormath, snuffled at the pockets of my tunic, hoping for a snack. I pulled them out to show him they were empty, and he yawned in disgust and plopped down next to me. I laughed, the wind catching the sound and whipping it away from me, down the slopes of the high Chalk towards the bloodstained grass of the valley below us.

I could feel them, the dead and the dying, out there in the darkness. Many had passed on swiftly, but some had lingered, lost and confused, not knowing the way. Any humans still living would be fleeing the battlefield, seeking out shelter in tents and around campfires. They feared the wandering souls of the fallen, the cold hands of ghosts both Roman and Briton creeping through the night. But I feared nothing, not even the dead. I was here for them.

Since I was called into being, many seasons past, I have guided untold numbers of exhausted souls, setting them on the path to Annwn, the afterworld. Most go easily, eager to find rest. Some fight, some curse, some threaten. They all go west in the end, for I am Mallt Y Nos, the Nightshade, Goddess of Death, and no soul on this island has ever escaped me. They go west, beyond the sinking sun, and none have ever returned to this mortal world.

I lingered a little longer on the hillside. Not because I dreaded the work ahead of me in the valley – blood worried me as little as water. No, I stayed because the night was beautiful, the wind was clear and cool, and the dead would wait for me. I had passed innumerable nights like this, perched up on the high places of the world, the dogs at my feet, the wind tugging at my clothes and rippling through my long black hair.

I dug my toes into the thin grass of the Chalk, enjoying the softness of the dusty rock.

Dormath shuffled a little closer to my side and I rested my hand on his back, stroking the pale, silky fur. The others pricked up their red ears, always alert for any special treatment their brother might be getting. I knew that they would already be smelling the blood on the battlefield – the iron and earth stench of it.

I heard a horn blowing in the distance, deep and eerie, and glimpsed huge, elongated shadows moving along the horizon. The Wild Hunt were abroad tonight. I strained my eyes but even my immortal sight couldn't discern more than the vague feeling of their shapes against the sky. I knew Gwyn ap Nudd would be leading them home from the battle. There would be feasting at his court tonight, as there always was after the mortals battled. I flexed my toes again and stood up. I had a long night's work ahead of me, but time moved differently with the Hunt. If I finished my task before dawn, I could run down the Wild Roads to wherever he and his queen had made camp and join in the celebrations. I wouldn't mind spending a little time with the Hunt this evening, perhaps courting one or two of the beautiful and unkind fae.

I ruffled Dormath's ears.

"Come on, boy, we've tarried long enough. There is much to do."

He yawned again at me then stretched out luxuriously and barked at his fellows. They jumped up, yipping and yelping at each other and causing general confusion. I stepped through them, sniffing the air for the scent of souls and blood. I gazed out at the glittering plains and considered my approach.

I would go down to the south-eastern corner of the battlefield and wind my way west and north as I tended to the dead. I called to the dogs, and they fell silent, forming a long line at my side. I took one last breath of the clean Chalk air and took off down the hill at a sprint.

The world tilted around me as I ran, down steep slopes and sharp river gullies. I didn't fall, I sprinted, each bound propelling me forward as I ran faster and faster. A human would have tripped, breaking an ankle at the least, a neck at worst, but my feet were sure. I felt the wind lift my hair and stream it behind me, rippling like a war banner.

The dogs trailed after me, baying as loud as Gwyn's war horns with the joy of the Hunt. They galloped along, legs outstretched, trying to overtake me. I laughed for the joy of the chase and sped up, pulling away from them though they howled.

I reached the base of the Chalk and rocketed forward, finding my pace over the rolling fields, dodging between hedges and great spreading oaks. I felt cold stone beneath my feet as we passed over the new Roman road that pointed north and heard the claws of the dogs skittering on the stone slabs. We were close now, the iron stench of blood burning in my nostrils. I could feel the dogs' energy change and sensed my own heartbeat quickening in my chest in anticipation. Then we were there and even the dogs pulled up in shock.

The field of battle was wide, tilted down towards the north from where I stood. I thought I recognised the place. A few weeks before it had been a meadow full of long grass and waist-high wildflowers. Now it was a marsh, the grass ripped up and the soil churned into a mire of mud and blood. Broken chariots were scattered across the field, wheels still spinning in the wind.

Spears and javelins forested the ground, forming spiky clusters where once cornflowers had bloomed. The smell was terrible, blood and shit and sweat, all mixed in with smoke and the bitter reek of the earth. Bodies were strewn everywhere, still fresh enough to twitch. A few were Roman, their gleaming metal armour and proud crests of horsehair spattered with mud. Most of them were Britons, men and women both, dressed in woollen trousers and leather boots.

Moonlight glinted on golden torcs, silver earrings, red blood.

There were thousands of them, tens of thousands. This was the end of the Firebrand's rising, I thought to myself. The Romans had crushed the rebellious tribes of the Iceni and the Trinovantes, ground any hope of resistance into the dirt for a generation at least. That cheered me a little: the massacres at Londinium and Camulodunum had resulted in months of long nights for me. Tonight was the worst of it, but would be the last of those for years to come.

There was a mewling sound by my feet. I looked down. A Briton was half curled into a ball, cradling the bloody stump where his left hand had been. From the shield still clutched in his right I could see he was one of the Trinovantes, and I remembered all of his clan brothers and sisters that I had helped over the past thousand years. He turned to peer up at me and I saw he had lost half his face, the exposed eyeball swivelling in the night air. I crouched down and laid a hand on his cheek.

"Come," I whispered, then strengthened my voice into a command. "Come." I lifted my hand from his face and pulled. His soul came free easily and his body shuddered and fell still, now no more than so much cooling flesh. I cupped the silvery fragment of light that had been the man's hopes and dreams, his shame and his fury, everything that had brought him here to die in this field of ruined flowers. I lifted it to my mouth and blew. The breeze caught the soul and carried it up and away. I watched as it floated off, slow at first, but then the pull of the afterworld caught it, and it vanished from sight. I could still feel it as it drifted, flowing westwards, riding the wind to Annwn.

An easy start. The man had wanted to be free of his agony but had not known how to let go. I clicked my tongue and the dogs fanned out around me in a wide arc. I whistled and they leapt forward, fae-quick, running in looping circles around the battlefield. Even all two dozen of them could not cover the whole space but they barked as they ran, snapping at the air. I sensed the lingering spirits drawing back from the edges of the carnage. Good. I had enough to do tonight without traipsing after some poor tribesman's soul before it twisted itself into something dark and horrific and started eating his countrymen.

I squared my shoulders and set off across the field. On average only one in twenty or so dead or dying had trouble departing and needed my assistance, but when the slain were as numerous as this I had thousands to release. I passed quickly, trailing my long fingers over hideous wounds and shattered bones, helping the souls trapped by pain to find their way out of their bodies and into the cool night air. I had stopped noticing the foul smell of the slaughter, focusing only on my work.

A handful of the Roman casualties were also in need of my aid. I paused at the first of them and looked down. He looked no older than twenty and a bronze amulet dangled from his fingers, bloody from where he had tried to hold in his intestines. I trapped his soul in my hands and called for Dormath. He broke off from the loop and padded over to me, his jaws dripping with gore.

"That better have been from one of the horses," I said to him sternly. He wagged his tail, and I decided not to check.

"Here, watch this for me," I said, floating over the Roman's soul. He bounced it off the top of his head and whined as I turned back to look for more.

Dormath shepherded the Roman souls in a separate group as I picked my way through the field, dashing around and preventing them from wandering. When I was satisfied I had found them all, I whistled to him again and he sat down, following the wispy shapes with a yellow-eyed gaze in case one dared make a break for it. I reached out and touched them. They were panicked, lost in a foreign land. I could tell these were soldiers who had not expected to die, they had not prepared themselves for death. I used a little of my magic to summon a breeze and lifted each of the souls onto it. Then I took a deep breath and pushed out, sending all of them south, back over the sea to the continent, to whatever afterlife they had believed in.

I watched them disappear then turned back. Dormath was rummaging in the ruins of a gilded chariot. I could tell from the way he was moving that he had found something else to eat. I sighed and went over. The owner of the chariot had apparently decided to take half a roasted chicken into the battle, presumably against the risk of feeling peckish as he rode down the legions. Dormath was wolfing it down as if he hadn't eaten in days. I grabbed him by the scruff of his neck and tried to fish the chicken out.

"Give me that, you'll choke on the bones!"

Dormath wriggled out of my grip and streaked away from me, rejoining his brothers as they ran endless circuits. A chicken leg dangled from his jaws. I considered going and catching him. I was the faster even if he was more agile, but there was still so much to do. I gave him the eye and turned back to my labour.

I soon gave up on my hopes of joining the Wild Hunt's celebrations as it was becoming clear that I would be working all night, would struggle even to finish before the sun came up. I was as at ease in daylight as in the dark, but soon the humans would start to trickle back to the battlefield, looking to loot the bodies or search for loved ones. I disliked live humans; I had no business with them before they died, and the dogs were prone to chasing them.

The eastern sky was beginning to blush with the light of a red dawn by the time I had finished combing the battlefield. Crows and ravens were clustering in the trees to the west of me, waiting for the dogs and me to leave. They would have a feast ahead of them, I thought, there would be enough meat to stuff every bird south of the Pennines. The thought didn't bother me, death would always lead to life. I straightened up from the last body, a pale-haired Iceni woman who had been split almost in half.

I sent her soul into the air and called the dogs to heel. They rushed at me, panting and wagging their tails. I bent down and patted them, enjoying how the doggish smell blocked out the stink of blood.

"Come on then, are we done? Ready to go again?" In my mind I was already planning out the next journey, intending to head north. Boudica's rebellion had occupied so much of my time of late that I had been forced to neglect the northern and western lands and there were bound to be souls there who needed my help. I would run through the woods taking a more circuitous path than I would at night, in order to avoid settlements. I flexed my toes and bobbed up and down again. The sun was threatening to rise at any moment, so I put the battlefield to my back and set off.

I had barely reached the edge of the trees when I felt something. A soul in pain, near death but too tangled up in itself to die. I slowed and looked back at the dogs.

"One more, then."

I followed the sense of anguish into the woods. The morning light was quickly blocked out by the leaves, and I found myself darting between the trees in almost total darkness. There was something else alongside the pain I was sensing, a kind of pressure, causing my ears to pop repeatedly as I approached. Dormath growled a little and I almost tripped over as he dashed in front of me, a pale blur in the gloom.

I moved closer and identified the cause of the pressure. It was magic. A strange kind of magic but magic nevertheless. I was used to my own power, and I knew well the enchantments and tricks of the fae, both high and low. This was different, imprecise and weak, though its meagre strength was building. It reminded me of the earth spells the druids had woven, using blood and tree sap to paint ancient symbols through which to channel their incantations. Ah! I knew it now. Witchcraft. I rarely saw witches or wizards; they almost never needed my assistance in finding the final path. I had heard of them, though, and I was surprised to find one whose power hadn't been diminished by whatever was killing her.

It was nothing to worry me, though, so I kept going, crunching twigs and leaves under my feet. The magic was growing as I neared, building in my ears and in my nose. Dormath sneezed and growled again.

A small glade appeared in front of me, well grassed and open to the dawn sky above. The light was a pinkish gold, bathing the slender elm trees and making the beads of dew sparkle like quartz in granite. I searched for the dying witch. A tall woman sprawled at the base of one of the trees, her long red hair splayed out around her. I moved out into the open and sniffed but her soul had long since gone. There was a sharp intake of breath from the side of me and I turned.

There were two more women in the shadows, one stretched on the ground beneath a spreading oak, her hand pressed to a bloody wound in the front of her dress, the other, barely more than a girl, crouched by her head. I moved a little closer, tasting the agony and confusion of death on the air. I had not bothered to glamour myself or the dogs and I heard the dying woman's breath catch in her throat. I waved to the dogs to stay back and knelt in front of her, reaching out a hand to touch her face. I noticed she was muttering something, her lips moving in a blur even as she stared at me.

I smiled at her, thinking she was probably praying. A calming habit for humans, though it didn't make much difference to me. The other girl leaned forward just as I laid my hand on the dying woman's forehead. I saw her open her mouth to protest, even as my palm brushed the skin.

There was a huge crash as the magic I had sensed exploded, ballooning out to encompass the three of us. I reached for the woman's soul, but it pulled back at me, draining power through the channel I had opened. I wrenched my hand back and there was a great cracking sound. I smelled burned metal and salt as I was flung backwards, my body arcing through the air until I hit something solid, and then there was nothing but blackness.

 Chapter 2

A human was groaning in pain somewhere close to me. They were making a terrible fuss; the sound was like an injured cow. I wished they would stop. There was some kind of problem with my head, and I needed to focus on it. I opened my mouth to tell them to be quiet when I realised the moaning was coming from me. This feeling in my head was ... pain? It was different from the sympathetic agony I was used to sensing from the dying, sharper and more debilitating. I could barely focus my thoughts. They seemed blurred and slow.

I reached up a hand and felt a new bump on the back of my head. It was sore, sending fresh waves of discomfort through me when I poked at it. I prodded it again, just to confirm I wasn't imagining it. I groaned again, without meaning to. No, it was definitely real. How strange, I had never injured myself before.

I cracked open my eyes and looked up. The sky was a very bright, very pale blue overhead, painted with long streaks of white clouds. Mid-morning at the very earliest. I must have been unconscious for a while. I tried to sit up, but my legs weren't working the way they ought to and as I raised my head the throbbing got worse.

"Oh," came a voice from my left and a figure appeared above me. It was definitely human and seemed strangely familiar.

Coppery hair framed a face covered in a truly astonishing number of freckles that made the grey-green eyes now looking down at me seem even brighter by comparison. I frowned and the face tilted to one side.

"You're awake, then? I thought you might be about to die." The woman didn't seem particularly bothered by the idea. "Here." She shoved out a hand. I inspected it, noticing the skin on the back of her arms was just as freckled as her face, then knocked it aside and sat up, making a great effort to ignore the pain in my head. My vision blurred and I swayed, suddenly unable to make the world stay still around me. I pushed through the vertigo and forced my vision to sharpen.

I inspected my surroundings. I was in a small forest clearing, the ground covered in grass and studded with daisies. I couldn't see my dogs anywhere, though that wasn't unusual; they were prone to wandering. As I looked around, I spotted another woman, lying dead between meandering tree roots.

My memories slotted into place: the trapped soul, the two other women, the magic. I snapped back to the freckled woman, still kneeling beside me. I struggled to my feet, clutching onto the tree trunk to stay steady, and looked for the third human, the dying one. She was lying near where I had seen her last night, still and pale. The freckled woman grabbed for my arm, but I threw her off and stomped over to the side of the glade, eager to do my duty and then leave.

Or I tried to. I managed the first stride, but with my second I felt my foot land on something incredibly sharp. I wobbled and fell, clutching my injured foot. I inspected the sole, finding a scrape in the soft flesh, and looked around for the cause. It must be an enchanted dagger, a knife of obsidian, something powerful that should not be left lying around. There was a rather angular stone beside me, but I had never been hurt by something so paltry before.

"What is this?" I said aloud, massaging my foot. The freckled woman looked over at me, her face blank with confusion.

"Well, if you will insist on walking about barefoot, what

do you expect?" Her tone was unsympathetic and more than a little rude.

I glared at her; humans were usually more polite when they addressed me. I still didn't understand what had happened to my sole. I always went barefoot.

A mystery for later. Now I wanted to leave. I hauled myself up again and set off for the dying woman, walking more tentatively this time. There was still something not quite right; my balance seemed off, and I was taking shorter steps than usual. It seemed to take an age to reach her side, and my muscles felt stiff and sore. I bent down next to the third woman, no more than a girl really, reaching out to touch her cheek.

It was warm and smooth, strange for someone on the brink of death. I listened but I couldn't hear her heartbeat, nor sense the condition of her spirit. Her chest was still and she wasn't breathing. I slid my hand under her chin, feeling for a pulse.

"Don't touch her," said the freckled one behind me. I ignored her again. There was no pulse that I could feel. I pressed my finger a little deeper, wanting to check I was not mistaken.

Something grabbed my arm and yanked me away.

"I said, don't touch my sister." She had grabbed my wrist, holding it in an iron grip. I tried to shake her off, but all my writhing had no effect. I turned to look at her properly for the first time.

She was tall, towering over me, and I was taller than most humans. I could see the muscles wrapping around her arms like ivy. Tall and strong as she was, she shouldn't have been able to pull me around like that. Something was wrong. I replayed my memories; the girl had been dying, brutally injured, I was sure of that. Now she was healed and not quite dead. It didn't make any sense.

"Who are you?" asked the woman, still holding my arm. I summoned up all the dignity I had and glared at her.

"I am Mallt Y Nos, Mallt of the Night. The Nightshade. I am the Shepherd of the Dead and Dying. I have been easing souls to Annwn since your grandmother's grandmother was a girl.

I am darkness, I am endless. Now, would you kindly let go of my arm!"

Her mouth fell open, and she stared at me. Then she let go of my arm and laughed. Peals of laughter echoed off the trees as the freckled woman bent almost in half, leaning on her knees and wheezing.

"You, the Nightshade, I can't, I can't." She broke off into further laughter. I rubbed my arm where she had gripped it, trying to soothe the circulation back.

"I am Mallt Nightshade," I said, unhappily aware that my voice was a little reedier than normal. She looked up at me again then snorted.

"You should be careful taking her name like that, a chit like you. The real Mallt is not to be trifled with. My word, and I thought I'd never laugh again."

"I am the real Mallt," I insisted. She straightened up and looked at me, her eyes skimming up and down, levity vanished. I wondered if it had been more a release of stress than real mirth.

"Mallt of the Night is ancient and beautiful, a goddess of dark mercy," she said, eyes stony. "She is said to be tall and slender as a young sapling, surrounded always by the Cwn Annwn, the hounds of hell. No disrespect to you, whoever you are, but you look like half the starved farm girls in Britain. You couldn't walk two steps across the clearing without tripping. How would you run from mountain to moor to guide the souls of the dead?"

"Firstly, I don't usually trip," I said, ignoring the rest of her insulting talk. "Secondly, the dogs were around here somewhere, they've probably just wandered off."

I pursed my lips to call them to me with my customary whistle, high and clear. It didn't come out as loud as usual. I waited for the dogs to appear from the shadows and bound towards me, but there was nothing, and the freckled woman rolled her eyes and turned back to her sister. I followed her, looking around for my companions. At the woman's feet lay a pile of fur.

"Dormath!" I yelped, falling to my knees. He rolled over and yipped at me, looking sleepy but otherwise unharmed. I felt a little of the panic subside, but where were the others?

"What have you done to the rest of them? There should be more," I hissed, turning back to her. I rarely got angry but when I did fae lords had been known to turn tail and run. This woman didn't so much as flinch from my fury.

"I haven't done anything to your stupid dogs. This one was here when I woke up. I haven't even touched him." She leaned over, peering at Dormath. "What breed is he? He looks big enough to be a wolf, but I've never seen one with that colouring. Pale fur, red ears, almost like . . ."

"I told you, he's one of the Cwn Annwn, my hunting hounds."

The woman glanced up at me again. "I could almost believe he was. But how can you be Mallt? You don't look like much, you're not even that tall."

"I am tall," I said, "you're just a giant. Not a real giant, I mean, although you could be. You're just taller than most humans. And I'm not human, can't you tell? Doesn't my face glow with ineffable beauty?"

The woman pressed her lips together, a smirk tugging at the corner of her mouth. She shook her head.

"No. I mean, not that you're not, I mean I wouldn't say ineffable." She seemed to be floundering a little. "But I'm not that tall. I'm big for a woman but I'm not nearly a giant. Half the men in my tribe are taller than me. You're just short."

I sighed. "Look, pointed ears." I tucked my hair back to show her. "Humans have sweet little round ears, no?"

She leaned forward. Her brows furrowed, like two ginger caterpillars inching together across her face.

"You have rounded ears," she said, almost apologetically.

I frowned, reaching up to touch my ears. The slanted points at the top had gone, rounded down. They felt wrong. This was why I couldn't hear that woman's heartbeat. I could barely hear anything. Mysteries began to slot into place: my hearing was weakened, my sight, too. I couldn't walk on sharp stones without pain, my strides seemed shorter.

I looked back at the freckled woman. I held out my arms, noting with horror how my tunic hung loosely where once it had fitted tightly.

"Something's happened to me, I'm not me any more." She nodded at me, still baffled by my reaction.

"What happened last night? I came to help. There was some kind of magic in the air."

She looked uncomfortable, shifting from one foot to the other.

"Magic is forbidden to all but the druids. It would not be appropriate for a daughter of my house to ..." She caught my eye and swallowed. "Yes, I was trying to help my sister. She was very grievously injured in the battle. I thought to heal her. My mother said it was a waste of time, that I should take poison with her rather than risk capture."

A healing spell shouldn't have had any effect on me, I thought, and from the glimpse I had caught of the injuries the night before it would have had to be incredibly strong to save her.

"Tell me exactly the spell you used," I said. "Leave nothing out."

She began to reel off the enchantment. It was in a very old dialect of Brittonic, old to her anyway. It wasn't quite a spell of healing, more a compulsion. There was a crux in the words that I thought she might have misheard, that would change the effect to suck in life from others rather than encourage the body to heal itself. I replayed the dim memories again. She must have pulled at my own power rather than hers, through the channel I had opened to free her sister's soul.

"Ah," I said when she finished. "Well, you're very lucky. That spell would have drained the life out of you to heal her. If I hadn't interceded you'd have healed her and died yourself."

She froze, stealing a look at her sister. I thought I detected a flash of guilt in her expression.

Probably some sort of survivor's remorse. I'd seen it before among humans.

"Unfortunately for me," I continued, "I appear to have lost my own power in her curing."

"You seem very calm," she ventured, taking a step closer to me. I backed away from her, turning so she could not see my face. If I had no power I was no longer me, no longer a goddess. I thought about my foot, my blurred vision. The answer loomed into my mind as inescapable as death itself. I was human.

Anger flooded through my body, red-hot and resentful.

"I am not calm," I said, turning back to face her. "I am trying to restrain myself from murdering you. You have absolutely no idea what you've done, the souls that will suffer without me to guide them. It's bad enough that this damned rebellion has distracted me from my regular work. I am already behind on my rounds, having been forced to spend my time on your battlefields. Now this."

She recoiled a bit from my glare but not as much as I felt appropriate. Clod-brained mortal. I waved a hand in dismissal.

"Go, you have caused enough damage. Tend to your sister and leave me in peace. I must figure out how to undo your mess."

My words would have banished any other human, ringing in their ears 'til their dying day, but this woman didn't so much as flinch. My heart constricted as I heard how small and weak my voice sounded.

I sat back down on the stony ground and rested my head in my hands. There must be a way out of this. I needed to go to Annwn and consult with the lord of the afterworld. He might be able to restore me. How to get there, though? It was an hour's run from here in my old body but somehow I doubted this mortal form could cover three hundred miles that fast. I could call on a friend. I had many old allies among the fae who would be willing to help. None of them lived in this particular part of the island, though, and without my power I could not call them here.

I noticed that the freckled woman was bent over her sister, trying to shake her awake.

"Cati, Cati, wake up!" she called, her strong hands gripping her sister's shoulders. She shook her again, more forcefully this time, then tried to prise her eyelids open.

"Cati, please, you're all healed now, wake up! You have to wake up. We have to go, we can't stay here. The Romans will be coming for us."

"Can you be quiet, mortal? I am trying to make a plan," I snapped at her. She looked over at me and I could see tears starting to bud in her eyes.

"Cati won't wake up. I don't understand. You said she was healed." Her voice cracked in pain.

I wasn't going to be able to concentrate if she started blubbering and making a fuss. I sighed heavily and went over on still wobbly legs to see what the problem was. The girl, Cati presumably, looked in perfect health. I opened her mouth to see if there was a blockage. Nothing. There was a very faint heartbeat, slow and weak as a kitten's. I took her hand and raised it above her face then dropped it, my lips thinning at the effort it took to lift it. Her arm flopped down without even a trace of resistance.

I glanced at the freckled woman. She looked back at me, hope battling despair. I peeled back the lids from Cati's eyes. She had the same grey-green irises as her sister, the shade of pine needles after the first frost. Of more interest to me was the shape of her pupils. They were wide, blown-out black circles and did not contract at the daylight. That was not a good sign.

"Bad news, I am afraid." I closed her eyes again and sat up. "Her body is healed but her soul has already gone. I must have dislodged it when I was trying to untangle her. She's not going to wake up. Best thing to do is smother her. Her soul will be stuck at the gates of Annwn until her body dies."

"What?" The freckled woman dragged her sister closer. "Don't touch her, she looks fine."

I shrugged and stood. "Suit yourself. You can sit here and watch her waste away if you like, but it will take months. Seems a little cruel to me but my work here is done."

She dropped Cati and rose faster than I expected, seizing me by the front of my tunic. "You sent her soul to Annwn. Call it back, you made a mistake, call it back," she hissed.

"Unhand me, wench. Do you know who you are assaulting?"

"Yes, yes, I know, and I do not care. Bring her back right now."

I blinked at her, surprised at the strength with which she had grabbed me. Dormath growled and stood up.

"Now be reasonable," I said. "Your sister, Cati, is it? She was going to die anyway. You may have slowed it a little with your spell but sooner or later it was going to start draining your life and you would have had to stop or die yourself. This has all been very upsetting, I'm sure, but you're not the only one in the world who's lost someone today. The Firebrand's whole rebellious force is lying scattered on the field just east of these woods. I spent most of last night helping thousands who will be just as mourned. So let me go!"

"How do I get her soul back?" she asked, ignoring my words. "You said it wouldn't have gone into Annwn yet. There must be a way to call it back before it does."

I gave the matter some thought. A soul that had passed through the gates of Annwn could never return to their mortal body, but one who merely lingered there? It was possible, I supposed, though I had never heard of such a thing.

"Perhaps," I said slowly, "though I could not order such a thing. My powers only extend to mortal Britain. Arawn would have to decide whether he would grant your request."

"Arawn?"

"Lord of the Afterworld. King of Annwn," I said, looking her up and down with all the immortal scorn I could muster. "Don't you know anything?"

She bridled at that.

"You shouldn't speak to me like that."

"Like what?"

"Like I'm some half-witted peasant. I'm not."

"Really?" I asked. "You're doing an excellent impression of one so far. Who are you, then?"

She let go of me and straightened up.

"I am Beliscena of the Iceni, daughter of Oak. This is my younger sister, Catrisca. You may call me Princess Belis, or your highness." She sounded surer of herself here and it took a great effort not to laugh at her petty little list of titles.

"I shall do no such thing. All mortals are alike to me, and I'm not interested in whichever insignificant names you've come up with. Iceni, hmm? Then your mother over there was . . . the one they called the Firebrand herself?" I paused. "Well, no matter, I must be off."

"Off where?" Belis asked. I moved back and brushed my tunic down.

"To Annwn, not that it is any concern of yours. I need to go and undo your mistake, regain my powers, before every lost soul on the island becomes some hideous ghoul without my guidance to send them home. I don't do this sort of work for fun, you know, nor out of the kindness of my heart. There are enough foul spirits lurking in Britain without human ghosts joining them."

Belis brightened.

"Well, that's perfect. It seems we have a common goal. You need to go to Annwn to get your powers back. I need to rescue Cati's soul. We should go together."

"Absolutely not," I said immediately. "You will slow me down. Not to mention every legionary in the south will be hunting you. It's a truly terrible plan. Listen to me: your sister is functionally dead. Let her go and head north. Seek shelter in the clans of the Highlands. The Romans will take a while to reach that far. Your family must have allies there, or at least those who would ally with their enemy's enemy."

Belis set her chin.

"I order you to assist me. I am Princess of the Iceni, you must obey me!"

I snorted. "Good luck with that, Princess. I might be stuck in this ridiculous human body for now but I'm under no illusions about the inherent nobility of your kind. Romans, Britons, you're all the same to me. Mayflies fighting over dog scraps while you breed like rabbits." I paused, having confused my metaphors. "What I mean is that you are barely a step above animals. Was that clear?"

Belis's shoulders slumped and she glanced back at her sister. She suddenly looked very tired, as if all the fire and fury that had sustained her had guttered out.

"Please, Mallt. I cannot abandon my sister. She is the only family I have left. It is my fault she's like this, my failure. I will risk anything to retrieve her soul." She looked at me again.

"Besides, I won't slow you down. I'm fast and strong and I have a little magic. I can protect us. I've trained as a warrior almost my entire life. You probably don't even have any money. I have. I can buy us supplies."

I paused at that. I had never needed money before, trading in kind with the goblin pedlars whenever our paths crossed. It was a ridiculous notion that she had. I would be very surprised if Arawn let one of his charges go. He took his work seriously and Belis would have a difficult case to make. Then again, I didn't need her to succeed, only for her to get me to Annwn. I had no idea if the human shape I had assumed really was mortal, if it could be damaged or killed, taking me with it. The idea of dying was not frightening to me; I had spent too much of my life helping others through it to fear it now. I wasn't done with my life, though. I wanted more, greedy as it might be for an undying goddess to say such a thing.

"Are you sure you can protect me?" I asked appraisingly. "You didn't do a very effective job with your sister."

Belis visibly bit back a reply, grinding her teeth. After a moment she spoke. "I don't see anyone else offering to help you."

"Fine," I said. "You can come with me to Annwn. If you get me there unharmed I'll speak to Arawn for you, though I doubt I can persuade him of anything he doesn't want to do."

Belis grinned.

"Really? Oh, Mallt, I promise you won't regret this."

"I hope that I won't. Now, collect your things. We have a long way to go and I'd rather not linger this close to your battlefield for any longer than we have to."

She hurried to her sister's side.

"Will Cati be all right without me?"

I considered the question. I didn't know for sure, but I could make a reasonable estimate.

"She's not quite alive, but neither is she dead. She's some kind of in between," I said. "Her body won't need food or water until her soul returns. The bigger problem is whether anyone will find her."

Belis crouched next to her sister, smoothing the hair back from her face. "This is a sacred place, full of old magic. It cannot be found easily."

"I found it," I said, then backtracked, realising this was unhelpful. "But I was following the trace of a dying soul. Most mortals probably couldn't, unless they were led here or followed a trail. Humans, anyway. I make no promises on wolves or lynx."

Belis nodded and bent to whisper something in her sister's ear. I looked away, not wanting to overhear. I glanced down to where Dormath was prancing at my feet. The other dogs had vanished when I had been splintered from myself. Only Dormath, caught in the spell beside me, had become a mortal dog.

"I'll leave my dog here," I said to Belis. "He can watch over her. He's run with the Wild Hunt enough times that wolves are common prey for him. She'll be safe with him."

Belis eyed Dormath suspiciously, not moving from her sister's side.

"He won't be a danger to her? I thought the Cwn Annwn hunted humans."

"We hunt human *souls*," I said, offended at her tone, "to guide them to the next world, to keep this one safe. Dormath won't touch your sister."

Belis looked down at her sister then stood up. "All right, if you think it's best."

I lifted Dormath's head towards me and looked into his big brown eyes. "I'll be back as soon as I can, pup." He pressed his face against mine and yipped. "The road's no place for you. Guard the girl for me." He looked offended and stalked off, flopping down in the shade of the trees.

I turned, trying to ignore the prickling sensation in my

eyes. Belis was standing behind me, holding a pair of boots in her hand.

"These are Cati's." She held them out to me. "They should fit you better than my mother's. Gods know she won't be needing them for a while. You can take my mother's cloak, though, your tunic looks rather thin.'

I considered explaining to her that the fabric of my tunic was crafted by the finest fae weavers, that it was perfectly suited for running, being both strong and light, but in the end I took the boots from her and sat down to put them on. Belis gave me a pair of knobbly woollen socks. I pulled them on, then the boots, and she helped me with the laces. I felt blood rushing into my cheeks at the humiliation of being helped like a child and mumbled my thanks. She shrugged and helped me up. I took a test stroll around the clearing. Not too bad, though I still preferred to go barefoot.

I slung the cloak around my shoulders. It was warm and I immediately felt a little better. I had not recognised that I was cold. I would have to keep closer tabs on the demands of this human body. I looked up to see Belis hurrying around the clearing. She picked up a pair of leather bags from where they had been left underneath the trees and began filling them with items scattered in the grass. Most of what she packed seemed to be knives, but I also watched her gather a clinking pouch of coins, a handful of dried leaves and a few things from her mother's pockets.

When she was done Belis came over to me and I stood up to meet her. The cloak slid from my shoulders and I caught it before it could fall. Belis reached out and pinned the cloak together. I looked down at my chest, admiring the golden brooch, carved into the shape of an oak leaf. A finer thing than I had expected to see in mortal hands.

"Another of my mother's things," Belis said. "A loan only. I want it back when we reach Annwn."

I shrugged. It was a pretty thing but paltry when compared to the work of dwarven smiths.

She passed me one of the bags and I heaved it onto my back. It had looked light in her hands, but I could already feel the weight cutting a groove in my shoulders.

"Ready?" she asked. "Which way?"

I set my shoulders and turned so that the morning sun was warm on my back. "We go west."

Belis Before

1

She is five years old and hiding from the commotion in her father's hall. Women rush to and fro, bearing armfuls of clean linen and steaming cauldrons of hot water. The men lounge near the fireplace, singing old songs to drown out the queen's screams. Her mother's screams.

Boudica is in the next room, giving birth to the little brother or sister Belis has been asking for for as long as she can remember. All the other children have siblings; instant teammates, comrades in the endless scuffles in the courtyards and stables of the Great Hall in Icenorum. Belis remembers sitting on her mother's lap, whining that she wanted a brother. Now she is huddled under the long table, eyes shut, hands pressed tightly over her ears, heart thumping in her chest so loudly she thinks it might crack her ribs.

Someone knocks on the tabletop and she blinks. Soft leather boots, spattered mud half hiding the intricate embroidery, stand before her, woollen trousers emerging from the tops. She recognises those boots. The legs bend and her father is crouching down in front of her, peering under the table. His smile is calm and soothing.

"What's this, little acorn?" he asks. "Hiding like a hare run to ground? Come out, little leveret, there's nothing to worry about."

She stumbles forward and he reaches out strong arms to catch her as she trips. Straightening up, he balances her on his side and removes a handkerchief to clean the soot stains and tears from her cheeks.

"I've been looking for you for half the day, child," he says. "You seemed to have vanished entirely in the commotion."

He walks over to the fireplace, one of the men immediately standing to leave him a seat. He sits her on his knees and smiles at her.

"Your mother is a strong woman, the best fighter in the land. She knows what she's about. You just sit with me and we'll wait for the babe to be born."

She nods and slides down to the floor, reaching out to one of the dogs lying nearby. It wags its tail at her and pads over to loll at its master's feet.

Above her the king claps his hands. "Well, while my wife is busy at her work we should be at ours. What can I do for the Iceni today?"

The men laugh and begin chattering. Her father makes judgements; he orders one man to allow safe passage for another's flock of sheep, he guarantees water rights to those who have always used a village well, he gives a purse of coins to a weeping widow and finds a place at court for her young son. All the business of the land continues even while the queen labours next door.

Belis sits, cuddling the long-suffering wolfhound, and listens to the king and queen at their work. Her father's voice is steady, but she can see the knuckles whitening as he clenches his cup of mead. The small evidence of tension makes her happy even as it worries her.

There is a final screech from the birthing chamber and the entire hall falls silent for a beat. The king pauses in his dictation and Belis feels her heart stuttering in her chest. Then there is that most joyful of sounds, the cry of a newborn babe.

The king leaps to his feet and his warriors cheer, calling a toast to the queen and the child. A midwife, her apron covered in blood and filth hurries, into the room and bows to the gathered men.

"A second daughter, my lord," she says. "Healthy and squalling. Your wife is in good humour though the labour was hard."

Her father grins and fishes a gold coin from the pouch at his waist. Flicking it towards the midwife, he grabs his cup and raises it high.

"To my new daughter! Princess of the Iceni, and to her mother, Queen Boudica!"

The hurrahs drown out the crying of Belis's new sister and for a moment she is afeared that she will be stepped on by the carousing men. Then her father snags her waist and lifts her back into the air, hurrying towards the next room.

Boudica sits in a carved wooden chair, a fur-trimmed robe wrapped over the thin linen birthing gown. Her hair is plastered to her head with sweat, but she looks triumphant and fiercely proud as she holds out the tiny bundle to her husband.

The king puts Belis down and accepts his newest child into his arms. Gurgling sounds come from the blankets and Belis cranes her neck to see. For a moment her father is completely lost, staring at the babe, and then he goes down on one knee and carefully tilts her so that Belis can meet her sister.

The baby is hilariously ugly, peony-pink and sticky with blood. Belis recoils a little but then her sister yawns and blinks open her tiny scrunched-up eyes. They are the same shape as hers, as her mother's. The curl of hair on the head is a pale ginger and Belis reaches out a finger and carefully strokes the baby's cheek.

Her father grins and pats her on the head with one hand before standing up and cradling the baby again.

"Another perfect babe, my love. Fine work."

The queen laughs at him, "You have barely looked at her, Taggie, not counted her fingers nor toes."

"How many toes does she need to be perfect? I am sure the gods have given her just as many as she requires and no more."

Her mother laughs again and beckons Belis closer.

"Here, my firstborn, do you like the new playmate your father and I have made for you?"

Belis climbs onto her mother's lap and snuggles into the reassuring scent of woodsmoke and sweat.

"I like her very much only she is too small to be much good at fighting yet."

The king nods seriously and moves closer to them, bouncing the babe in his arms.

"That's very true, Belis, and you must be gentle with her. You are her older sister and that is a sacred duty as well as an honour. Just as your mother and I will protect you, so you must protect her. That is the way of the family. And all of us will protect our people, for that is the way of the Iceni. We are the oak that stands tall and shelters them from the storms."

Belis nods and her mother drops a kiss onto her forehead and rocks her back and forth.

Chapter 3

"Could you be more specific?" Belis asked. "More detailed than simply 'west'?" How far west, a day's walk? A month?"

"Over two hundred miles," I said snippily. This mortal had no sense of occasion. "An evening stroll for me as I was. I don't know how quick humans can move over long distances. How fast can you walk?"

"A few miles an hour," Belis said, rubbing her chin, "but I can't walk day and night. I can probably do fifteen or twenty miles before stopping for a rest."

I considered this for a moment. Twenty miles a day was painfully slow, and the breaks were another delaying factor. I tried to parse out the timing in my head; it would take weeks of inching across the land. I sighed and squatted down on my heels.

"Here," I said, pointing in front of me and sketching a line in the dirt. "This is where we are, on the eastern tip of the Chalk uplands. We need to follow the crest of the Chalk west, walking for eighty miles, then cross through the ten miles of lowlands to the Cotswold hills. We should be able to hire a boat to take us across the River Severn at Glevum and from there walk along the south coast of the land of – what is that tribe called?"

"The Silures," Belis said, frowning at the sketched lines. "If I'm reading this right."

"Silures, yes, that sounds familiar. We walk the entire length of the coast to the furthest point of the land. There lies Caer Sidi, the physical entrance to Annwn."

She peered at the rough map again, tugging at a coppery lock of her hair.

"Won't we be exposed up on the Chalk? There's only a handful of villages up there to get supplies from. Wouldn't it be easier to walk straight from here to Glevum? It would certainly be faster."

I nodded. "True enough, but the Chalk is well wooded still, and I know the land well. The red cloaks have never liked it. They take the old road south of the hills or the oak road north of the Thames. Even if they follow us they'll go slow and careful. We'll have an advantage."

Something was still bothering her. I could see the struggle in her face as she decided whether to speak. Perhaps she was finally learning some respect.

"Isn't the Chalk, well, haunted? The stories say that it belonged to the old kingdom." She lowered her voice. "Giants, redcaps, wights."

I chuckled. Not respect, then, just mortal suspicions. "The only thing that haunts the Chalk is the dogs and me. It's one of our favourite spots in the south. The giants have long since migrated north or intermarried with the humans. As for the rest, well, they can be found anywhere in Britain, whether inhabited or not. You are just as much at risk in your own bed in the marshes as up on the Chalk."

She looked a little unsure still. The Iceni lived in the fens and flatlands of the east. They misliked hills. I knew she would feel safer on the plains and I was certain the Chalk was the best path. If a Roman patrol followed us, then we would stand a better chance out in the wilds than on the main roads where reinforcements could appear quickly. I looked back at Belis and waited for her to give in.

She nodded and straightened up, grabbing a long oak spear from where it was leaning against a tree. The weapon seemed to comfort her and she squared her shoulders as she wrapped long fingers around its smooth grip. "The Chalk it is."

We started walking. It was slow going at first, picking our way through the trees. The woods were thick, and the only paths were the occasional deer trails, footprints showing where a herd had wandered through. I kept tripping over my new boots, my feet unused to the constriction as well as the itching of the knobbly socks. I had started out in front, assuming my rightful place as goddess and leader of the expedition. Belis had accepted this without complaint but after the third time I got caught in a trailing bramble she stepped around me and began cutting a path for us with a long knife, slinging her spear over her shoulder.

I didn't understand it. I ran through deeper forests than these almost every day and never got tangled up or twisted an ankle. There must be something different about these woods. I made a note to come back when I was restored and inspect them thoroughly for pucks and wights.

Perhaps I could gather some of the more civic-minded members of the Wild Hunt to assist me. I refrained from mentioning my suspicions of an infestation to Belis, not wanting to scare her fragile mind.

The ground began to steepen underfoot, and the trees were thinning around us. I was glad to be getting out of the forest, even if there was something strange happening to my breathing. It was quickening, though I hadn't changed my pace. My mouth was a little dry, too. Once we got up on the Chalk I would feel better. The fresh winds would blow away the closeness of the dark woods.

Belis paused on the very edge of the trees and put down the pack she had been carrying. I stopped beside her and peered over her shoulder. As the woods had thinned out she had sheathed her blade and begun plaiting her hair. Now it sat in two neat braids, arcing from her forehead all the way down to her midback. Each plait was as thick as my wrist and I was struck by the strange urge to tug on them as if to ring a bell. Belis pulled out a thin grey scarf and wrapped it around her head, knotting it in a small bow at the nape of her neck.

"Red hair isn't that common," she said, noticing me watching her. "I'd rather not be immediately visible from a distance, not when there's a Roman legion camped nearby. I imagine they'll still be picking over the battlefield today but soon they'll notice they're missing three rather important bodies and start sending out search parties. These aren't my lands and I wouldn't blame a peasant farmer for giving me up if a patrol had him at sword point."

I considered her words and decided to pick up my pace. Romans had never bothered me before, but I had seen their gift for organised destruction. I had no wish to be on the sharp end of one of their javelins in this fragile human body.

Judging from the position of the sun it was just after midday. At the speed Belis had suggested, we should be able to reach the valley of the River Boulburn before nightfall. I hoped she could keep up with me.

I made it almost a quarter of the way up to the crest of the Chalk before I had to stop.

Something was seriously wrong. I slumped to the ground, unable to carry on. Belis, who had been plodding along behind me, caught up in a moment.

"What is it?" she asked, looming over me like a storm cloud.

"I think this body is dying," I said, clutching my chest. "The heart is beating so fast I think it's going to just explode. My lungs feel like they've been peeled raw but also somehow like there's a wasp nest inside my ribcage. My stomach hurts, my legs, my thighs, my calves are burning, literally. I think they might be on fire."

"Oh, really?" Belis looked surprisingly unsympathetic.

"Yes," I continued, "there are stabbing pains in my side. I think some evil creature has cast a death spell on me. I thought there was something strange in those woods. You were probably too slow to notice it. So this is the ignoble end of the Nightshade, after thousands of years. You'd better go on without me. If my soul makes it to Annwn I'll tell the lord you're coming."

Belis bent down and took me by the arm. She pulled me to my feet with no discernible effort and brushed the chalk dust off my cloak.

"You're not dying," she said. "You're just a little out of breath. You are as red as a strawberry in case you wanted to add that to your list of symptoms."

"What? No, I run all the time, I run over mountains and gorges and steep valleys. The problem isn't me. This is my fate, my final end." I made to slump back to the grass.

"Well, maybe your old body could." She held me up. "But this one isn't used to it. Come on, I'm not leaving you here to feel sorry for yourself. I need you, remember? We'll take it slow but we're not stopping 'til we get to the top of the hill."

We did have to stop three more times before we finally crested the hill. The second time I actually had to vomit, a deeply unpleasant sensation and a part of human existence I had no wish to repeat. Belis was impatient with me, her eyes darting behind us to check for pursuit. When I was retching for the second time she yanked the pack from where I had dropped it beside me, adding it to her own bag. I wanted to complain, to insist that I could manage it, but the weight of it had ground welts into my shoulders even through the thick woollen cloak and I doubted I could have carried on with it.

We passed no one on the slopes but a young boy, minding a small flock of wiry sheep. He nodded warily at us and I watched his hand go to the knife in his belt. I pointed uphill and he relaxed, watching us go. As we scrambled over the crest of the hill I paused. I bent down and began to scrape away at the grass. It was thinner here and it took me only a moment to expose the soil. I brushed it away, revealing the bright white chalk beneath. I pressed my hand against the soft rock, trying to feel for the power I knew was trapped there. The Chalk is made of the bones of old creatures which lived before even the giants walked these lands. Their life is in this rock, a source of strength to those who remember to claim it. When I had walked here before it had felt as if I was paddling on the banks of a great river, full of a sense of life and movement and power. I called for that power now, trying to remake myself or even to soothe my aching muscles.

Now there was nothing. I sighed and picked my hand up. Chalk dust traced the lines of my palm, the creases in my fingers. I brushed it off against my leggings.

I looked out grumpily at the increasingly picturesque view in front of me. We were high enough now that I could see for miles. The Chalk was ringed with thick woodland, but beyond that small fields and villages had been cleared. Smoke trickled into the air from the east, above a plain flashing with steel. I was grateful for the westerly wind that would keep the smell away. Belis had paused to look back. She stood there, gazing down at the plains, her face carefully immobile.

I called her and she turned from her lookout and began walking towards me.

"Hurry up, I don't want to linger in the open this close to the battlefield. We need to make better time," she said as she caught up.

"I'm walking as fast as I can," I snapped. "These legs are less than a day old. I'd like to see you climb up the Chalk when you were a babe."

"For certes I could hardly have been slower," she jibed. "We'll have to adjust our travel time. That or I'll have to steal a cart and push you."

"I don't need to be pushed like some mortal grandmother," I said. "I can make it. It would be easier if I had a little support from you."

"I gave you socks and boots, put my own mother's cloak around your shoulders, took the pack from you and now I'm standing around waiting for you to get your breath back hoping that a cohort of Romans don't appear. How could I be more supportive?"

"You could stop snapping at me," I said. "It is most impolite and I don't have the breath to argue and walk at the same time."

"You seem to have plenty of breath to complain but, fine, we'll walk in silence."

She turned on her heel and strode off up the hill. Muttering under my breath, I followed, trying my best not to fall too far behind. As we climbed, the grass grew still thinner underfoot and the wind picked up. It whistled as it rushed past me, pressing my tunic to the back of my legs and trying to snatch Belis's scarf from her head.

Walking on the crest of the Chalk was a little easier on my legs, the pain in my calves easing, but that merely allowed me to think more about how much my feet were hurting. The wind, which I had dearly loved to feel on my skin, was beating at my ears, rubbing them raw. My tunic and leggings had not shrunk with me. The tunic, which had finished just above my knees, now flapped irritatingly at my ankles and I kept having to stop and roll up the leggings as they sagged.

Worse still, I just could not seem to keep my hair out of my face. Usually it wafted delicately behind me like a sheet of spider silk, well behaved even in a thunderstorm. Now it seemed to be constantly buffeted around my head, strands flying into my mouth, my nose, my eyes. I glared at Belis, tramping away in front of me. Her curls had seemed much more unruly than mine, but the braids had tamed them and the headscarf kept even the few loose tendrils out of her face. I paused to catch my breath again and pushed my hair back for the thousandth time.

I staggered on. Belis was clearly reining her pace in, walking slowly so that I wouldn't lose sight of her. It didn't make me feel any better. All of this mess was her fault. I was tired and sore and miserable and sick of humans. Their endless infighting and murdering and battling had led to this. I could have been bathing in the crystal streams of the Eryri mountains by now, playing with the dogs. Instead, I was actually sweating! Me, sweating, like some common dwarf, and panting like one, too. Even my eyesight seemed to blur as I swayed back and forth, tramping along on this endless walk.

The sun was beginning to dip below the western horizon when we approached a wooden hut, tucked into the lee of a hill. It was small and squat, no more than a few wide planks nailed together, with a shallow leaning roof.

"We may as well stop here for today," Belis said, sliding off her packs. "I don't think you've got any more steps in you, and this is as good a place as any to camp for the night. We're lucky to have found it."

I peered inside the hut. There was a three-legged stool in the corner, with a carved cup sitting on it. Beside the stool stood a rough bucket and a small pile of chopped logs. The rest of the single room was completely bare except for the ashes of an old campfire and the faint but unmistakeable scent of ferrets.

"Maybe I'll just sleep outside," I said doubtfully. I was already starting to feel the evening chill close in around me, but the hut looked very small for two people. Especially if one of those people was a large Iceni warrior who looked as if she might snore.

"Up to you," the large Iceni warrior said, ducking into the hut and throwing her packs into the corner. She leaned her spear against one of the walls and picked up the bucket. "You'll freeze outside, though. It'll be much warmer in here, especially once I've got a fire going."

I sniffed and stepped inside after her, aiming to nab the stool before she got ideas above her station. Belis shoved the bucket at me before I could sit down.

"Here, go and fill this. I saw a well not fifty yards back down the way. I'll start the fire."

I looked at the bucket with derision. I did not fetch or carry for humans. I wasn't a common brownie.

"You go. You're better at heavy lifting. I can start the fire."

She glanced up from the log pile where she was already pulling out smaller pieces of wood and kindling with an expert hand.

"How? Have you ever lit a fire without magic?"

I didn't want to answer that so I grabbed the bucket and stomped off, grumbling not quite under my breath. The well was closer to a hundred yards away, which gave me a long time to complain to myself. It was an old-fashioned ring of stones, built up in a cylinder with a rope to tie the bucket to and a handle to pull it back up. I checked the rope before I threw the bucket in, not wanting to have to slink back without it. The rope looked newish, the hut must be popular among the local shepherds in the spring and summer. We were lucky that it was empty now, though I supposed it was near the end of the grazing season. Soon the lowlands would be burnishing from green to gold as autumn passed through the island.

I tied the bucket carefully and lowered it into the darkness until I heard a faint splash. I jiggled at the rope a bit until I judged the bucket was full and then began hauling it up. It was incredibly heavy work for such a small bucket, and I felt fresh sweat break out over my forehead and slide into my eyes. My arms were pretty much the only part of my body that hadn't been sore from the day's walking, but by the time I got the bucket out of the well they were screaming at me just as much as my legs, and my palms were scraped raw. I inspected the bucket.

Unbelievably, it was only about three-quarters full. That would have to do. I wasn't starting the whole ordeal again.

I squinted at my reflection in the pail. My face hadn't changed that much, I decided. I had the same straight nose, large dark eyes, blue, though you couldn't tell the colour in the rippling water. My hair was an unmitigated disaster and the rest of me was windswept and sunburned. Beneath that was a deeper change. There was something missing. I had definitely been beautiful before, my features striking and my skin glowing pale as the moon, my whole being giving off an air of dark power. Now I just looked soft and weak. I didn't like it and my new face frowned back at me.

I leaned a little closer to my reflection, trying to see the shape of my new ears, and jostled the bucket, shattering my image. Just as well: the idea of Belis coming to find me and seeing me staring mournfully at my reflection was too humiliating to bear.

I lugged the bucket back to the hut. By the time I got there, it was less than half full, but Belis took it without comment. She had somehow managed to trap a rabbit in the short time I had been gone and was already halfway done skinning it. The fire was roaring away in the centre of the hut, filling the room with a smoky warmth that made me cough.

I sat down and took my boots off before Belis could ask me to do anything else. My feet were sore and blistered. I pulled one of them into my lap and began to try and rub a little feeling back into it. As I massaged my poor soles then moved my way up to the aching muscles of my calves, Belis finished skinning the rabbit and divided it into quarters. She set up three sharpened stakes above the fire and then pulled a leather cauldron from her pack and hung it from the tripod. Finally, she poured water from my bucket into the cauldron and added the rabbit, along with a handful of small root vegetables, also from her bag.

"Do you just carry all that around with you?" I asked, incredulous at the contents of this unassuming-looking pack.

"The cauldron, yes, it folds up small so I always keep that in there when I go riding. The vegetables, no. I picked them when we were wandering through the forest and climbing up here. They're easy to spot if you know what you're looking for."

I frowned. "I didn't notice you digging for turnips."

"That's because you were too busy gasping for breath or retching," said Belis, her eyes still on the stew.

I couldn't think of anything to say to that, so I shuffled a little closer to the fire. My stomach was yowling at me. I rarely felt hungry, though I ate when I wanted to. I could eat fae and human food as I pleased; neither was necessary for me to sustain myself but I generally enjoyed it. This body, however, clearly wanted more and the smell of the rabbit stew was beginning to fill the hut. Saliva was filling my mouth by the time Belis judged the stew was done.

She only had the one spoon so we took it in turns to fish out bits of rabbit and ladle the watery mixture into our mouths. It was unseasoned and slightly undercooked, and I would have turned my nose up at it a few hours ago, but my stomach was completely empty and I ate everything, even the turnip peelings.

I sat back and leaned against the wall of the hut, wrapping my new cloak around me. Belis wiped her knife on her trousers then offered the hilt to me.

"You should cut your leggings shorter; you can't walk two

hundred miles hitching them out of your boots every few steps. And you can use the scraps to tie back your hair. You can't go around looking like you just fought your way through a hedgerow, it will attract too much attention. Tidy yourself up."

I puffed up, insulted.

"That's rich coming from a great ginger giantess," I said. "Many have called me the most beautiful of creatures, lovelier than the night sky. If you hadn't—"

"Yes, yes," she snarled, brandishing the blade at me. "If I hadn't messed up you wouldn't be here, you'd be off combing your hair with the fae. Just shut up and take the knife."

I took her knife with a scowl and began sawing at my leggings. The material was tougher than it looked and I almost stabbed myself a few times, but I managed to take about six inches off each leg. I looked mournfully at the offcuts.

"The finest cloth on the island," I said, struggling to rip them into strips. "Made by the hands of Lady Creiddylad herself and her attendants."

"Much good it'll do you now," Belis grumbled. I ignored her, fingering the fine cloth.

"How do you know so much about this anyway?" I asked, waving at the fire and the stew and the rabbit skin. "Do all princesses learn this stuff? I'd have thought it would mostly be weaving and learning to be polite to old men with bad breath."

"My father thought his daughters should know their land," Belis said, staring at the fire. "He said that a person couldn't rule a country if they didn't know how to live off it."

"Sounds surprisingly sensible," I said, "for a human."

She nodded. "The land of the Iceni is very different from here but some things are the same. It is a wide, flat land, not so steep like this place." She gestured to the view beyond the hut door.

"You can see for miles and miles on a clear day, watch approaching rainclouds cross the horizon and have enough time to hurry home before the storm hits. I was born in the open. My mother was visiting one of our vassals, a horse farmer, when she was expecting me. On the way home her waters broke and she gave birth to me out under the blue sky. When my father rushed out with a cart full of midwives, he found her leaning against an oak tree, cradling me in her arms, having cut the cord with her eating knife."

Belis rubbed her chin, leaving a smear of rabbit grease. For a long while she said nothing. I waited, unsure whether she would start again and unwilling to press her. Humans were very prone to complaining about their troubles and I decided I wasn't in the mood to listen to it after the terrible day I had endured. She looked as if she were about to speak so I yawned widely, stretching my arms out above my head.

"Better get some rest," I said gruffly, pulling back and shuffling on the floor to try and find a comfy bit of ground. "We've got a long walk ahead of us tomorrow. I should be able to walk a little faster with a full stomach."

It was cold comfort even to my ears, but Belis nodded and began tidying up the remnants of our dinner. Before long she was stretched out on the other side of the fire, tucked under her own cloak. As I drifted off to sleep the last thing I saw was her face, still staring into the fire.

Chapter 4

Belis showed no inclination to talk the next morning as we packed up our possessions and set off. We walked in silence for much of that day, and the ones after. The Chalk was wide and empty and we saw no more than one or two shepherds a day. They kept their distance, whistling to their piebald sheepdogs to keep their flocks away from us. I watched the dogs streaking lightning-fast across the turf and missed my own hounds. They had been with me all my life and their absence felt as deep a wound as my own mortality.

The second day of walking was by far the most painful. My blisters had burst, my muscles had seized up and it took me an hour to walk the first mile. Belis was twitching with impatience by the time I finally settled into a steady pace. I was just as frustrated. My body was betraying me, not obeying the orders I gave it to leap, run, jump. When we crossed the Bournbrook river valley I almost wept with fury at how long it took me to climb back up the hill.

It got better slowly, inch by inch. My feet hardened and my legs, though still sore and clumsy, gained a little new strength so that I was less of a total embarrassment. I was still significantly slower than Belis, but I no longer had to pause for breath every time the angle of the land steepened beneath me and I had taken my pack back from her for small stints, carrying my share of the weight.

We seemed to have used all our good fortune on the first night, for we never found another shepherd's hut to stay in. I had spent more nights sleeping out in the wilds than under cover, but my immortal blood had always kept me warm and I had had two dozen hounds snuggled in around me. In this new body I tossed and turned all night, trying and failing to find a comfortable position, and I woke each morning tired and sore. Worse still was the cold, which crept in through the stony ground and sucked all the warmth from me. The second night found me shivering so hard that my teeth chattered against each other loud enough to prevent Belis from sleeping until she insisted we sleep back-to-back and share warmth.

I was loth to listen to her but it was becoming clearer every day that Belis was much more suited to this life than I was. I would barely have reached the top of the Chalk on that first day had she not carried my pack and I would be close to starvation by now without her. The berries and mushrooms I had picked and eaten in the past were now poisonous to me and the wild beasts that had come eagerly to my hands for a caress now fled in fear.

This was difficult for me to accept; I had been bitter enough about accepting Belis as a travel companion when I had thought she would slow me down. To find that she could outpace me at every turn, striding tirelessly across the Chalk, was somehow harder to take. To have yew berries slapped out of my hand before I could toss them in my mouth was even worse. I had yelled at her about that and she had snapped back that a goddess of death should know her poisons better. I sulked at her rudeness, hugging the resentment to me like a cloak. I could hear myself being unreasonable, but it was difficult to stop my mouth from spitting whatever hurtful words I could think of at her. I couldn't control the new emotions that were raging through me, was as ill practised at managing human feelings as human limbs.

Late on the third day we moved into the woods above the Misbourne and were considering stopping for the night when we came across a huge brown bear. He was standing up on his back legs, nosing at a bees' nest set in the branches of a slender elm tree. My immediate reaction was delight at seeing the beast and I kept walking towards him, intent on getting a share of the honey. Belis caught me by my pack and pulled me backwards. I turned, trying to shrug her off, and found she had her spear out, held in her free hand.

"Move back into the woods," she said, "quick and quiet. I'll cover our retreat."

"Don't be so dramatic," I said, tired and eager for some honey to sweeten whatever dreadful stew Belis had in mind for tonight. "I won't be a moment. I'll just get him to share whatever he has found so far."

Belis actually took her eyes off the bear to stare at me in disbelief.

"Are you mad? You can't take food off a bear. This is trying to pet that lynx all over again." I looked down at the scratches on my arms. I had forgotten about that.

"Humans and bears don't get along?" I asked.

"Gods give me strength," she muttered. "No, we don't. Get back into the trees, we'll go around, keep walking for another hour or so."

I opened my mouth to argue but the bear growled, a low huff of warning, and an unfamiliar feeling swept through me, a cold kind of stiffness. I shut my mouth and ducked behind Belis before I could even process the instinct. She rolled her eyes and began stepping back out of the clearing. The bear turned back to his feast.

I kept quiet for another hour of walking, puzzling over my curious response to the bear's cautionary growl. I hadn't experienced anything like that before, a visceral urge to flee, to put something solid between myself and danger. Was it fear? I had never thought of myself as cowardly but as I trudged through the woods in the dim light of the evening I considered that there had never been any true cause for fright. I had felt exhilaration, anger, pride, but never fear. I felt revolted at its power over me.

Ahead of me Belis stopped walking and put her pack down.

"We've gone far enough. Let's sleep here tonight and start fresh tomorrow," she said.

I nodded and, dropping my own pack, began to gather wood for a fire. By the time I had returned with the third armful, Belis had the cauldron bubbling over a flame and was sitting on a fallen log, chopping up the vegetables she had gathered during the day's walk. I took a seat beside her and stared into the flames. I didn't say anything; I was still mulling over the memory of fear and its hold on me. Belis stayed quiet while cooking the evening meal, speaking only to ask me to pass more wood. We spoke less than a dozen words before turning in for the night, lying back-to-back, both cloaks piled on top of us.

Belis fell asleep quickly and the feel of her steady breathing beside me soothed my racing mind so that I slipped into dreaming without noticing.

In my dream I was back in the glade with Belis and her sister, but both of their lips were stained with the dark poison that had taken their mother's life. I was immortal again, leaning over Belis's limp body to loose the soul within. Suddenly her eyes snapped open, not grey-green but the amber eyes of the bear, and when she smiled it was with ursine teeth that opened to let out a guttural roar. I fell backwards and scrabbled for a weapon, but my hands found only yew berries and rabbit bones and I felt the chill terror flood through me.

I awoke with a shudder into the inky black of night. The fire had burned down to the faintest embers and the woods were cold. I had rolled out from under my cloak and found myself lying in the dirt. I sat up. Beside me Belis had pulled the cloaks around herself in her sleep. I shuddered at the memory of her with the bear's eyes and decided not to try and wrestle my cloak back.

I crawled towards the fire and poked at the coals with a stick, releasing a torrent of bright sparks into the air. I shoved a few more branches onto the embers and blew on them, waiting for the flames to catch. When I had built up the fire enough to put out some more heat I sat there and tried to calm myself down. It had just been a dream, probably brought on by the shock of the last few days. Humans had dreams all the time that meant nothing. There was no need for this one to symbolise anything at all. I fumbled in my pack for an apple and bit into it, the sweetness pushing new strength into my blood.

Across the fire something moved in the darkness. A deeper black than the night, unlit by the dancing flames. The sound of rustling leaves came from my left and I turned to see the tattered edge of a cloak slipping between the trees. A foul scent drifted towards me on the wind, the sour taste of rotting flesh. It was faint but I could smell enough to recognise it. Wight.

A common enough problem in my old life. When a human died a quick and violent death sometimes their soul would not recognise its body had perished. It would not be strong enough to animate the fresh corpse, but if the body was not burned or buried, was left to rot, then the lingering spirit could re-enter it later. Demented by the pain of existing in such a form, the wight would attack any creature in its path.

I had put down hundreds of wights over the years, using the dogs to herd them away from human settlements to where I could quickly and easily prise the soul loose from the body and send it on to Annwn. I had even occasionally reunited with one of the souls when visiting Arawn and they had always thanked me most politely for my aid.

This wight didn't look like he would be thanking me this evening. Branches snapped behind me and I jumped to my feet, keeping the fire to my back. Belis was still asleep, her spear propped against a tree beside her. I measured the distance between us, no more than a few yards. I didn't want to call out to her lest I provoke the wight. The smell got worse and I felt my mortal heart begin to drum in my chest, pumping the blood faster and faster.

I dashed towards Belis, shaking her awake.

"Wake up, wake up, there's a wight in the trees."

She was dizzy with sleep for a moment, but her eyes focused on my face and in a moment she was on her feet, spear in hand.

"Where is it," she whispered, tracing the spear point through the night. I pointed to where the smell was strongest.

"Over there, it came up from the south." I moved closer to her. "Have you fought one before?"

"I've never even seen a wight," Belis said. "You're sure that's what it is?"

For once she didn't sound patronising, speaking as one equal to another. Still not appropriately respectful but better.

"That smell can only mean one thing."

Belis nodded and fished a knife from her belt. "Here, guard my back. I've heard they're wicked quick when they want to be."

I took the knife from her. It was heavy and cold in my hands, and I doubted I would be particularly successful in wielding it.

"Anything else you can tell me?" Belis muttered, moving closer to the fire.

"Don't let it near you, they bite."

"Great advice, Mallt," snarled Belis as the wight emerged from the trees and lunged towards us. "Whatever would I do without you?"

The wight had been a man in life, tall and broad-shouldered, though the muscles had withered down to gristle and his skin hung loose. I could easily see his death: half of his skull had been stoved in, the bowl of his head was empty. His eyes had long since been plucked out by birds and the teeth marks of scavenging rodents patterned his face, but there was a terrible twisting rage in his decaying features.

Belis ran him through with her spear before he got within a yard of us. The wight barely paused at the blow, pulling himself along the shaft, snaggletooth jaws snapping at Belis. She kept gripping her end of the spear and levered him backwards, grabbing for her sword with her spare hand. The wight moved faster and Belis had to drop the spear before she could raise her sword. The spear slid to the ground and the wight leapt forwards, raising his arms to claw at Belis's face. She took one hand off with a swing of the blade but the other kept coming and backhanded her across the cheekbone, knocking her to the ground.

The cold thrill of fear had rooted me to the spot, but now the wight was turning towards me. He was no larger than dozens of his kind I had faced before but now I stood alone in the woods, my hounds long vanished, my only ally still sprawling on the floor. I raised the knife, my hand shaking. Sweat coated my palm and I dropped the blade. The wight was almost on me now, the stench of rot so strong I could barely breathe.

Its remaining hand gripped my arm, dragging me forward. I stared up at its eyeless face, unable even to scream.

A bright sword appeared in the corner of my vision, sweeping the wight's head from its shoulders. Belis stood behind it, the still snarling head of the wight in one hand. The body kept going, its hand moving to my throat. Belis dropped the head and pulled me loose, turning to slice the body into fragments.

Even as she stood over the dismembered limbs of the wight, it still twitched, trying to pull itself back together.

"Does it never die?" she asked, panting.

I was still shivering but managed to find my voice.

"Not by mortal hands. Shove it onto the fire and we can burn the body. The soul will linger, looking for another body to inhabit."

Belis looked at me aghast. "One of ours? Can we protect ourselves?"

I shook my head. "It's not strong enough to push out a living soul; it'll find another body, human preferably, but I've seen them in dogs, lynx, horses."

"So how is Britain not overrun with them?"

I frowned at her. "Because of me. That was one of my tasks, to keep the land free of such creatures and send the souls of the dead on. Now that I can't do that . . ."

Belis paled and she looked down at the still jerking wight. "There is no one else who can do this?"

I sat down heavily and reached for a waterskin.

"There are other beings who could slay them, but they are not inclined to take on the duty of hunting all of them, nor of dealing with the menace in good time. It has been five hundred years since I last let a wight slip past me and harm a living human. I fear that my ability to protect has gone with my immortality." I took a draught of water. "This is why we must get to Arawn, and fast. Wights are not the only fate that can befall a stranded soul. It is my responsibility, my purpose, to keep this land safe, to keep them safe."

"What about Cati?" Belis said, something like panic entering her voice for the first time. "She's an empty body. Could this wight find her?"

So typical of a mortal to think of themselves first, I thought.

"She should be safe enough with Dormath guarding her. He might be a mortal dog now but he's still wily and fierce enough to chase anything smaller than a dragon away."

Belis nodded and bent to push the fragments of the wight into the fire. Sleep seemed unlikely to return so I sat back on the log and watched as the remains of the wight melted into the flames, the smell of burning flesh filling the night.

Around noon on the seventh day of the Chalk I called to Belis, who had paused to grub for what she thought were onions.

"Come on up, here's a sight you'll not soon forget."

She hurried up to join me where I stood, looking to where the green hills sloped down to the north. I heard the sharp gasp as she saw the great white horse carved into the chalk. It was drawn with long, smooth lines hundreds of feet high, as if some celestial being had traced the shape into the hillside with a finger. As I watched, the sun came out from the clouds and the horse seemed to move, running in place. It wasn't anatomically correct, but the shape captured the essence of the creature, of the feeling of running free, thundering hooves and rushing winds. I had often wandered this way, spending an hour here and there weeding along the cuts. It made my heart sting a little to see it again now.

"The Vale of the White Horse," said Belis, from beside me. "I had always hoped to see it. It's enormous, so much bigger than I thought it would be." She looked at me. "Was it your kind that made it? The fae, I mean?"

"I'm not fae," I said. "I'm a goddess. And, no, it was made by humans, magic ones, but humans nonetheless."

"Druids?"

"No, witches, I think." I looked down at the horse, remembering the story. "It was, what, a thousand years ago? The lowlands were being terrorised by a herd of horses that ate human flesh. The warriors gathered together and managed to kill all but one, the stallion. The beast was enormous, pure white, and no fighter in the land could bring him down. Eventually a witch, I forget her name now, sold the warriors a spell to defeat him. The second bravest of them scattered meat beneath a tree and waited in the branches until the stallion came to feed. When the horse was eating, the warrior leapt onto his back and, saying the words of the spell, rode him into the hillside where the Chalk captured him and turned him into the carving you see now."

"The second bravest?" said Belis. "Why the second bravest? Why not send the bravest?"

"The bravest warrior was the meat," I said.

She blinked at that. I let her stare at the horse a little longer before clearing my throat.

"The White Horse marks the next stage of our journey," I said. "From here we turn north, head for Glevum and the River Severn."

"How far is it?"

"To the Severn or to Caer Sidi?"

"Both."

I thought about it, picturing in my mind the lands we had to travel.

"If we maintain my current pace we should reach the banks of the Severn in three days' time. Then another two weeks travelling through Silurian territory."

Belis flexed her fingers, then balled them into fists. I could see the tension running through her like a vein of tin ore through granite. She set her jaw, making a decision.

"So far to go. We need to make better time. Come on," she said, striding off down the hill.

So brusque still, I thought, as I gingerly followed her, taking small, tentative steps. Walking down slopes, especially those as steep as these, was tricky and Belis was forced to wait for me at the bottom. She was looking up at the horse as it gleamed in the sun.

"Someday I'd like to bring Cati here," she said, half to herself. "She would like it, I think. I might keep that story to myself, though."

I gave a noncommittal mumble of agreement. It was the first time she had mentioned her sister in five days. She sniffed and set off again.

The sloping hills around us flattened into arable land, wide golden fields of wheat and barley. Belis insisted that we walk next to the hedgerows, in order not to stand out against the horizon. I complained a little, just to show I couldn't be ordered around, but I didn't mind it much. It was a relief to get out of the wind and walk in the cool shade. There were the beginnings of the autumn berry crop and we feasted on blackberries, raspberries and blackcurrants as we walked. The juices stained my fingers and I could tell from looking at Belis that half of my face must be as well. The sweetness seemed doubled after a week of watery stew and even the thorns that tore long scratches on my arms couldn't douse my good mood.

We stopped early that day, in a stand of trees between four fields. Belis weighed the urge to cover more ground against the risk of us not finding somewhere with cover to camp. Eventually I decided for us, sitting down and beginning to unlace my boots.

"It'll be at least a few more miles 'til we find somewhere else to stay for the night," I reasoned, sliding off my socks with a sigh of pleasure. "And I'm beat for the day."

"You could move with a little more urgency," Belis snapped, rubbing her chin as she thought.

"I could. I could have run there and back a dozen times a night. I can't now. And whose fault is that?"

She snarled at me and took off into the wood. I shrugged off my pack and sat back against a tree, stretching out the muscles in my legs. I doubted Belis would go far; she'd collect some dead wood for the fire and maybe try to trap something. I hoped she caught a wood pigeon; I couldn't face rabbit again. I let my eyes flutter shut and tried to relax and enjoy the solitude. I could imagine things as they were before.

Something snapped behind the tree. The wind carried the faint but characteristic clink of plate armour towards me. I froze, unsure whether to risk running. I would have little chance of escaping. I felt absurdly vulnerable, alone.

A hand came down over my mouth. I jumped, but it was only Belis, crouching beside me and holding a finger to her lips. I nodded and she removed her hand. She dipped her head towards the east, where the sounds had come from, then mimed something walking towards us. I nodded again and she pointed up the trunk of the tree: she wanted us to climb it. As quietly as possible I slid my boots on and grabbed my socks, stuffing them into my tunic. Belis made a lattice with her fingers and boosted me up to the first branch. I swung myself up then leaned back down to pull her up behind me. The effort almost knocked me back down again, but we managed it in the end. The elm was old enough that the branches were thick and easy to climb and we clambered higher until the curtain of leaves hid us from view.

I looked over at where Belis had stretched out on her branch. She held a finger to her lips again then pointed down and pretended to hold a hand to her ear.

Below us the metallic clank of armour was growing louder, along with the stomping of hobnailed sandals. A male voice filtered up through the branches.

"Come on, sir, let's take a breather." The voice was deep, rounding out the harsh Latin consonants of the words.

"We saw them walking this way, they can't be far ahead of us," a second man snapped back.

"They'll be stopping for the night in a few hours, we'll have a better chance at catching them then," the first man cajoled. "The men are knackered, centurion, they've been marching for two days straight. Give them a few minutes to take a drink."

"A moment, then," the second man, the centurion, agreed reluctantly. "But boots stay on and no wine."

There was a general grumbling and the sound of soldiers collapsing to the floor. I looked over at Belis and stretched out both hands, indicating about ten Romans. She shook her head and flashed one hand three times. Fifteen. Far more than anyone could handle in a fight. I leaned my head down, trying to catch the conversation.

There was a fair amount of grousing from the soldiers: sore feet, bad rations, unattractive local women. I managed to glean that the troop had followed us from the Iceni battlefield but seemed to have had trouble keeping up with us over the Chalk. There was much complaining about haunted British uplands and general agreement that any people who lived up there were barbarians.

"Boots stay on!" The centurion's voice cut like a whip through the hubbub.

"Sir, I just need to bind a blister," a soldier whined.

"I said boots stay on, soldier. Any more backtalk and you'll be lashed for insubordination and I'll have you digging latrine trenches when we get back."

There was silence for a while and then the general chatter started again.

"Bloody Croser," came the voice of the complaining soldier. "There's a blister on my toe the size of a sestertius. You can bet he's got fancy shoes that don't rub."

"It's your own fault for talking back," cut in another man. "Never give a centurion any lip, they take it worse than anyone. Higher-ups ignore it and the Decani will just box your ear. Centurions have the authority to make your life hell and the spite to do it. Especially when we're out here with just two contuberniums' worth of men, you can't blend in like you would in a century."

I glanced over at Belis. I wondered if she understood the

meaning of the ranks; it made no sense to me. I shifted a little, trying to get more comfortable on the branch.

"I still don't understand why we're out here in the sticks anyway," grumbled the man with the blister.

"We're chasing that Icey bitch," said his friend.

"Iceni!" corrected the deep-voiced man who'd called for a halt. "Don't you know anything?"

"What does it matter, Terrasidius? They're all uncultured brutes, barely good for slaving. Let her scurry off to some cave somewhere to rot. What do I care?"

"Tell that to the pile of ashes we used to call Londinium," said Terrasidius. "Tell that to the boys of the Ninth, rotting outside Camulodunum. Better yet, try telling that to Centurion Croser."

"What's he got to do with it?"

Terrasidius lowered his tone, and I had to strain my ears to hear him. "He brought his family over last year. Mother, wife, three kids. Thought the province was settled enough that they'd be safe in Londinium."

"No!" whispered the blistered soldier. "Did they . . ."

"All of them died during the sack. His whole line wiped out overnight. The sound he made when he found out." Terrasidius gave a low whistle. "Never heard a man make that sound before. At least, not one who wasn't being cut up by the torturers' regiment."

"Is that why he volunteered to hunt the wench down?"

"The governor thought he'd be sufficiently motivated," Terrasidius said, "then he sent the rest of us along to stop Croser killing her on sight. Got to do these things properly. Rebel leaders go back to Rome, to be properly humiliated and cowed. Can't have them running around the provinces stirring up more trouble. The Firebrand's rebellion almost succeeded. If it had, the repercussions back home would have been immense. You'd have had tribes rising up in Gaul, Iberia, Dacia. There'd be trouble along the Rhine again and the Parthians would be grabbing at our eastern borders. The empire's a mighty thing but it's fragile in its way."

He launched into a complicated explanation of the tribes along the Rhine, clearly an expert on the topic. I tuned his voice out, attempting to stretch my leg which was beginning to cramp. I very much did not want to fall from the tree. Belis waved at me, trying to get me to stay still. I noticed the conversation below us had paused and wondered if I had accidentally made some noise. I froze, trying not to breathe.

"So after Teutoburg Wald," continued Terrasidius's voice, "we stayed west of the river."

"But why—" A loud whistle ended the conversation.

"On your feet, soldiers," the centurion barked. More clattering rose up to us as the Romans stood and formed ranks, fresh waves of complaints floating through the branches.

"Ready to move out, sir?" Terrasidius asked. The centurion must have nodded because the soldiers began to march. Within a moment the woods were quiet again, the clattering of armour fading into the distance.

I waved at Belis and she sat up on her branch. She mouthed something at me and I realised she was counting under her breath. I guessed she was planning to count to a hundred before letting us climb back to the ground. A little dramatic but I understood her nervousness. I was not eager to introduce myself to a troop of Roman legionaries in this form.

Belis made me wait to the count of two hundred before she jumped down from the tree. I half climbed, half slid down, fully falling from the last branch. I hit the ground on my back, driving all the air out of my body. I groaned and closed my eyes. There was a new set of bruises I could expect tomorrow.

"Get up," said Belis, her voice vibrating with nerves. I stayed where I was, still catching my breath from the fall.

"Why? They set off to the north. They won't stop for hours yet. That centurion seems even more of a tyrant than you."

"We won't be stopping either. Come on. We need to put some distance between us. We're going west." She leaned down and hooked a hand under my arm, hauling me up.

"You're being ridiculous." I tried to shake her off me. "We've walked far enough for one day. Sit and rest."

Belis grabbed me by the shoulders, looking straight into my face.

"They've been following us across the Chalk. Someone must have seen us passing and told them. It's an insane bit of luck that we heard them coming. They must know we are close by. If they march north and find no trace of us, then they'll come back this way. Believe me, you do not want that to happen. Me, they want alive. You?" She paused, her green eyes blazing at me. "If you want to live long enough to regain your immortality then we need to move right now."

"Fine." She let go of my shoulders and thrust my socks at me. I'd dropped them when I fell out of the tree. She did at least let me put them on before we set off.

The reminder of the enemy had soured Belis's mood and quickened her pace. If I fell behind now she would pause, but fidget uncomfortably, looking up at the sky and tapping her foot until I caught up some more. We walked through the night and met the next morning's sun on the edge of the Cotswold hills.

"You have got to slow down," I gasped, looking up at the forested slopes ahead of us. "We must have put at least fifteen miles between us and that patrol, not to mention that they think you're heading north. We have some time."

Belis ignored me, eyeing the thick woods.

"Come on, this way," she grunted, striding west along the forest's edge.

"I think not," I called after her. She spun on her heel and glared at me.

"And why not, O Mallt, the wise one? Since you know so much better than me about everything, yet have not ceased in complaining for the last week. *'Oh my feet hurt, oh my ears are sore, this stew is tasteless and the fire is too smoky.'* My sister is a moment from death, there are Romans snapping at our heels and you whine about your feet hurting. Could you not, for one single moment, stop talking about your paltry problems and let me walk in peace? Believe me, I like this arrangement even less than you do, but I need you to get to Annwn, so you're stuck with me. We are going this way if I have to drag you."

"As you like," I said, deeply offended. I didn't complain that much. "I only meant to let you know that the fort of Corinium is a mile and a half over yonder hill. I didn't realise I was so poor a travelling companion that you'd rather deliver yourself straight to the wolves' den than listen to me."

Belis froze, then snatched a look behind her as if there would already be cavalrymen riding towards us. She looked back at me slowly, and with an expression of utter frustration on her face.

"When were you planning on telling me this?" she spat out from between clenched teeth. I met her fury with my own.

"I was about to when you went off on your little rant," I hissed at her. "And I do not appreciate your tone of disrespect. I am a goddess and should be spoken to with deference. If this is how your mother taught you to speak to others, then I am not surprised the Romans would not deal with her."

She lunged at me then. I stepped back and tripped over something, landing flat on my back for the second time in one day. I glowered up at her from the ground, vaguely aware that I may have spoken a little harshly but absolutely certain that I would not be apologising. Belis grunted, visibly pushing down her anger, and turned away, her shoulders shaking with emotion. I clambered to my feet, keeping a wary eye on her back in case she lost her internal battle of wills and tried to attack me.

I dusted myself off and set off into the forest, aiming my feet north-west. After a moment I heard Belis follow me. The Cotswold woods were old even to me, gnarled oaks and broad-canopied beeches. What light filtered through to the forest floor was green-tinged gold and the air was thick with the sounds of songbirds. It was an incongruously peaceful scene, compared with the short but bitter argument we had just had.

I replayed my words inside my head over and over again. Perhaps I had been a little mean. I pushed it to the back of my mind. She had just made me walk for a whole day and a night after all; she could forgive me being snippy, especially with the disrespectful way she kept speaking to me.

We stumbled on in icy silence for a few more miles, pausing only to cross the newly paved road the Romans had built a decade or so previously. I let Belis decide when we should dart across, not wanting to provoke her any further.

I waited until we'd walked about a mile from the road before speaking. "*Now* can we stop and rest?"

Belis was about ready to drop – her footsteps were starting to slow, her eyelids shuttering open and closed. She looked as if she would argue just on principle but then shrugged and sat down right where she had been standing.

"If we're going to stop during the daytime then one of us should keep watch," she muttered eventually.

"I'll go first," I said, giving the vaguest suggestion of a peace offering. Belis nodded, already stretching out and wadding her pack under her head.

"Wake me at midday," she said, eyes closing, "or if you see anything." She fell asleep almost instantly, her chest rising and falling steadily under her cloak.

I curled up against the trunk of a beech tree, tucking my feet underneath me. I was tired, too, more tired than I ever remembered having been before. Every muscle in my body seemed wrung out, completely depleted of energy. Worse still was the constant racing of my mind. I could barely sort out my thoughts, my feelings, the strange emotions that were rocketing through this body.

The aching in my feet began to subside a little but I noticed a new sensation in my chest. It felt deeper than a muscle pain. Could it be some kind of indigestion? I thought back to the last thing I had eaten, the handfuls of berries the day before. I could feel hunger pangs in my stomach, but they were different. Human bodies were always aching in one way or another, I thought. No wonder they were so bad-tempered

The sun was almost directly overhead. I decided to let Belis sleep a little longer. She could have my hour and we would go when she woke up. I was pleased with my altruism. Let her try calling me selfish again after this. I began to sing, under my breath at first and then louder when it became clear Belis wasn't going to be disturbed. It was a song I'd learned a few dozen years ago, while visiting Gwyn's court, a merry tale of derring-do with an extremely whistle-able tune. The melody had stuck in my head, though I had forgotten more than half of the words.

"I haven't heard that song since my childhood."

I started, looking around for the source of the voice. A woman was standing right beside me. She looked to be in her late fifties, grey-haired and with lines radiating across her tanned skin. She smiled at me, her fingers twitching strangely in a gesture I didn't recognise.

"I didn't mean to startle you. I thought I was making a fair amount of noise as I came up the hill."

My human hearing really was terrible. I should have heard her coming. I retrieved my manners and returned her smile.

"I was miles away. My name is Mallt."

She bowed towards me. "Vatta. What are you doing in my woods?"

"Your woods!" I exclaimed. "Well, I like that, what a foolishly human turn of phrase! I didn't realise these woods were owned by anyone. We're on the run from the Romans, heading out to Caer Sidi. That's Belis over there, she's the one who the Romans are after. We're trying to go and get her sister's soul back from Arawn, as well as my powers." I clapped my hands over my mouth before I could say more.

"Wait, I didn't mean to say all that." I looked Vatta up and down, my eyes narrowing. "You put a compulsion of truth on me. How dare you!"

She looked unrepentant. "I find it saves a lot of time. I'll admit I was expecting something more along the lines of taking a shortcut to mushrooms rather than a tale of desperate fugitives from Roman justice."

"Well, I don't appreciate it at all." I nudged Belis with my toe. "Wake up, I need you to kill this witch."

Belis yawned, opened her eyes, saw Vatta and scrambled for her knife, almost slashing her hand open as she fumbled the blade from its hilt. She held it out in front of her, moving between us.

"A witch?" she said, looking frantically from me to Vatta.

"Yes. I told her who we are and that the Romans are looking for us. You'll have to kill her. Quick, before I say anything else."

"What else would you say?" asked Vatta, interestedly. I stuffed one hand in my mouth to stop the words spilling out and pointed the other fist at the knife and then at Vatta, miming a stabbing motion.

Belis held out her knife but stayed where she was.

"You're a witch?" she asked. I rolled my eyes. I had covered that already. Humans were so slow.

"Indeed I am," Vatta said. "You can put that away, child, I'm no friend to the Romans. The Dobunni chiefs may have given over control of the villages and the roads to their allies, but these woods are still mine and I keep them."

Belis sheathed her knife. I took my hand out of my mouth and wiped it on my tunic.

"Belis is a witch, too, you can talk about that. Teach her some spells to make her cooking taste better."

Belis glared at me. "I can do some magic. Not enough for everyone's liking."

"What is enough?" Vatta said. "There are always more things that we wish we could do than we can. Who's your angry friend with the bad hearing?"

"I'm not her friend. I'm Mallt Y Nos. That mortal somehow stole my power when I was trying to collect her sister's soul. Now I'm trapped in a human form and . . . Stop that spell right now!"

Vatta raised her eyebrows and turned to look at me more closely.

"The Nightshade? I'm honoured, my lady. I have made many offerings to you over the years, even seen you run through the woods a time or two with your hounds. I thought you looked familiar. Though you're a great deal shorter than I remember."

She bowed towards me. I made a great effort not to be soothed, but the bow was nice. Finally someone was treating me with proper respect. I patted my hair, wishing I didn't look so messy. When she rose she flicked her fingers and I felt the compulsion release me.

"Come," she said. "My home is not far from here. I can offer you a more comfortable place to rest and some supplies. You shall be safe there, I swear it on my power."

Belis shifted awkwardly. "You're very kind to offer that but we have a long way to go. We must cross the Severn and keep heading west. We have a Roman patrol out looking for us. I would not lead them your way."

"Let me worry about the Romans. Besides, you'll be slow on foot. I know someone who'll sell you a pair of horses. You can make up the time you spend resting and more." Vatta turned and began walking down the hill. "Come!"

I looked at Belis. She shrugged at me.

"Horses will be faster. And I'm sick of hearing you complain about your feet." She grabbed her pack and followed Vatta, hurrying to catch up.

I sighed and trudged after her.

Belis Before
2

She is nine years old and holding a spear for the first time. For years she has been pestering her parents to let her train in the courtyard with the other youngsters. Her father has tried to distract her with pony rides and new toys, but Belis will not be bribed. She wants to be a warrior like her mother. Eventually the king threw up his hands and ordered the carpenter to make her a practice spear, blunted at both ends.

On presenting the much-longed-for weapon to Belis, her mother warns her that this is not a toy.

"A spear is not just a weapon, it is a life, a duty. I had it carved from an oak tree that had stood for a hundred years. You must respect that, honour the strength of the oak when you fight. A warrior may wield it in war but must do so with purpose, with truth in their heart. To be a spear maiden is to understand when to stand down as much as when to fight."

Belis nods, her brow furrowed in concentration. The queen stands before her, her long hair swept up in battle braids, her own spear in hand. She wears practice garments, deerskin leggings and vest, leaving her limbs free to move. She spins on a toe and strikes so hard that the air sizzles.

"I do not speak only of choosing your opponents with care," Boudica says, twisting the spear above her head. "Any warrior with a scrap of honour knows not to attack the weak and the sick. I should not have to tell you that."

She throws the spear and it flies through the air, thudding into the hitching post on the other side of the yard. She turns back to Belis.

"I speak of more cunning things. When to retreat and regroup, when to let an opponent think he has beaten you and concede. When to fight with all the strength and all the blood in your body."

Belis grins, still clutching her practice spear. The queen smiles at her and suddenly the fierce warrior is gone and her mother is kneeling before her. One hand comes down to tuck back a loose curl.

"I know you will make me proud, little acorn."

Belis practises for hours, striking, blocking, fighting opponents a year or two older than her. Her mother sits and watches as the weapons master drills her and the other children. Cati, now four summers old, has wandered out into the sunlight and flops to the ground at her mother's feet.

Belis waves at her little sister and takes a spear butt to the chest. Sprawling in the dirt, she gasps for breath then scrambles back to her feet. She can feel her mother's eyes on her and she forces herself to calm and reset to the basic defence position, feet in a wide stance, crouched low.

The weapons master is the one who struck her and he looks down approvingly.

"Don't get distracted, Princess. But if you do take a fall, that's the way to do it. Straight back on your feet. If you stay on the ground then you'll never win."

She nods and moves back towards her fellow trainees. The old warrior watches her go, tugging thoughtfully on his braided moustache.

"She's got guts, your girl," she hears him say to the queen. "Lacks a little focus but she'll get there."

Boudica doesn't answer but out of the corner of her eye Belis can see a smile flicker across her face. She feels a swell of courage and pushes forward with renewed vigour.

The yard is filled with the clatter of wood on wood, of grunts and gasps and the occasional stifled sob. Belis feels the fading sun on her back and uses the evening glare to temporarily blind her adversary, knocking them down with a lucky blow.

The other child rolls on the floor and Belis reaches out a hand to help them back up. This is what she is made for, she thinks to herself, not clumsy embroidery or tilling the land. She is a spear maiden, wild and free.

Chapter 5

Vatta led us another half-mile or so through the woods, down through heavily vegetated gullies where even the songbirds fell silent. I had to clutch at the exposed roots of the trees in order not to trip, but Belis had no problems keeping up with Vatta. Both of them bounded down like spring lambs and looked irritated whenever they had to pause and wait for me.

Eventually we halted in a patch of woodland seemingly no different from any other. Belis looked around, clearly confused as to why we had stopped again. Vatta paused to check I had caught up. Then she went up to the nearest tree, an enormous spreading oak, and rummaged in the thick ivy that coated the trunk. She pulled out a rope and tugged on it. A ladder tumbled down from one of the branches above. I looked up, squinting through the leaves. There didn't seem to be anything there. I could see through the leaves all the way to the chinks of blue sky.

These days my eyes had become significantly less reliable at seeing things that were hidden, so I followed Vatta up the ladder. My second tree climb of the day was less successful than my first. Even with Belis holding the ropes taut on the ground the ladder wriggled underneath my hands and feet and it took me an embarrassingly long time to haul myself up to the branch.

Vatta ended up helping, gripping me under my shoulders

and heaving me up the last few rungs until I finally collapsed, frustrated and exhausted, at the top.

When I got my bearings I found that I was sprawled out on neat wooden planks, nailed in a wide circle around the main tree trunk. I took Vatta's outstretched hand and let her help me to stand. She smiled at me then leaned over to help Belis who was swarming up the ladder behind me as if she did it every day of her life, the show-off. My old body would have leapt up without even the need for the ladder, reaching for a branch and swinging myself up.

I squinted at the tree trunk, trying to see past the glamour. The air shimmered and rippled and suddenly I was staring at a small cottage, built from blocks of creamy limestone and thatched with thick golden straw. It looked as if a giant had picked up a completely ordinary peasant's house and dumped it in the middle of the tree, with no regard for how it would stay up or whether the tree could bear the weight. That was possible, I supposed, but unlikely. I took a step closer, one hand on the railing, and peered out. Parts of the house seemed to be hanging out over the air. Vatta clapped me on the back.

"Welcome to my home, Mallt Y Nos. It is an honour to host you."

I smiled back at her. "Yes, it probably is."

She laughed and stepped towards the whitewashed front door. It swung open before she had even reached out a hand to touch it and the witch disappeared inside. I glanced at Belis and then followed her in. The cottage was artificially stretched out, much larger than I had expected from outside. Even the additional space seemed cramped as it was absolutely packed with things. Piles of vellum scrolls covered in a spidery acorn-ink handwriting littered the floor, drying herbs hung from the rafters, an entire deer skeleton wired together with gleaming copper string stood in front of a wooden bed piled high with blankets. Half-completed knitted scarves were draped from the skeleton's antlers and a gently turning potter's wheel spattered clay across the floorboards in the corner of the room.

I skittered backwards on instinct as something on the floor moved towards me, then relaxed as I recognised what it was. A fully grown chicken was pecking at a half-opened scroll. I looked closer and saw more chickens, scratching on the table, nesting in between cushions and on windowsills. Looking out over the entire mess, with all the royal disdain of Gwyn ap Nudd himself, was an enormous ginger cat lounging in the very centre of the kitchen table, flicking his tail and glaring at the intrusion of strangers into what he clearly considered to be his domain.

I picked my way through the chaos and took a seat at the table. Then I stood up again and removed the speckled chicken egg that had been left there. I handed it to Vatta and sat down again. She put it into one of her pockets and beamed at me.

"What can I get you? Water, wine, mead, apple juice?" she asked, clattering about in a cupboard.

"Water, please," I said, at the same moment Belis asked for "Wine if you have it."

We glared at each other then looked away. Vatta set three smooth earthenware cups on the table, filled one from a ewer of water near the roof and the others from a jug of wine. Belis moved to sit down at the opposite end of the table. She picked up a scroll that the chicken had been pecking at.

"Is this Greek?" she asked, turning it over in her hands.

"Yes, Plato's *Republic*. One of the earlier volumes." Vatta puttered over to peer at the scroll. "Do you read Greek, my dear?"

Belis shook her head, holding the parchment as if it was as delicate as a butterfly's wings.

"No, only Latin and some runes. I just recognised some of the characters. How did you come to learn Greek? There can't be many traders this far west and you said you didn't speak with the Romans."

I detected an edge to her voice and realised without knowing how that she had tensed, ready to grab for her knife again.

Vatta yawned. "Oh, I intercepted a wagonload of goods going along the road to Glevum a few years back. Mostly records and logistics but a few interesting books here and there. I taught myself the basics with a spell of understanding."

"Intercepted?" I asked. Vatta grinned at me then nodded to the cup of water she had poured. "Replaced the whole lot with chicken dung. They stopped disrespecting me after that. Drink up. You will stay here tonight, and tomorrow I will direct you to a farm that will sell you horses."

I took a sip of the water. It was clear and fresh, with the slight acidic tang that water from this part of the world always had. Belis drank her wine and eagerly accepted the tranches of bread, meat and cheese that Vatta served us.

I offered a piece of the cheese to the cat, who deigned to take it from me without biting my hand. I muffled a yawn of my own. Sharp-eyed Vatta saw it.

"Go and rest. I am sure Belis and I will find something to talk about."

I glanced longingly at the bed and realised it had been almost two days since I had slept, then back at Belis. She nodded.

"Go. I would say we are as safe here as anywhere in Britain. Besides, I want to talk witchcraft with Vatta and I doubt that will interest you."

I slid down from the seat and padded over to the bed. I kicked off my boots and collapsed onto the blankets. It was warm and cosy and the clucking of chickens was surprisingly soothing. I fell asleep almost instantly.

By the time I woke, the shutters were closed and flames were burning merrily in the brick fireplace. It took me a moment to remember where I was – it had been the first true rest I had had since losing my immortal form. There was a comforting warmth in the bed beside me. I sat up. Belis was lying next to me, her head on a pillow next to my feet. Her hair was loose, covering her shoulders in a wave of copper curls She looked younger, gentler than I had seen her before, the fatigue and grief of the last week smoothed away by sleep. I felt my frustrations with her fade, just a little, and something knotted inside me. Probably hunger.

I gingerly picked myself up out of the bed, trying not to disturb her, and padded over towards the kitchen table, wiggling my toes on the smooth polished floorboards.

Vatta was seated on a long bench, fingers busy making what looked like a fishing lure out of twine and chicken feathers. I took a seat beside her and she nodded towards a bowl covered with a fine linen cloth.

"Your dinner. We didn't want to wake you."

I lifted the cloth, revealing a lamb stew. I spooned some of it into my mouth. It was delicious, still warm and well salted. The best food of the fae courts could not compete with this fresh fare. We sat in silence for a while as I ate, disturbed only by the clucking of the roosting chickens and the faint growling purrs of Vatta's cat.

I finished my bowl and pushed it away, resting a contented hand on my stomach. "Thank you," I said, keeping my voice low so as not to disturb Belis. "I appreciate your offerings. I will repay your faith when I am restored."

Vatta smiled at me then stood up.

"Come, let us talk outside. That princess of yours needs her rest."

I glanced at Belis then grabbed my cloak from where it had been hung over one of the antlers of the deer skeleton. Vatta opened the door for me and we slipped out onto the planked decking. She led me around from the entrance to the back of the cottage where a pair of rocking chairs had been placed in front of a gap in the canopy.

I sat in the left-hand chair and looked out. The sky was clear and the stars were bright in the firmament. My eyesight was not as good as it had been, but it still filled my heart to see my old friends. I had spent countless nights staring up at the stars and they were one of the last links back to my old life left to me. Below them the woods of the Cotswold hills faded into the floodplain of the Severn, which glittered silver in the starlight as it wound its way into the west.

"Pretty view, isn't it," said Vatta, taking the other chair and leaning back. "I can see all the way to the Brecon Beacons on a clear day. Mind you, it's bitter cold when the wind is in the west."

"How is it we've never met before?' I asked, turning away from the vista. "A witch with your obvious powers, you should be known by every small fae and human with half an ounce of magic south of the Humber. I should have been listening to gossip about you for years. Yet I've never heard your name mentioned by even the nosiest pedlars."

Vatta tucked in her cloak around her legs, a half-smile on her lips.

"You mean why am I content to live in obscurity in a treehouse rather than leveraging my magic to rule over half of the island?"

I nodded.

"Well, it all sounded like a great deal of work. I came into my powers late, after my children were grown and gone to homes of their own. My husband had passed away when they were young and by the time I had learned just how much strength I had, the idea of ruling over anything seemed extremely dull. Besides, even my powers could not hold against the might of Rome. They have their own magic users."

She paused to pick up the cat, which had followed us out and was rubbing against her legs. It settled into her lap and blinked slowly in pleasure.

"No doubt had I been younger when I found my magic I would have got myself into the sort of trouble you talk of, but at my age I knew that happiness for me was living in anonymous peace. And having the wherewithal to protect those dear to me: my children, a handful of the local villages, the wild places of these woods. I'm a fundamentally selfish and lazy person. If you don't interest me, why should I bother myself with you?"

I pondered that. It seemed eminently sensible to me, so much so that I was surprised a human had come up with it.

"Maybe Belis can do the same thing," I said. "Her family

hasn't done very well at conquest so far. Maybe she should try something else. She could go north and build her own treehouse." I paused. "But she's not very patient and she's rather angry with the Romans. I think she's quite set on fighting them again."

"She's got a way to go. She only knows a handful of spells and most of them are not particularly useful. Perhaps you could suggest that she come back to study here."

"I doubt she'll listen to me. We don't get on very well. She thinks I complain too much. But I am a goddess, I don't do anything too much."

Vatta grinned.

"And now we come to the things you should have done differently," she said. I frowned at her, but she kept going. "Before Belis, when was the last time you spoke to a human?"

I considered the question, leafing back through my memories.

"I will assume that you do not include the dead or dying? I do occasionally buy food or goods from them if I can't find a pedlar."

Vatta raised her eyebrows.

"And when was the last time you spoke directly to a human for more than a moment? About something other than a jug of goat's milk."

I turned it over in my head. Nothing came to mind. Surely there must have been something.

"May I take it from your silence that you can't remember such a time?" Vatta asked. "Then I think we have identified the source of the tension between you and Belis. Every human you interact with is either dead or about to be. You are too accustomed to human suffering, it is all you see. Belis is alive and whole but what you cannot see is that for her the pain is within."

I shook my head.

"I understand that she's upset, but that doesn't excuse her lack of respect."

"Upset!" cried Vatta so loudly that the cat in her lap stopped purring and stretched out his claws in displeasure. "She's devastated! She's lost every person she ever loved. Her people have been wiped out. And you might think that you understand that, but deep down you feel that she's overreacting."

I went over the last week in my head, thinking about what Vatta had said. I had seen so much human grief and death throughout my life that I no longer considered it much to worry about. Belis had had a hard few months, to be sure, but I had encountered many humans with worse luck over the long years of my existence.

What I had perhaps forgotten was that Belis almost certainly hadn't seen worse. Her being alive and unhurt might seem like good fortune to me after spending night after night fishing souls out of twisted and broken bodies on the battlefield, but Belis had lost everything in the course of one day. I should perhaps have tried a little harder to understand that. It still rankled with me, though.

"Haven't I lost everything, too? My immortality, my power, my hounds, my connections with the other immortals?"

"Of course you have," said Vatta. "Don't you grieve for it?"

Vatta's words were gentle but I felt them like a knife in my ribs. I did mourn my lost life: every moment in this human body was a reminder of what I had lost. Each morning I reached out for my dogs and felt their absence; each night I shivered in the cold, remembering when I had run through the darkness barefoot and free. I was doing everything to regain my old life. So was Belis. Perhaps we were not as dissimilar as I had thought.

"I think I am ... sorry? I'm sorry," I said, tasting the unfamiliar sentiment on my tongue. Vatta let the words hang in the night air for a moment before she sighed.

"My lady, I am not the one who deserves your apologies. I am sure Belis bears a proportion of the blame for this coolness between you. Were you still in possession of your powers then I would not presume to offer you advice. In the body of a human, though, with all the strange and unfamiliar feelings that must be coursing through you, I dare share a little of my observations."

"It is a very strange thing," I said, "full of aches and pains.

Do you know that when I walk uphill my thighs hurt but when I walk downhill my calves hurt. Oh, and whenever Belis is angry, I get this feeling like indigestion in my chest. It's terrible: no wonder you humans don't live long. Who could bear such a whirlpool of emotions for more than a few decades. I'm already exhausted from it."

Vatta smiled at me and stood up.

"It may not be a long life but there's a sweetness to it. I think you may discover that as you continue to travel west."

I nodded and followed her back into the cottage, turning at the door to take a last look up at the stars.

Vatta waved us off the next morning with our packs filled with fresh supplies and bellies full of fried eggs and bacon. Belis seemed much calmer for her time spent with the other witch and we walked in companionable silence for a while, occasionally stopping to snatch an apple from one of the trees that grew wild in the woods. The chill of the morning burned off after a while and I wrapped my cloak up and stowed it in my pack.

The rest had done me good and Vatta had taught Belis a handful of cantrips, including one to heal blisters. I was pleased to be moving more easily again, even if I was still slower than my companion.

Eventually the trees thinned out and then stopped entirely. We followed Vatta's directions and took a footpath to the south. At the end of the road I saw a long wooden house, surrounded by pens. Horses grazed in the fields. As we approached the house I saw a young woman lunging a horse on a rope as it cantered in wide circles around her.

She paused when she saw us and glanced back up to the house. Belis bowed politely towards her. The woman gave a long, low whistle and waved an arm towards us. A pair of shaggy hounds ran over, stopping a few yards away. Clearly we were not to go any further.

I crouched down and held out my hands to the dogs. One of

them made to come closer but his fellow snapped at him and he fell back in line. I stood again, disappointed but understanding. The sight of the dogs had sent a wave of longing through me for my own hounds. I wanted to run my hands through their fur and bury my face in their scruff.

We waited in the sun. A second figure emerged from the house and headed towards the dogs. He calmed them then beckoned us closer. The farmer was broad-shouldered and tall enough to look Belis in the eye. She explained that we had been staying with Vatta and had come to trade for horses and he visibly relaxed.

"The lady sends a few of you my way every year or so. I don't sell my horses lightly, but I can probably spare a couple. A favour from the lady is worth a year of good luck. Follow me."

He waved back at the young woman, and she started lunging the horse again. The farmer led us to a low-set barn, split into stables.

"If you've had dealings with the lady Vatta then you'll be keeping off the main roads," he said, sizing Belis and me up. "Nothing flashy or expensive-looking. You want reliability. Have you ridden before?"

Belis nodded. I gave a weak smile. I had ridden often and well on the fae horses of the Wild Hunt whenever I visited them, great stomping beasts who could run faster than the wind. I doubted my human muscles would have retained those memories, though. I decided to hedge my answer, not wanting to jump in over my head.

"A little, mainly mules or donkeys," I said.

The farmer laughed. "This will be an upgrade, then." He unlatched the nearest stall and clicked his tongue. A sturdy-looking pony trotted out, his coat a burnished bay with three white socks.

"This for you, then." The farmer patted the pony on the rump. "His name's Weasel. As for you . . ." He glanced at Belis thoughtfully then walked up to the end of the barn. He returned a minute later leading the scruffiest gelding I had ever seen. It stood about thirteen hands, with a long, tattered mane and tail. I eyed it dubiously. The farmer caught my expression.

"Yes, I know, but there's nothing wrong with him, he just likes looking that way. I can't tell you how many hours my daughter has spent grooming him, brushing his mane and polishing his coat. He'll just go off and roll in the mud. He's a good horse, though, and eye-catching is not what you want on the roads these days."

Belis stepped forward and offered her hand to the horse to smell, before stroking his nose. She checked him over with an expert eye. The muscles in his legs and shoulders were strong beneath the dust.

"What's his name?" she asked the farmer, finally turning back.

"Carrot," he said, a little abashed. "My daughter named him. He's got a chestnut tinge to him under the grime. We don't go in for fancy names around here."

He wiped his hands on an apron.

"I suppose you'll be wanting some tack for them, too? And we didn't discuss how you'll be paying for these horses."

He endeavoured to loom over us and seemed surprised that Belis was the same height. Belis opened her pack and fished around. She withdrew a handful of golden coins and held them out to the farmer.

"I recommend you rub the faces off before you try and use them," she said, dropping them into his outstretched hands.

He picked one up and bit it, inspecting the toothmarks in the soft gold.

"Well, that'll more than cover it, and my silence, too. Thanks for the tip. I take it this face isn't popular among our new overlords?"

"They're looking for me. It'd be better for you if they never know I was here."

The farmer scratched his head. "I reckon so. Don't tell me any more, then. Lady Vatta's got a firm grip on these parts, but you don't want to push your luck."

He held out his hand for Belis to shake, then headed off back to the house. Carrot nosed into the open pack and I closed it before he could snaffle the last of the apples. He gave me a doleful look and I relented and fished one out for him. He ate it from my palm and I stroked his soft nose. It wasn't quite as good as having a dog, but his animal smell and obvious love of treats made me feel a little better.

Riding was exactly as uncomfortable as I had feared, but Weasel was a quick little thing and Carrot could be enticed into some speed with the rankest bribery. We made excellent time and reached the banks of the Severn before nightfall. I remembered Vatta's words and tried hard not to complain too much when we finally slid out of the saddle. I had thought I'd identified all the muscles in my legs that could possibly give me pain but a day on horseback proved me wrong.

Belis found a boatman willing to transport us across the river and I led the horses down to the waterside, hobbling and trying not to slip in the mud. The river was a muddy-brown in the greyness of the day, a far cry from the silver snake I had seen in the moonlight from Vatta's balcony last night. When we had boarded and the boatman had begun to punt us across, I turned and waved back towards the woods.

"What are you doing?" Belis asked, raising her eyebrows.

"Vatta might be able to see us. I want her to know we're safe!" I nudged her. "Wave!"

"You realise that we're a good fifteen miles away?" Belis said.

"You realise that she's an incredibly powerful witch? Wave!"

She sighed as if I was being ridiculous but put her arm up and waved to the east. I thought I detected the ghost of a smile on her lips and I felt a bubble of happiness in my chest.

We landed on the far side of the river and began disembarking. The light was almost gone but we climbed back into the saddles and put another mile between us and the river, riding into the Forest of Dean.

Belis still wasn't talking to me much, but I thought she was a little less angry with me than she had been. I let her be quiet, unsure of the right words to say, but I could hear Vatta's voice in my head telling me to try harder. I decided I had waited long enough and shuffled a little closer to her.

"I wanted to say," I began, trying not to sound too rehearsed, "that I have been very upset since we first met. Living as a human has been difficult for me to accept. It's horrible, I really don't know how you all do it."

Belis blinked then narrowed her eyes at me. I dragged myself back on track.

"What I meant to say was, I've not been acting as a goddess should. I've been rude and unpleasant company and I'm sorry for that."

"Is this a joke?" Belis sounded suspicious.

I shook my head, struggling to find the words.

"I'm serious. And to be clear, this is not about you being the daughter of a king. I still dramatically outrank you. I should have been politer to you because you're a person." I remembered what Vatta had said. "A person with a lot of feelings."

Belis's mouth quirked and I wondered if I had misspoken.

"Thank you, Mallt. I should have been kinder to you, too. I know that we're in this because of me and it must be hard being in a new body. You're entitled to complain a bit."

"I really don't think I complained that much," I said before I could stop myself. "What I mean is, thank you."

She leaned over, easy in the saddle, to knock her shoulder against mine. I felt absurdly pleased with myself at the gesture.

Belis reined in her horse and dismounted. She leaned her spear against the tree and dropped her pack.

"I think we can risk a fire," she said. "Mallt, will you gather some dead wood? I will see if I can find something to eat."

I nodded. By the time I had collected enough dry wood and built the base of the fire she had returned bearing wild garlic, tubers and several kinds of non-poisonous mushrooms. For a final prize she revealed a handful of late wild strawberries.

We ate the berries first, carefully dividing them between us, trying to eat slowly and savour the sweetness, then we dug into the fungi.

We sat in silence, munching on the mushrooms while I roasted the tubers on the fire. The rain was still pattering on the thatched leaves and the light had faded. For once the lack of conversation did not feel heavy, but comfortable. We were being quiet together, not at each other. Belis had tucked her knees up to her chin and was staring into the fire. Her face took on the look of melancholy that had become so familiar to me. I remembered her smiling on the boat and wanted to see that again. I wished I could cheer her up, or at least lessen some of the burden she carried. Before I could think of anything, she spoke.

"I've been thinking," she said, "that I should try and give you a little instruction in fighting. If we run into the Romans again you ought to be able to defend yourself. You weren't much help against the wight."

My face must have fallen because she gave me another half-smile.

"I'm not saying you'll become a master fighter overnight. I can just teach you a little of the basics. Right now, you don't have a spear or sword of your own, or even a knife. You need to start with what you have, so that you'll never rely on weapons."

She stood up and adopted a fighting stance, legs wide and slightly bent.

"You know I'm a goddess. I've fought fiercer opponents than you before."

She didn't move so I sighed and stood up. From her slouching position Belis's eyes were the same level as mine.

"Fine. What's my first lesson?"

"You need to learn how to fall down," she said.

I frowned at her, confused. If there was one thing I had absolutely proven I could do in this frail human body it was fall over. She beckoned me closer.

"Try and push me over. Use all your strength."

I hung back, unsure whether this was a trick. She rolled

her eyes. "I promise I won't defend myself. I just need to demonstrate."

I moved a little closer. Belis smiled at me encouragingly. I reached out, then hesitated. "Come on, Mallt! I won't get hurt. Humans aren't that fragile!"

I pushed her, using both hands. I doubted I had really landed it with enough force to knock her over, but she fell backwards, rolling over her shoulders and springing back into position as gracefully as any fae.

"Again, this time from the side," she said, flicking a strand of coppery hair from her face. I pushed her again, and again she went down, this time rolling over her right shoulder.

"You never want to be on the ground. You should avoid it at all costs," Belis said, jumping back to her feet. "But sometimes you will get knocked down and you need to know how to get back up. Use the force of your attacker to fuel your movement. Again."

I pushed her a third time and she dodged, missing my hands by inches. Faster than my mortal eyes could track, she doubled back and pushed me hard on my shoulders. I went down, hard and fast and without any of Belis's grace or purpose. I landed flat on my back, the breath knocked out of me.

"Ow!" I complained, struggling to sit up. "You said that you wouldn't defend yourself."

"I was lying," Belis said cheerfully. "Never trust anyone to fight fair and never fight fair yourself."

"I thought you were a princess," I grumbled. "Shouldn't you be more invested in nobility in combat?"

"My father was noble," she said, the smile dropping from her lips. "He put trust in his enemies and, after he died, they betrayed him. Again!"

Belis came at me, fast and threatening. We continued until she decreed that I could fall acceptably.

"Perhaps tomorrow we will start on blades," she said happily. "You should carry my sword, get used to the weight of it."

"I'm beginning to regret making amends with you," I muttered but took the weapon she offered me and settled by the fire. Belis sat opposite me and wrapped her cloak around her shoulders.

"It's your turn to teach me something now," she said. I frowned, looking up at her; she hadn't shown much curiosity about me so far.

"What do you want to learn?"

"Tell me about you. Do you always live in the mortal world or do you flit between here and Annwn?"

"Here mostly." I considered how to frame my response. "Very few can travel between the realms and it must be done carefully and with a purpose."

"What purpose could take you there?"

"Think of those who should be in Annwn but remain here: wights, ghosts and ghouls. If they were in Annwn they would be normal souls but if they are trapped here then they become dangerous." I shuffled a little closer to the fire. "Most who need my help require only to be set on the right road and they can find their way, but for those few I must take them right to the gate. For only the most fearsome and lost souls do I escort through the passage and into Annwn itself. They are rare, arriving maybe once a generation, and with them I go through to speak with Arawn so that he can care for them appropriately while they recover."

Belis nodded thoughtfully, an odd look on her face. "And now you are returning there with me, the greatest monster of them all."

"That's a strange thing to say." I glanced at her, the light of the flames reflected in her eyes so that they seemed golden.

"Didn't I kill you? Your immortal self, damning all lost souls to wander and all the living to fear them?"

"Well, yes."

I paused, trying to marshal my thoughts. Belis was saying no more than what I had been grumbling to myself and aloud to her for weeks, but I had never considered her monstrous because of it, merely foolish and human. Now Vatta had talked a little sense into me and I felt differently. I looked at Belis again and saw the sadness cut deep into her expression. I wanted to ease some of that pain if I could.

"Perhaps for now we can forget what we were and simply be two humans travelling together, at least for a little while. I am sick of fighting. I would rather be at peace with you."

For the first night since we had met I watched a little of the tension lift from her face, and she fell asleep easily while the fire crackled between us.

Chapter 6

The next morning my legs were even more brutally sore and stiff than usual, but I got back up on Weasel as soon as Belis and I had broken our fast. After much hesitation Belis had agreed that we could ride along the road. She paused again as we left the forest and touched the back of her head, checking that her braids were tucked under her scarf. She caught me looking and flushed, urging Carrot forward onto the road.

Out in the open we passed other travellers every few hours, greeting them with nods and a mutual unease. Most were small merchants, riding on carts piled with bales of carded wool or cages of chickens. The wealthier ones rated a guard trotting along beside them who invariably glared at us until we were out of sight. After three days on the road we saw our first Romans, a covered carriage escorted by a small squadron of legionaries. They barely glanced at us as we scrambled off the road to let them pass, taking our obeisance as their right. I saw Belis grinding her teeth and heard her fingers tapping the sheath of her dagger. She was jumpy for the rest of that day and I let her take a long time to find a campsite that felt safe without complaint. She insisted we keep a watch and it was only with great effort that I talked her into letting me take the first half of the night. She tossed and turned for a while before eventually lapsing into a restless sleep.

A few hours later she started screaming. I scrambled up from where I had been sitting, leaning against a tree and staring out into the blackness, and hurried over to her. Belis's eyes were clamped shut and she was all tangled up in her cloak, pinning her arms to her side. Her face was damp with sweat and she was howling in fear.

"Belis, wake up!" I grabbed her shoulders and shook her, but she was too lost in the dream. She managed to free one hand from her cloak and started grabbing for the spear beside her. I kicked it away and slapped her in the face.

"Wake up!" I yelled.

Belis's eyes snapped open and in one fluid movement she had spun me over, pinning me beneath her. I squinted up at her, watching as the terror in her face ceded to recognition.

"Mallt?" she whispered, letting go of my wrists.

"You were having a nightmare," I said, pulling myself into a seated position. "You were screaming. I had to wake you up."

"Screaming?" Belis looked confused. "I never screamed. I kept quiet the whole time. I didn't want to give them the satisfaction."

I regarded her for a long moment, watching as the pulse in her neck slowed back to normal, as her breathing became less ragged. I thought I understood what she meant.

"Well, do you want to break camp? In case anyone heard us? You were making quite a lot of noise."

Belis glanced at the dying fire and then shook her head.

"We're half an hour's ride from the main road. I made good and sure that we were alone before we lit the fire."

She put her hand to her head, rubbing at her eyes.

"I'm sorry, Mallt, I didn't mean to disturb you. I'll take the next watch."

"Are you sure?"

Belis nodded. "I'm sure. I don't want to go back to sleep just yet."

I stood up and made my way back to where I had left my pack and started unrolling the sleeping mat Vatta had given me. The night was cold and I wrapped my cloak around me and dragged the mat a little closer to the fire.

"Here, take my bedroll as well." Belis tucked it around me. "I'll be fine with my cloak."

I thanked her and snuggled into the extra fabric, still warm from her body. I watched as Belis picked up her spear and went to the edge of our clearing, her features bright against the darkness of the night. I tried to stretch out my mind, to understand the emotions that must be tussling within her. All these years I had run, guiding my lost souls, I had seen every stage of human life in every possible permutation. Yet I still didn't understand them. That hadn't seemed to matter to me before, but, looking at Belis now as she leaned against her spear, I found that I wanted to understand.

We rose early and rode west, meeting the road as we went. The land continued to unspool ahead of us until suddenly we were there. The cliffs dropped away and all was the silver sea, shining in the grey daylight. Belis slid out of the saddle and tiptoed right up to the edge of the land. I eyed the ground suspiciously, but it seemed solid.

Gulls swirled overhead in the pale sky, screeching at us. Belis's eyes were wide and the grey-green of her irises seemed luminous with wonder.

"So this is the sea," she said, not turning away from the view. "I always wondered. It's so much more than I thought."

"More what?" I asked.

"Just more." She stretched out her hand as if to touch the air.

"Didn't you see it in the east?" I said, remembering what she had told me on the Chalk.

"We stayed in the fens, in the marshes and rivers. My father always said he would take us one day but there was never time."

She stayed where she was, breathing deeply. I waited a while then coughed gently. Belis sighed and looked over towards me.

"Well, this is the coast. Is Caer Sidi far from here?"

I shook my head. "Another fifteen miles or so further west."

"West?" Belis glanced up at the sun then back at the sea. "How much further west can we go? Is there a headland somewhere?"

"No. Caer Sidi isn't on the mainland. There's an island, the locals call it Grassholm, about fifteen miles from here."

"An island?" She frowned. "Do you have a boat?"

That was a strange question, I thought. Why would I have a boat, and even if I did, why would I keep it here?

"No..."

Belis stared at me and I wondered if I had missed something.

"Then how do you get to the island, to Grassholm?" She slowed her speech as if I was stupid. I bridled at that. I thought we had moved past this.

"I run, of course. I don't go often, every ten years or so. I just wait for a full moon and then run across the path. You can do it in a half- or crescent moon, too, but the path is widest at full."

"You could run on water?" Belis shook her head. "No, of course you could. Goddess, I remember. What I mean to ask is: how were you planning on getting there now?"

"Well, it's a full moon tonight so I'll just—" I broke off, finally understanding. "It won't work any more, will it? Humans can't run on water."

"No." Belis looked as if she was going to continue, then slammed her mouth shut before anything else could slip out. I appreciated that.

I swung myself off Weasel and down to the ground, wincing as my legs straightened out after hours in the saddle. I tiptoed up to the edge and looked over. Below me the waves were enthusiastically smashing themselves onto the rocks, the sea churned into a roiling foam. I stepped back smartly and went to grip the reins of my pony. My head was spinning at the height and I wanted to cling to something solid. Weasel nuzzled at my hair, whiffling comfortably.

"Well?" demanded Belis.

"I guess we can't run. Unless you can magic the water to hold us?" I asked hopefully. Belis dismissed the idea without consideration.

"No, and definitely not while running for fifteen miles. I'm not sure I can run fifteen miles on land."

"We could swim," I said, chewing on my lip. I liked swimming usually but hadn't done more than bathing in a stream since meeting Belis.

"Not for fifteen miles of open water."

"Do you have a boat?" One look at Belis told me she didn't think this question was any less stupid coming from me than I had when she'd said it.

"Sorry, I forgot to bring it with me when I fled my home."

"We need to find a boat then." I scanned the horizon. The land was completely empty of human habitation. "Could you make one? Your tribe uses little coracles and suchlike on the fens, no?"

"I can make a coracle," Belis said. "Just give me two deer hides, a basket of cat guts, a stack of aged willow branches, some hooves to boil down for glue and about three months."

I thought that over.

"Could you use the horse hides instead?" I nodded at the knife on her belt. "And the hooves, horses have hooves, too!"

Belis looked shocked.

"We are not skinning the horses! I was being facetious anyway. I can't make a boat."

I sighed. It was difficult not to complain when she said confusing things like that.

"Then we'll have to go find someone who can. Or at least someone we can borrow a boat from."

"We haven't passed anyone on the road for three days. Where are you going to find this fantastic shipwright?"

I considered. It was rare for any mortal dying so close to Caer Sidi to get lost. The pull to Annwn was stronger here, and so I did not have cause to come by often. There had been an incident about fifteen years ago, however, a woman murdered by her husband. Her soul had been so tangled in fear and fury that it had metastasised into something dark and had haunted the community that had failed her. By the time I had arrived and sent her to her rest, the ghost had taken a bloody revenge on her killer, along with half the men in the village. I tried to remember where the village was in relation to here. A lot of my navigation had been helped by my sensitivity to the background magic of Britain. One more thing that was now lost to me.

"I think there's a fishing village about ten miles north of here." I said. "They have boats, or at least they did the last time I visited. We can go there and try to buy one."

"Buy one? I suppose we could. We could trade the horses. I guess it's better than the alternatives," Belis said, stroking her horse's neck. "Ten miles, you say? We should get there by nightfall. If we set sail tomorrow we'll only have lost one day."

That agreed, we mounted again and turned our horses to the north. The coastal path wound worryingly close to the edge and though Weasel's hooves were steady I couldn't help but worry. Riding along the cliffs made my human stomach flip-flop like a landed trout and I gripped the reins with white knuckles. It was a relief to trot down the winding goat track towards the village.

The houses were tumbledown, shutters flapping in the wind. Wood pigeons cooed down from threadbare thatch as we trotted between the houses towards the sea. A half-sunken wooden jetty floated in the water, tied to posts with rotting ropes draped with seaweed. The village was completely empty.

"There's no one here," Belis said, twisting in her saddle. "How long ago did you say you were here?"

"Fifteen years," I said. "Maybe twenty. No longer than that."

"The villagers must have gone," she said, jumping down and looping her reins over a gatepost. "Take a look around. They might have left something."

I hitched my horse next to hers and began to peer into the houses. They were all completely empty: no furniture, no log piles, nothing but drifts of leaves and spiders' webs. I found the shards of a clay cup in a smaller hut near the beach, the old wine stains still spattered on the floor. I leafed back through my memories, trying to remember the inhabitants of these houses. It was useless: they had barely registered at the time and the years had merged the thousands of human faces into one.

I knelt down to peer into a small alcove beside the fireplace. A lump of bone sat inside. I reached in and picked it up, bringing it outside into the light. It was a crudely carved figurine of a woman, circles etched into the torso for breasts and a triangle just above where her legs parted. I recognised it, having seen similar idols many times before. A tiny mother goddess, wrenched from her little altar. I turned it over in my hands, wondering why it had been left behind. They were rare these days and whoever had carved this had not been especially gifted. There were echoes of past effort, though, in the charcoal rubbed into the engraved lines and in the faint smell of animal fat that had been used to polish it. Belis called my name from the beach and I turned to go. Then I paused and propped the figure back in her alcove, wishing my unknown sister goddess well.

When I returned to the beach, I found Belis dragging a rowboat out onto the sand. Her arms were covered in scratches and there were cuts on her face. Her headscarf had come undone but she looked triumphant.

"What happened to you?" I asked, hurrying forward. She blew loose curls out of her face and grinned at me.

"Found it hidden under an overgrown blackberry bush. I reckon whoever left it must have meant to come back but never did."

"And you decided to go in after it yourself?" I asked, incredulous at her injuries. "You're all scratched and cut up!'

"Well, it wasn't going to get out on its own." Belis saw my expression and touched her cheek, wincing as her fingers found a particularly deep scrape. "Don't worry, Vatta taught me a good spell for this. I'll patch myself up this evening."

I went to help her flip the boat over so we could check it for holes. It was covered in algae and moss but the wood beneath felt strong enough and I couldn't see any obvious damage. When we turned it back over an oar fell out. Belis picked it up and drove it into the sand next to her spear.

"One oar is a bit light for a twenty-mile sail. I don't suppose you remember what the currents around here are like?"

I didn't: such things were generally beneath my notice. Belis wandered back to the bushes and emerged happily gripping the second oar. There was a fresh cut above her eyebrow, beginning to dribble blood around her eye socket and down her cheek.

"That's enough. Go and sit down," I said. "We can do the rest tomorrow."

"You're very worried about a few scratches. Aren't you the Goddess of Death? Surely a little bit of blood shouldn't upset you."

"This is different. I get upset if one of the dogs get a thorn in their paw, too."

Belis began to complain but I took the oar off her and stuck it beside the other in the damp sand. She shrugged and followed me back up the beach.

"We should camp here in one of the old houses tonight and set sail tomorrow. If we hug the coastline 'til we get back to where we were this morning do you think we'd still have time to reach Grassholm by tomorrow night?"

I considered this. I wasn't sure how fast Belis could row, or if she would be expecting me to help. I doubted I would find long-distance rowing any easier than walking or riding.

"Let's see how long it takes to get back to the cliffs, then we can decide."

She dropped her pack and dug around in it for her waterskin. She began washing sand out of the scratches on her arm. Next, she traced a finger over the worst of them, a long red line that ran from her elbow almost to her wrist. She muttered something too low for me to hear. As I watched, the flesh began to mould back together until the cut had completely vanished.

Belis looked pleased and began on the next.

"I'm glad to see it works. I've never tried a healing spell before." She frowned in concentration as her skin repaired itself.

"What about Cati?" I asked.

Belis stiffened and stopped her muttering. "Apart from that."

"That's quite a spell to forget. It's the reason we're here, after all."

"It wasn't strictly speaking a healing spell," Belis said, prodding her arm with her finger and not looking at me.

"Then what was it?" I asked, alarmed. "What were you trying to do?"

"It is not important."

I stood up, resting my hands on my hips and glaring down at her.

"Tell me the truth!"

Belis looked down. Her finger pressed against a scratch, causing blood to pool around her nail. I grabbed her hand and pulled it away, smearing her blood on my own hands.

"Tell me!" I said, still holding her hand.

"The spell I was doing, I learned it from a druid, like I told you." Belis hesitated. "But it wasn't a healing spell. It was a spell of sacrifice. It takes life from one source and gives it to another. I saw them kill a goat once to try and make the crops grow. I remembered the words. I heard the chief of the Trinovantes had three slaves killed to save his own life. I thought it would work for me."

"I don't understand."

"You truly don't know?" She gave a short laugh. "I thought you had figured it out. Humans really all look the same to you, don't they."

"What does that have to do with anything?"

Belis dropped my hand and lifted up her tunic. The skin of her stomach was pale and freckled, but a jagged scar sliced across her abdomen. It had almost healed to a fine silvery line.

"Cati wasn't the one who was injured in the battle. I was. She and my mother carried me to the clearing. My mother took poison."

At first I didn't understand the implication of what she had said, but then it struck me like a blow from an axe.

"You – you used her life force to heal yourself? You weren't trying to heal her, you were trying to kill her!"

I tried to keep my voice steady, but it wavered. I was surprised by how shocked I was at her confession. I had seen horrifying things in my thousands of years of life, acts of violence between lovers, parents, siblings. I had thought there was no horror left to shake me, but all those nameless, numberless bodies had been nothing to me and this was Belis, who had become a comrade to me.

She hung her head, the words spilling out now as if she had broken some internal dam. "I didn't mean to kill her. At first I was trying to pull from the trees, from the life around us, but it wasn't enough. The spell was already in progress and I was so desperate to live. I tried to pull at my mother. She had already taken the poison by then. I thought she wouldn't care either way, but Cati was right beside me. Once I'd realised that I had grabbed onto her instead. I thought to just take a little of her life. Just a little. But then I couldn't stop."

"Couldn't?" I said softly. "Don't lie to me, Belis."

"I . . ." she gasped. "It *was* a mistake at first but then I didn't want to let go. I didn't want to die. Oh, gods, Mallt! I wanted to live so much, more than I loved Cati, more than I wanted to make my mother proud, more than anything else. I clung to life like a rat. I didn't know that it would kill Cati, but I don't know that it would have made a difference. I was too far gone to care."

I sat down beside her again, looking out at the sea.

"I thought a chance at life was worth any price. Now I have nothing but shame and regret." Belis turned to me, grabbing at my hands. I tried to wriggle free but she was stronger. I stared at her face, struck by the pain in her expression.

"I'm tortured by my sister's face. I see her everywhere, her hair in the burnished leaves of the autumn trees, her eyes in the mossy stones, her laughter in the bubbling streams. I was her other half and I betrayed her. I was supposed to be the oak that sheltered her, but I let my fear choke me and now I am hollow. I cannot go on without Cati. I will journey to Annwn and offer my own soul for hers and then go gladly into death. Only then can I find peace."

She glanced over at me. "And that doesn't even cover what I've done to you."

"Destroyed an immortal goddess and risked all the lost souls on this island?" I said coldly. "Yes. That's quite the weight to carry. I need to think this through, Belis. I'm not sure I can take you to Annwn any more. I was helping you because I thought it was a mistake, that it was more my fault than yours."

"Please. I know I don't deserve your help. But Cati does, she's never hurt anyone, never betrayed anyone. I swore to her before I left that I would bring her back. I swore I would spend my entire life, give every drop of blood, every breath in my body, to protect her. If you won't take me with you, I won't force it. You can take the boat. But I'll get there myself, I'll swim, I'll do whatever it takes."

Her cheeks were slick with tears but she seemed surer of herself now. I wished I could have been as confident in her words but there was the taste of her falsehood in my mouth now and I could not spit it out. I was truly, deeply shocked.

"Let me think, Belis. I can't decide right now."

She let go of me and sat back, returning her gaze to the waves crashing on the beach. Then she froze.

I followed her gaze to the other side of the beach, where the cliff path wound down from the hillside. A Roman patrol, at least a dozen legionaries, was storming down the trail. Their plate armour glinted in the weak sunlight.

"Gods save us," swore Belis, her hand dropping to the knife in her belt. She looked around wildly before lunging up the beach to where we had left the horses.

"No, Belis, wait!" I leapt after her. "There's no time, we'll never make it."

She stopped, measuring the distance back into the village with her eyes, then cursed again and nodded.

"The boat?" Her voice wavered.

"It's the only way." I grabbed our packs and took off back down the beach to where we had left the boat. Behind us the Romans were yelling. I sneaked a look over my shoulder. They were on the sand now, running steadily towards us. I could see their unsheathed swords, then there was a hissing sound and a javelin thudded into the wet sand not five yards to our left.

I tripped and almost fell. Belis caught my arm and hauled me up without breaking stride and I stumbled along beside her.

New strength flooded through my body and I tasted bitterness in my mouth.

We reached the boat and Belis began pushing it out into the waves, heaving at the stern. I grabbed the oars from where we had driven them into the sand and carried them to the side of the boat, throwing them in with our packs. Then I ducked around the side to help Belis push. It was maddeningly slow. We were still a dozen yards from the waves when more javelins began to fall. They smashed onto the beach, horrifyingly close to us. Belis let out a terrible cry and threw herself at the boat, forcing it into the water just as the soldiers crashed towards us.

"Get in the boat," she screamed at me, grabbing her spear and turning to fight.

I counted the legionaries: fourteen wearing the red-crested helmets of the rank and file and one who must have been an officer. His helmet was crossed with white horsehair.

"Fan out, cut off their retreat," the officer barked. I recognised his voice, though it had been weeks since I had heard it in the woods: the centurion who had lost his family at Londinium. He was too far away for me to see his face but there was bloodlust in his voice. Belis knew him, too. I could tell from the tension in her shoulders when she heard his voice.

"Take her. Try to keep her face intact, she'll be worth less if that's damaged. Kill or capture the other, I don't care."

The soldiers advanced, swords drawn. Belis swung her spear at them, a wild sweep that they dodged with ease. A particularly burly man grabbed the end from her and wrenched it away, dropping it in the surf. Belis flashed her knife, crouching slightly as she tried to step backwards. I was holding onto the oars, trying to punt the boat further into the water. Her sword was still belted at my waist but I didn't dare try and throw it to her. Belis was up to her knees now, the white foam of the waves frothing against her thighs.

"Get in the boat," I yelled. "You have to come *now*!"

Belis glanced over her shoulder at me then slipped and went up to her chest in the water. The Romans didn't rush. They knew they had no need to. They kept advancing slowly. The centurion had stayed on the beach, his pale crest fluttering in the wind.

"It's too late, Mallt," Belis called, spitting out seawater.

"Come *now*. You'll have to swim for it!" I screamed, the wind tearing at my words and carrying them away. Belis turned sideways, keeping her knife pointed at the soldiers, but looking at me. Her face was calm.

"Promise me you'll help Cati," she said, and I began to understand what she was planning to do. "Promise me you'll set her free."

I shrieked wordlessly at her and began to try and lever the boat back towards the shore. "I'm not leaving you." I stood up, leaning against the side of the boat, and screamed at Belis again. She met my eyes and I could see she had already given up. She'd decided to sacrifice herself, just like she'd said.

"You have to try!" I called, but she had turned away. Fury built inside me and I knew I wasn't going to let her give up.

I jumped out of the boat. The saltwater stung my eyes and burned down my throat as I breathed in a large quantity of it and broke the surface, coughing and spluttering. The water was deeper than I'd realised and I floundered, trying to reach the seabed. I tried to push forward, to swim back towards Belis, but the current was strong and it was already pulling at the fabric of my clothes, dragging me down. I went under, came up gasping for air then slipped beneath the surface again. I pedalled my legs madly, hitting the ground with one foot. I was only inches below the surface but there was no air left in my body and I couldn't find the strength to swim up. I swiped desperately through the water, fingers splayed wide as if I could claw my way through it. My chest felt as if it was about to implode, the weight of the sea crushing my ribs and forcing burning seawater down my throat.

As the water filled my lungs the pain receded a little. I felt my hair drifting around my face, blocking my view. I was perversely embarrassed. I – who had once swum the entire length of the River Thames, who went diving with the selkies in the sea lochs – I was going to drown here, in seven feet of water. I giggled and the last few bubbles fluttered out of my mouth and rose to the surface, sharp seawater flooding into my throat. Arawn was going to laugh if my soul ever made it to Annwn.

Then strong hands wrapped around my arm and pulled me up towards the light. I gasped as air filled my lungs and I was thrown through the air, landing hard on the boat. I coughed and retched, trying to get out the water that still sloshed in my chest, but even as I did I was hauling myself up, reaching for the oar. Belis launched herself at the side of the boat, dragging herself out of the water and rolling onto the planks. She leaned back over and grabbed at her spear which was floating beside the boat.

I looked up. The soldiers were wading towards us but the waves were affecting them, too, and the armoured chestplates were dragging them under. The burly man tore his armour from his torso and kicked forward, swimming towards us with strong strokes.

He reached the edge of the boat and grabbed the side, trying to pull himself in alongside us. I smacked him with my oar and he howled and let go, slipping beneath the water. Belis was suddenly beside me, taking the oar from my hands and starting to manoeuvre us further out. I let her do it, falling to my hands and knees and retching seawater into the bottom of the boat.

By the time I thought I had brought it all up we had reached the edge of the bay and were beginning to round the coastline. I could see the red cloaks of the legionaries in the distance, lining up on the beach.

"They'll follow us around the coast, I should think," said Belis, puffing a little from the effort of rowing. "If we keep out of range of the javelins we should be fine. We'll have to row all night, though, and there'll be no breaks. We can't afford that now."

I nodded, sitting down on the bench opposite her. She paused in her rowing, droplets streaming off the oar as she held it out of the water.

"Why did you jump?" she asked.

"You were giving up. You were going to let them take you, drag you back to Londinium, to Rome even." I met her gaze. "I didn't want you to give up."

"But you could have drowned, they could have taken you, too. Then everything would have been lost – you, me, Cati. You should have left me."

Her reasoning was logical. I could probably have eventually drifted my way to Grassholm. I didn't understand it myself. Every logical thought said I should have stayed on that boat. I hadn't realised I was going to jump until I was in the air. I tried to reason it out to myself, but I couldn't. It had to be some strange mortal instinct.

I realised Belis was still waiting for an answer.

"I didn't want to leave you," I said simply.

"Even after everything I've done?"

"You don't need to kill yourself to make amends. I'll talk to Arawn. We can get your sister's soul back without a trade. He wouldn't be interested in it anyway. He knows he'll get it eventually."

"So you'll let me come? To Annwn? You can forgive me?"

"I can't forgive you," I said. Belis looked down, hope dying in her face. "I can't forgive you for hurting your sister, that's something you will have to work through with her. For myself, I can't pretend to understand why you did it, but I know you are trying to make it right. I'm grateful that you told me, and now that there is no lie between us I think we can work together and try again."

Belis stuck her hand out towards me. "Peace? Pax Brittanica?"

I gripped her forearm and smiled. Her arm was warm under my hand, and I could feel the muscles contracting. It felt strange to touch a human in the full strength and vigour of their life. Her skin was softer than that of the fae, and as I met her eyes I noticed that her irises were speckled with silver the same way her skin was covered in freckles. I replayed the memory of finding her and Cati in the glade.

Strange to think that I had once found all humans so similar that I couldn't even tell them apart. Now that Belis's face was more familiar to me than my own, I would have known her anywhere.

Belis dropped her gaze. I leaned back on the bench, noticing that the feeling of indigestion in my chest had come back and was burning worse than ever. The seawater must have turned my stomach. Then I realised I had forgotten something.

"Belis," I said, sitting up. She looked back up at me.

"Thank you for rescuing me from drowning. It is not a pleasant way to go." She smiled and started rowing again.

"You're welcome. Thank you for coming back." I snorted at that.

"I was worse than useless. All I did was jump in the water and almost drown."

"Nevertheless," said Belis, still smiling, "thank you. For rescuing me, too."

# Belis Before
3

She is fourteen years old and radiant with excitement. Her father has brought her with him to meet with the new governor in Londinium. She flicks her heels against her pony's sides and the beast trots forward, almost as eager as its mistress to take in the new sights and smells of the city. She has never been so far from her father's hall at Icenorum. Her father laughs as she surges past him and calls out.

"Not too far, Belis. Gods know I don't have the energy to chase you after two weeks in the saddle!"

She reins in her horse and looks out over the valley. Londinium nestles against the riverbanks, squatting in the low ground between several small hills. The skies are grey and the wind carries the briny smell of the saltwater of the lower Thames. Her father stops beside her.

"This is a very important city," he says. "Sacred and ancient for many years before the Romans came. It will last long after they have gone. It is larger than our home and you must not wander off."

Belis nods seriously and her father grins.

"But there will be time for some fun as well. Stay close and we will explore once our business is concluded. Hurry now, it looks like rain."

As they ride nearer she begins to make out the old ditches and the new walls budding up above them. The Romans have been busy. The freshly placed bricks are an orange colour, so bright that the city seems to glow in the morning sunlight. There is a constant stream of people entering and leaving the city: Britons, Gauls, slaves, Romans. The king barks an order and the warriors and scribes accompanying the Iceni keep the crowds at arm's length.

They pass under an arched gate wide enough for a team of carthorses to walk through. She stares at the flash of a red cloak, her first city Roman, a legionary, leaning on his spear and yawning. He hardly blinks as the Iceni ride past.

The king stables the horses near the gate, swapping a bronze coin for a parchment chit that attests to their ownership. Belis pats her pony before they lead her away, taking comfort in the familiar equine smell. Londinium is so loud, so smelly, so much. She half wants to call the stable boy back, jump on the horse and ride all the way back home. But she is a princess, her blood is royal and so she straightens her spine and prepares to turn away and step into the street.

Londinium is squalling with life. Small factories hum with the sound of brickmaking and the heat of glass furnaces. Slaves hurry in and out, carrying neatly packed crates of glossy red pottery and smoky glass goblets. When they turn to the right, to head towards the temple district, she sees a slave trip and drop his burden. Hundreds of tiny glass tiles, intended for the mosaic in some rich man's house, spill out into the muddy street. A second slave, taller and with an overseer's paunch, smacks the unlucky man into the dirt, yelling at him to pick them up, quick smart.

She bends to snatch a handful of tiles from the dirt, holding them up to her face as they stroll away. They are as bright and colourful as butterfly wings and she pockets them to show Cati when she gets home.

Her father walks comfortably ahead, barely looking at the strange sights. Belis hurries after him, gazing up at the houses on either side of the street. High walls separate them from the muck of the public areas and bored-looking guards slump in narrow porticos. They give way to a cart loaded with cages full of miserably damp chickens and Belis tugs at her father's arm.

"Is it far from here?" she asks, trying to keep her voice steady. He nods and keeps walking. Belis glances at the others, none of whom seem to share her nerves. She pushes them down and follows.

They pass a cluster of temples, old and new, the cart of chickens stopping to deliver the creatures intended for sacrifice, then turn through the food markets, where animal carcasses swing gently in the sun. She pauses to look at a stall selling caged songbirds, unsure if they are for food or entertainment.

When she turns around her father is gone: no sign of any of the Iceni. She spins on her heel, looking around for a glimpse of them. She is tall for her age, already almost six foot, but in the close market with the stalls blocking her gaze she cannot see. She darts back and forth and realises she cannot even see the way she came into this market, let alone find the exit. She begins to panic, her heart thrumming in her chest.

Someone touches her arm and Belis yelps, bringing up her fists in defence. A young woman stands beside her, a baby balanced on her hip. She looks Roman, with her hair pinned up in what Belis vaguely recognises as the Latin style.

"Sorry! I didn't mean to startle you," she says. "You just looked upset, and I wanted to see if you needed help."

Belis puts her hands down and tries to calm her heart.

"My apologies. I seem to have become separated from my companions. They were headed to meet Governor Gallus. Do you know where they might have gone?"

The woman nods and Belis realises she is older than she had first thought, late twenties at least. Her skin is olive-toned and her hair is an inky black. She's pretty and Belis flushes a little at her smile, feeling gawky and awkward and fourteen all at once.

"Of course I do. My husband is a centurion in the Twentieth, he is accompanying the governor with a few cohorts as he attends to business in the city. I can take you to him now if you like."

Relief floods through Belis and she smiles shakily. "Yes, please."

The woman shifts the babe to the other hip and holds out a hand in greeting. "My name is Echo. This is my youngest, Claudia. Named for the old emperor."

Belis takes her hand and introduces herself. The woman picks up her basket of purchases and sets off through the market, moving through the crowds as if they weren't there. She chatters as she goes and when she pauses for breath Belis has a chance to address her.

"You speak excellent Brittonic. How long have you been here?"

"Oh, four years or so? I came over from southern Gaul where Croser, that's my husband, had left me. I was born in Rome, but I've been all over." Echo tucks a loose strand of hair behind her ear.

Belis feels very young and naïve.

"I've never been further than Camulodunum before," she confesses. "It must be wonderful to have travelled so much."

Echo smiles at her. "Oh, well, home's the best place of all. When Croser retires we'll be heading back to Rome, get a little wine shop and watch the grandchildren grow."

They have left the market and are walking up to a huge house, built from carved blocks of limestone. A pair of legionaries guard the door but at a nod from Echo they step aside and let the women pass.

Belis steps into a wide atrium, supported by smooth, narrow pillars. In the centre is a square pond, an impluvium, with a slightly blurred image of a dog set into the floor. Cushions are scattered on couches that line the richly painted walls. Her father is there, talking to a tall man in a soldier's uniform, his horsehair helmet tucked under one arm. The other man glances up and sees Echo. For a moment his face softens, and Belis can tell instantly that this is her centurion husband. Then his eyes flick to her and he nods towards her father.

The king turns and his whole body sags with relief.

"Beliscena," he cries, hurrying forward. "I told you not to wander off." He turns to Echo and inclines his head.

"You have my gratitude, lady, for helping my daughter."

Echo flushes to the roots and the centurion comes over and winks at Belis. He is craggily handsome and there is kindness in his face when he looks at Echo and Claudia.

"This is my wife, sir. I am sure we are very happy to be of service." The king kisses Echo's hand and gently pinches the baby's cheek.

"Ah, well, that explains it. I see you too have a beautiful daughter. I hope that one day I may return the favour."

He smiles at them both and then the centurion whisks him away to speak with the governor. Echo waves goodbye, collects her basket and is gone. Belis sits on the edge of one of the couches and watches as rain begins to fall on the impluvium.

Chapter 7

The outline of the island appeared on the horizon like the wide back of a whale. From my position at the helm of the little boat I could see clouds of seabirds rippling above it and then dispersing as they dived into the water. I turned back to Belis who was taking a breather, leaning forward heavily across the oars.

"Look." I pointed behind me. "That's the island of Grassholm. We're almost there."

Belis looked up and squinted into the distance. Her face did not adopt the look of stunned awe I had expected from a human seeing Caer Sidi for the first time.

"Are you sure? It doesn't look like much. I thought you said there was a castle." I nodded, impatient.

"Completely sure. You can't see the castle from the sea. Only those who land and know how to look for it can find it." I grinned. "And there are no living folk who know where to look. Except me. No one knows the way to Annwn until they die."

Belis shrugged and stretched out her arms then resumed rowing, cutting the oars through the dark water. She had pulled off her cloak and rolled up the sleeves of her tunic and I could see the strong muscles of her forearms flexing and tensing.

"I don't suppose your wisdom extends to knowing which side

of the island we should land on? I'd rather not capsize the boat onto the rocks and have to swim for it. My arms are weak as a babe's from all this rowing."

I considered this, though I doubted arms that strong could really be as tired as she said. I had always just run straight across the water and climbed up the cliffs on the east of the island. I wasn't totally sure what made an area suitable for boats.

"The north," I said, hazarding a guess but trying to seem sure. "There are some little inlets we should be able to row into."

Belis grunted. I swivelled on my seat to look out at the island again. We were close enough now that I could separate the dark mound into parts. Closest to the water was a thin layer of black rock, stained by seaweed and algae. Above that layer, the island was split into the grass-covered east and the pale west, completely white from the guano of the thousands of nesting gannets. Above us the sun emerged from a bank of clouds and lit up the sea so that it glowed an emerald green. I took a deep whiff of the salt air, remembering my last visit here, when the porpoises had come to the surface to race me and the dogs to the island. I nearly reached out a hand to stroke Dormath before remembering he wasn't there.

I watched the gannets lift off from the rocks and throw themselves into the air before slicing, bladelike, into the water. Each movement was precise, the wide wings drawn back, the long neck stretched out; even the resultant splash seemed contrived to set off the elegance of the dive. Moments later the birds would break the surface again, swallowing down fish and leaping back into the sky.

I had always loved to watch the gannets, loved the rare journeys to Caer Sidi, if not the destination. Now I felt awkward and lumpen, unable to run and leap alongside the birds and wild creatures of the sea. I turned away and stared at the water swilling in the bottom of the boat.

It took less time than I had feared for Belis to make landfall on the island. She was surprisingly skilled at manoeuvring the little boat through the craggy rocks until it was close enough for her to reach out and grab an outcrop with one hand so that I could clamber onto the island. When she was sure I was not going to fall into the water, Belis tossed me a coil of rope we had found in the boat and then followed me onto the rocks. She retrieved the rope and tied the boat off with practised ease.

"With a bit of luck that should last for a few days if the weather keeps. If we're much longer than that I doubt I'll have the strength to row us back anyway with no food and no fresh water."

"Once I regain my power I can carry you back across the water," I said, bouncing back and forth on my toes.

"Really?" asked Belis. I nodded, beginning to twitch with nervous excitement at being so close to our destination.

She straightened up, silhouetting herself against the afternoon sun. I raised a hand to shade my eyes and looked at her, hair wild and curly from the salt spray and the wind.

"Can you find this castle before nightfall? I don't particularly want to spend another night without shelter, especially out here in the open."

I nodded and stood up.

"Caer Sidi, the entrance to Annwn, is on the eastern side of the island. It shouldn't take us too long to reach. Be careful where you step, the rocks will be slippery with gull shit."

Belis wrinkled her nose but followed me as I began to climb up the slope. It was steep and uneven and I had to use my hands, jamming my fingers into cracks in the rocks to haul myself up. I paused for breath several times, conscious that Belis would be impatient to carry on. She said nothing, though, stopping whenever I did but always quick to move when I had caught my breath.

As we reached the crest of the island the winds picked up, hurrying the gannets home. They ignored us but the clattering howls they gave as they returned to their roosts filled the air.

Finally I paused about halfway along the eastern cliffs. The rock outcrop formed a rough circle, the grey stone jutting from the thin grass. From where I stood I could see straight across it, the blue-green sea and beyond, on the far horizon, the rise of the mainland. Belis came up beside me.

"This is it?" She didn't sound impressed, but I was getting used to that.

"The Western Isle, the Castle of the Gate. Here all living things come in their own time," I said, remembering the old words.

"I still can't see it."

I sighed. This woman had no sense of drama.

"Wait just a moment," I said. "Here, come and stand where I am."

I moved to the side and Belis obliged, shifting to where I had been. I tugged on her arm and she bent down. I leaned over her shoulder.

"First, close your eyes. Done? Now open them just a little, so that there's a crescent moon of light at the base of your vision."

I checked to see that she had followed my instruction then half closed my own eyes. The sound of the waves seemed to increase, the wind whistled louder in my ears. I reached out and placed a hand on Belis's arm, feeling the heat of her skin under my fingers.

"Now, we will walk forward, step by step. Each time you put your foot down imagine that you are walking on paved stones. Listen for the sound of it, expect it. The wind will fade because you will step inside the castle, so ignore the senses that tell you otherwise. Don't open your eyes until I say so."

Belis opened her eyes and blinked in the light.

"For example, don't do that." I sighed. She stared at the cliff, measuring the distance between us and the fall.

"It can't be more than ten paces across." She looked back down at me. "How long will it take us to reach the castle?"

I shrugged. "It depends. I usually just walk straight in. The handful of times I've had to escort a soul right to the gates we've approached from over the water."

Belis walked around the side of the ring of stone and peered over the edge of the cliffs. I followed her. Below us the furious waves crashed against the rocks, seething with white foam. I felt the undertow of nausea at the height and moved back.

"Straight onto the rocks," Belis said, her voice wavering. I clapped her back.

"Come on, we're wasting time. I thought we were in a hurry."

I pulled her back to the entrance and waited for her to half close her eyes again. I reached for her arm once more but to my surprise she took my hand, lacing her fingers through my own. Her grip was firm and strong, her palm larger than mine. I paused for a moment, unsure if I liked it, then squeezed her hand. She smiled, her eyes still half shut.

I closed my own eyelids, 'til only a splinter of light peeked through. I imagined the high walls of Caer Sidi, the arching gate before me, the cold stone of the floors. I took a step forward. The grass muffled the sound of my feet but in my head I could hear the click of boots on stone. Belis had taken the step as well, keeping pace with me.

I took another step, then another, all the while listening for the echoing sounds of my footsteps, the muted wind howling at the thick walls. The only sense I allowed myself to notice was the gap of light sliding under my lashes. I moved forward again, five more paces, each step noticeably landing on the grassy cliffs. Belis stopped beside me again. I could feel a slight tremor in her hand. I wanted to look, to check if she had kept her eyes shut, but I knew I couldn't. As soon as I opened my eyes we'd have to go back and start again, and once I lost confidence in her, I'd want to keep checking.

I took the ninth step, concentrating hard on the castle. I wished I had gone barefoot. I had never done this wearing boots before. It was harder to imagine the flagstones beneath my feet. One more step and we were at the edge of the cliff. My hand was slick with sweat, and I couldn't tell if it was Belis's or mine. For the first time I felt worried that with the next step we would simply topple over and onto the rocks below. I would never return to my old self, never see the dogs again. The souls of the restless dead would linger in the mortal world. I would have let Belis down.

I couldn't wait here much longer. Belis could count ten paces just as well as me. If I hesitated, she would lose faith. If she lost faith, then we would fall. I had to make a decision.

I squeezed her hand and we stepped forward together.

My boot came down on smooth, solid rock and the sliver of light in my eyes darkened. I opened my eyes. A familiar scene lay before me. We were standing in the vestibule of Caer Sidi, a stone corridor hung with grim tapestries. In front of us was a wide arched door that looked east, out over the shimmering sea and beyond to Britain. I glanced back and saw, ten paces away, a second door leading to the grassy slopes of the island.

"Are we—?" Belis spoke from beside me. "Are we there? Can I open my eyes?"

"Yes," I said. "We're here."

I watched as she slowly opened her eyes and looked around, her pupils widening as they adjusted to the dim light.

"This is Caer Sidi?"

"The gate to Annwn. No mortal has ever seen this place with their living eyes."

Belis shivered and I realised I was still holding her hand. I let it go and bent to tighten my bootlaces. Belis was still staring around at the walls, running her fingers over the smooth, glassy blocks of stone, marbled with thin veins of white quartz.

"Come on," I said, getting back to my feet. "That was the hard part. Let's go and see if we can track down Arawn."

Belis hesitated, drawing her hand back from the walls.

"Are there any rules I should know? Could I get stuck here?"

"What, like not eating or drinking? This isn't a place of trickery, it's a land of rest. Arawn isn't interested in trapping anyone here. Don't expect to see anyone you know. Those living this close to Caer Sidi are the oldest of the dead, the newer arrivals head further out. Stay by my side where possible."

My words seemed sparse, too little to guide Belis through the endless land of the dead, but she nodded and we began to walk down the corridor into the afterworld.

The light from the twin doors to the living world faded fast and soon we were walking in near total darkness. I thought about how long it had taken me to come this way in the past. Of course I had run everywhere so my sense of distance was a little skewed. I could hear Belis's breathing next to me, shallow and a little uneven.

"Are you all right?" I asked. "I don't think it is too much further from here."

"I don't mind," she said, her voice surprisingly steady. "I find that I am not afraid with you."

The darkness began to lift as the floor below us angled downwards, lightening by degrees until we were no longer standing on castle floors but on a wide balcony at the top of a winding staircase that looked out over the land of Annwn. Belis gasped and stopped walking.

Above us the sky was periwinkle-blue, studded with pale clouds. The land around us was a rolling series of meadows, half farmed and budding with golden wheat, half left fallow to produce a miasma of wildflowers. Clusters of woodland broke up the quilt of fields, orchards of apple and pear trees, vineyards groaning with clusters of grapes. The laughter of streams bubbled up to us from where they moated green hills and irrigated the land like silver arteries.

I turned back to see the towers of fine grey stone behind us, pale granite glittering in the sunshine.

"Well, this is it." I looked over towards Belis and was shocked to see tears welling in her eyes.

"This is Annwn?" Her voice trembled. "It's so beautiful."

"It goes on for thousands of miles," I said. "You could walk until your feet wore down to the bones and you'd never reach the end. Even I have not seen much of this place."

Belis rubbed her eyes with the back of her hand and sniffed the air. She turned slowly on the spot, still staring up at the sky.

"It's nearly dusk but the sun seems to be rising."

"The sun rises in the west here and sets in the east. Their day is our night." I paused to give her a few moments to breathe it all in. "Come, we must find the lord of these lands."

We began down the steps and walked out into the countryside. It had been half a century since I had visited Annwn and it remained as lovely as I had remembered.

I found Arawn exactly where I had expected to, in a field of bronze wheat a few miles' walk from Caer Sidi. The ruler of the afterworld was stripped to the waist, sweat shining on the long muscles of his tanned arms as he bent to parcel and scythe the crop, twisting it into bundles and tossing them back on the ground. Around him other men and women laboured, some in fine purplish tweeds, others in drab linens or animal skins.

"Hail, Arawn, Lord of Annwn," I called out as we approached. He turned and peered at me, shading his eyes with one hand from the early-morning sun.

"Mallt? Mallt, is that you?" His face split into an enormous grin and to my surprise I saw an expression of relief pass over his features. "The fates are kind to send you to me now, Mallt. We have been waiting for you."

He broke off and squinted at me. "You look different, Sister of the Night. Is it truly you?"

"In the flesh, which is a surprise to me, too." I balled my fist over my heart and bowed to him.

Belis copied me, looking around nervously at the harvesters.

Arawn shoved the handle of his sickle into his belt then strode over to us. To my irritation I found that, where once we had been the same height, he now towered over me. "Blood of my ancestors, Mallt, have you shrunk?"

I glowered at him. "It's this human form I'm stuck in, it's terribly inconvenient."

"Human? It can't be."

He looked at me again, crouching a little so that his eyes met mine. They were a liquid gold, no whites nor pupils. I flinched a little under his gaze. He grabbed my hand, raised it to his mouth and bit down hard. I yelped and tried to drag it back.

Belis hurried forward but he had already released me. I inspected the injured finger – a shallow cut on the tip. I looked back up to Arawn.

"Your blood proves the truth of your words. There is no taste of magic in you, no scent of the ages." He stepped closer. "Tell me what happened."

I scowled, unhappy with how strange and unfriendly he was being. Belis pushed her way between us and to my surprise I felt a little better. She was not quite the same height as the Lord of the Dead, but it was comforting to have her there.

"It is my fault," she said, meeting Arawn's eyes. "My mistake. We are here to ask you to help rectify it."

Arawn stared at her then threw his head back and laughed. Birds were startled from the trees at the sound and a murmur rippled through the dead. He was almost gasping for breath by the time he regained control of himself but there was no mirth in his face.

"You have come to ask me for help, Mallt Y Nos? After years and years of praying and hoping for you to come, you arrive powerless and mortal. Truly you are the Nightshade, for you have brought darkness to this land.'

I recoiled, gripping Belis's arm and pulling her back. Arawn covered his mouth and cast a quick look at the dead.

"We cannot talk here. Come." Arawn beckoned us over to the edge of the field where a huge barrel had been filled with water. A set of wooden cups floated on the surface and the king dipped one into the water and handed it to me. I dropped my pack and took it gladly. The water was cold enough to sting my teeth. He gave a second to Belis who was still looking at him as though he might attack again.

"Apologies, my lady," Arawn said to her, "you have not caught me at my best. I am usually more composed. I don't believe Mallt has introduced us. A living mortal?"

"This is Beliscena, Princess of the Iceni," I said. "She's the reason I'm in this mess."

"I am Arawn. Welcome to Annwn."

"Thank you," said Belis, bobbing another bow. Arawn nodded at her then turned back to me.

"So, Mallt, care to explain?"

I described the battlefield, the events in the glade. Belis hovered next to me, casting anxious glances around her. When one of the dead reached into the barrel to help herself to a beaker of water she flinched backwards, staring at the woman.

"She won't hurt you," Arawn said, interrupting my story. "Be at peace."

Belis nodded and smoothed down her skirt nervously.

"As I was saying," I cleared my throat, "when I appeared and had reached out for the distressed soul, somehow the three of us got tangled up. Belis was healed, but her sister's soul was tugged loose and my powers were dislodged, leaving me helpless and human."

"Indeed," Arawn said, looking from me to Belis. "You must have strong magic indeed to have done such a thing. Powerful yet extremely foolish. If Mallt had not been there you both would have died."

Belis flinched and dropped her gaze.

"I will never forgive myself for it," she muttered, still staring at the ground. "I was mad with fear. I wish I could excuse myself by saying I didn't know what I was doing but I doubt it would have made a difference."

Arawn raised an eyebrow at me. I sighed.

"Mortals near death do desperate things. And I should not have intervened. I was in rather a rush."

"Oh, I don't doubt that you have more than your fair share of the blame for this, Mallt. Now for your joint foolishness many will suffer. The souls of the lost will continue to wander the land, in torment and tormenting, and so death will pay for life, pain for indulgence."

I shuffled my feet, unable to think of a good response to that. Arawn was so often jovial that his seriousness cut deep. He turned his dark eyes back to Belis.

"And that is not the worst of it. There are problems here that you do not understand; that I had hoped ..." He paused and shook his head. "I cannot help you. You would have done better to forget your sister, to carry on with what remained of your life. As for you, Mallt, I have no power to return you to your form, nor can I permit you to leave."

"What!" I said. "I'd like to see you try to stop us. We're mortal, not dead. We could just go back through the tower."

Arawn spread out his hands. "Believe me, it is not my choice. Annwn has changed, it has ..." His voice petered out. "Let me start afresh."

He squatted down in the dirt and began sketching a map.

"This is Annwn," he said, tracing the lines through the soil. "Here is Caer Sidi, here is where we are now. All this land is under my rule, peaceful and ordered, where those who have passed can linger as they please until they are tired of even this final plane of existence and give themselves back to the world. This is what the living picture as the afterlife."

Arawn rubbed his forehead. "For thousands of years it has been this way." He marked out another set of lines. "Then, not twenty years ago, something began to change. A strange corruption took hold of the land. It started with dying plants, trees and crops choked by thorns, then the fields furthest from Caer Sidi fell under a shadow, the soil blew away into a dust that rose to block out the sun. I walked the damaged earth, trying to encourage new growth, but my power stuttered and I felt myself decaying.

"Then came the sickness; the inhabitants of the damaged areas grew malformed of body and soul, turning into twisted beasts that fell on their companions and passed on the infection.

"I gathered those souls who had been warriors in life and we marched on the shadowlands, intent on burning out the corruption even at the cost of the lost souls."

"What happened?" I asked, horror-struck.

"My power is tied to my role as Lord of the Dead. When I tried to fight I discovered that I cannot harm those under my care even if they are changed beyond all reckoning. Worse still, the more of them that become corrupted the more I am changed. I am an avatar of this land and as it sickens so do I.

"When we crossed into the darkness my sight grew dark and all those with us began to fall to the shadow. Our forces were thrown back, more becoming corrupted or *shadowbitten* every day. The entirety of Annwn was on the brink of collapse until my seneschal, a powerful witch in life who has retained some of her power here, dragged me back from the brink and split the land in two."

Arawn scratched a jagged gash through the map. "A vast schism now cuts across Annwn, a canyon border. Her magic was enough to weaken any *shadowbitten* who crossed over, but it could not keep out the wind which blew corrupted seeds into our lands. We have spent the last dozen years in constant fear, tearing out seedlings before they can take root. Last year my seneschal was lost in a dark forest that sprang up not fifty miles from here. Whenever I approach the trees I feel the corruption taking hold of me and none of the dead have been able to get her out. When her magic along the border fails, then we will be overrun."

Belis crouched, reaching out a finger to touch the line of the canyon. Arawn fell silent, letting the sound of the wind whistling through the willow branches fill the silence.

"Why didn't you ask for help?" I said. "Surely Gwyn or Arianrhod would have aided you if you asked for it. They may not be selfless but even they can see the damage will affect the whole of Britain."

Arawn smiled, but there was no joy in his eyes. "I cannot contact the living world, and visitors here are few. Only one person comes to Annwn with any sort of regularity . . ."

It took me another heartbeat to take his understanding. "You were waiting for me?"

"I knew you would come. I prayed it would be before the situation was beyond repair." He shook his head. "But you came as a mortal, unable to flit between worlds as you had before. You were our last hope, Mallt."

"I don't understand," Belis said, standing up from where she had been staring at the map. "Mallt can still go back and tell the others. We can take Cati's soul and go."

Arawn dropped his gaze. He seemed to be struggling to find the words. I was shocked. I had never seen the Lord of Annwn so lost before. Finally, he lifted his head back up and met my eyes.

"The way is shut," he said. "You cannot get out. I had to seal the passage back to the mortal world, to make it one way only. Your old self could have passed through, but as a human . . ." He shrugged. "I had to close Caer Sidi before one of the *shadowbitten* broke through. It is only a matter of time."

"So we are trapped here?" I said. Arawn nodded.

The realisation thudded inside my skull like clods of earth falling onto a coffin. A life of immortal freedom and I had thrown it all away in a moment of foolish impatience. I staggered backwards. It wasn't fair. I deserved more after all my labours. I opened my mouth to complain but then my eyes fell on Belis.

There was a look on her face I had not seen there before. It took me a moment to place the expression. I recalled the face of a man I had seen years ago as I had visited the bedside of his dying wife. I had come to collect the soul of the stillborn babe that now lay in a carved cradle as the husband held the woman's hand while midwives tried to staunch the bleeding below. That despair, the death of hope, was mirrored in Belis's face now. I knew it was more than her own life she mourned; it was her sister's.

As I stared, I felt the pain within her echoed in my own heart. I shoved it away. Arawn was right: he had done the only sensible thing. I could not let the emotions of this human body distract me from my task. I shut my eyes so I would not have to see her face but found that the image of her grief was still etched on my mind. There was still work to do. I ground my teeth and turned back.

"What can we do?" I asked. He frowned at me and Belis met my eyes. There was a fierceness in her now.

"Mallt is right. We must help you. What can we do?"

A smile flickered across the king's face. "There's iron in your stomach, child. What could you do? My own strength has failed, as has that of my soldiers. What can any of us do but sit here and wait for the border to fall."

Chapter 8

The Lord of the Dead dropped his cup back into the barrel of water and strode back to the harvest. I didn't turn to watch him go. My legs felt so weak it was taking all my strength to remain standing. I opened my mouth to say something, swayed and fell. Belis caught me and lowered me to the ground. I tried to thank her but there was a cold pressure around my throat, choking the breath from me. Invisible bands of steel seemed to have wrapped themselves around my arms and legs. I couldn't form my thoughts into sentences, not even into words; the inside of my head was a hurricane, uprooting everything I thought I knew about myself. I curled in on myself, trying to block out the world.

Belis grabbed my shoulders and hauled me into a sitting position. She propped me against the water barrel and shoved my head between my knees.

"Breathe deep," she said, her voice almost drowned out by the panic. I gasped for breath, panting like a dog.

"I've doomed us all, Belis," I gabbled, the words tripping out of me. "I should have come sooner, should have taken more care. I should have told someone we were coming this way, no one who could help will even know this is happening. It's my fault, my fault, my fault." The words were ragged but I kept forcing them out.

Belis looked around for help then crouched down in front of me. "Take a deep breath, Mallt, you need to stop panicking."

I screwed my eyes shut and fought for control. It was a losing battle and my eyes snapped open again.

"Can't breathe," I choked out. Belis took my head between her hands and stared directly into my eyes. Then she leaned her forehead against mine.

"Breathe in with me, yes, that's it. Now let go. Again, breathe in, then out."

I only managed a shallow breath, but my panting was slowing. I felt her palms on my cheeks, coarse from years of gripping a spear. Her eyes were very green in this light and I could count the flecks of silver in her irises.

"That's better, Mallt, one breath, then another. Slow. Don't think about anything else, focus on me. In and out." Her voice was soothing and I felt some of the tension leaving my muscles, the bands of steel around my throat loosening.

"Sorry about that," I muttered, once I had regained control of my lungs. I half expected her to smirk but she sighed and sat down next to me, leaning back against the barrel.

"Things are not going according to plan," I said. She barked a short laugh.

"I'll say. I was hoping we would not linger here long, that we could convince Arawn to release Cati's soul and be gone before the next sunset. I was already thinking about how to avoid the Romans on our return voyage."

"Wishful thinking," I said. Belis nodded.

"You know all that I have done. You understand my urge to remove this stain from my own soul. Now it appears that there will be no redemption for me. Worse still, no second life for Cati, and, most terrible of all, I have managed to pollute whatever chance she had of a peaceful afterlife."

I leaned over and nudged her shoulder with mine. "I thought I was the one blaming myself for all this."

"Is there not guilt enough to go around?" Belis didn't shift away and I found a little comfort in the feel of her warmth next to me.

"So what are we going to do?"

"We?"

"There's no point fighting it any more. I'm a human now, just like you. It seems that won't be changing, even if we find a way out of this. You and I are humans together, the only living humans in Annwn."

"If we weren't here then I'd tell you being a human wasn't so bad. You've only really met me and Vatta. I wish you could meet Cati properly, you'd like her, I think. Humans are the best part of being human," Belis frowned, "though they can be the worst part as well."

"Tell me a bit more about her then," I said.

"Now?"

"We have nowhere to go, nothing to do. For the first time in weeks there are no Romans on our tail. Since we are sitting here together waiting for the end, why not pass some time. So, what is your sister like?"

Belis took a deep breath and began talking. At first she was stoic, but as the sun traced its way across the horizon she seemed to settle into her stories. She told me about Cati, how she had spent her whole life protecting her, proud to be her older sister. She spoke about her family, her brilliant and beloved father, Prasutagus, and his reign over the Iceni. Her mother, the firebrand Boudica, teaching her to fight, to survive. The rise of the Romans and the gradual understanding that her father would be the last of the independent Iceni kings. Her voice broke as she talked about his death and the betrayal of the Roman governor that sparked the rebellion.

I liked listening to her talk, the sound of her voice humming through the warm autumn air. When her throat grew dry I fetched us more water from the barrel, and when her eyes grew damp I put my hand on hers and she gripped it tight.

When Belis ran out of stories she asked me for mine and I talked about the ages I had spent running across the islands of Britain. I laughed as I recounted adventures with the Wild Hunt and the old kingdoms when the line between fae and mortal had been blurred. Belis laughed, too, and I found I liked the sound of her laughter. It felt precious, hard-won.

At last I fell silent. The swallows were darting back and forth in the evening sky, black silhouettes against the lavender. Arawn's group of farmers had moved on. I could see them in the next field lighting a fire and erecting a small spit.

"Could we do that?" I said, breaking the quiet.

"Light a fire?" asked Belis, shifting her arm out from where I had leaned my head against it.

"If you like. It's not very cold here, though."

"No, I mean, could we live here like that? Work during the day and then sit by the fire all night. They look happy enough." I peered towards the distant blur of the flames.

"We could," said Belis, moving her arm back, "but they won't be happy for long. Arawn said the darkness would break free soon enough, spreading across this whole land."

"Then I suppose we'd better stop it." I sat up, twisting around to look Belis in the face. "If I'm going to be human, I'd like to enjoy it properly. Find a patch of land to farm, maybe up in the north, where the Romans haven't reached yet. You could come and stay if you wanted, teach me some of the landcraft."

She blinked at me and I felt a little of the closeness we had built in the last few hours shake. This friendship was a fragile thing.

"Or not," I said, hurriedly. "You and Cati could travel further, up into the Pictlands and the islands."

"That wasn't my problem, Mallt," Belis said to me, her mouth quirking up at the corner. "Have you forgotten what Arawn said? There is nothing to be done."

"I don't accept that. There must be something we can do. Maybe we can find Arawn's seneschal or cure this sickness. We've still got a few weeks before your sister will be beyond help, and who knows how long before these *shadowbitten* overrun us. I'm not prepared to give up just yet."

I scrambled up and held out a hand to Belis. She frowned for a moment then took my hand and I pulled her up.

"Where should we start?" she asked, then continued without

waiting for an answer. "We should consider our strengths, that's what Mother would say. Other than the druid's spell, I only know a few cantrips, but I'm still a trained warrior, I have my spear and my sword . . ."

She glanced at me and I patted the sword's hilt where it was strapped to my belt. "Well, you have. What are your strengths, Mallt?"

I considered. I seemed to have left most of them back in my old life: speed, strength, power over souls. I had been wrong about pretty much everything since meeting Belis, from trying to eat poisonous mushrooms to forgetting humans couldn't run on water.

"Not much," I said. "Perhaps we should focus on your skills for now."

Belis frowned. "I see we've moved on from towering self-importance to self-pity. You have lots of strengths, Mallt. You're stubborn as a donkey, you're smart as a crow, you're tough as—"

"An old boot?" I suggested. "Or did you have another unflattering comparison in mind?"

Belis grinned at me. "There you go, you're as old as the hills themselves but your mind hasn't gone yet. You might not be a goddess any more but you're still formidable. And I haven't mentioned the one thing that separates us from every other creature in this land, even the *shadowbitten* themselves."

"What's that?" I asked. Belis shrugged.

"We're alive. Maybe that's the missing piece. Arawn can't fight his own people, nor can the uncorrupted dead. But we're neither, we're alive, the first living mortals ever to set foot in this world. We don't belong here yet so we can't be corrupted so easily."

She clapped me on the shoulder. "Come on, let's go and find Arawn and tell him we want to fight."

Arawn leaned back over the map he had drawn in the ashes next to the fire, conjuring the dirt into hills and valleys with a wave of his hand, water trickling out to form rivers and streams.

It was near dawn; we had spent most of the night talking with him. The Lord of the Dead did not seem entirely convinced but we had persuaded him to let us try.

"The most trouble we've had is along the canyon, the current border with the shadow," he said, pointing to the deepest slash in the map. "I have sentries stationed along there to watch the line, but I cannot guarantee your safety there. You think that living mortals can fight the shadow. That's a possibility I want to explore but let's start somewhere more controlled. Then we can consider a bolder move."

Belis looked at the map with a warrior's eye.

"I think we should strike hard and fast, before the *shadowbitten* know we're here. Use surprise to push into their land and—"

"And do what?" Arawn cut in. "You are only two women and only one is in the least bit trained in combat. Mallt has spent her existence trailing battlefields like a crow, always late to the feast. This is my land, child. We will do things my way."

Belis looked as though she wanted to respond but bit her tongue. Arawn stabbed his finger into the map.

"Here: this is where we shall start you off. It is a few hundred miles north of where we are now, a good fifty from the current border. There is a corruption there that I have been unable to root out. Come."

Arawn strode from the field. Belis and I hurried after him.

"If it is hundreds of miles away," I said, "it will take us weeks to get there. I have lost my old speed and—" Arawn grabbed my arm in one hand and Belis in the other and the world seemed to spin around us.

Chapter 9

Trees, rivers, valleys whooshed past us as Arawn moved. He led us through a blur of fields of wheat and barley, between apple orchards and vegetable plots. I was used to moving fast but even in my old body I could not have matched this pace.

We stopped so abruptly that I tripped, fell forward and would have careened into the dirt had Arawn not grabbed my collar. He helped me right myself and I brushed down the front of my tunic which was completely covered in dust.

"What was that?" I coughed. Arawn grinned.

"That was *rushing*. You were always so proud of your speed, Mallt. I never mentioned that I can outpace you." His smile died as he noticed Belis trying to peer past him.

Arawn stepped aside, revealing a wide-open paddock, completely overrun with thick black brambles which had grown up around trees, now cut down to stumps. Red ribbon had been strung around the edge of the miasma of thorns, dividing the fouled land from the fair.

"It grew up overnight. Seeds of darkness must have blown across the border. Only my strongest magic has been able to confine it within the ribbon and yet it edges a little wider every day." Arawn eyed the knots of thorns with distaste. "When I send a work crew to cut it down, the thorns slash their skin and turn them to the shadow. When I take up a scythe and start to work, my mind clouds the same way it did when we attacked the *shadowbitten*."

I stared at the field. I had little experience of farming, knowing only what I had gleaned from years of wandering through homesteads on my travels, but this seemed like more than a week's work for a hundred farmers than for two women.

"We tried setting fires, but the brambles suck water from the earth and do not burn. I had leather gloves and aprons made but they are so cumbersome that we could cut only a small amount each day and the thorns bloomed again at night, doubling the land we had cleared."

Belis glanced at me and then approached the thicket. She reached out a hand to the vines. A breeze shifted them and they seemed to curl in on themselves.

"We should test our theory," she said. "See if the thorns can poison us."

"Careful," I whispered. Belis nodded at me then dropped her hand into the brambles.

She picked up a trailing branch, thumb-thick and covered in thorns. With a wince she closed her hand around it. I moved towards her but Arawn caught my shoulder.

"Drop the branch and come back towards us," he said. "Let me see."

Belis held out her palm. The thorns had bitten deep and the calloused skin was dotted with blood. Arawn picked up her hand and cradled it between his own. I felt tension building in my chest as he closed his eyes, concentrating on the rips in Belis's skin. If this didn't work, if Belis fell to the shadow . . .

"It's clean," Arawn said, and the relief in his voice was echoed in my sudden release of breath. "The corruption isn't working on you. I can't sense it in your blood."

Belis grinned at me. "I told you it was a good idea."

"It's a start." Arawn let go of her hand and stared over at the thicket. "You haven't fallen to the shadow but it still injured you. If it hurt you badly enough you could die and then you would be as vulnerable as the rest of us."

"We won't then," I said. "Belis has been teaching me how to fight, and I'm getting stronger already. We should come up with a plan, strike now!" Belis nodded eagerly beside me.

"No." Arawn looked back at us. "One pinprick is not enough to prove you're strong enough. We should wait. I will *rush* us back to Caer Sidi and call a council."

"We are ready!" Belis insisted. "I've fought in battles, besieged towns, killed Roman soldiers with twice my experience. And Mallt was the Goddess of Death. We can do this."

Arawn gave a half-smile. "You are very young, child."

"I'm not a child," Belis snapped, and in the morning sun she seemed to glow with fury. "I am a princess of the Iceni, baptised in the blood of battle. I have tasted defeat and victory and defeat again. Let me prove my mettle."

Arawn glanced at me but I was still staring at Belis. "Very well then, my lady." He gave the honorific enough of a twist that it hovered between respectful and ironic.

"If you want to prove yourself then here is a task for you. If you can clear this land by nightfall then I will consider moving faster. I want the thicket gone and the stumps uprooted or it will regrow in the darkness. When you have done that, it must be ploughed and sown with linseed. It must be sown by nightfall, so the crop will grow overnight, pushing out the corruption and ready to harvest by the time the morning dew has dried."

Arawn nodded to his right. "You will find pitchforks and spades and scythes over there, beside a bag of seeds." He extended a long finger towards the next field.

"By nightfall," I whispered. Arawn grimaced and ran a hand through his hair as he stared out at the field.

"No citizen of Annwn could do this thing," he said, "nor could I, the lord of this land. If you can do this then maybe there is a hope."

He turned on his heel and was gone. Belis and I stood alone at the edge of the thicket, staring up at a sky that was suddenly filled with a twisting flock of starlings.

"Well," I said after a moment. "We had better begin."

I began by pacing out the length of the field in the ultimately vain hope that it was smaller or less ravelled than we feared. It was worse. I could not even reach the ribbon for much of the length of the sides, having to make great detours around particularly heinous brambles. Belis had collected a scythe and was trying to cut her way along the fence line but without much success. She had not cleared more than a yard in the time it took me to walk the entire perimeter.

"We need those gloves," she said, already panting from the effort. "It's all very well slashing at these vines but I can't pull out the roots without ravaging my hands – look!" She displayed her palms which were already brutally scratched. A few of the deeper cuts were beginning to drip blood.

I eyed the undergrowth warily. I had never bothered about it much in my old body, but I had encountered bramble hedges enough during my brief sojourn as human to rankle at the thought of plunging my bare hands into it. I remembered Belis's effort in removing the rowboat from the thorns at the fishing village. That had been a patch of daisies compared to this.

"Should I see if I can go and find some gloves?" I asked, picking up the other scythe. Belis ran a hand through her hair.

"There's no time to lose! I don't even know where you'd go for them. Arawn's gone, and there's no one to ask for help."

"Gods be good!" I dropped the scythe and grabbed one of the pitchforks. "If I move the vines around can you reach them without cutting your hands?"

Belis tried it. It took a bit of manoeuvring but combining the fork and a shovel seemed to hold off the worst of the thorns. We cleared another two yards that way, working together. I took a step back and leaned on my spade.

"I'll have to take a break soon, this is terribly hard work."

"No, Mallt, look!" Belis stared up at the sky. "It's midmorning already. We've barely made any progress."

"Dammit." I looked around. We were not even a hundredth of the way through clearing the brambles. If we kept going at this speed we would still be working at the thicket for a month. I felt panic rising in my throat, wrapping phantom vines around my arms that stung almost as much as the real ones.

"We'll have to split up, both of us use the spades," I said. Belis looked like she was going to cry.

"It's no use, we still won't be fast enough." Her knuckles tightened around the scythe. "We're not going to make it."

"This was your idea and now you want to give up? Before we're halfway through our first day?" I snapped at her, letting my panic turn to frustration. "Would your sister give up? Would your mother? I thought you Iceni were made of stronger stuff than that."

She stared at me. I was a little shocked at my own words. She was usually the one who pushed me to keep going. But her strength had made me stronger and now I could give it back. Belis gritted her teeth. "Fine. We keep going."

I nodded and turned back to the brambles, hacking at the roots with my spade. She retrieved the other one and joined me. We worked side by side, stabbing and cutting at the thorned vines. Before long my hands were torn to ribbons and blood was trickling down my forearms to my elbows. The thicket was almost thigh-deep, clawing at the fabric of my leggings and scratching my calves. I kept going until the shovel was so slippery with blood that I could barely hold onto it.

I paused and dabbed my hands on my tunic. I'd made more progress than I had expected: I'd cleared a ten-yard strip. Belis had done even more: she was almost as far again into the bramble patch. I glanced up at the sky, expecting the sun to be overhead for midday.

Strange. It hadn't moved. I stepped backwards into the area I had cleared, dodging a thick tree stump and moving to where we had stood before switching back to the spades. I wasn't mistaken. The sun was exactly where I would have expected it to be at mid-morning. Something else caught my eye, a hawk hovering over the field, but as I stared longer I realised that it wasn't riding the wind. It was flying, beating its wings but so slowly that it seemed frozen in the air.

"Belis!" I called. "Look up!" I watched as she paused from her work. As she stared into the sky I noticed the movement of the hawk begin to quicken, until it had swooped over the whole length of the field and landed in a stand of trees. Belis looked at me quizzically.

I grabbed my shovel and ran to join her, skipping through the piles of cut branches.

"I know how we're going to do this!" I called to her. I pulled up, panting for breath. "I know how we can clear the field before nightfall."

"How?" Belis looked unconvinced. She wiped the back of her hand across her forehead, leaving a streak of blood which mingled with the sweat.

"Time! Look up at the sky. We've barely taken any time to clear since we started again."

Belis looked up and frowned. "So?"

"So, I didn't understand how we are so much faster now. It feels like we are moving much more slowly, each movement hurts, it seems like it takes forever. But it's the other way around!"

"I don't understand," Belis said, "we're slower but we're faster?"

"Did you ever have a day that felt like it went on forever? A bad day that you just wished would end but seemed to drag longer than a day should? Or the opposite. A day that was so good you wanted to hold onto it but it was gone in a snap?"

"Yes." Her eyes were wary and I saw the flash of pain behind them. "But it's not real, it's just how you perceive time."

I grinned at her. "Here it can be real! When we're digging by hand, cutting our hands to pieces and wishing for it all to end, the time moves slower. We can achieve more in less time, we can buy time with our suffering. Clearing these thorns is so terrible, so painful, that we have almost infinite time to complete it."

"That can't be right?" Belis snorted.

"Oh, no? Look up at the sky. The sun's moved more since

we've been talking than in the time it took me to clear these ten yards."

She looked up again. The sun had indeed moved, maybe a degree towards midday. She dropped her eyes.

"We can do this?"

"Yes," I said. "But we can't stop. We have to be suffering, desperate for the task to be over. If we pause, if we break, then we'll be wishing for more time and it'll go the other way." I held up my hands, strafed with deep cuts. "It is not going to be easy."

Belis took my hands, holding them palm up in one of her own. Her touch was gentle as she traced one of the scratches with her finger.

"I'm sorry for getting you into this," she said, still looking down at my hands. "I'm more grateful than you could know to have someone here beside me, to have you."

She glanced up and met my gaze. Above me I felt the sun moving overhead. "Come on," I said, withdrawing my hands. "We must get to work."

It was brutal. The skin of my palms was almost completely flayed by the time we had cut the whole length of the field, completing about a quarter of the clearance. I paused to tear rags from the tattered remnants of my tunic and wrapped them around the spade handles, to prevent them slipping from my grip. The pain was close to incapacitating, so that each blow to the brambles seemed to fall in slow motion, and hoisting the spade up again felt like rolling a boulder up a cliff.

I remembered estimating the whole job at over a week for a village, at least a month for the pair of us. It certainly felt that this morning had stretched far beyond that already. I wondered how much longer I could go on, whether my body would give up before my mind did.

Beside me, Belis worked tirelessly. We had settled into advancing at the same pace, though she cleared twice as much width as me. We were nearer the centre of the brush now, the brambles thickening so that they caught at my spade and wouldn't let go. I had to slice at the same vines again and again before they would break. I glimpsed the sun through lashes dripping with sweat. It was nearly midday. Even the pain, all the longing within for this to be done, wasn't slowing the morning enough.

I ripped the bandages from my hands, exposing the bloody flesh beneath. In patches I could see the white glint of bone through the flesh. I stuffed the rags into my mouth to stop me from screaming and gripped the shovel tight.

Somehow, inch by bloody inch, we finished clearing the brambles. Belis helped me with the last of my patch, swapping her spade for a pitchfork to remove the last cuttings.

I leaned on my spade, gasping for breath. The red ribbon fluttered in the breeze, now surrounding an acre of scrubby land still dotted with tree stumps. Above, the midday sun had gathered strength, beating down on us.

"We've still got half the day left," Belis said. "We need to dig out those stumps and plough and sow. If we can keep the pace up we can do it. The worst is the brambles and that's done."

I flicked my gaze towards her, too exhausted even to turn my head. Belis looked in terrible shape. Her thick arms were scored with red, lines of blood criss-crossing her face. It hurt to see her in pain, almost worse than my own agony.

"Bel, I can't, I—" The words had to be pushed out of my mouth. "I'll try, I really will."

We dug the stumps out, first with shovels then by hand, scooping handfuls of dirt away from the knotted roots. When the final stump lay outside the boundary there was perhaps an hour 'til dusk. Belis fetched the plough, an ancient wooden thing, and pulled it herself, while I followed on behind, pushing with all my strength. In the last few moments of the day we ran up and down casting handfuls of linseed across the freshly turned soil.

The sun sank below the eastern horizon, leaving only the faintest wash of light over the field. I keeled over and collapsed onto the ground. The pain and blood loss had made me weaker than I had ever been before, but a small part of me felt a little stronger for all that I had endured. Belis sat down beside me, lolling back so that we were both staring up at the evening stars as they appeared above us.

"Everything hurts," I muttered, feeling I had earned the right to a few complaints. "If we ever do get back to the living world I'm never going to eat blackberries again. I'm done with thorns. If anyone comes courting with a handful of roses I'll slap them out of their arms."

"Is that a problem you anticipate happening regularly?" asked Belis, with a smile in her tone. I stuck out my tongue, though I didn't really mind. I liked the sound of her voice when she was happy.

"You don't understand my struggle! Mortals are always falling for me and leaving me bouquets of flowers and presents of food. It's a real problem trying to stop the dogs from eating them."

Belis laughed, rolling back and forth on the soft grass.

"Oh, the trials of Mallt, the incandescently lovely. So roses are out. What should your admirers bring you instead? Golden torcs? Wildflowers?"

"Usually dog treats are a good start. You need to get the hounds on side." I smiled, thinking about the pack of dogs I had left behind me. "After that? Apples are nice. Apples and, I don't know, foxgloves. Although now I suppose I won't ever be a goddess again, I won't have all those worshippers. I'll have this face forever and no one will think I'm beautiful."

"I think you look just fine," Belis said.

"If I remember correctly, when we met you said I looked like half the starving farm girls in Britain."

"Well, I was quite upset," Belis admitted. "And I had only just met you."

I turned onto my side. She was still gazing up into the sky, her face silhouetted against the stars, but I could hear the blush in her voice.

"What about you? Do you have someone waiting for you in the east?"

"All my admirers wanted was my land, the title that would come with me. Roses would have been much appreciated."

She hesitated as if she wanted to say more but there was a rumble behind us and I sat up. Arawn was standing behind us, looking out at the newly ploughed field.

"You sowed the seeds?" he asked. Belis scrambled to her feet and nodded. He let out a long breath. "We will wait until morning to be sure, but this is a good omen. Mortal blood, living blood, may be able to help us turn the tide. Sleep here tonight and I will think on what to do next."

I held out my tattered hands to him.

"And these? What do you expect me to do? Can you heal them?"

He glanced at the bloody fragments of my skin.

"Injuries heal fast here. Yours may be slower than one of the dead but they should be scarred over by sunrise."

I scowled but Arawn ignored me, turning on his heel and vanishing with the same rumble that had announced his arrival.

"And some dinner would have been nice!" I yelled at the empty air.

Belis Before
4

She is nineteen years old and her father is dying. Her sister clutches at her arm, fingers tight on the muscles of her biceps. Before them the king's breath is slow and ragged, each inhalation painful, each exhalation perilously close to a death rattle. Her mother stands at his bedside embroidering a woollen blanket with long nimble fingers. There is grey at the corner of her temples and starred through her long red braids, grey in her face, but she is holding the court, holding this family together with the calm, neat stitches.

At her father's left hand a scribe is writing down a letter, smoothing the king's half-gasped words into an eloquent missive to the Roman emperor. Belis sits there silently as half her kingdom is written onto a thin curl of parchment in acorn-inked Latin. Each scratch of the quill she feels as a lash on her back, but it is the only way to hold onto what remains of her world. The representatives from Londinium have assured the king that the will is a formality. It will bring the Iceni under the cloak of Rome, sheltering them beneath the Eagle's wings. Belis thinks the Romans less eagles than wolves, slavering at the gate, picking off the weak and the sick. She tells herself that they are not weak, that her mother can hold the line.

The scribe is finished. He reaches for a tin of sand to scatter over the damp ink. When he is satisfied he raises the letter to her father and the dying king grasps the quill with hands ravaged by the killing thing and makes his mark.

She wants to let out a long sigh but she holds it in. This is not about her, she tells herself. Even though this letter will dictate the rest of her life, this moment is not about her. At her father's deathbed she is a bit player in the drama of kings and emperors.

Her father sags back against the pillows and blankets and her mother reaches out to stroke his hand.

"It will be all right, beloved, this is for the best. The Romans keep their word."

Her mother's voice is strong and her father manages half a smile, twitching his fingers to lace with hers.

The scribe takes back the letter and rolls it up, slotting it into a leather tube. He hands it to a messenger and the two of them leave the room.

The king looks over at her and she knows he wants her to approach. She hurries forward, kneeling beside the bed. She feels useless and ungainly; the muscles she has worked for on the training ground, the strength she is so proud of is worthless here. She can fight any man on the island and win but she cannot save her father's life.

Cati sits beside her and their father grimaces in what she thinks is a smile.

"Little Cati," he gasps. "My precious second girl. So funny, so gentle. Don't let the world burn the heart out of you."

Her sister is crying properly now, tears pouring down her cheeks. She leans forward and kisses his hand.

"Don't be too sad," her father manages to say. "There's a world of peace and plenty waiting for me. You just look after yourself, Wildcati girl."

Her sister shuffles back and her father's eyes flick to Belis.

"Now, my firstborn, my battle cry, my warrior girl. You have your mother's strength, my dear; some day you will make a fine queen. I know you will make me proud."

Belis nods, blinded by sudden tears. She moves to press her lips to her father's cold fingers, noticing how thin they are, with none of the strength that had tossed her into the air as a child.

She sits back down and her father looks at his wife.

"Beloved," he whispers. He doesn't say anything else, just holds her gaze. Belis sits with her family and waits for death.

 Chapter 10

We snatched a little sleep, dozing off here and there into an unconsciousness plagued by vividly colourful dreams. I finally flinched awake just before dawn. Belis was already up and checking her pack. I could feel the nervous energy rolling off her.

"How are the cuts?" I asked.

"Not so bad now," Belis said. "Another day and I think they'll be gone." She held out a hand covered in purple lines, the fading scars of our work the day before.

I looked down at my own arms. I felt strangely proud of myself. The hard-won strength of the journey to Annwn had kept me going. The newborn Mallt of a few months ago could never have cleared the brambles. I wondered if the immortal form I had worn before that could have either. I had always been diligent in my work, but it had never been physically difficult.

Belis finished her checks and shuffled over. She picked up my hand and turned it over in hers, running strong fingers over the scars.

"I am glad it heals so fast here," she said, still staring at the cuts. "It is a hard thing to see those you care about injured."

"Indeed," I pressed my palm to her palm, "but these wounds were chosen in order to help others, not forced on us by an enemy."

"Pain is pain," Belis said, but she looked a little more cheerful. "Come, Arawn should be here soon."

She scrambled to her feet and pulled me up next to her. Behind us the field of thorns was filled with pale green stems, the newly planted flax already knee-high and waving gently in the breeze. The dawn was rising behind us, painting the plants in a golden light. As the sun broke from the horizon the flax stems began to bloom blue, tiny flowers unfurling as they reached up to the sky. In a few moments the whole field was a wash of azure.

"Beautiful, is it not," said a deep voice from behind me. I jumped and turned to see Arawn staring out at the view. "You have done very well."

"We have proved ourselves then?" Belis said, hurrying towards him. "You will let us head towards the gorge?"

"Not quite yet. There are still a few things we must do."

Belis ground her teeth. "My sister is waiting for me. We must try soon."

"I understand your urgency, Princess, but it will do your sister no good if we fail and Annwn falls to the shadow. We have proved that living mortals can be effective against the corruption, but you will need more help to win out."

"Help from where?" I asked.

"I will show you." Arawn reached out and I took his arm. I looked back at Belis and she sighed and linked up with us, our packs slung over one shoulder and her long oak spear in her spare hand.

"Now take a deep breath." Arawn stepped forward smartly and the world flickered around us again. All the blood in my body seemed to shoot into my head and I would have fallen were it not for Arawn's arm. I took a moment to centre myself and then looked around.

We were standing next to a huge wooden pavilion, a fluted roof held up by intricately carved pillars. The twisting knots of the carving had been merrily painted in yellow and white. Fine netting had been strung between the pillars, through which filtered the sound of birdsong. Bright colours flashed inside the aviary as birds fluttered back and forth.

I stepped a little closer and peered in. Robins, blue tits and goldfinches darted from perch to perch above a wide pool crewed by mallards and geese. A gyrfalcon gazed down at us from the lofty heights of the rafters, looking over the quail and pheasants and chickens that scratched comfortably in the grass and dust of the floor. Behind the falcon huddled a parliament of owls, snoozing peacefully in the shadows of the roof.

"Birds?" Belis said, peering through the netting.

"Birds," confirmed Arawn. "These are the Adar. Every morning their song wakes the dead and lulls the living to sleep. They are cared for by my seneschal, a powerful witch. I spoke of her before." He nodded behind us and I turned around.

I had seen mazes before, usually grown by druids to hide holy places. They were twisted hedgerows and oak trees, patched up with ivy and holly trees and pearled with mistletoe. What lay before me now made those look like herb gardens. A vast forest spread out across the whole valley, a patchwork of thousands of trees in every shade of green from seafoam to pine.

"This is where she vanished, while gathering herbs in the maze. It has always been a dark place. Most of the dead chose to avoid it but she liked it. We hadn't realised it had become corrupted until she failed to return. I went after her but the shadow came down on me again. Rescue parties did better but they get hopelessly lost and the longer they spend in there the more they forget why they went in. If they don't find their way back within a few hours, they come back *shadowbitten* or simply never return at all."

His voice was bitter and he suddenly slammed his hand into the wood of the pavilion so that it shook and the birds began to clamour in alarm.

"I am supposed to be the Lord of Annwn but this affliction has left me helpless as a fox kit. I cannot do anything to help but send those I am supposed to guard into danger and linger where it is safe while they fall."

"Sometimes that is a leader's position," said Belis, moving a little closer from where she had jumped back at his outburst. "A general does not always lead from the front. They need to see the whole battlefield so they can call the orders."

Arawn looked up at her, surprise in his face.

"That's kind of you to say, but if this is a battle then it's a fighting retreat. We need reinforcements and you two alone will not be enough. We need my seneschal back."

I stared out at the wood. "You cannot expect us to clear the whole forest. We almost died doing the thorns."

"I agree that is beyond you," Arawn said. "And the labyrinth is an ancient and sacred place. I do not wish to destroy it. But you must rescue her. We will need her magic if we are to root out the cause of this corruption. I believe that your living strength will have the capacity to resist. Do not trust what your heart or mind are telling you to believe. Look closely, listen clearly. Only then can you be sure of what is ahead of you."

I glanced at Belis. She looked as worried as me at Arawn's words. "Do you have any idea where she might be? The wood is large."

"Head to the springs then turn east. The oldest paths should lead you to the centre of the labyrinth. I would guess that she is there. Beware the darkness inside, it will try to lead you astray. I do not think there are *shadowbitten* still within the bounds, but I cannot guarantee it."

He picked up Belis's spear from where it was leaning against the pavilion and handed it to her, then passed me her shortsword.

"You can cut them down long enough to run for it and lose them in the maze. Try not to lose yourselves."

I nodded and set my shoulders. We had done so well against the thorns the day before, pitting our will against the corruption. I felt confident we could be proof against it again.

We bade farewell to him and set off down the hill. An arch of rough stone reared up before us. The positioning of each rock seemed fragile, almost tentative, but the moss covering the western edges hinted at the great age of the structure.

Inside the woods seemed no different than before. The trees were still ancient, old and twisting against each other. The sunlight that spotted through the leaves was pale, dappling Belis's skin as she headed into the heart of the springs. Her hair was beginning to escape from its plaits, the strands shaking free like tongues of fire. No, it was fire, lapping at the nape of her neck, as if to burn the pale skin.

I shook my head and hurried to catch up with her. My thoughts were not entirely my own. Belis looked over at me and on an impulse I grabbed her hand, needing the comfort. She started slightly but didn't pull free and a moment later she started walking again.

The temperature in the forest was increasing now, the cool of the early morning growing into a damp heat that began to drop beads of moisture along my forehead and down my spine. My hand in Belis's grew slippery and I had to blink sweat from my eyelashes.

I could tell we were getting close to the springs, the ground underfoot getting steadily muddier, sucking at my boots with every squelching pace. The humidity had blossomed into a white mist, thickening with every blink until I could no longer see Belis, only feel her hand in mine and hear the quickening of her breath.

With a splash I stepped into warm water, swirling up to my ankles. Belis stopped, yanking her foot back from the mud.

"Don't panic," I said. I was whispering but the fog seemed to magnify my voice so that the words echoed. "Keep walking, head east."

She squeezed my hand and moved forward. I followed, not wanting to lose her to the mist. The water deepened and soon we were wading up to our thighs. It grew hotter as we splashed onwards, the mist forcing itself down my throat, pressing down on my chest with each breath. Beside me I could hear Belis panting, but she kept her grip on my hand even when she tripped into the water and surfaced spluttering. I helped her to her feet, still blinded by the mist.

"The spring floor drops off," she murmured. "I think this is as far as we can go."

A sound came from behind us and I whipped around. A girl was wading towards us; she looked about six or seven, I thought. Her long coppery hair trailed in the water. She seemed familiar to me and I tried to place where I had seen her before. Belis gasped and turned as pale as the mist.

"Cati!"

I looked back at the girl, recognising her now. She looked ten years younger than when I had last seen her, but the lines of the adult she had become were present in her face. She stared up at Belis with pale, unseeing grey-green eyes.

"Cati." Belis went as if to throw herself towards her sister. I grabbed at her wrist, trying to hold her back. She almost pulled me over but I jammed my heels into the mud.

"It's not real, it's an illusion," I shouted at her, trying to break her concentration. She kept moving and in a panic I dug my nails into her arm. "Belis, please, look at me!"

Belis froze, glanced at me then back at the girl. She shut her eyes, and an expression of terrible grief passed over her face. Then she opened them again and looked down.

"It's not her?" she whispered. I shook my head.

"Her soul is trapped at the gates. Arawn wouldn't have allowed it in till her body died and if that had happened he would have told us. It's just a trick." I waved my hand through the girl's shape, passing through it like the mist it had sprung from.

The un-Cati smiled and beckoned us further in. Belis hesitated then yanked us both away. "This will get worse before it gets better," she muttered. I grimaced.

"I'm sorry. You knew this would not be an easy task," I said. She nodded. I watched her as she traced the branch where the image of her sister had vanished. Then she squared her shoulders and turned back to the path.

After an hour of walking the path before us split, offering no obvious direction to take. We halted, gazing first one way, then the other. I considered suggesting that we split up to try and cover more ground but dismissed the idea. We would do better to stick together. I was about to say that we should just pick the right-hand path when a flash of bronze caught my eye.

About thirty yards down the left path, sitting high in the branches of an elder tree, was a huge bird. I narrowed my eyes. It was enormous, perhaps a yard from beak to tailfeather, with rust-brown wings tucked back as it glared down at the path, amber eyes searching for prey. For a moment I thought it was a creature of the shadow but it seemed so vibrant. I remembered what Arawn had said about the birds, that the witch we were looking for had cared for them. Perhaps this eagle was a sign.

I nudged Belis and pointed towards the eagle. She didn't respond. I elbowed her in the side, keeping my eyes fixed on the bird. Still nothing. Exasperated, I turned to hiss in her ear.

Her eyes were locked on the right-hand path and it took me no more than a moment to understand why. Her mother was standing at the edge of the woods, barefoot and bareheaded. In this facsimile of life, Boudica was terrible and wonderful to behold, her dark eyebrows furrowed as she looked down at her daughter. She stretched out a hand to Belis, inviting her closer.

"Is she real?" Belis murmured to me. "Is that really her?"

I looked at the ghost of the last queen of the Iceni, her long red hair blowing gently in the wind. I wanted to lie, to say it was only a dream, only a trick of the shadow.

"I don't know," I said. "It could be, but, Belis, if you go to her now that'll be it. We'll never find this witch, we'll lose your sister, lose everything. If you go to her now you'll never leave."

"But she's my mother," Belis whispered, "she's calling to me."

I felt my heart constrict painfully in my chest. I could feel her heartache as if it was my own and the realisation hit me that I could not drag her away from this.

"I can't tell you not to go, Bel, you have to choose."

Belis reached out a hand to her mother. Then she drew it back and turned away. The ghost vanished back into the trees. Belis shut her eyes, tears trickling down her face.

I spun back to the eagle. Miraculously, it was still on its lofty perch, scanning the path below.

I hurried towards its tree, towing Belis behind me. For a moment it simply eyed me, then it launched itself from the branch and wheeled into the air. Its outstretched wings were wider than my arms and it landed heavily on my shoulder, causing me to stagger. The eagle regarded me with those glowing golden eyes and blinked. I tried to repress a shiver at that cruel beak so close to my face and looked back at Belis.

She had her spear out in front of her, ready to strike. I didn't fancy her chances of killing the thing before it could rip my eyes out and hoped that I hadn't made a mistake. It blinked at me again and chirped, then tugged at the collar of my tunic.

"I think it wants us to go this way," I said, trying not to speak too loudly.

"You want us to take navigational advice from a bird?" Belis sniffed, still gripping her spear. "Based on how it cheeps at you?"

"Just trust me on this, Belis," I said, still staring at the bird. "I think I'm making a connection."

The eagle had strong opinions on which way we should go, digging its claws into my shoulder if I took a path it disapproved of. The sun was low in the sky by the time the eagle croaked in triumph. Before us was a huge, gnarled oak, the largest in the whole forest. The great flock of starlings I had seen earlier was encamped in its boughs, covering almost every inch of the branching arms of the tree. I came to a halt, the eagle chittering in my ear. Belis stopped next to me.

"Has your eagle run out of ideas?" she said, glaring at the bird. It blinked back at her and beat its wings.

"I think this is the centre of the forest." I looked around, unsure where to turn next.

One of the starlings hopped down from its branch, landing at the foot of the tree. It stood on a protruding root that had wrapped itself around a small pond as if the tree was hoarding the water for itself. Belis approached the tree, pausing at the edge of the water. Something swished beneath the surface and Belis glanced at it then froze. I looked down, my spare hand flying to my knife.

Belis's reflection floated in the spring, smiling back at us. Not a reflection, another Belis. Slowly she rose, water sloughing off her like snakeskin. She yawned loudly and grinned at the Belis standing next to me.

The other Belis seemed to grow taller and older. Golden bracelets appeared on her wrists and heavy torcs wrapped around her neck. The rough linen dress she was wearing brightened, then vanished behind heavy velvet robes. A thin circlet grew to crown her head, spikes fanning out like the rays of a sunrise.

"What are you?" Belis cried, staring at the copied form before her. The eagle on my shoulder screeched and tightened its talons into the soft flesh of my arm.

The other Belis smiled, and when she spoke it was as harsh as the howling of the wind.

"I am your true self. You cannot save your sister for there is no love in you. You are cold and cowardly. I know your heart and it is carved from stone. You are not the hero of any story. Give up, go back, run from these lands as you ran from the battlefield and seek a small life where none will find you."

The other Belis smiled once more and then lunged towards us. Belis brought her arms up but as the doppelganger reached her she shattered into a swarm of buzzing flies. They flew at Belis's eyes, her mouth. She clawed at her face, trying to get them off. I grabbed her arm and dunked us both under the water. When we resurfaced the flies had scattered.

"What was that?" Belis asked, panting.

"Neither shadow nor ghost nor anything that ever lived," I said, picking damp hair off my face and calling back the eagle, which had leapt off me as I threw myself at the water. It was sitting on the tree roots, scratching at the wood with long talons.

I squinted at the tree. The bark was twisting around, seeming to form a long arch, almost like a door. I stepped closer and placed my hand on the rough trunk. My fingers slid through the bark and I closed them into a fist and pulled back. The tree vanished and a figure slumped forward, landing on top of me.

Belis hurried over and peeled them off me, lowering the body to the ground. They were covered in a thick woollen cloak, a scarf pulled over the face. Belis knelt over them and looked up at me.

"It must be the witch," she said. I nodded, wiping sap from my hands.

"Unwrap the scarf. She must be struggling to breathe."

Belis pulled the scarf back but a hand, thin and birdlike, reached up to grab hers. Belis shrank back and the figure sat up, looking over at us.

"You are not *shadowbitten*?" The voice sounded vaguely familiar to me, female but deep and strangely rasping. I shook my head.

"We came here to rescue you, on behalf of Arawn," Belis said. "We're alive, humans come to beg a favour from the lord. You've been in here a while. Did something lock you in the tree?

"I wrapped it around myself as protection from the corruption," the figure said, then pulled back her scarf. She grinned at us, revealing a mouthful of pointed teeth. It took me a moment, but I recognised her. Rhiannon, an old queen of Britain, who had died perhaps a thousand years ago after a long and eventful life. The teeth had been an inheritance from her fae mother, the crown from her mortal father. We had met a handful of times, rarely under pleasant circumstances.

"Rhiannon?" I asked. "What are you doing here?"

"Mallt, it's been years. I haven't seen you since you pulled my husband's soul from his decapitated head." She flashed her teeth at me. "And mortal? There must be a tale to tell there."

Rhiannon had been demanding even for a queen. I doubted death had softened her.

"You're Rhiannon Half Fae, Queen of Dyfed?" Belis asked, standing up and peering at the old woman.

"I was, when I dwelt under the living sun. Now I am merely another of the souls that live in the afterworld."

Belis smiled at her. "I think you might be my great grandmother, give or take a few generations. My father's mother came from Dyfed."

Rhiannon sniffed. "Possibly. I only had the one son but he was rather more profligate with his affections than I would have preferred. I am sure I have descendants all over Britain and even the mainland." She brushed off her cloak. "You needn't think I will grant you any favours. I owe fealty only to Arawn these days."

Belis blinked, a little upset at having this offer of familial connection slapped down. I watched as she swallowed the emotion down then stepped back and nodded. I rolled my eyes at the old queen, annoyed at how she had spoken to Belis.

"Death suits you, Rhiannon," I said. She grinned toothily at me. Belis held out a hand to help her up.

"We had better leave."

"While you've been hiding in a tree," I paused to shoot a glare at her, "things have deteriorated in Annwn."

"So you've noticed at last." Rhiannon crossed her arms, tapping slanted nails against her sleeves. She smiled at me, revealing all her pointed teeth, and reached back into the split trunk to pick up a satchel. "The shadow will not easily give us up. We may need to fight our way out."

"We can sustain injuries from them without becoming corrupted," Belis said. "We'll get you out."

"Perhaps, but you can still be killed," Rhiannon countered, "and once dead you'll be just as susceptible as me. Are you ready?"

I looked back into the shadows, watching the dust motes dance on the air. I was hardly eager to step back into the woods but I could not see another way out. Belis nodded; her grip on her spear was steady. I unsheathed my sword and held it out in front of me.

Rhiannon fetched a knife from her bag and pricked the edge of her forefinger. She squeezed the flesh so that a bubble of blood formed on the tip and dabbed it on her eyelids, the tip of her nose, the bridge of her lips, all the time muttering in old Brittonic.

"Half-fae blood," she said, noticing us watching her. "Acts as a protection against the corruption. Only works on me, though, more's the pity."

She held out an arm and the eagle hopped from my shoulder to hers. She stroked its beak affectionately and looked up at us.

"Follow quickly and do not fall behind."

She strode into the darkness. Belis met my eyes and smiled before following. I hesitated for a moment, then hurried after them.

The woods were loud now, the eerie silence replaced with a cacophony of screeches and snapping twigs. The undergrowth was alive, leaves twitching as strange, scaled things crawled beneath. Lines of ants wound around the tree trunks, rolling over larger insects and tearing them apart.

Rhiannon moved quickly, turning left and right through the maze with an old familiarity. Belis and I stayed close. I ran my thumb over the hilt of Belis's sword, unsure if I was ready to use it. I had felt confident that I was, out under the blue skies of the open, but here in the darkness of the maze I wasn't so certain. What was I now, no longer with my strength and speed? I had tried to fight with Belis when the Romans chased us into the sea and all I had managed was to almost drown. I was weak. Belis deserved a better person to fight beside.

Something moved to the side of the path and I paused, peering into the blackness. There was a pale man stepping neatly between the trees, white hair gleaming in the low light. I hissed a warning to Belis and she turned back, following where I pointed.

"You see him?" I whispered.

Belis shifted her spear, eyes locked on the strange man.

"Should we strike? Or hope he doesn't come after us?" I asked. Belis chewed her lip, trying to make a decision. Rhiannon was still walking, chittering under her breath to the eagle.

"I don't want to start something this far from the entrance," she said, keeping her voice low. "I don't know if the witch could run all that way if we pick a fight we can't finish. I'll watch our backs, you catch up with Rhiannon and look out at the front. Whistle if you need me."

I nodded and darted back along the path to Rhiannon. Behind me Belis was stepping backwards, keeping her eyes on the figure in the trees.

We'd walked a little while longer when I caught hold of Rhiannon's arm and pulled her to a halt.

"Over there." I dipped my head to the left. A second man, this one with long dark hair, was wading through the undergrowth. Belis caught up with us, her eyes locked on the road behind.

"There's another one," I muttered.

"The first is still following," Belis said. Rhiannon's face turned from one to another.

"They're hunting us," she said, "waiting to strike. We should hurry."

We set off again, scurrying through the forest. The pale men followed. They didn't seem to be speeding up, but they stayed at the same distance. I could see more of them appearing through the trees, all of them bare-chested, with the same white skin and their eyes on the ground.

"Faster," called Belis, and we broke into a run. The woods were getting louder and louder, strange birds screaming as we sprinted under the canopies. There was a clattering behind me and I turned to see the first of the men come onto the path. He raised his eyes and I could see they were dark red, blood trickling down like tears. He bared his lips and his teeth were broken and rotting in his mouth. A second stepped onto the track and then a third, and then there were six of them, blocking the whole path as they staggered forward.

Belis dropped back, whirling her spear, and shoved me in front of her.

"Get Rhiannon to the arch, don't wait for me."

"Are you mad? You can't fight them all off." I tugged at her arm. "Besides, it's only worth getting her out if you survive, too. You're a far better warrior than me. If anything, I'm the disposable one."

"Not to me," she said, but she let me drag her forward, starting to run.

The pale men were sprinting now, no more than a few yards behind us. Rhiannon was just in front. She whispered something and an enormous elm tree began to teeter, before crashing to the ground just as Belis and I ducked beneath it. The vines whipped at my legs and I staggered but Belis caught me and pulled me on. The pursuing *shadowbitten* slowed to clamber over the tree and we gained a little distance. Rhiannon called out again and two more trees uprooted themselves, crushing a couple of the pursuers as they fell. I began to feel a little hope, though my chest was burning with the effort of running.

Then a pair of *shadowbitten* burst from the trees in front of us. I stalled, fumbling for my sword, but Belis was already in motion. She launched her spear and it sailed through the air, sinking with a thud into the chest of the leftmost man. Before he hit the ground she'd loosed a knife that hit the other man in the eye, causing him to stagger forward, clutching at his face.

I managed to recover my grip on my sword and half fell forward, running it through him. The man juddered and gasped as I tried to drag the blade back out, collapsing as it slid free. Belis bent to retrieve her knife, picked up her spear and then caught my arm, tugging me on as Rhiannon darted past.

"Can't you pull down more trees on them?" I panted as we caught up with the witch. "Or open another ravine?"

"I don't have the strength for that," she hissed at me. "You'll have to fight them off."

I glanced over my shoulder. The two we had attacked were crawling back into the undergrowth, but there were still four on the trail and they had made up some of the distance when we stopped to fight past the others.

"Outnumbered," muttered Belis to herself. She was barely panting, running easily as Rhiannon scrambled on and I fought desperately for breath to keep going. "How much further?"

"Still a way to go," Rhiannon called, "but there's a shortcut through an old hole in one of the hedges. If we can squeeze through there we'll be close to the arch."

Belis looked back and nodded. "All right, let's make for that."

We hurtled to the right, heading down a long, narrow path that pointed due east. It was too tight for us to run side by side so Rhiannon went first, then me, then Belis, running sideways to keep her spear pointed at the *shadowbitten* who were pushing past each other to get after us.

Rhiannon skidded in the dirt and began clawing at the base of a bush. She tore at the new leaves and vines and cackled with delight as they came loose in her hands, revealing a small gap. She began to squirm through just as the *shadowbitten* reached us.

Belis caught the first of them on her spear, pinning the man to the ground. The second ran right over his fellow and leapt at her, mad hands clawing even before he was within range. Belis brought up her knife and slashed at his arms, opening great cuts in the pale flesh.

Rhiannon gave a grunt of relief and slid through the hedge. Then she ducked her head back to our side.

"Quickly, Mallt, get in here."

I swung my sword at the man fighting Belis, slicing through his neck before the blade got caught in the column of his spine. He dropped and I yanked it free. Belis grabbed my shoulders and pushed me to the ground.

"Get through, I'll follow when I can."

She picked up my sword and was already turning to face the next attack. I caught the end of her spear and passed it through to Rhiannon, then crawled through myself. For once I was glad to be small and scrawny as I slid through easily.

"Belis, come on," I called, crouching down in the dirt and peering through the gap.

It was too small to see what was happening, but I could hear the clamour of blades and the growling of the *shadowbitten*. There was a thud and I saw red hair hit the ground. Belis groaned and I could just about glimpse her wincing through the tangle of branches.

"Here," I screamed, reaching out to her. She rolled over and gripped my hand. I pulled with all my strength. Rhiannon knelt next to me and grabbed her other arm and we dragged her through the dirt towards us.

She was too broad-shouldered and the branches of the hedge were too close together. Rhiannon let go of her hand and said something short and sharp. The branches widened and Belis shot through to our side of the fence, one of the remaining men still clinging to her heels. I grabbed for the sword and stabbed at him, sending him howling back under the scrub.

Rhiannon repeated some more words and the gap sealed, fresh vines curling out to separate us from the *shadowbitten*. She sagged back, clearly still exhausted.

"Which way?" I asked. We couldn't afford to linger here. Belis staggered to her feet and pulled up the old queen, who was now gasping for breath, and slung her onto her back.

"Follow the eagle," she gasped. The eagle, which had been perched atop the hedgerow, jumped back down to my shoulder and nipped at my ear. I set off again, praying that we were as close as Rhiannon had said. We would not survive another encounter with the *shadowbitten*.

The stone arch loomed ahead of us, silhouetted against the setting sun as we burst through it. The eagle loosened its grip on my shoulder, stiffly detaching the talons before launching itself into the sky. It flew up the hill before us, skimming over the ground like a dragonfly before landing neatly on the roof of the aviary. Belis hurried after it, eager to leave the shady trees behind.

Arawn was waiting outside the pavilion. He kept his face clear, but I could see a little of the tension leave him as Belis put Rhiannon down beside her.

"Thank heavens." He bowed deeply towards the old queen. "You are not hurt?"

She shook her head, silver earrings chiming slightly with the movement. "But we have much to discuss. I have had a garbled account from these two."

The Lord of the Dead glanced at us. "There's food and drink in the pack over there. I will be over once I have consulted with my seneschal."

Belis opened her mouth to protest, but I pulled at her arm and she shut it and followed me over to where Arawn had pointed.

Arawn and Rhiannon spoke for almost an hour. I heard little of their conversation as I attacked the soft bread rolls and hard cheese we found in the pack. Belis was still shaken. She sat hunched over, her long fingers shredding a bread roll into crumbs until I finally took it away from her and forced her to eat something.

When they were finally finished talking, Arawn laid a hand on Rhiannon's shoulder then turned and vanished, *rushing* off into the dark. Rhiannon walked over and stood looking down at us.

"Arawn tells me that not only have you safely extracted me from the maze, but you have also cut down one of the bramble patches that has infested our lands."

She eyed the pile of crumbs next to Belis and whistled for a moment. A small flock of sparrows flew out of the pavilion and set to work eating up the mess.

"As I was saying, it seems you have my gratitude. There may be a little hope for this land after all."

"What do we do next?" Belis asked, her voice low in the twilight. Rhiannon spread her hands.

"There is still much to discuss on that account. Arawn believes we should wait for the next incursion of the *shadowbitten*, test your strength against them in battle—"

"We don't know how long that will be," Belis interrupted, balling her hands into fists. "We must strike first, not wait to be attacked."

"Is that what your mother taught you?" Rhiannon asked. Belis looked as if she had been struck and she half rose, reaching for her spear. I caught her arm and she sank back. Rhiannon continued as if the young warrior had not moved.

"Yes, Arawn has told me all about Boudica's rebellion. Wiser heads must prevail this time, child. I do not intend to let whatever corruption has poisoned Annwn dictate the terms of battle, but neither shall we be *rushing* in without thought."

I glared at Rhiannon, and she flashed her pointed teeth at me.

"So what do you think we should do then, Half Fae?" I snapped. I decided I didn't like it when other people were rude to Belis, especially now that I had promised to be polite to her.

"I haven't determined what I think yet. I need to consider all our options, then of course the final choice will be up to Arawn. Things would certainly be easier if you had managed to hold onto your own powers, Nightshade."

It was Belis's turn to hold me back then. The old witch really was infuriating.

"In any case there can be nothing done for at least one more day. It is most auspicious that you have come to us now, on the eve of Annwn's greatest celebration. Arawn has gone on ahead of us to prepare the way. As the harbingers of hope, you two will be our guests of honour. Get some rest here and I will wake you at dawn."

Chapter 11

I dreamed in red, in shades of crimson and vermilion. I saw Boudica and Cati as they had been in the forest clearing, their flaming hair trailing through the grass like a river of blood. I saw the battlefield where thirty thousand of their countrymen lay, now nothing more than crow meat. I saw Londinium burning, the heat of the fire so real and close that it seemed to scorch my lungs. I saw the cloaks of the Romans, flashing like a flock of robins as they marched down their long straight roads. I saw Belis sitting in a tower, bent over a spinning wheel. At first she was twisting fibres from the pile of red flax Rhiannon and I had harvested, but as I watched the threads thickened until she was spinning from a mound of viscera, her fingers sticky with blood.

I woke yelping, clawing at the strong hands that were shaking me from my dreams. Rhiannon glared down at me.

"Calm, Mallt, it's only me."

I sat up, my cloak slipping off me. It seemed to be shortly before dawn. I didn't feel rested but when Rhiannon held out a hand I let her help me to my feet.

"Where's Belis?" I asked, looking around for her. Rhiannon sniffed.

"She's already gone. I can only *rush* one of you at a time. You were fast asleep and snoring so I decided not to wake you."

I groaned and stretched out my arms. My muscles had cramped overnight and were tight and knotted.

"Where are we going exactly? And do we have to travel by that horrible dizzying way of yours?" I asked Rhiannon, dropping my arms.

"*Rushing*? We surely do, unless you know of some other path that will bring us to our destination before sunrise."

"I don't understand how you can stomach it. Every time it makes me dizzy."

Rhiannon raised an eyebrow at me. "You have changed, Mallt Y Nos. Once you would have laughed at those who were nauseated by speed. I remember how you would race the Wild Hunt across the high moors of Britain, outpacing even the fastest of their horses. Now you cannot bear a simple *rush*."

I shut my mouth and took the arm she proffered me. Rhiannon hummed under her breath and the world squeezed in around us. When I felt steady enough to open my eyes, I found we were now standing at the edge of a meadow buzzing with activity.

Long trestle tables were being manoeuvred into place, forming a rough circle around a huge pile of logs. Crates of goblets and casks of wine were being unstacked from a caravan of wagons. In the very centre of the circle a tripod was being erected, with seven men heaving a huge cast-iron cauldron beneath it. As I watched they attached thick chains to the sides and hauled it into the air so that it swung gently below the tripod. The cauldron was big enough to bathe in and the metal was blackened with use.

I tore my eyes away from it, looking for Belis. There were so many people in the field that it took me a moment to pick her out. I finally saw her helping a group of women as they carried bales of cloths down to the tables, stray red curls peeking out from beneath the mountain of embroidered linen she was carrying. I watched, smiling, as she stood patiently while the smaller women distributed first their own armfuls and then hers, her face appearing as one tablecloth after another was removed from her pile and spread out over the benches.

She looked as tired as I felt, purple bruises of fatigue under her eyes, and I noticed now how thin she had become over the last few months, beaten down to lean muscle. I lifted a hand to wave at her and she saw me and went to return the gesture, almost dropping the last of the cloths. She caught them and placed the pile on the nearest table before striding towards me.

"Mallt!" she called, and I felt some of the tension in my muscles relax at the sound of her voice.

"Belis, they're keeping you busy, then? Has Arawn told you what's hap-mmpfh!"

My words were cut off as Belis reached me and enfolded me in a hug. Her arms hadn't grown any less strong and they held me tight as she tucked my head under her chin. I started to complain but gave up and breathed in her scent of fresh grass and honey.

She let me go, looking a little embarrassed at her reaction. I straightened my tunic. "What is it?" I asked, grinning. She flushed but smiled back.

"It's Calan Gaeaf! My favourite festival. I never thought to celebrate it this way, but I find it makes me happy, even in Annwn."

I beamed at her and was about to say something stupid when Rhiannon tapped me on the shoulder.

"If you're quite finished, I believe there is some work for you."

We followed her through the trestle tables, dodging between laughing children who chased each other between the feet of their elders. Rhiannon stopped in front of the hearth, where the enormous cauldron had stopped swinging, hanging still as stone beneath the tripod. There was a wave of laughter from behind the cauldron and Arawn, Lord of the Dead, emerged, a puppy in one arm, a toddler in the other.

"Something for the pot!" he bellowed and both dog and child wriggled in his grip. I saw Belis's mouth drop open in horror even as Arawn's twisted in a grin.

"A jest, a jest," he said, plopping the puppy on the ground and swinging the little boy up on his shoulders. The toddler wound his fat hands in Arawn's hair and screeched in delight.

Arawn patted his shoulders to check the child was secure then looked back at us. The mirth left his face and he placed a hand on the side of the cauldron. The iron sang quietly under his touch, a low baritone that echoed in the body and billowed out through the crowd like a shockwave. The chattering of the folk around us died and the puppy at Arawn's feet whined and fled to hide under a table.

"What is that?" Belis asked. Arawn stroked the blackened iron.

"This is the Giant's Cauldron. It is Calan Gaeaf tonight, the beginning of winter in the living world. The best thing to do today is to celebrate as we always have. Traditionally we feast here before the mortals do, as winter is the time of death. These fine souls have prepared bread and wine to feed all in Annwn, but without meat there is no feast."

Arawn waved behind him at a wagon piled high with pig carcasses, neatly gutted and ready for the pot.

"You're the guests of honour. Cook the meat for us in the cauldron. It's the only one big enough to have the meal prepared for sundown when our banqueting begins. You'll find all the herbs and spices you need in the wagon with the pork."

He lifted his hand from the cauldron and the singing stopped. I squinted at the great pot, trying to remember what I knew of it. The Giant's Cauldron, one of the great treasures of the high fae in the old world. Now it was here in Annwn. There was always a twist, though, a cost or a challenge to the use of these fae items. Needlessly complicated things, I thought, but the fae had always delighted in them.

"The cauldron," I said, the words coming to me slowly as I thought back, "not many can use it. It won't cook the food, no matter how hot you stoke the fire."

Arawn nodded. "Few can get this cauldron to boil. Only those who are brave of spirit will succeed. If I am going to send you into the shadows alongside Rhiannon, I need to know you are strong in mind as well as body." He scooped the child from his shoulders and set him on the ground. "Best of fortune with it."

He took the child's hand and led him away. I exchanged glances with Belis.

"Only those who are brave enough can cook with the cauldron?" she said. "What kind of terrible system is that? Who would make such a thing? Since when is bravery prized among cooks?"

I shrugged. "The fae made all kinds of strange things before humans came to Britain. Best not to look for mortal reasons in their ways."

"Will it cook for us?" Belis looked worried, chewing her lower lip. "How high are its standards? How does it even know if we're brave or not?"

"How should I know?" I asked, a little disgruntled. "It's magic. I was magical but that doesn't mean I understand it. Besides, you've fought in battles, you're a blooded warrior, I wouldn't worry overmuch."

Belis rocked back on her heels, casting concerned looks at the cauldron. I knew she was thinking about her sister. I was harbouring my own doubts about the cauldron's judgement but I thought it would be unhelpful to say so. I sighed and clapped her on the shoulder.

"Let's bring the meat over and begin preparing it," I said, "and I'll light the fire. The best way to start is to start."

She said nothing but when I headed towards the wagon I heard her sigh and follow me. There were six large pig carcasses, each dressed and ready for the pot. Tucked in beside them were bushels of sweet-smelling sage and rosemary, dill and thyme. Small barrels of wine and pots of honey sat beside a bag of coarse-grained sea salt and a sack of parsnips.

I hoisted the parsnips over one shoulder and gathered the herbs in my arms. Belis heaved one of the pigs onto her back, her biceps straining at the weight.

"Is there a particular order we should add in?" she asked, gritting her teeth. I considered the question, reviewing my own meagre knowledge of cooking and the weeks of Belis's tasteless stews.

"Just throw everything in the pot," I said eventually. "It's a magic cauldron. It can work it out."

Belis grunted and set off back to the fireplace. I left the meat to her and began ferrying the herbs and barrels of wine to the cauldron. There I hunted down a footstool and began adding everything in, leaning on the rim as I glugged the wine into the pot. Every few minutes Belis would bring over another side of pork and I helped as she shoved it into the cauldron.

Once the entire contents of the wagon were in the pot I bent down to start building the fire. I stacked the smaller logs into a pyramid and filled the centre with dead leaves and wood shavings, remembering the way Belis had built her fires on the journey through Britain. I concentrated hard on the structure, trying to make sure it wouldn't collapse in on itself when the fire caught.

Belis crouched down next to me, turning over her kindling pouch in her hands. I waited for her to make adjustments.

"Not bad," she said, surveying the pyramid. "Here." She tossed me the pouch. "Set the spark."

I caught the small leather bag in my hands and opened the drawstrings. Inside was Belis's fire steel and a chunk of flint, nestled in a pile of soft tinder. I picked out a handful of the tinder and leaned over it. The fire steel was about the length of my thumb, a rough rectangle of metal with an elegantly curved handle so the user could hold it while striking. I gripped it in my left hand and took the flint in my right.

I struck the steel against the sharpest edge of the flint, the way I had seen Belis do. It sparked immediately but the tinder didn't catch. I tried again, striking over and over. I ground my teeth in frustration.

"Here." Belis put her hands over mine and moved them lower so that they were almost touching the pile of wood shavings. "Try now."

I struck again and this time the tinder caught, a handful of sparks catching the edge of the soft fibres. Belis picked it up, cupping it in her hands and blowing gently so that the orange pinpricks blossomed into flames. When the fire had truly caught she slid it into the pyramid I had built and I leaned over to help her blow more air. After a few minutes the rest of the kindling had caught and the thinner logs were beginning to glow orange and yellow.

"Nicely done," Belis said, sitting back on her heels. "Did you put all the food in the cauldron?"

"All apart from the honey." I looked around for the pot. "Hang on, the lid's stuck."

Belis held out her hand and I gave her the honey jar. She twisted it off with no discernible effort and handed it to me. I climbed back on the footstool to drizzle it into the cauldron, enjoying the sweet smell of it, the spirals of gold pouring into the pot.

"More water, too, I think," I called down to her. Belis nodded and grabbed a pitcher from one of the trestle tables and filled it at the water barrel. I took it from her and poured the water on top of the pork, using a long ladle to stir it in.

"How does it look?" Belis asked, jumping to try and see over the side.

"Good." I clambered down and handed her the ladle. "Besides, I don't think that the quality of the food is that important, just whether we can get it to cook."

Belis nodded and added a few more logs to the fire. It had built in the short time it had taken me to add the honey and the water and I could already feel the heat of it licking at my exposed hands and face.

I reached out to test the surface of the cauldron with the back of my hand. It was still cool. I glanced at Belis but decided to keep this to myself. The metal pot was thick, thick enough to take time to heat up. I would give it a while before I started worrying her.

*

An hour later as we sat tending to the fire I was trying not to panic. Around us the preparations for the feast were ongoing. Long strings of flowers were being hung between poles, low benches were carried in to serve as seating for the tables and in one corner of the field a small platform was being erected, a stage for the bards and players.

My face was hot from sitting so close to the flames and Belis had turned as red as her hair, but no matter how high we built the fire the cauldron wouldn't heat. I tested the surface again and cast a worried look at Belis.

"Still nothing?" She wiped some of the sweat from her forehead. "Dammit, it's never going to work."

I moved away from the heat, trying to think clearly.

"The cauldron thinks we're cowards," Belis said, coming over to join me. "It will only cook for those it deems worthy, those it deems brave. We've been found wanting."

"I can't believe I'm getting judged by a lump of iron." I glowered at the pot. "What would it know about bravery, it's a cooking utensil! Arawn is just going to have to let us fight anyway, it's not like he's got any better options."

"He could delay us. We'll need Rhiannon with us if we're going to make any progress and she's sworn to him. Every day we wait, the chances of rescuing Cati are smaller. Besides, maybe it's right," muttered Belis.

"What do you mean?" I asked.

"I said maybe it's right! I am a coward! I'm not worthy and the cauldron knows it." She dropped her head into her hands. "The wrong daughter survived. Cati could do this in a heartbeat, she's always been brave."

I put a tentative hand on her shoulder, struggling to find the words to say.

"You're a warrior, Belis, a veteran of the fiercest rebellion Rome has ever faced. How can you say you're not brave? Think about everything you've told me!"

Belis remained slumped over. I swore under my breath and turned on my heel. I strode up to the cauldron and punched it in the side. It made a dull ringing sound where my fist hit the metal and I swore even more loudly at the impact on my wrist.

"You want bravery? Have this! And this!" I hit it again and again. It remained cool to the touch. "You want me to fight something else? I'll do it! I'll fight—" I scanned the field for someone who might impress the cauldron. "I'll fight Arawn? That would be brave. Hey! Over here!"

Arawn didn't look up from where he was hammering at the stage.

"Stop that," said Belis, standing up. "You're not going to fight Arawn."

"Why not? A mighty warrior, challenged in single combat — how would that not be brave?"

"Because you're not frightened of him." She looked over to where the Lord of the Dead was now supervising a trio of lute players. "He might be powerful but he's not cruel or unfair. He holds true to his oaths."

"I could fight him anyway," I suggested. "Just to check?"

She gave me a wan smile. "Bravery isn't about fighting. It's not about battles and killing and blood. It's about being afraid, about being frightened, deep down in the marrow of your bones, and acting anyway."

I frowned at her.

"Then what are you afraid of?" I asked.

"I—" She broke off. "I'm afraid I'll fail and never get Cati back."

"Well, there's not much you can do about that that you aren't already doing." I tapped the side of the cauldron. Still cold. "Try again."

"You try!" she snapped at me. I bit back a response and gave it some thought.

What was I afraid of? There were things I didn't want to happen: I didn't want to die, I didn't want to feel pain and I didn't want to fail Belis. I remembered the feeling of fear when the Romans had caught us on the beach, the metallic taste of panic in my mouth.

"Ugh, I'm worried something bad could happen to Dormath without me." I tugged at my collar, suddenly feeling warm. "I'm nervous that a human life might be too much for me, that I'm not strong enough." I caught Belis's eye and winked. "I'm afraid of getting more blisters."

I turned back to the cauldron. "Did you hear that? Now cook the damn food!"

"Almost hard to believe that didn't work," said Belis, a smirk breaking through her frown.

"Feel free to try something else," I said, bridling at her words.

"Very well." She tucked her hair behind her ears. I noticed her hands were shaking. "I was afraid to die. I was so terrified that I stole my sister's life, tried to drag myself back from the brink by offering the most precious thing I could think of instead. I sacrificed my sister but even that great evil didn't stop the fear. I'm more afraid than ever. I am afraid to live with the guilt. That's why I am here because I am too much of a coward to try and make my own way."

The fire crackled and spat as she spoke. I touched the smooth iron of the cauldron. It was a little warmer than before.

"That's a start," I said. "Anything else?"

"More?" Belis sighed. "What more is there to tell? And yet there are still more depths to my cowardice."

"You have to face it," I said, "to say it out loud." Belis looked at me and there were tears in her eyes.

"I can't say it," she whispered. "I can't watch you realise how worthless I truly am."

"I could never think that." I crouched down so that our faces were level. "Belis, whatever you have to say, whatever you've done, trust that I have seen worse. Trust that I cannot be shocked, that I will not forsake you."

"I'm afraid," Belis said, her voice so low I had to strain to hear. "I am afraid that we will succeed. If we should bring Cati back I'll have to face her as I tell her what I did to her. Afraid that she will never forgive me. Isn't that terrible? A part of me would rather my sister died than that I should have to face the consequences of trying to kill her."

I was silent for a moment, trying to find words of comfort. I wanted to help her see what I saw, but the emotions were thick and heavy in my throat and I struggled to frame them.

"I can't pretend I understand," I said, slowly, "and that is certainly a cowardly thought. But, Belis, you are not beholden to it. You are afraid to fight but you go into battle anyway, girding yourself with love and duty to your sister. You gave your blood to the thorns; you walked through the maze. You do not let your fears guide you any more. You're braver today than you were yesterday. Tomorrow you'll be braver still."

Belis was still, then she nodded. She stood, straightening to her full height. I placed a hand on the cauldron and the iron burned beneath my fingers.

Belis Before
5

She is twenty years old and her world has gone mad. She lies on the flagstones of the courtyard at Icenorum and feels the blood seeping from between her legs, from the cuts and bruises on her face and arms. She knows it must hurt but she cannot feel anything; she is carved from stone, like the marble statues of the emperors she has seen in Londinium.

Belis tried her best to stay silent, to go somewhere else and pretend it wasn't happening. Using the strength she saved by not resisting, she is able to roll over, struggling up to her hands and knees. Her mother stands at the hitching post, her hands tied above her head, her dress pulled down to her waist. Her back is more blood than not; the lashing whip has all but scourged the skin from her bones.

The courtyard is empty of any other living souls but Iceni corpses are scattered across the floor. Belis sees old warriors who drank with her father, her childhood nursemaid. Any who tried to interfere with the disgrace of the House of Prasutagus were cut down. Inside the hall she can hear the carousing and pillaging of her home and she knows she and her mother will not be the only ones outraged tonight.

But now it is growing dark and she thinks she has enough left in her to get away while the Romans have moved on. She crawls to her feet, leaning over with her hands on her knees and breathing heavily. She goes first to her mother, who is half conscious, sagging against the post. The sweat and blood and strain has tightened the ropes around the queen's wrists and Belis cannot get them undone. She swears under her breath then fetches the kitchen knife that a ten-year-old squire had been clutching in his hand when he came out to defend his queen. She devotes half a second to closing his eyes then returns to her mother.

It takes longer than she expects to saw through the ropes but at last her mother is free. She winds her arm around her shoulders and half carries her towards Cati. She leans her against an overturned barrel then kneels down beside it. Inside her little sister is curled up, hands still clapped over her mouth to stop the screams. Belis finds a smile. Her sister at least is safe. Belis threw a punch at the first of the soldiers; it made her own treatment even more savage but it gave Cati time to hide and that's the most important thing.

Cati slides out of the barrel and stares at their mother, then at her. Belis shakes her shoulders, gently at first, then harder.

"We have to go, Cati, we cannot stay here," she whispers, terrified that her voice will draw their attackers back. She looks around desperately for a cart, for a horse.

Boudica struggles back upright.

"We need to move. Cati, grab some supplies. I can't walk on my own yet. Can I lean on you, Belis?" she asks. Her voice is hoarse from screaming but it is strong still and Belis gladly gives up control of the situation.

"I think so." She loops her mother's arm around her shoulders, glad that they are the same height. Boudica sucks in a breath of pain but Belis doesn't have time to be gentle. At last she is positioned and Belis takes a tentative step forward.

Cati picks up a cloak from one of the dead warriors, a sword from another, a waterskin from a third. Then she nods to Belis and the three of them walk out through the gate, into the dark night.

Above them the sky is clouded, covering the stars and the sliver of the moon that should be lighting their way. The new

Roman road finishes a few hundred yards from the town and Belis feels the stone turn to cold mud beneath her feet. She can hear the hooting of owls, frogs calling in the marshlands to the east. It is a chill spring night, the trees still too young in the year to have budded leaves. They wave skeletal arms in the easterly wind as the Iceni women pass.

When the lights from their home are lost in the darkness Belis wonders if they will stop. Her numbness is fading and she is starting to grasp the enormity of the pain dwelling within her, in her body and in her head. She wants to put her mother down and crawl into a hole and let the foxes take her. Ahead her sister paces endlessly. Belis is jealous of the strength she still has, the absence of pain.

Her mother's wounds have stopped bleeding and her back is one great slab of raw flesh. Belis can't imagine how she remains upright and walking but as long as the queen leads Belis will follow.

It is midnight by the time they stop, when Cati sits down on the road, refusing to go on. They have walked only three miles, each step slow and painful. Her mother turns towards her and indicates she should let her down. Grateful for the rest, Belis unlaces her arm and stretches out.

"Get up," her mother says. "We cannot stop 'til dawn."

Her sister groans but Boudica drags her back to her feet. Cati moves to slump back down but the queen slaps her hard across the face.

"We do not give up. We do not lie down and wait for the end. I am a queen, and you will be, too. You will stand and you will walk until I say stop."

Cati opens her mouth to complain and her mother slaps her again. The crack of the impact echoes against the clouds. She nods meekly, her eyes clearing a little.

"Good." Her mother wraps the cloak around Cati's shoulders and gives them both a sip of water.

"Now go. There is much to do."

Belis looks at the only two people left in her world.

"What is there to do, Mother?" she asks, feeling like a child again.

Her mother touches her cheek and there is sorrow in her eyes, sorrow and a savage rage. "Blood must pay for blood, my daughter," she says. "We will find our revenge."

Chapter 12

The stew was delicious. The pork had simmered for hours until it was so tender it fell apart in my mouth. I took a seat at one of the long trestle tables and focused on nothing else until I had wiped my bowl clean with a crust of bread. Stuffed but still eager for more, I looked over at where Arawn was still serving ladlefuls from the Giant's Cauldron into the neat wooden bowls. The queue for food had stretched as far as the eye could see, although most people had taken their portion and left. Even the the small fraction who sat down to feast with us still numbered in the hundreds, with every table packed.

I picked up another slice of soft manchet bread and began to chew on it mournfully. "Room for one more?"

I looked up to see Rhiannon shooing someone from the opposite side of the table and sitting down. She plopped her bowl of stew in front of her, seized the intricately carved spoon sticking up from the pile of meat and tucked in.

"Delicious," she said, swallowing. "Not at all bad for your first time cooking, Mallt. You can come back and work at Calan Gaeaf any time."

"I've never seen so many people at once," I said. "Outside of an army, I mean."

"Calan Gaeaf is a festival most enjoy celebrating," Rhiannon said. "The dead believe the greater the feasting here the gentler the winter months will be in the living world. They rejoice in helping their relatives. And everyone loves a party, no matter the reason."

I looked around at the crowds.

"There should be more still, no? In all the thousands of years I have been shepherding souls I must have escorted more than this and I only help the handful of lost spirits. Most make their own way."

"You don't know much about Annwn, do you?" Rhiannon took a sip of mead and waved a hand at the dead. "Annwn houses the spirits of the unquiet dead, those who died early or unfulfilled. Those who are waiting for loved ones or are simply not ready to rest. Most people stay here for a couple of decades, some for centuries, a rare few longer still. But in the end they all fade. Only Arawn endures."

"Can you stop people from 'fading'?" I asked. "Where do they go?"

"They just disintegrate, their spirit passes and the life force goes back into the living world." Rhiannon wiped her mouth and smiled at me. "It's a good thing. People want to find peace."

I inspected her face, the deep lines and tired eyes. I had known Rhiannon briefly in the living world, thousands of years ago. I hadn't questioned her presence before, but now it seemed strange.

"What—" I cut my words off before I could insult her. I was learning human ways. She smiled at me, pointed teeth gleaming.

"What am I still doing here? You can ask, I don't mind people asking. My husbands, my son, all my grandchildren are long passed. I stay because there is work to do. I was queen of Dyfed and that doesn't go away with death. I still feel a responsibility, a duty, to my people. One day I will have done enough and I will rest."

"Aren't you tired?" I asked. Rhiannon shrugged.

"I've been tired all my life and all my death. It's never stopped me from my labours before."

She took another draught of her mead and squinted at me appraisingly.

"Surely you can empathise. You have been shepherding the spirits of the dead since long before I was born. Do you wish to stop?"

I considered. Had Rhiannon asked me such a question a year ago I would have immediately and fervently said no. Even before I had met Belis, I had thought I was perfectly contented to wander Britain until the ending of the world. Now I wasn't so sure. I remembered Vatta telling me this life of mortals was sweet. Maybe it was in the nature of humans to crave an ending, a definite finish to a life. I had known only a very few high fae who had abandoned their immortality. This new body of mine seemed full of strange desires, emotions that I did not know how to comprehend. The idea of going on the same way forever seemed less pleasing than it had.

I realised Rhiannon was waiting for an answer. "I don't wish to die," I said.

"That was not my exact question," she replied and drained her goblet. "Regardless, the feasting is almost done and it is time for the dancing to begin so I will not delve any deeper. Calan Gaeaf to you, Mallt Nightshade."

Rhiannon nodded at me and stood. I watched as she headed over to Arawn, who was tipping his own bowlful of stew directly into his mouth. He dropped the empty bowl back onto a table and called for quiet.

The gathering silenced almost instantly. Thousands of revellers turned their eyes towards him. Arawn crooked a finger at the stage, which was now filled with musicians, and they hurried to their posts. There was a brief cacophonous confusion as instruments were tuned. Then they crashed into a song.

Arawn bowed deeply to Rhiannon and she sank in an equally deep curtsey. She took his outstretched hand in hers and began to dance. It was an old song, and an older dance, modelled on the spinning wheel of the seasons. Arawn and Rhiannon whirled around the centre of the clearing, turning sharply right at the edge of the laughing crowd and dancing back into the centre before wheeling out again. When they had spiralled a full eight times, other couples joined them, dancing back and forth, missing each other by inches.

The onlookers began clapping in time, stamping their feet to the beat of the drum. One of the musicians put down his instrument, standing to wave his hands over his head, directing the crowd in the tempo of the song. More couples took to the floor and the remaining feasters seated drew back, allowing them more space. In the back of the crowd I could see porters hurrying away with the empty tables, widening the area for dancing.

I felt the music beginning to wind me in. I was tapping my toes already and now I could sense the dance pulling at me, begging me to join in, to dance the summer away. I had ever loved to dance but it had been the artful stylings of the fae. This called to my human heart, itching at my feet, and the rhythm thundered through my veins. I turned, looking for a likely partner, and found Belis at my elbow.

"My Lady Nightshade." She made a deep bow.

"Princess Beliscena," I said, curtseying just as I had seen Rhiannon do. It was harder than I had thought and my legs almost tangled but Belis had already held out her hand and I caught it to stop myself falling.

"Dance with me," she said, and I lifted my arms into hers.

For the first few steps I worried that my human legs had lost the grace and speed that had made my dancing the toast of the Wild Hunt. I didn't want to embarrass myself in front of the entire kingdom of the dead. After a minute of dancing, though, I had cast aside my concerns. I was clumsy and graceless in this mortal form but I no longer cared. I was dancing, and dancing with Belis.

She led us through the dance, darting and ducking as we swung through the matrix of couples, moments from collision but never tripping. I had been smiling at the start and now joy bubbled up in my chest like a geyser and I laughed out loud. Belis grinned back at me, colour rushing to her cheeks until they were as red as her hair, which had spiralled into a cloud behind her.

More and more people joined us, old men spinning toddlers,

young warriors partnering grandmothers, giggling teenagers and war chiefs all dancing together to end the summer and bring the living world as much joy as they could muster.

There was a great crescendo of drums and the band roared to a halt. The crowd cheered and the dancers fell apart, sweating from their efforts. The musicians began a slower tune and about half of the dancers headed back to the tables to swill more mead and beer.

I looked up at Belis, still holding me in her arms. "Do you want a drink?" I asked. She shook her head.

"Another dance? Maybe just one more?" she asked. I smiled at her and we began again.

One more turned into another and then another. We danced as long as the band played, 'til the stars spun overhead. Part of my mind remembered that we had more work to do tomorrow, that we should probably be saving our strength, but the rest of me ignored it. I danced until my feet were slipping in my boots and then I kicked them off and danced some more. I knew that I would never forget this Calan Gaeaf, this inverse feast in the land of the dead, would remember this night until I forgot my own name. Belis never tired. She was always there above me, smiling and whirling us back into the melee.

At last, when the western sky brightened with the dawn, Arawn strode into the centre of the floor.

"Souls of Annwn! You have feasted and drunk and danced enough to welcome in the winter! I warrant that the winter in the living world will be gentle enough that your descendants will think it nothing but a second summer!"

The crowd cheered, if a little tiredly.

"We have one last dance to do and I ask everyone to join us, shepherd and king, druid and drudge. Join your hands together!"

The crowd streamed back into the dance, forming huge concentric circles of dancers. Belis was whipped away from me and I found myself holding hands with a laughing farmer and a dark-eyed youth. Across the ring from me I could see Belis. I grinned at her and she smiled back at me. Even the musicians had joined the circles now, and the only music was the song we were suddenly singing.

> *So we watch the old year go, let it rain and let it snow,*
> *still our crops will grow and grow.*
> *Sing the songs our fathers know,*
> *Dance the steps our mothers show,*
> *Hand in hand through life we trow.*

"What is this?" laughed Belis, swooshing past me. "The dead sing children's rhymes?"

"It's older than that," I called, when the circle took me back to her. "It's a counting song, humans have been singing this song since they came to the island. The living—" I broke off as we parted again, waiting for the rings to turn. "The living world has forgotten its origins but the dead have a longer memory."

The rings of dancers were wheeling faster now, bellowing out the words

> *Sing the songs our fathers know,*
> *Dance the steps our mothers show,*
> *Hand in hand through life we trow.*

The song finished and about half the dancers stopped with it, gasping for breath. The others kept going and all was cheerful chaos. I could see Arawn still spinning in the centre, holding hands with a pair of young children and wheeling them around until they were breathless with giggling. Behind him a man was forcing himself towards the king, elbowing his way through the dancers. I focused on his expression and frowned. None of the joy of the festival was visible on his face, only grim determination.

"My lord," the man called, shoving his way forward through the exhausted crowd.

Arawn turned and I watched as the mirth left his face. I dropped the hands of my companions and hurried forward.

The man had reached Arawn now and was reaching up to say something in his ear. I stopped beside him. The Lord of Annwn looked grim, his skin greying as the blood faded away.

"Ill tidings indeed, Luc," he said, nodding to the messenger, "you must have ridden hard to arrive ahead of them."

"What is it?" Belis reached my side. Around us the souls of the dead were still celebrating but here in the centre the air had chilled with the arrival of the messenger.

"News from the borderlands," Arawn said, keeping his voice low so that I had to strain to hear him. "I need Rhiannon, she— ah!"

The witch queen had appeared beside him, the pleasure of the dancing already leaching from her face.

"A breach, along the border. Luc says they've tricked it into the canyon but it won't stay there for long."

Rhiannon nodded. "What kind of breach? I can be there by daybreak." Arawn shook his head, and I was shocked to see fear creeping into his eyes.

"It is beyond any of us. Come, let's get somewhere we can talk more privately."

Arawn and Rhiannon strode quickly away, the revellers parting before them like a bow wave. I grabbed Belis's hand and tried to follow. The dancers were less eager to get out of our way and by the time we had broken free Arawn had vanished from view. I looked around, trying to see where they might have gone. Belis tugged at my hand.

"Over there."

I spun to see Rhiannon vanishing beneath the fronds of a weeping willow. We hurried after them, slipping between the trailing branches.

Arawn sat on an upturned log, his left hand gripping the long scythe he had been wielding when we had met him in the fields. It seemed sharper now, cleaned of the chaff of the harvest, more a weapon than a tool. Beside him Rhiannon was peering into a pool of water at the foot of the willow's trunk. The messenger was gulping down a mugful of something.

"I can't see it," Rhiannon said, bringing her face so close to the water that her nose almost touched the surface. "The corruption must be hiding it from me."

Arawn ground his teeth.

"Try again, try to see the path of where it was. That should help us a little."

"It cut quite the swathe of destruction," Luc interrupted, putting down his cup. "I've never seen anything like it. When it flew it almost blotted out the sun."

"It flew?" Belis said, then put her hand over her mouth. The others turned to look at her, seemingly just noticing that we had followed them. "There's trouble at the canyon, isn't there, Arawn? Tell us what's happening, we've earned the right!"

Rhiannon's nostrils flared and she half rose but Arawn waved a hand.

"Go back to your scrying."

Arawn rubbed his forehead. "This beast on the borders, Luc, this *shadowbitten* monster, tell our guests what form it has taken. What horror has befallen one of my charges."

The messenger looked startled to be called upon. "My lord?" Arawn nodded at him. "The *shadowbitten* has taken the form of a great white wyrm. A fire drake, winged and sulphurous. It crossed over from the shadow side of the rift and has been tormenting the surrounding lands."

A dragon. I had never much taken to the beasts, though they were common enough in the wilder parts of the island. Vicious, smelly creatures which had occasionally chased us away from their lairs when I had ventured close enough to retrieve the souls of their prey. I had no wish to repeat the experience in this human form.

Belis nodded, not even flinching. "A dragon. So we must drive it back or defeat it."

"You say it like it would be an easy task," Arawn said. "The drake is only a symptom of the problem. Of the poison. As long as it infects the land such creatures will continue to be twisted from the souls of the dead. Even should you succeed against this dragon we cannot hold out forever. More and more will come."

"We've a better chance than you," Belis retorted. "I'm willing to try. Maybe if we buy more time then one of the high fae will notice."

"I have a different suggestion," Rhiannon said.

"No," said Arawn. He stood up, leaning his scythe against the tree trunk. "I know what you want to do. It is too soon. You have only just returned to us."

"The dragon is a worrying development. We cannot leave this problem much longer. Instead of going in numbers we should slip into the shadowlands, make for the centre and see if we can cure whatever is causing it once and for all."

Belis narrowed her eyes. "Why have you never tried it before?"

"We have," rumbled Arawn. "No one has made it more than a league across the canyon before being corrupted or overrun. There are simply too many of the *shadowbitten* and my own powers are useless against those I am sworn to protect. Rhiannon has never been strong in martial magic. I doubt you'll have better luck."

"I think we could, Arawn." Rhiannon moved in front of him. "You've seen the bramble field. I think they can cut down the *shadowbitten*, just like mortals in the living world can. No other guards you could send can resist the corruption."

She knelt down and sketched another rough map in the sand. She built a mound of dirt and tipped over her scrying bowl so that the water formed a moat around it.

"Here, this is the point where the poison first started. If Belis can get me there then I can break us free of it."

"Just you and Belis?" Arawn folded his arms. "I don't like it."

"And me," I cut in. "I'm not staying behind."

"You're not a fighter," Rhiannon said, "you've spent your whole life chasing death, not facing it. You'd do better to wait here."

"Annwn is my responsibility, too," I said. "Every soul I have brought here is my responsibility. I will not shrink from battle."

Belis cut Rhiannon off before she could respond. "Mallt comes, too." She looked over at me. "I need someone to watch my back."

I smiled. Rhiannon didn't look pleased, but Belis's tone had a finality to it, a command. I wondered if she'd learned it from her mother.

"It's settled then." Arawn stood up. "Belis, Rhiannon and Mallt will head south from here, crossing the ravine near the vineyards. We can *rush* you to the canyon, then it's two days' walk on the other side to reach the hill. I'll field a company to raid the north. Maybe that will draw more of the *shadowbitten* out of the heartlands."

"Arawn, that's terribly risky," Rhiannon said.

"If you are cut down by a creature who could otherwise have been attacking us then all hope is lost. We have one roll of the dice left. I am prepared to stake everything on it." Arawn's face was fierce but he laid a gentle hand on Rhiannon's arm. "We have been waiting years for a chance. I will not miss it."

The witch took a deep breath and nodded. She bent down, swiping the map in the sand until there was nothing left.

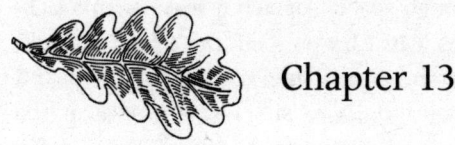

Chapter 13

The festival had sunk into embers by the time we stepped out from the privacy of the willow tree. Revellers had simply lain down to sleep where they had been dancing, considering the feasting grounds as safe as any other part of Annwn. A few with the look of soldiers huddled around the main fire, poking at the glowing remnants of the logs while passing around a skin of liquor. They nodded to us as we passed, pressing hands to chests in a casual salute to Arawn. He beckoned them over and exchanged a few low words. In a moment they had scattered across the grounds, wrapping up food and filling waterskins from barrels. Others dug ropes and knives from packs and handed them over to us. I gave Belis back her sword, swapping it for a razor-edged bronze blade that seemed to slot into my hand as if it had been made for me.

"Gather as many as you can and set out along the north road," Arawn said to the leader, a spade-faced woman carrying an axe. "I'll catch up with you as soon as I can. See if you can pick up a few others from the watchtowers. There's a big push coming."

She grunted an assent and began calling orders. Arawn turned back to us.

"Here, take my hands. I can *rush* us a mile or so from the canyon. Beyond that we'll have to go on foot. Rhiannon will meet us there."

Belis and I exchanged looks, then she took his outstretched hand. I winced pre-emptively at the nausea and cast a final glance around the field. Nothing appeared to delay the inevitable so I placed my hand in Arawn's. The dizziness hit immediately as Arawn pushed us through space, surfacing again with a sickening yank at my insides. My ears popped and I held on tight until I was sure I could stand on my own.

Arawn had stopped in a shallow depression between two drumlins. The ground was thick with a knee-high grass the colour of dust, covering the hills with an ever-waving blanket of stems.

Belis was already up and scanning the land. Her spear was in her hand now, seeming just an extension of her arm. She scampered up the rise of the hill, pausing on the crest and going down on one knee.

"Over there." She pointed to the west and called down to us. "Is that it?"

Arawn strode after her, dropping to a crouch. "Yes, that's the gorge Rhiannon created. It runs for a thousand miles, cleaving the afterworld in two."

I hurried up the hill and stood behind them. The drumlin field extended another half a mile or so in front of us before the wavy landscape flattened into a plain. The lowlands should have gone on for miles but something had shattered them. A great rift had hewn the lands in two, snaking back and forth like the path of a lightning bolt. The land beyond the rift was grey, so overcast with clouds and ash that it was difficult to discern either distance or landform in the miasma.

"Get down," hissed Belis, yanking at my leg. "Don't stand on the top of a hill, you're just asking to be targeted."

"I only followed you," I said, hurt by her tone.

"We're below the ridge line, much harder to spot."

"Peace," Arawn said, an undercurrent of warning in his tone. "We're far enough away and no one will be expecting you. Look, you'll need to reach the eastern rim. I don't know how long it will take you to find a path to the bottom."

There was a faint pop from behind us and I turned to see Rhiannon padding up the hill, keeping her body low to the ground. She took a knee beside Arawn and the Lord of the Dead turned to look at her.

"Wait here 'til tomorrow. I'll attack in the north at dawn, see how much of a commotion I can cause. If you leave when the sun rises the way should be clearing by the time you reach the canyon."

Rhiannon nodded and held out an arm. Arawn gripped it tight.

"Best of luck, my old friend," he said, voice rumbling. "I would hate to lose you."

The witch patted his hand and then beckoned to us, rising and padding down the slope. I nodded to Arawn as I passed him.

"If we survive this, I will be holding you to your promise to release Cati."

"I keep my word, Nightshade. You keep yours." He stood and I felt the air ripple around me as he prepared to *rush* and then was gone.

We spent a miserable day and a restless night in the drumlin field. Belis and I sparred as she tried to fit a decade's worth of training into a single day. Rhiannon sat and watched, weaving the long grass into braids, muttering spells of protection and luck into the bands. The witch queen insisted we both sleep as much as possible while she kept watch. It was cold in the hollow and we huddled together for warmth, talking quietly in the night. When the first light of dawn came we rose and waited for Rhiannon to come down from the drumlin she had been perched on, her face newly striped with her blood. When she did she handed out charms on leather thongs, explaining one side would feel the pull of Caer Sidi and go warm. If we got lost we should follow the cold side, heading directly into the heart of the shadow.

We were still technically in Annwn, but it no longer felt like it. There were no birds overhead, no crickets singing in the undergrowth. The only sound was the breeze whistling through the grass and the faint thump of our own feet. We crossed a little stream at the edge of the hills, winding its way towards the canyon. I stopped to scoop up water for a drink.

"Ugh." I spat it back out. "It's bitter, smoky."

"It's ashfall in the rivers," Rhiannon said. "When the wind blows from the west it whips up dust and cinders from the other side, carrying it over the border to pollute our lands. Seeds of the shadow on the wind."

She waved a hand at the plains in front of us. "All this used to be forest, but the smoke blocked out the sun and the trees withered and died. The only thing that grows here now is this grass. And the thorns, of course, but we come along and burn them out every few months."

"All along the border?" Belis asked. Rhiannon nodded.

"The north lands are chalk, so they were never used for much other than pasturelands. The winds grow fiercer every year. Even without the *shadowbitten* raids the corruption would begin to encroach on us."

I bit my lip, staring at the rift, swirling mists veiling the wastelands on the other side from my sight. I had brought souls to Annwn on the understanding that it was a place of rest and beauty. This was as cruel as the mortal world, without even the promise of an ending.

"We should keep moving," Belis said, hurrying us onwards.

The grass thinned as we approached the edge of the canyon, growing dryer so that it crunched underfoot. I felt very exposed out on the plain. Rhiannon kept glancing up at the sky and Belis gripped her spear tight as we ran.

We paused about ten yards back from the edge. Cracks were splintering back from the cliffs, suggesting that the slopes weren't stable.

"Stay here," Belis said, tilting up her spear. She extended it ahead of her, probing at the ground, checking each spot before she stepped into it. I drummed my fingers against the knife Arawn had given me, sure that at any moment the ground would fail. Belis reached the edge and peered over. I held my breath but nothing flew up from the darkness. I saw her smother a sneeze and she inched her way back.

"It's pretty foul down there but I can't see anything moving," she said, accepting a swig from Rhiannon's water bottle. "We should cover our faces, mouths and noses at the very least."

"What else? Is there a way down?"

Belis shook her head. "It's almost vertical on this side. Funny thing, but I can see paths on the western cliffs. Something has been coming down regularly but they haven't managed to climb up here."

"Should we move on?" I asked. "Find a better place to cross?"

"I think this might be as good as any," Belis said. "At least here I can see a way out. I don't want to find a way in but then get stuck at the base. We can rappel down and then walk up the path."

"What about whatever made those paths?" Rhiannon asked.

Belis looked grim, her hand tightening on her spear.

"If it comes to it, I'll deal with them."

Rhiannon shrugged and began rummaging in her pack. I frowned at Belis, remembering the last time we had had to fight, on the beach in Wales. I wanted her to be more careful of herself than she had been then. She ripped off a strip from the bottom of her tunic and handed it to me. I tied it over my nose and mouth. Belis covered her own face, looking over at me.

"We look like bandits," she said. I patted the rough fabric to check it was tight.

"Better than breathing in that filth."

Rhiannon was hammering a stake into the ground about five yards back from the rim. She tied one end of the rope to it and gave it an experimental tug.

"Excellent," she said. "Here."

I snatched the rope as she went to hand it over to Belis.

"I should go first. I'm lighter, I can test the strength. Besides, if it doesn't reach the bottom you'll be able to pull me back up. Rhiannon next, then you can climb down the rope."

Belis opened her mouth to argue but Rhiannon nodded. "Very well, you can certainly try."

"Thank you, Rhiannon," I said, stepping over to the cliff's edge. It looked very steep; the rock face was almost vertical. I thought back, trying to remember if I had ever seen humans doing this sort of thing before. They had wrapped the rope around their waist, I thought, then leaned back and just walked down the cliff. I twisted the line behind me, looping it back between my legs. As long as I held onto the rope this couldn't go too badly wrong, I reasoned. Belis could always pull me up. Then I stepped off the edge.

The rope held, going tight around my waist and almost squeezing the breath from me. I still had one foot on the rim, the other dangling below me. Belis stepped forward but I managed to slam my free foot into the side of the cliff, finding a toehold. I dropped the second leg beside it, now completely standing on the side of the cliff.

"Not bad," said Belis. She'd wound the top of the rope around her forearm, presumably so that the weight would be on her rather than Rhiannon's stake. "Just keep going, one foot after the other. I'll let out the rope slowly, but if you need to stop just tug twice on the rope. Tug once at the bottom and I'll pull it back up."

Her voice was encouraging. I took another step down.

I kept moving, walking down the cliff face. The rocks in front of me were layered sandstone and limestone, strong and easy to find footholds in. Above me Belis and Rhiannon vanished from sight as the smoky grey air closed over my head. I kept going, trying to ignore the rope burns on my palms. A few steps more and I felt my boots hit flat dirt. I gripped the rope, reaching out with my legs to check I hadn't just hit a ledge. It seemed to be the base of the canyon. I tugged on the rope then let go.

I peered around me. The air was still murky but I could see tracks in the dust, too mangled to tell the number or even size of the feet that had made them. The canyon floor was only a few paces across, narrowing down from the gaping ravine at the surface. I crossed over to touch the other wall. Belis had been right: there were handholds in the rock, a clear path to follow. I jumped as gravel slipped loose under my hands, clattering to the floor. The sound echoed in the quiet of the canyon.

I ducked back and pressed into the cliff face, trying to stay quiet. I could hear scuffling above me as someone, presumably Rhiannon, climbed down. The wind groaned through the base of the canyon, blowing dust into my eyes. I blinked hard, trying to clear my vision. A pair of boots appeared above me and Rhiannon clattered to the floor. She leaned on the wall to steady herself then tugged on the rope again.

"Have you seen anything?" she asked, her voice muffled by the dust mask. I shook my head.

"Nothing, just shapes in the wind."

Rhiannon looked around. "Foul smells and foul humours. I do not think it will get better as we advance into the shadow."

"I'm sure you're right," I said, glancing up to see if I could spot Belis climbing down the rope. I felt vulnerable down here without her. Rhiannon didn't look as if she'd be much use in a fight. I realised with a jolt that until Belis got down here I was supposed to be protecting Rhiannon. I gripped the hilt of the sword Belis had given me, wishing I had practised with it more than a few times. I imagined what forms the *shadowbitten* would take and peered desperately up the cliff.

Rhiannon tugged on my arm. "There's something down here," she whispered.

I leaned out onto the pathway, taking a few tentative steps. I couldn't hear anything but the howling of the wind.

"Are you sure?" I hissed, turning back to her. There was movement in the shadows and I ducked, spinning away from the cliffs.

Something struck where my head had been, driving at the wall. I squinted through the dust, reaching for my sword.

An enormous serpent was rearing above me, black and silver scales glinting in the dim light. I stared up at the creature, pressing myself back against the canyon walls. It ducked down and I saw the full horror of the *shadowbitten* for the first time. Instead of the head of a snake, the creature had half retained the face of the human it had been, warped and stretched into something monstrous, eyes mad with pain and malice. Tufts of hair sprouted from between the scales on its neck, snaggled molars peppered the gaps between long fangs dripping venom.

I felt horror warring with pity inside me. This was what I had always worked to prevent, to bring souls to a safe place where they could rest, ready to pass on. The hideous creature before me would find no peace, would inflict terror on others. It shook its head at me, a lolling black tongue flickering out as its panicked eyes darted back and forth.

I pulled Rhiannon beside me, fumbling for my sword. I dropped it and it clattered to the floor. I cursed and scrambled forward to pick it up. It felt very small in my hand compared to the foot-long fangs of the *shadowbitten* snake.

"Where is that damned spear maiden?" muttered Rhiannon from behind me. "Isn't she supposed to be fighting these things off?"

"I don't think it's going to wait," I replied. "I'll distract it. You run off down the canyon. Belis should get here before it comes after you."

Rhiannon didn't argue, much to my irritation. I knew it was my job to protect her but some sympathetic protests that we should stand together would have been nice. I towed her out into the centre of the path, keeping the sword between me and the serpent. It hissed at me, coiling its body up ready to loop over us. Saliva dripped from its tongue.

"Now!" I shouted. Or, rather, I tried to shout. The words seemed to dwindle to a whisper in my mouth. Rhiannon took off down the path. I held out the sword, praying that it wouldn't slip out of my sweaty palm. The snake looked past me to where Rhiannon had run. I had to do something now to make myself the target. All my fine words echoed stupidly around my head, and my arm looked spindly and weak as I held the blade. I was an idiot for getting myself into this situation, I thought. I had never been a fighter. All I could do was take long enough to die so that Rhiannon could get away. I remembered Belis telling me it was all right to fall down as long as I got up again, remembered her showing me how to hold the sword. She'd be disappointed if I didn't even try.

The malformed face of the *shadowbitten* snake roared at me and I threw myself forward before I could let myself delay further. I tried to stab at the viper's side but my sword skittered along the keel-backed scales, glancing off as if on plate armour. I did manage to distract the snake, however; it turned its head to strike at me again. I hit the ground and rolled, just as it lunged for me. I dropped my blade in the dust, hands too slippery with sweat to hold onto it. I pulled myself up to hands and knees, scrabbling around on the floor for it. The worm circled me, cutting off any retreat. Strange energy flooded through my body as any hope of escape was removed and I found the hilt just in time to bring it around. This time I hit the fang itself, using the momentum of the impact to swing me out of the path of the jaws. The reverberation jarred my arm and I staggered. The snake's tail lashed into me, pinning me to the ground. I tried to stab at it with the edge of the sword, jamming it under the scales, but the snake hissed again and moved above me.

Venom dripped onto my face, viscous and foul-smelling. I coughed and tried to catch enough breath to snarl at the creature, determined to make a good show of defiance for Belis's sake. I wondered if I would stay here after death, leaving my body for the *shadowbitten* to feast on. I saw Belis's face in my mind, strangely glad that she wasn't here to see me so helpless.

The snake reared back for the killing blow, but a projectile hit it just under the eye. It screeched and turned towards this new aggressor. I peered through the mist.

"Over here!" called Rhiannon, throwing another stone. This one bounced off the snake's neck, falling harmlessly to the ground. The creature lunged but I dug my sword back into the tail and it snapped at me again, unsure who to focus on.

Rhiannon threw another stone and I managed to prise loose one of the scales, driving my sword deep into the unprotected flesh. The snake decided I was the greater annoyance and I saw it lunge for me again, jaws wide.

Belis leapt from the side wall, her spear in her hand. She landed on the snake's neck, driving the javelin directly into the creature's skull and through the upper jaw. The serpent thrashed wildly, its whole body scrunching up as it flung itself back and forth, crashing into the rocky sides of the canyon. Belis clung on grimly to her spear, riding the death throes of the beast. The snake kicked up so much dust that I could barely see her, nothing more than a flash of red hair in the gloom.

With a final whine the snake crumpled to the ground and was still, apart from the occasional twitch. I tiptoed forward, peering at the thick coils of flesh. Belis was standing on its back, tugging her spear loose.

"Next time I go first," she said, glancing up at me. I swallowed and nodded. She pulled the spear out with a sickening sucking noise and jumped down. "You did well, though."

I nodded again. My mouth was suddenly full of dust and my heart was skittering in my chest. I sat down heavily in the dirt.

"Hey." Belis crouched next to me. "Are you hurt?" She grabbed my chin and turned my face back and forth, checking for wounds.

"No, I just – that's the first time I really thought I was going to die."

Belis didn't smirk or say she'd told me not to come. She sat down beside me, resting one hand on my shoulder.

"It's all right. You did well in the moment, it's normal to panic afterwards. It's a sign you're not taking it too lightly. It's when you start laughing things off. Then you have to worry."

"It's different from when you see it and when it happens to you. I was . . ." I paused. "I was quite worried."

Belis snorted, then looked contrite. "Worried! My word, Mallt, what a thing to say. I'll freely admit that I was scared when I saw you being attacked. What were you telling me about how the only way to be brave is when you're scared? Be brave with me, Mallt."

I smiled wanly at her. Rhiannon appeared, climbing over a coil of dead snake.

"We need to move," she said. "There are handholds in the western wall and for certes this snake didn't make them. Besides, it seems dead now but *shadowbitten* never stay that way for long. I don't think you'll want to be here when the corruption reanimates it, even more twisted than before."

Belis met my eyes and I nodded, trying to appear calm. She didn't seem convinced, but she helped me up and we left the giant corpse behind us and headed to the wall.

The steps I had seen were crude, as if whatever had made them had simply stabbed rough claws into the rock rather than carving them out deliberately. Each was large enough to provide a toehold or something to grab onto. Belis scrambled up the first few yards to check the path. She jumped back to the ground before the mist could swallow her.

"The distance between the footings is the same as far as I can see. You should be able to reach." She looked at Rhiannon and me. "I'll go first, then Rhiannon, you follow me. Try to use exactly what I touch. Mallt, you bring up the rear. If something at the top clobbers me, get Rhiannon back to the floor and run like hell. There'll be another crossing somewhere and you can try there. Understand?"

"Yes."

"Good." Belis jumped back onto the wall and pulled herself up. Rhiannon followed, examining the holes in the rock before putting her hands in and stepping up from the floor. Belis moved another few steps up and Rhiannon clambered awkwardly after her. I watched the old queen: she was ungainly but there was strength in her arms. I breathed out in relief. I hadn't wanted her to fall on me. When she had cleared the first steps I took a final look around the ravine, eyes flitting over the twitching body of the snake, then reached for the wall.

The rock was coated with ash and dust but the filth provided a reasonable grip. I was grateful for the assistance; my hands were still clammy with the cold sweat of the fight. Rhiannon took another step above me and I grabbed for the hold her foot had vacated. Climbing was harder than Belis had made it look and the cliffside seemed a lot higher on the way up. One reach after another, my arms started burning with the effort, my legs to wobble and cramp. I snatched a glance back down. It barely seemed like I'd covered any ground but the height made me dizzy and I clung to the wall.

Rhiannon stumbled above me, causing a shower of pebbles and rock shards to fall on my head. I shut my eyes in time but enough dust slipped beneath my mask to choke me. I coughed hard, desperately wishing for a gulp of water. I could feel my waterskin sloshing around in my pack but I couldn't reach for it now. It was maddening to have water so close but not to be able to drink. I tried to put it out of my mind and pulled myself up another few inches.

We crawled up the face, step after agonising step. My arms were screaming at me now and I was battling the urge to cough again. I was sure that I could hear something scuffling below us – a harsh gnawing sound floated up on the clouds of ash. I wondered if something had found the snake and was enjoying a meal. My throat was bone dry, too dry to breathe without coughing. I struggled to keep climbing on the same breath but my chest felt as if it would burst. I took one final step and my left hand landed on flat ground. I looked up, realising Rhiannon and Belis had hauled themselves up to the top of the cliff. Belis was leaning back over, reaching out her hand to me.

I sighed with relief, remembering too late why I had been holding my breath. A horrible cough racked my body and burst out of me. I shook, almost falling from the wall. Belis seized me by the collar of my tunic and swung me up. I coughed violently again for a few more moments before Rhiannon thrust a waterskin at me. I took a deep glug of the sweet water. The scratching sound below us stopped.

For a moment we were silent, listening to the quiet. Then

screeches ripped through the air, first from the rift then from around us.

Rhiannon grabbed the waterskin back from my hands and Belis pulled me to my feet.

"What do we do now?" I whispered, staring through the clouds of dirt that were even thicker up on the rim.

"Now?" Belis said, unslinging her spear from her back. "Now we run."

Belis Before
6

She is twenty-one years old and her family is broken. They are camped in the fens, close to where the Nene meets the sea. Belis sits at the edge of the tents, staring out across the pale yellow reeds, still gilded by the early-morning frosts. Behind her slumber perhaps four hundred men, women and children. They have been gathering slowly since she and her mother first arrived, two weeks ago. Mostly they are Iceni but a few from the Trinovantes have come, and there are at least four huge old Catuvellauni warriors, still bitter from the Roman defeats some twenty years ago.

The queen welcomes each one, embracing the adults and bending to pat each of the children on their heads. She walks through the encampment in a robe open at the back and her hair pinned high so that all may see what the Romans have done to a British queen. In the evening she gathers the oldest and fiercest fighting men and women in her tent and talks strategy late into the night.

Belis joined her at first but for all the training and practice she has no experience at war and her mother sent her away. Now she spends her nights lying in the sedge grass and watching the secret paths for more pilgrims, more blades to pledge to this sacred endeavour.

Cati is half ghost, rarely straying from their mother's side. She flinches if men come too close, hands creeping to the knives she hides under her robes. The men of the camp are understanding; they don't take offence but Belis hates seeing the death of youth in her sister, the innocence that faded as she huddled in her barrel, listening to the world end around her.

So she sits and watches the wind blow through the marshes and watches the herons fly low over the horizon and watches another day in her life pass away.

In another week they are a thousand-strong, in two there are more of them than can be supported by the fenlands and Boudica gives the order to move out. A band of warriors meet them south of Elge with chariots and ponies and from then on Belis and Cati ride beside their mother, wielding spears and shortswords.

Hundreds are coming every day now, the lands of the Iceni and Trinovantes emptying of all their warriors, all their rage focusing on this one point. Even the queen cannot greet each one individually, but she drives the chariot up and down the line, showing the still raw scars on her back, talking of the wrong done to her daughter. Belis stands silently next to her; every day her fury grows and she longs to quench it, to drown it in Roman blood.

She has barely practised with the spear since Icenorum but now as soon as the army stops – for it is an army, there can be no longer any doubt about that – as soon as the army stops she leaps to the ground and calls for a sparring partner. She fights with her battle tip, scorning the blunted wooden staffs used for training. She drills daily and has defeated every man who dares face her. This time, Belis promises herself as she runs laps of the encampment and sharpens her long knives, this time she will fight back. This time they will do the screaming.

They approach Camulodunum at midday. The lords of the Trinovantes know the city well for it is their own capital and they have come up to the front of the column to speak with the queen.

Belis listens eagerly as they explain the layout of the city, the earthworks built by the occupying forces, the new temple to the last emperor built on ground sacred to Adraste.

Boudica arranges her forces around the city. She calls for the

Romans to come out and fight her. Word comes that there are less than two hundred soldiers left in the city. The queen grinds her teeth. There is little glory in that, but the messenger continues. The soldiers are the personal guard of the Procurator.

A howl goes through the ranks; the Procurator is hated above all others. He has been the personal ruin of many of them, his soldiers are the ones who came to Icenorum and tore Belis's world apart. She stares at the city. She can taste metallic battle lust in her mouth, sees the same madness reflected in her mother's eyes. Even little Cati grips her knives and gleams with anticipation. They are going to drive these wolves back into the sea.

The queen calls for the charge and suddenly they are flying towards the city, blades flashing at their chariot wheels. Belis barely has time to take a breath and then there is nothing but blood and fire and death.

Chapter 14

We fled. The misting ash was too thick to see through so I had no frame for where we were going, only that I had to follow Belis. The ground was soft underfoot, thick with ash and tangled with dead grass. I kept stumbling as I ran, unable to keep my feet beneath me. Twice I fell and Rhiannon helped me back up. I returned the favour when she tripped and went face first into the dirt. Only Belis seemed steady, loping ahead of us, untiring and wary.

Behind I could hear yowling, the snap of serrated teeth against bone from whatever had followed us from the rift. There was a wet panting that grew closer whenever I staggered, pushing fresh strength into my legs. Worse still was the opaque air around us, veiling its threats, so that every step forward seemed to hang on the edge of a knife.

The chittering mouths that chased us closed in and I found new speed in my feet, dragging Rhiannon beside me. Belis dropped a little so that she was running behind us, flashing glances back into the haze.

I tripped for a third time and landed on my hands, sinking my fingers into something soft and sticky. I ripped them free, holding my palms up to my face. They were dripping in a gelatinous black blood, clots of viscera lodging under my fingernails. I looked down at the ribcage of some rotting beast, riddled with fat white maggots. A shriek tore from my throat before I could stop it. I held my hands out in front of me and threw myself back, trying to distance myself from the gore. Belis dropped down beside me, pushing a hand over my mouth. I managed to hush myself and for a moment there was silence. Then a great pining wail started up to the left of us, like the scream of a rabbit in a trap. The ground trembled and only the entrails on my hands stopped me from clapping them over my ears, trying to block out the terrible sound.

Belis dragged me backwards and grabbed my hands, shoving them into the dust to wipe off the worst of the blood. I calmed down enough to let her do it, and in a moment she was pulling me back up.

"Run," she hissed in my ear, "go right!"

I stumbled forward, away from the howling. Belis yanked her spear from where she had stabbed it in the ground and followed me. Whatever I had disturbed was still ululating, groaning as it joined the chase. It sounded big; even the layers of ash and silt couldn't muffle the sound of enormous feet.

"This isn't working," Belis whispered to Rhiannon, running alongside us. "We can't run forever, we need to hunker down and hope they won't find us."

Rhiannon nodded, too short of breath to speak.

"I'll make a commotion and head forward then double back and see if I can lose them. You and Mallt run a hundred paces on and then find somewhere to hide. If I get free I'll come back for you."

"Belis, that's not—" I broke off, wheezing from the effort of running. I wanted to tell her that it was a terrible idea, that she shouldn't go off on her own, but Rhiannon nodded and veered to the north. Belis sped up and I hesitated, unsure if I could catch her up. It felt wrong to leave her, but she'd already vanished into the fog and Rhiannon needed a living mortal to protect her. I turned right and began counting paces. The keening and then chittering noises faded a little as I padded into the gloom. Ahead of me Rhiannon paused and looked back at me. I came to a halt beside her.

She pointed ahead of us. Something loomed, dark and angular against the grey mist. I squinted and made out the shape of an uprooted tree, earth still clinging to the great morass of roots. I trotted forward, carefully peering around the trunk to check for inhabitants. It seemed to be abandoned. I jerked my head towards Rhiannon and she followed me over. We climbed down into the hollow the roots had left, keeping them as a shield between us and the way we had come.

I wiped sweat from my forehead and dabbed at my throat. I hadn't noticed before, but the air here was warm and moist, forcing long humid tendrils down my throat with every breath.

Rhiannon's hair was plastered to her scalp, dark with sweat. I realised I was panting and forced myself to slow my breathing, to inhale deep and hold the air inside for a moment. My heart steadied and I regained enough control to fumble the waterskin from my pack and take a sip. I swirled the water around in my mouth, washing away the taste of ash. I offered the bottle to Rhiannon and she took a small draught before handing it back.

The mist around us had gone quiet. I could no longer hear the sound of whatever had been chasing us, nor feel the thudding of heavy feet echoing through the earth. Was that a bad sign? Had Belis been caught or had she managed to lose them? I imagined her surrounded, whirling her spear in a desperate attempt to break free. I thought of the rabbit scream, the grinding of teeth, my mind filling in the horrors that would be attacking her. I gripped the hilt of my knife and climbed back to my knees, determining that I had to go out and find her.

Rhiannon caught my eye. She was sitting still, her hand on the pack she had brought, full of whatever she thought would be useful for the spells. I remembered what Arawn had said, that this was our only chance. Belis had trusted me to keep Rhiannon safe so that she could save all of us. I couldn't let her down by stumbling around in the grey clouds of ash, getting myself killed and leaving Rhiannon undefended.

I sat back down. Rhiannon didn't say anything but I saw her shoulders sag a little. I felt a curl of shame in my stomach and shuffled back to sit next to her. We sat in silence, listening to the breeze whisper through the mists, ears straining for any approach. I kept my hand on my sword, ready to draw. I could taste the sickness in the air, feel beads of perspiration dripping down my back. I wriggled a little, trying to get more comfortable. My hands were still sticky with traces of blood and I looked for something to wipe them on. There was nothing so I settled for digging my hands through the ash and scraping the worst of it off with the blade of my sword.

Rhiannon's lips were moving, her eyes shut tight. I realised she was counting under her breath. I wondered if she had given up on Belis and was waiting for enough time to pass so that we could move again. I tried to shut that thought out but it rattled around my skull. I tried to summon happy thoughts – running with the hounds over the moors, feasting with the Wild Hunt. Dancing with Belis at Calan Gaeaf. The first time Belis had smiled at me. Her eyes meeting mine as she made me inhale slow and steady when I couldn't catch my breath. Belis sitting by the campfire, the flames lighting her hair so it glowed.

The mist permeated the images so that Belis shrank in on herself, becoming a grinning skeleton with wisps of red hair. I slammed my eyes open and stared into the grey.

We huddled in the grave of the tree for what felt like half the day. Every moment I was terrified that Rhiannon would insist we start moving, leaving Belis behind. Every crack and whistle seemed to herald new monsters. Something snuffled around behind us for a while, rooting in the dirt. I gripped my sword so hard that the muscles in my arms spasmed and I almost dropped it. When the thing finally left, Rhiannon let out a long sigh.

"I think we should go now," she murmured, "before we're discovered."

"I'm not leaving without Belis," I said, trying to keep my voice steady.

"Mallt . . ."

"She'll be here, I'm sure of it!" I folded my arms, determined to show I would not be moved.

Rhiannon rolled her eyes at me.

"A little longer, then."

I relaxed slightly and crawled up to the edge of the hollow, peering out into the gloom. No warrior maid appeared through the mists. I slid back.

"Maybe she's looking for us? I could just do a quick ring around the tree, to see if I can find her."

"Mallt, I don't think that's wise."

I chewed my lip. I felt horribly helpless, just sitting here and waiting. Belis might be yards away and not know it. Worse still, she could be injured or dead, lying cold in the dirt while nameless creatures gorged on her flesh.

There was a rustling from behind us and I sat up. Something was probing at the edge of our pit, causing the piles of silt and ash to trickle down the sides. I unsheathed my sword and crept towards it, waving to Rhiannon to get behind me. I prepared to spring, hoping I could lodge the blade deep and prevent any screaming. I leapt forward, just as Belis jumped down into the hollow.

I dropped my sword and flung myself at her. I hugged her tight, feeling the solid thud of her heartbeat. Belis patted my shoulders and I remembered myself and stepped back. She looked tired but unhurt, no visible blood or bruises.

"We were about to move," Rhiannon whispered. "Did you manage to lose them?"

Belis nodded. "Led them a merry chase, then ducked back and lay on my stomach in the dirt for an hour. Since then I've spent most of the time looking for you." She smiled at me and I felt the anxiety in my chest settle.

"Do you need to rest?" I asked.

"No, better we keep moving. I want to cover a few more miles before dark."

Rhiannon nodded and climbed out of the hollow. I reached out for Belis's arm.

"Are you truly all right?" I asked. I could hear my voice wavering. "I wanted to come and find you."

Belis put her hand over mine. "I am. And I'm glad you didn't. There are bigger things at stake than my life." She grinned. "Besides, I can take care of myself. You should know that by now. Come on, let's go."

We stepped back to the surface level. The dust had cleared a little but the light was already beginning to fade. Belis organised us into a marching order, her leading, Rhiannon following and me at the back. She gave my hand a quick squeeze before setting off. I waited for Rhiannon to begin moving then followed.

Belis set a steady pace, leading us between piles of boulders and around stagnant ponds.

The ground was soft underfoot, coated in drifted piles of ash, so that every step pulled at my calf muscles, sucking at my feet. The only benefit was that it muffled our footfall. Around us, but out of sight, the *shadowbitten* whimpered and whined. Flies droned in my ears, landing on my lips and clustering around my nose and eyes. I tried to ignore them, to save my energy, but it was too irritating and I swiped at my face, causing them to lift off for a moment only to settle again as soon as I lowered my hands.

Belis padded ahead of us, peering through the darkness, her spear clenched in one hand. Every couple of hours she called a halt, giving us a few minutes to catch our breath and take sip from our rapidly emptying waterskins. Then we were off again, traipsing through the night.

I found my mind wandering. I had spent so much of my life doing almost exactly this, travelling across the land, first as the Nightshade, then the weeks of walking to Annwn with Belis. I had always loved the sensation of the world unfurling before me, no matter if it was through places I had been a thousand times before. Every step, every breath, was new, the landscape changing around me. Even in my mortal form, with weak legs and burning lungs, my eyes had always been greedy for beauty. This place was different. Walking here was dull; the unchanging grey, the sulphurous stench of the air sapped my will to carry on. I could barely muster the energy to put one foot before the other. I didn't even want to run away; I simply sought to give up, to lie down in the dirt and wish myself home.

I paused, looking down at the drifts of ash and silt. It did look comfortable, surely better than this endless walking. Belis would be all right without me. She hadn't even wanted me to come in the first place. Maybe I should just have a little rest, let her and Rhiannon keep going. I swayed forward, sinking to my knees. My eyelids sagged, suddenly unbearably heavy. My fingertips trailed in the ash. It felt soft, fine, like river sand.

A strong arm wrapped round my waist and hauled me up. "On your feet, Mallt," Belis said in my ear. "Can't stop yet."

I moaned and almost toppled forward again but Belis gripped me tight. Rhiannon pushed back my hair, looking into my face.

"What's wrong with her?" Belis asked. I could hear the frown in her voice, but my eyes had slid shut again.

"I'm not sure." Rhiannon sounded concerned.

"Should we stop and rest?"

"No, if we stop now I'm worried she won't get back up." She paused. "Do you have any food left?"

"Some, but I don't think she can chew right now." Belis tightened her arm around me.

I wanted to reassure her that I was fine but I couldn't find the strength to open my mouth. I gurgled, trying to force out some words, and my head flopped forward.

"How much further do we have to go?" Belis asked. I heard Rhiannon sigh.

"A few more miles at least, and we'll need to save some energy for when we get there." Belis ground her teeth.

"She's not going to make it."

Once again I tried to protest that I would be fine but I couldn't so much as wriggle. "Belis, maybe we should—" Rhiannon broke off.

"No." Belis's voice was quiet but firm. "We'll do another mile then reassess the situation."

"Belis, she can't even stand."

Belis grabbed my wrists, lifting them above my head, then

draped them over her shoulder. Then she bent and scooped up my legs, shifting my whole weight onto her back until I was wrapped around her shoulders. I tried to force enough strength into my fingers to grab on but she caught my right hand in hers, tucking it against my legs to secure me.

"You can't walk a mile like that!" Rhiannon hissed.

"Watch me," Belis retorted. She grabbed her spear from where it was standing upright in the ash. "Come on, we've wasted enough time."

She started forward, settling into a loping stride. I stopped trying to fight whatever had paralysed me and focused on taking deep, steady breaths. The dust in the air irritated my chest but I tried to draw on enough saliva to keep my throat from drying out. In a few minutes we passed into an area where the air was clearer, though the rotten-eggs stench of sulphur worsened. I ignored it, counting breaths in and out. Belis kept moving, taking long, steady steps forward into the darkness. I could hear Rhiannon following just behind us, hear the susurration of her boots sinking into the piles of ash.

After a while I found I could open my eyes again, though I shut them quickly before I grew dizzy. Gradually the strength seeped back into my muscles, filtering down my limbs into the tips of my fingers and toes. I patted Belis's hand.

"You can put me down now, I think I can walk again."

"You're sure?" she said, though she sounded out of breath.

"I think so. I feel much better."

Belis knelt and I slid down off her back. I held onto her shoulder with one hand while I found my feet, letting the blood recede from my head.

"You're recovered?" Rhiannon asked. I found a wobbly smile.

"Yes, thank you. I don't know what came over me."

"This land is full of foul airs and vapours. It could have happened to any of us."

I nodded. It was kind of her to say so, even if it wasn't true. I was the weak one. She and Belis had kept going. I was useless, slowing down my friends, reducing our already slim chances of success. Belis had tired herself out for my sake. They should have left me.

I shoved my thoughts aside; self-pity wasn't going to help anyone now. "How much further?" I asked. Rhiannon nodded ahead of us.

"I'd say just over that crest." She sniffed the air. "I can sense the magic, it's very close." Belis gripped her spear.

"I'm ready. Mallt?"

I patted the knife sheathed at my hip and tried to look fierce.

"Good. You and I will lead, keeping Rhiannon behind us. Stay quiet as long as you can but if something attacks then act on instinct. I will try and keep larger beasts at a distance with the spear, so you'll have to mop up anything that gets past me."

I nodded. Rhiannon stretched out her hands, sparks flying from under her fingernails. She looked surprisingly calm.

"All right, then," she said. "Here we go."

Chapter 15

We scrambled up to the top of the crest and peered over the edge. The land sloped downwards in a bowl shape, the base blocked from view by a thick blueish mist. I could hear streams trickling over the ground, and if I squinted I could make out the gouges the water had raked through the rocks. Belis tapped my shoulder and pointed at the nearest creek.

"We'll follow that to the bottom. Stay close."

She padded off through the piles of ash. I skipped after her. We ran low to the ground, trying to stay below the line of the horizon. I could see the vague shape of my companions ahead of me as we stumbled down the hillside into the heart of shadow. The valley was silent except for the murmur of the water and the swish of our feet as we walked through the ash.

The streams wound back and forth across the valley floor, carving a complex network of channels into the earth. The gaps of dry land got narrower and narrower until we had to jump between them. I eyed the water suspiciously. The creeks should be shallow but the water seemed to soak up the light as if it was fathoms deep.

In the centre of the bowl was a single hill, perhaps fifty yards across. Belis paused on the last footing before it, waiting for us to catch up.

"Rhiannon, I think we're here?" she whispered.

The old queen peered at the hill. I couldn't see anything special about it. It was covered in the same drifts of ash and silt as the rest of the landscape and ringed entirely by a spiralling moat of water. All the same I felt my gorge rising in my throat as I stared at it, an anxious nausea sliding down my spine and wrapping iron bands around my arms.

"This is it," Rhiannon said, keeping her voice low. "Where the corruption first spiralled out from."

Belis nodded, preparing to jump onto the island. I caught her arm and she looked at me impatiently.

"I think we should go together," I said. "All together."

Belis glanced at Rhiannon then grunted. "Very well. On the count of three."

We leapt through the air, landing on the soft turf of the island. For a moment nothing happened and I told myself I had been foolish to worry. Then the ground started to shake, the ash rippling into dunes that began to slough off into the moat.

I staggered forward, grabbing Rhiannon and Belis and tugging them with me as the edge of the island crumbled, falling into the water. I tripped, going down on my hands and knees in the dirt. Beside me Rhiannon had fallen, too; only Belis was left standing, leaning hard on the spear she had driven into the earth. She stretched out a hand to me and I jerked my head towards Rhiannon. She was the one we needed to preserve in order to make it to the centre. Belis gritted her teeth and caught Rhiannon by the shoulder, propelling her further inland.

The island shook again and I turned back. The still air had exploded into movement, winds buffeting the ash into stinging clouds of dust. The water was rising now, the current whirling around the little island, curdling into choppy waves and drowning out the path we had taken. Dark shapes rushed past, pale teeth and fangs flashing beneath the surface. Something brushed my shoulder and I jumped, hand flying to the sword at my belt. Belis was reaching out to me, her fingers just touching the hood of my cloak. Ahead of her Rhiannon was crawling to the centre of the island, dragging herself forward by the daggers she was methodically stabbing into the dirt. I grabbed Belis's hand and she pulled me up. I slammed into her and caught the handle of the spear, using it to support me.

"We need to get to Rhiannon," I shouted, the wind snatching my words away. "She won't make it on her own."

Belis shook her head and pointed behind us. I swivelled my head. The dark creatures in the water were breaking the surface now, beginning to writhe up onto the land. They were eel-like in shape, damp grey skin covering thick cylindrical bodies. Their blind heads were almost split in half with mouths lined with sharp black teeth. The first of the monsters launched itself onto the island. It squirmed back and forth, coating itself in the grime and dirt of the earth. I shrank back as the beast sniffed at the air, a wormlike tongue running along the innumerable teeth. Then it hissed and began to slither towards us.

Belis drove her spear into the ground and drew her sword. She staggered forward against the wind, leaning down to slice the creature in two with a single stroke of her blade. The disjointed halves thrashed in the dust, rolling back down the slope. More eels had landed now and the morass of mouths devoured the corpse before it met the water. Belis paled and took a step back.

I shivered in disgust at the repellent creatures and grabbed my sword. The eels were landing all over the island now, squirming their way uphill towards Rhiannon.

"We have to stop them here," Belis called, waving an arm at the old queen. "You cover this half, I'll go there. Kill them before they reach her."

I swallowed, looking down at the gelatinous black blood that coated her weapon, then nodded.

"We can't keep them off forever," I yelled back. Belis met my eyes then turned back to the roiling knot of eels. I knew what she was thinking. We didn't have to hold them off forever, just long enough to give Rhiannon some time. I moved forward, giving my sword a tentative swing, and then the creatures were on me.

I spun wildly, carving the blade through moist grey flesh, juddering as it hit bone. I hacked down, swinging the sword clublike at the eels. Each time I injured one its fellows would turn on it, consuming it even while it screamed. The worms were clearly trying to reach Rhiannon and I dashed around the ring of the hill, cutting them down as fast as I could. On the other side of the island Belis's sword arced in a silver blur, raining death onto the eels.

I paused to catch a breath and something squirmed at the corner of my vision. One of the innumerable eels I had slain was beginning to twitch. I turned to look closer and saw the thin flesh begin to suck in the blood that had drained through the grass, the tendons stringing themselves together. It was already snapping at the air as its jaw rehinged and I staggered back, trying to put more space between me and this nightmare thing.

Sharp pain flashed in my ankle and I stabbed downwards on instinct, impaling another wriggling eel on my sword. I flicked it off into the morass, where it was instantly shredded, and allowed myself a second to look at the injury. It hadn't cut an artery, but black venom was already spiralling through the capillaries near the surface, forming a dark webbing under my skin. I prodded the skin and cried out as a wave of agony rippled through me.

A pair of eels tried to go past on my right and I moved on instinct, decapitating them both in a single blow. I risked a glance behind me. Rhiannon had reached the top of the hill and was crouched down. I could see her gesturing with her hands and a pale light was beginning to glow in the ground beneath her.

There was a sharp yell from the other side of the island. I whirled just in time to see Belis flinging an eel back into the moat. Bloody toothmarks were printed around her wrist. I wasn't close enough to see for sure, but I knew the same dark venom would be spiralling through her bloodstream. I could already feel it dampening my reflexes. I had to keep going, had to fight as long as I could. Rhiannon needed all the time we could give her.

I threw myself forward, ploughing through the eels, carving a great rent through the mass of squirming, writhing, snapping mouths. Wherever I turned to bring down my sword more of them were sliding from the water. I felt another bite, then a third, more bites coming as the venom slowed me down.

I slashed a few more times then staggered. My vision was beginning to darken at the corners of my eyes and my heart was stuttering in my chest. I stepped backwards, waving the blade to hold off my retreat, then sat down heavily in the dirt. The eels wound closer and I tried to slice at them but I no longer had the strength to hold the sword. Some were already past me, climbing the hill towards Rhiannon. I heard a thump in the distance then screams and knew Belis was down, too. I wanted to crawl towards her, to try and help. I wished for the clouds of ash to clear, to grant me a final glimpse before the worms took me. I felt the first of the beasts crawling over my boots, winding up my legs, and took a deep breath.

A wave of white light blasted down from the top of the hill. I blinked hard, blinded by the cataclysmic flash. I covered my eyes and tried to squint through my fingers. The eels were writhing, their flesh shrivelling up until only the bones remained, long strings of vertebrae and teeth-studded skulls. I dropped my hand to my ankle. The bite was still painful but the black webbing had faded. Whatever Rhiannon had done seemed to have burned the eel venom from my body. I stabbed my sword into the ground and struggled up, running towards Belis. She was lying flat on her back, her sword held loosely in her hand. There were more bitemarks along her arms and legs.

"Belis." I dropped to my knees and shook her shoulders. "Belis, are you all right?" She groaned and her eyes fluttered open. I pushed her hair off her forehead, cupping her face in my hands. She blinked up at me and I felt my heartbeat slow a little.

"Am I dead?" Her voice was faint but steady and I smiled at her.

"I don't think so."

"You don't think so?" She sat up and looked down at herself. "I don't look dead. But how would I know?"

"Better assume you're still alive for now." I tilted my head towards the top of the hill. "Come on, Rhiannon might need us."

Belis kicked off the bones that had collected on her feet and stood up, yanking her spear from the ground. She followed me up the slope where we found Rhiannon kneeling down to blow dust from a piece of rock, a pale marble slab embedded in the hill. She glanced up as we approached.

"I trust you're not severely injured? I appreciate you holding them off for me."

"Of course," said Belis, tugging her sleeves down over the bitemarks on her arms. "What have you found?"

Rhiannon finished cleaning the stone. "Pass me a waterskin," she said.

Belis fumbled in her pack and handed one to her. I crouched down, looking at the slab. There were deep lines carved into the stone, interlocking like knots. They seemed familiar but I couldn't quite place them. Rhiannon pulled the top off the skin and emptied it onto the marble. I sighed. That was all the water we had left.

The water sank into the lines, trickling around until the entire carving was covered. Belis squatted beside me.

"It's the valley we're in," she said, "that's the path the streams were making."

I looked more closely and saw she was right: the pattern swirled to an inner circle. Even now the water was beginning to flow the way the streams had before we'd stepped onto the island.

"So that's us, in the middle?" I pointed towards the centre. Rhiannon slapped my hand away.

"Don't touch it," she snapped. I withdrew my stinging hand. "Yes, I think so. This is the heart of the corruption. I've never seen it before. It's more than just some disease, I think, it's a fundamental wrongness. I thought that it must have been fae mischief but it's not. I think it stems from the living world . . ."

"You said this began almost twenty years ago. When exactly did you notice it?"

Rhiannon screwed up her face in concentration. "Nineteen, no, eighteen summers ago. Early in the summer, when the blossom was beginning to fall."

Belis slammed her fist on the ground. "Eighteen years ago was when the Romans invaded, Rhiannon! I was five years old. I remember the druids whispering that troops were massing on the mainland. My father told them not to worry, that ancient spells girded the island, that no invading army could pass through."

"That's true," Rhiannon said. "I was there the last time the spells were renewed, written in the blood of forty chieftains."

"The Romans must have undone the spells, perhaps allied with one of the rulers who lost their land under Cymbeline," I said. Belis glanced at me, surprised.

"You know of Cymbeline?"

"I do pay some attention to the kingdoms of men," I muttered. "Especially when their armies clash and leave me a thousand souls to collect."

"It doesn't matter how it happened," Rhiannon said. "Those spells were braided into the heart of the island, both living and dying realms. If they were broken the worlds would begin to splinter. The living island lost its protection, and the dead began to rot."

"So the Roman greed for empire has brought pain and destruction even to the land of the dead," said Belis, her voice sharp with bitterness.

"Less Roman greed than British treachery," Rhiannon countered. "But we should put away our disgust at the past. There may yet be time for us to repair the future."

"How?" I asked.

"The enchantments must be sung again," Rhiannon said. "The worlds shifted back into their places."

"Can you remember them?"

"I never forget a spell. The words aren't the problem, nor the magic."

"What else do you need?" Belis asked. Rhiannon stared at her.

"The magic requires more than mouthed words. It requires a sacrifice. I told you I saw the spells cast all those years ago. Forty kings and queens gathered together to pay the price. Each gave a cup of blood. There's power in royal blood. Not from the ruler but from the ruled. Each of those chieftains bore within them the love, the assent, of those they represented so that through them all the inhabitants of Britain came together to bind the island anew."

"Royal blood," Belis said softly. "You need me."

"You are the only one who can serve." Rhiannon's voice was quiet.

"You can't take all the blood from Belis alone," I said. "You need pints of the stuff, you'll kill her."

"Like I said." The old queen looked at my friend. "It requires a sacrifice."

"No." I grabbed her arm. "You can't do it. You're a queen, why can't we use your blood, too?"

"Because I am already dead," Rhiannon said, brushing my hand off. "I have no blood in me to give. Believe that I would take this from you if I could, my child."

"Belis." I turned towards her. Her face might have been carved from the same marble as the stone. "Be sensible, there'll be another way to solve this!"

"How?" she asked. "You and I are the only two living mortals in Annwn. We can't bring more in and we can't get out. This is the only way."

"But you'll die," I said.

"Then I'll stay here in Annwn, except it will be safe enough that I'll be able to find peace eventually. It's not so bad. I'd rather live in the mortal world but I'd only be coming down here a little earlier than scheduled. I should have died at the battle on Watling Street. Maybe this is the best thing."

"You won't necessarily die," Rhiannon interrupted. "It will take a lot of blood and I can't guarantee you'll survive. You've got a chance, maybe one in ten. If you survive it there'll be no more magic in you, though, it will go into the spell."

Belis smiled at me. "You see, one in ten. That's better odds than a battle, and magic has brought me nothing but trouble. I am happy to give it up."

My chest felt like it was burning, bursting with fire. "I don't want you to do this. I want you to live, to come back to the mortal world with me and save your sister. Remember that farm in the north I was going to find? You were going to come and stay with me. I can't do it on my own." I ducked my head down to hide the stinging tears that came unbidden.

"I think you can do anything, Mallt Nightshade," Belis said. "I wish I could be there to help you do it."

She moved closer and tilted up my chin so that I was forced to meet her eyes. They seemed even brighter than ever in the gloom of the shadow.

"I've failed to do the right thing so many times already, Mallt. I failed my sister, failed my mother. Before we came here, I already wanted to die. This would have been no sacrifice. Now ..." she paused, and I felt my heart cracking open in my chest, "now I have something I want to live for, someone. I want that farm in the north, too. I swear I'll try to hold on but if I don't, promise me that you'll try to save Cati for me. Take her somewhere safe. Promise me?"

I nodded, almost blinded by the tears that spilled down my cheeks. She smiled at me and turned away. I gasped for breath, fighting a losing battle for control of my face. I wanted to be strong, as strong as Belis. That was all I could do for her now.

Rhiannon cleared her throat. "Are you ready?"

Belis drew back her arm and offered Rhiannon a knife. "Yes. Try not to kill me if you can."

"I'll do my best."

I lurched forward, wanting to say something, but I couldn't find the words. I felt the panic bubbling up in me just as it had beside the water barrel our first day in Annwn but this time Belis wasn't there to calm me down.

Rhiannon took the knife, pressing it into the freckled skin of Belis's wrist. She muttered something under her breath and pushed down, splitting the skin and neatly severing the vein.

Belis clenched her jaw, trying not to wince as the blood began dribbling into the carved channels of the rock. Rhiannon positioned her hand in the centre and then let go, allowing the blood to drain freely. She stepped back and began chanting, singing in the oldest language I remembered, an ancient form of Brittonic.

I hovered at the edge of the rock, watching as the blood spiralled out, flowing along the interlocking lines of the carved knot, then trickled down further, branching like tree roots through the earth, red lines breaking through the ground and down into the waters that still surrounded us. The new capillaries of blood went further, rising up the sides of the valley and into the sky, like inverted lightning.

It should have looked terrifying but instead the blood glowed softly, the red light a hearth fire to keep the whole world warm, like a womb cradling an unborn child. Except this fire was burning Belis for fuel. She was a mother who would die in the birthing.

Belis staggered, her face pale. I rushed forward, looping a hand around her waist to hold her up. I remembered how she had carried me through the ash, holding me at my weakest. I wanted to do more to help her but all I could do was pray for Rhiannon to hurry, to finish the spell before the last of Belis's lifeblood leached into the earth.

The old queen lifted her hands to the air, calling the fractal lines of blood back towards her so that we were trapped within a scarlet torus, flowing in an unending circle of blood and magic and song. The spell built to a crescendo and I felt Belis sag, unconscious in my arms. I wanted to yank her still bleeding wrist from the stone but I dared not. Dared not risk ruining this one chance she was giving her life for.

Rhiannon stopped singing and the torus exploded, shattering into red crystals that flew out then fell like rain. The marble slab, now dyed a gleaming ruby-red, glowed and sank into the ground. The central circle grew, expanding until it was wider than the slab, eating at the ground beneath us. Rhiannon, Belis and I were left floating in the air. The yawning gap below us kept growing until it was the size of the entire island. Ash began to tumble down the slopes, then the cliffs themselves were tumbling, falling into the void. More and more of the rot was sucked down, hideous shapes half glimpsed through the mist, straightening and reforming into human bodies.

Belis moaned and I tore my eyes away from the spell to look at her. Her skin was milk-white, blood still dripping from her wrist. I grabbed the cut and clapped my hand over it, applying pressure to stop the flow of blood. I remembered the fae-woven fabric of my tunic and tore off a strip, binding the wound as tightly as I could.

"Hang on, Belis," I whispered.

When I looked back down the void was pulsing as the entirety of the fractured realm was pulled back in and then shifted and the lost part of Annwn started to back. There was a second flash of blinding light and Belis was ripped away from me as the circle shut and I fell backwards through the air.

# Chapter 16

I woke with a jolt, still feeling the echoes of the magic thrumming through me. I tried to sit up but my limbs still felt weak. I rolled over and crawled onto my knees. The landscape had changed utterly. The piles of ash had vanished, revealing fields of bronze grass that waved in a breeze that had only the faintest taste of sulphur. The few trees within sight were still upended, but birds were already beginning to return to them, nesting in the mess of roots and singing out at the lapis-blue sky. The bones of the *shadowbitten* had gone; in their place lay sleeping mortals. I staggered up and looked around for Belis.

She lay flat on her back beside the stone slab. I rushed towards her, tripped over and crawled to her side. Her hair waved delicately in the wind, and she looked pale as death. I felt my heart almost stop beating. If this had killed her, how could I go on?

"Is she all right?" asked Rhiannon from behind me. The old queen sounded exhausted.

I frowned, sliding a hand under Belis's chin, feeling for a heartbeat. For a long moment I couldn't find it, only the smooth skin of her throat. Then, weak and unsteady but dogged, a pulse pushed through her veins. I sagged in relief, leaning over to press my forehead to hers.

"She's alive," I sighed.

The old queen grinned through her spiked teeth and closed her eyes in relief.

"Excellent. Good job." She sat down on the ground and stretched her hands. "Not a drop of magic left in me. We'd better hope the journey home is uneventful. Your girl is stronger than I thought. The magic in her blood was very powerful indeed. She would have been a great witch given training."

I felt Belis's breath on my cheek and her eyes fluttered open. "Is it done?" she said sleepily. I smiled at her.

"It's done. You did it. Rest now."

She grinned and closed her eyes again. I lifted her head into my lap and released a long breath. Rhiannon was staring out at the world around us. One of the sleeping mortals twitched, then sat up. I frowned at it and felt for my sword as the woman stood and began to walk towards us. She paused a few strides away and looked down at Rhiannon.

"I dreamed I was a monster," she said, her voice dry from lack of use. "Lady Seneschal, it was not a dream, was it?"

Rhiannon shook her head. "You have been lost here for some years, but we came to bring you home. Will you stay with us a while?"

The woman smiled. "I think not, I am ready now." She glanced at me and I thought I recognised her, just one of the many souls I had brought to Annwn. Her face relaxed when she saw mine and then she was gone, leaving nothing but a ripple in the wind where she had been standing.

Rhiannon muttered a few words of prayer and I nodded. A feeling of pride swept through me. I might not be the Nightshade any more but I had still helped this woman find peace. That was a good feeling. I looked down at Belis. Her eyes were closed. Perhaps that was something I could bring into whatever life I found next.

We rested for the whole day. Rhiannon brewed a potion to replenish some of Belis's blood and made her drink the entire foul-tasting thing. She complained heartily but the colour came back into her cheeks almost at once and she insisted on standing up to see what we had done.

Rhiannon and I helped her to her feet and looked around us. More of the dead souls were standing now, wandering around and embracing each other. No others faded into the wind; these were smiling and talking, still full of energy.

"It looks as if hardly anything happened here," Belis said, staring out at the plains

"Just as well. Those who were *shadowbitten* have been healed, they will forget their sickness as a bad dream. That is how they will go on until they are ready to pass."

"I guess." I bit my lip, trying to frame the emotions tangled up in my chest. "But if they forget about this then how will people know what we did?"

"They won't," said Belis. Rhiannon nodded.

"No songs will be sung, no stories whispered around bonfires. The three of us have saved the afterworld and all who reside in it. The old protections have been renewed and no one will ever know."

I squirmed, uncomfortable with how this thought made me feel. It seemed incredibly selfish to say how much I had wanted to be a hero.

Rhiannon patted my arm.

"I'll know, Mallt. And so will Arawn, and Belis here. Most importantly, you'll know." I found a weak smile and Rhiannon turned back to the east.

"We should leave. There's a long walk ahead of us."

Belis frowned. "Can't you *rush* us? Now that this is all Annwn again?"

"I don't have the energy left. I spent everything I had on the spell."

I groaned. "So we have to walk all the way back?"

Rhiannon answered by setting off down the hill, into the waist-high grass that carpeted the slopes. Belis laughed.

"Come on, Mallt, I thought you enjoyed travelling! Or do you want me to carry you again?"

I wrinkled my nose and followed Rhiannon. Belis padded after me, humming to herself and twirling her spear. She seemed in an irritatingly good mood. I could understand it. We had beaten impossible odds and had merely to collect Cati's soul from Arawn and head back to mortal Britain. I didn't know why I was so on edge, why the sound of her singing grated on me. I felt a little awkward. I wanted to speak to her in private, but I couldn't think of a reason to send Rhiannon away.

It took half a day for us to reach the western side of the rift. The wind still howled through the gap in the land.

"So this place didn't mend?" Belis said, wrinkling her nose.

"It appears not." Rhiannon peered down one of the canyons. "It was my magic that created it not the corruption so I suppose it makes sense it didn't reform when I burned that out. I shall have to come back later and try to push it back together, or perhaps Arawn can build some bridges. In any case there doesn't seem to be anything left down there; all the *shadowbitten* should have been healed. We should be on our guard, though."

Belis spotted a footpath down into the gorge and we half climbed, half fell down it. When we reached the bottom Rhiannon looked around, frowning. Where the southern rift had been a single canyon, this was a labyrinth of alleyways and crevices. The smell of sulphur was stronger here than up on the plains.

I leaned against a boulder, listening to Belis and Rhiannon debate the best way out. Belis wanted to climb straight up the cliffs, cutting handholds for us to follow. Rhiannon wanted to try to find a more leisurely route, arguing that we were no longer racing against time.

"I'm in a hurry, Rhiannon," Belis said, testily. "My sister is still waiting for me. I am eager to take her soul and leave this place."

Rhiannon flushed but stood her ground. Belis had escaped death only hours before. She was far too weak to be climbing another cliff.

"Very well," Belis said, giving in. "We'll split up and walk a mile or so in each direction, looking for a way out. After an hour we'll come back here and regroup. If we don't find anything in that time," she paused to glare at Rhiannon, "we'll come back and try climbing."

"Agreed," I said, keen to end the argument. "Belis, you should wait here and preserve your strength in case we have to climb."

Rhiannon headed south, while I went north, leaving Belis sitting on the floor and rubbing her feet.

It was surprisingly interesting walking along the foot of the rift. The rock layers had folded back on themselves like a coiling snake, alternating black and white. I remembered having seen something similar on the south coast of Britain and my mind wandered back to the times I had spent travelling through the living world. I paused here and there to look for an easier route to scramble up the cliffs. The limestone layers protruded more than the mudstone, forming a makeshift ladder to the top of the canyon. It was still steep enough to be almost vertical, though, so I kept walking. After almost half an hour I was about to give up and turn back when I heard a rustling ahead of me.

Not good, I thought, unsheathing my sword. I glanced around, wondering if I could run for it. Now the sound was coming from behind me. The warren of passageways could allow whatever it was to circle me completely unseen. Breathe, I told myself, forcing deep gulps of air into my chest. The thrumming beat of my heart was pounding within me, almost drowning out any other sounds. I dug my nails into the soft skin of my palm, levering the pain to try and focus. I wished I could think of anything other than how to fall down.

A grinding sound came from my left and I turned. I could see nothing but shadows. I raised my sword to hip height and waited. I sniffed the air and winced. There was something sulphurous on the wind, rotting flesh. Had one of the *shadowbitten* been trapped here rather than being drawn back, perhaps? I dived to my right on instinct, rolling in the mud and filth.

Flame billowed forth, shooting straight as an arrow towards where I had been standing. The fire licked at the ground, baking the wet mud into dry, cracking clay. As the flames dissipated I stared back through the smoke. The white dragon the messenger had warned us about was standing at the edge of the canyon.

It stood as tall as a house, somehow both solid and sinuous. The glassy white scales glowed with the pale heart of a fire, the air above them shimmering with the heat that rolled off the dragon's body. Its head was viper-like, broad at the jaw and narrowing towards the nose. A long tail, edged with spikes, whipped behind it, churning the baked mud into dust. The white dragon unfolded vast wings and shrieked up at the sky above. It leaned back on legs wide as tree trunks and leapt into the air, beating its wings to break free of the ground and blasting another wreath of flame towards the sky.

I rolled back onto my feet and crouched in the mud. My head was spinning but there was no time to worry about it now; the dragon was still hovering, but soon it would leave. I grabbed rocks from the ground beside me and hurled them into the air. They missed, arcing harmlessly past the dragon. I tried again and this time, through pure luck, hit a dangling leg.

The dragon turned back to me and roared. It folded its wings and landed heavily on the ground. It roared again in outrage, sending out a fireball that scorched the air. Then it shook its head back and forth and turned to stalk around the valley floor.

I rolled behind a boulder and tossed out another rock. I scrabbled at the floor again but, finding nothing, gripped my sword tightly.

The great wyrm paused, lashing its tail back and forth, then began to mince forward. Its movement was smooth and delicate now, like a cat walking along a fence. It lowered its head to the ground, sniffing at the air, keeping its eyes fixed on me. Slowly, carefully, I stood up, bringing the sword in front of me and gripping the hilt with both hands. I stepped back, moving away from the wall, taking steady paces.

The dragon sniffed again, opening its mouth so that I could see the long, curved fangs beginning to emerge from the upper jaw. Its nostrils flared, an incongruously shell-like pink. It half spread its wings and I realised it was preparing to pounce rather than to strafe me with fire. I tensed my legs, rising up on the balls of my feet.

Just as the dragon sprang I darted forward and to the side. Its head shot forward but I was already beside it, jamming my sword at its throat. The scales were too hard to pierce, however, and the blade slid along the dragon's neck. I kept my forward momentum and pressed on, slipping in the mud. The edge of the sword scraped along the chitinous plates then caught in a divot at the shoulder. I drove the sword in with all my strength and the dragon screamed.

It sprayed fire in a wild arc, spinning on the spot to try and grab at the sword. I was knocked over and rolled away, leaving the sword jammed into the beast. I scrambled up and ran for it, wiping mud from my eyes as I went. I caught a brief look behind me, enough to see that the dragon appeared furious but not mortally wounded. It snapped at the hilt of the blade, bending its neck almost double to try and reach it. I realised I should have ripped the sword out, to try to bleed the dragon dry. Too late now. I had done nothing but enrage the beast and lost my only weapon in the process.

The dragon gave up trying to remove the sword and reared up on its hind legs, loosing another bolt of fire into the air. It crashed back onto all fours and scanned the area, searching for me. Clear lids criss-crossed over silver eyes and the dark slash of the iris thinned as it looked into the sun. I pressed myself against the wall, sliding back around towards the dragon.

The dragon roared and stampeded forward, ploughing the baked mud into furrows with its claws. Its lips rippled back, exposing the fully extended fangs as it prepared to strike at me. It dived just as I leapt. I threw myself at its tail, landing about halfway along. The dragon shrieked and whipped its tail up and down. I clung on, digging my fingers into the gaps between the scales and wedging my feet onto the tail spikes. The dragon snapped at me, baring its fangs and spitting fire. I ducked as scarlet flames licked the air above my head and I felt the murderous heat.

I needed to move further up. I pushed with my feet, reaching for the next row of spikes, and stepped up. I caught my breath as the dragon beat its wings and rose into the air, dangling its tail and lashing it back and forth. I grabbed for the spines then wrapped my legs around the tail and began to pull myself up with my arms. It was like climbing a ladder, I told myself, or a tree. A tree that was on fire, a ladder that could bite.

I reached the base of the tail just as the dragon threw itself back to the ground. My legs slipped and I shot forward across the dragon's back. I flung out my arms and managed to grab onto something. The dragon shook itself like a wet dog; my grip loosened and I slid sideways, falling against its left wing. It squawked in triumph and shook again but I had the measure of it now and the bones of the wing were easier to hold on to.

I swung myself to my feet. The dragon was still roaring as I stepped from its wing to its back. I sat down right at the nape of its neck, gripping on with my thighs as I would sit a horse and wrapping my arms around it as far as I could reach. The scales were burning hot, scorching the exposed skin of my palms, but I held on. The dragon was outraged. It threw itself back and forth, rolled in the mud and dust. It leapt into the air and crashed back to the ground and roared again and again until I thought my flesh would melt. Eventually it stood still, panting yellow flames. I checked my palms. They were blistered and burned but I could still move them.

I stroked the smouldering scales of the dragon's neck as it shook out its wings, spreading them wide.

"Calm," I whispered, "we just have to sit here and be calm until Rhiannon comes back. She'll know what to do."

The dragon screeched and twisted, screeched and twisted in fury. I clung on, digging my feet in more tightly so that I wouldn't fall. The beast reared back then ran forward, picking up speed as it raced across the canyon. It howled once more and I felt the scales beneath me burning as the furnace within began to heat up.

"No!" I yelled, realising what it intended "No, stop, wait, we have to stay here!"

Then the dragon leapt through the air, skimming over the edge of the canyon and into the sky above.

The wind whipped through my hair, knotting it into snarls and tangles. The dragon had turned east, following the path of the setting sun. The air was thin and the constant howling of the wind in my ears had beaten a brutal ache into my head. Only the warmth of the dragon's scaled neck beneath me kept my battered fingers from losing their grip.

Below us the landscape had shifted from the shattered canyons to what seemed to be high chalklands, pale green and deserted.

The dragon flexed its shoulders a little and banked to the right. I peered down. We were nearing the edge of the chalk, the grassy land puckering as it sloped down.

Something white flashed below us and I looked down. A white bull was etched on the chalk, a hundred paces long, a brother to the white horse I knew from the mortal world. The carving had captured the creature mid-charge, head down and legs stretched. It looked free, even as it was caught in perfect stillness. I peered down, shielding my eyes from the rays of the sunset. A pair of figures stood at the base of the bull's neck. I could see Belis, staring up at the sky. Beside her was Rhiannon, arms outstretched, silver hair streaming in the wind. They must have *rushed* here. Rhiannon must have found some vestige of strength.

I twisted around the dragon's neck, trying to see. The dragon dipped and I scrabbled to regain my hold. I wanted to yell to Belis but I didn't dare upset the dragon. The wind carried speech towards me, strange, old words, from songs that I had forgotten ever hearing. I recognised the voice, too: Rhiannon was singing. There was a power in the song, both in the language and in the melody. I felt it drawing me closer, pulling me towards her.

The dragon leaned again to the right, circling lower over the chalk bull. I pressed my arms even tighter around its neck, cursing my bad luck. How could I be so close to help and yet beyond it?

The dragon growled and I felt the fire within it begin to burn a little hotter. I scanned the ground, looking for what had provoked it. A bird was flying towards us, riding the rising air currents with widespread wings. As it soared towards us I saw that it was Rhiannon's eagle, amber and gold feathers bright against the sky. The dragon grumbled again but didn't seem threatened and the scales beneath me cooled.

The eagle angled its wings and banked heavily to the left until it was mere feet from my head. There was a yellow ribbon tied to one of its feet, a scrap of parchment threaded through the silk. I raised my arm out and the eagle landed neatly on my fist, watching me with bronze-eyed malevolence. Its vicious talons dug into the skin of my hand but I refused to flinch, glaring right back at it until it looked away and grudgingly held out its leg. I fumbled for the parchment, winding the ribbon in my hands. In neat, perfectly calligraphic Latin, it said, "at fifteen feet, jump to the south".

I looked at the eagle.

"She can't be serious. All the trouble of sending you and this is all the information I get?"

The eagle blinked at me then took off, skimming over my head so low that I had to duck to avoid the trailing claws. The dragon murmured unhappily and I patted its neck.

"I know, you should have roasted it."

I shoved the message inside my shirt and pushed my hair back, using the yellow ribbon to tie it out of my face. Rhiannon's voice came again but now there was more than one note to her song. Dozens of tones, layering on top of each other, high and low, sweet and rough. The song seemed to resonate in the cavity of my chest, in the hollow of my skull. It called to me and I leaned down against the dragon's neck, reaching out through the open air.

The dragon opened its mouth and keened. It drew in its wings and began to fly in lower and lower rings. I trailed my fingers in the air, brushing against the delicious sound. I closed my eyes to concentrate on it better. Something sharp prickled my collarbone. I yelped and grabbed at my shirt. The parchment letter was irritating my skin. I shook my head and cleared a little of the enchantment of the song. Fifteen feet. I had to be ready to jump.

We were lower than I'd realised by now, close enough to the ground that I could see the powdery chalk beneath the thin grass. I loosened my grip and levered myself into a crouching position on the back of the dragon. Below us Rhiannon had moved to the west, into a wide-open space opposite the charging bull. The sun was almost below the horizon now and the last of its beams washed the hillside in gold so that the figure seemed to glow, seemed to move.

The dragon turned one last time and came in to land. It stretched out its claws, reaching towards the hill where Rhiannon was standing. I had to trust in her plan. I sprang to my feet and half ran, half fell down the back of the dragon, diving towards the chalk.

I hit the ground hard and rolled, tumbling back and forth so that sky and grass seemed two sides of a cartwheel, but the slopes dipped to the north and my momentum could only carry me so far before I stopped. The pain of the landing hadn't hit me yet but I knew it was coming.

I looked up, eyes still rolling in my head, just in time to see the dragon land. Its wings were splayed out behind it like battle flags and its talons extended, just to the hem of Rhiannon's tunic. The old queen's face was warm and gentle and she held out her hand. Her lips moved, framing the final words of the spell.

The dragon struck the ground and sank like a stone through clear water. No sound came from its mouth, no fire burst from its chest, it simply sliced through the earth and was gone. The sun set and the hillside was dark.

I heard Rhiannon mutter something and pale wisps bloomed in the air, casting their pearlescent glow over the ground. Beneath our feet a new carving had appeared. The long lines of a dragon's wings spread out across the chalk, shining white in the darkness. The old queen looked at me and smiled.

"It's done," she said. Then she was gone, too.

I fell back against the stubbly grass and looked up at the sky as the wash of fear and panic drained away from me, quickly replaced by the reality of my injuries. I was badly burned and the leap from the dragon's back had jolted my left arm. I flexed it tentatively and stifled a yelp as a rush of cramping pain rocketed through me. There was truly no end to the delights of a mortal body. I took a long shaky breath and focused on steadying myself.

I managed to convince my stomach not to empty its contents and looked up. Belis was running towards me, panic on her face. She clattered to a halt in front of me, falling to her knees.

"Mallt, thank the gods you're alive. When the dragon came I thought—" She broke off, seeing my arm. "You're hurt, Mallt? I'm so sorry, this is all my fault. I shouldn't have let you go off alone."

"I'm fine, really," I said, trying to stand up. My legs were wobblier than I had expected and I stumbled forward, almost falling on top of her. She caught me and lowered me back to the ground.

"Where's Rhiannon," she asked, looking back around. I shrugged and felt my eyes begin to sting. I raised a hand to my face and it came away damp. Tears, I realised. One of the few things I hadn't experienced since I had become human.

"She's gone," I said, stumbling over my words. Belis pressed her eyes shut for a moment.

"Did the dragon take her?" she asked after a minute. I shook my head.

"It went into the chalk alone. I think she was just ready to fade. She'd worked for so long."

"That's a good thing, right?" Her voice wavered and I felt more tears trickle down my cheeks.

"I think so."

She leaned forward and hugged me. We sat for a while in the darkness, watching the moon rise.

"Hey, Belis," I said, breaking the silence. "I fell down. I fell off the dragon just like you taught me. It is the most important thing, after all."

She smiled. "Not quite, Mallt. The most important thing is how you get back up."

Chapter 17

We walked back across Annwn, as the sun rolled overhead and the landscape changed from the scrubby grass of the chalklands to lush paddocks where cattle grazed, back to the rolling fields of crops. Already there were wagonloads of people heading towards us, spreading back out into the lands that had lain fallow under the infection of the shadow. They greeted us happily as they passed, faces smooth and unworried. They had brought food for the road and gave us bread and cheese and fruit. Neither of us had eaten since the drumlin field and we fell ravenously on the food, washing it down with cups of watered wine that another group of travellers shared out.

When they had gone, leaving nothing but dust kicked up on the road behind us, I turned to look after them. I was glad they didn't know how close they had come to the *shadowbitten*, even if it meant our work would be forgotten. They seemed so peaceful, families reunited and on their way to a long, easy existence, followed by a final rest. Maybe that wasn't so bad. Maybe I, too, could accept this death as the cost of the rich gifts of a human life.

I glanced up at Belis who was singing to herself as she walked. Rhiannon's potion seemed to have half cured her and the renewed strength of Annwn was closing her cuts and bruises, but she was still a little pale. I decided to suggest we take a break soon so as not to exhaust her.

We were still coated with ash and sweat and I stank of dragon and smoke, so when the road brought us alongside a bubbling stream I dragged Belis into the water with me. It was cold and fresh and she screeched with the shock of it. I laughed and splashed her, then stripped off my clothes to scrub out the worst of the dirt. The once beautiful fae fabrics had been worn down to rags, stained with blood and filth.

Belis swam up behind me, trailing her own tattered clothes.

"We can trade for new ones when we get back. I still have some coins left," she said, leaning over my shoulder to see what I was looking at. "And you can always go and find your old friends and get some more fairy clothes."

I bit my lip and pushed the clothes under the water, scrubbing at them ferociously. Belis drifted around in front of me.

"What is it?" she said, reaching out to take the tunic from me before I ripped it. I stared into the water.

"Belis," I started, then lost courage. She swam a little closer to me and I found the strength to look up at her. She was so beautiful, her hair darkened by the same water that threw lights into her eyes. I wanted to count the freckles on her face, to run my hands along the muscles of her arms.

"Mallt." She met my gaze and I felt my heart twist in pain at the sound of my name in her mouth. I floundered in the water, suddenly almost too weak to swim.

"That farm we were joking about," I stuttered, trying to get the words out. "Will you come with me? To the north?"

"I'll go anywhere you want with you," Belis said. "Just tell me what you want."

"I think I want you." I let the words fall out of my mouth before I could stop them.

She ran a hand through her hair, freeing a long tendril from her braid. I reached out to tuck it behind her ear again, my fingers skimming her face. She caught my hand before I could take it back. Her eyes were full of turmoil, racked by indecision.

I leaned forward and kissed her. At first it was just a graze, just my lips skimming over hers, asking a question. Then I felt her arms wind behind my neck, and she pulled me close. Her mouth was so soft, her tongue dancing against my own. I wrapped a hand in her hair, moving the other down to tug her waist nearer to me. She pulled back then kissed me again and again. I smiled and our teeth knocked together.

Sorry," she whispered, and I laughed, pulling her up the bank and onto the grass.

I sat back on my heels and drew her close, taking her hand and moving it to my throat, my waist, my thighs. Her fingers traced down my stomach, her touch light but my skin almost burning beneath it. She kissed me again and my mouth was trembling beneath hers.

"Can I?" she asked, and I nodded desperately as she pressed her lips to my throat, my collarbones. I was dizzy with Belis, drunk on her. All the pain and fear of mortality that I had struggled with, now I could understand how the humans could bear it, for this moment was worth it all.

When we finally paused for breath the sun was high in the sky, casting golden light over where we lay on the soft grass beside the river. I lifted my head up and looked down at Belis as she lay beneath me, marvelling at the long muscles of her arms, the sharp line of her nose, the myriad freckles that starred her skin. It was too much to look at, I wanted to taste, to touch, to smell her. I wished for the thousandth time that I was still Mallt Nightshade, not to run but so that I could love Belis in my immortal form. Yet even in the wishing a part of me knew this feeling was greater than my ageless heart could bear, that these emotions were entirely mortal, entirely human.

"It's too much," I burst out, still looking at Belis. She frowned at me, a dent of worry appearing between her brows.

"Is it? Mallt, we don't have to . . ." She paused as I shook my head at her. "Not that, this." I gestured at myself. "It hurts, why does it hurt?"

Belis sat up, alarmed, pulling me into her lap. "What hurts, Mallt?"

"Everything! I thought humans only felt things with their chests! That's what all the songs say. Your heart is where you're supposed to feel things, but I feel all over!"

"What do you feel?"

I stuttered, trying to find the words. "You! I feel you in my legs – they're weak as kittens. I feel you in my arms – they ache to hold you, I mean physically hurt to not have you. My stomach is a whirlpool, my throat is a wildfire. I can feel you in my fingertips, I can feel my mouth aching to kiss you, to say your name. It's not just my chest, or my head, it's all of me. I can feel you in my elbows, Bel – what does that mean?"

"What do you think?" Belis asked, her gaze dark and very serious.

"This is your stupid human love, isn't it?"

She smiled at me and I felt my traitorous mortal heart beat so hard that I thought my ribcage might crack.

"For what it's worth, Mallt, I love you with my elbows, too."

I groaned and kissed her again.

I woke from a sweet, dreamless sleep to a faint tickling in my ear. It took me a moment to realise it was Belis's breath, each exhalation ruffling a loose lock of hair over my cheek. The sky was still light, with only the slightest tinge of orange in the west to herald the coming dawn. I stayed still, enjoying the comforting warmth of my lover beside me. Belis had wrapped herself around me, tight as ivy clinging to an oak. One of her legs had nestled between mine and my head lay against her left arm. Her right hand rested gently on my stomach. I snuggled back and laid my hand over hers. The touch of her hand on my stomach was somehow more intimate then all the pleasure we had shared. The feeling of her palm filled a gap I hadn't known was there, healed an old scar I had forgotten I bore.

I lay in Belis's arms and watched the western skies bloom

with red and orange sunlight. After a while I felt the tempo of her breath quicken and I knew she was awake. Neither of us moved to get up, only shifting slightly to fit more comfortably against each other. I felt my heartbeat thudding in time with hers, steady and true. Only when the sun had broken free of the horizon, sitting low and heavy in the sky, did I finally sit up and stretch out my arms.

Belis smiled up at me, drowsiness still clouding her face, the yellow light setting fire to the crown of scarlet curls mussed up by sleep.

"Come back and lie with me," she said, reaching out a hand to my leg. I closed my eyes as she traced her fingers along the muscles of my thigh, trying to ignore the shiver of delight shooting through me.

"It's the morning, Bel," I said, grabbing her hand and pulling her upright. She came up easily but then distracted me by kissing my neck, working her way to my ear and nipping playfully at it.

"It's daytime, we've spent almost a whole day here," I said again, fighting for my rapidly diminishing willpower. "We have to get back to Arawn. He'll be wanting to know what happened to us, to Rhiannon. Not to mention we can claim your sister's soul."

"He's waited eighteen years to solve the problem of the *shadowbitten*. He can wait a little longer. Besides, it's still too dark to travel," Belis murmured, placing her palms over my eyes. "I can barely see. We should wait here a little longer."

I pulled her hands away and she grinned and lifted me back into her lap. I opened my mouth to explain exactly why we had to go but she had returned her hands to my thigh and I soon forgot anything I had wanted to say.

When Belis finally rolled back onto the soft grass, I managed to formulate my thoughts enough to insist that we leave.

Belis smiled at me lazily then jumped back up.

"Come on, then. No time to waste lying about all day, Mallt, I've got a soul to collect. You should know about the importance of that. I don't know why you've been dragging your feet so much!"

I stuck my tongue out at her and she bent down and scooped me up in her arms. She spun me around like a bridegroom then dropped me on my feet. I swayed, still a little light-headed, then concentrated on standing straight and slipping on my tunic. My boots had been kicked off a few yards away and I went to retrieve them then leaned on Belis while I hopped on one foot to get them on.

I patted my head, tucking wisps of hair behind my ears. Somewhere I had lost the strip of fabric I had used to tie it back. I glared at Belis then grabbed her wrist, stealing the spare leather thong she had wrapped around it. I twisted my hair into a long braid and secured it with the scrap of leather. Belis caught the end and tugged on it gently.

"Immortal thievery," she said, "my father always warned me about it."

I sniffed. "If you hadn't lost mine like some big lumbering human I wouldn't have had to steal it. Besides, I'm not a goddess any more, that's very offensive. I'm just as human as you."

"A human forever!" She pulled me close and I beamed up at her, counting the silver flecks in her eyes.

We found Arawn much as we had on that first day, stripped to the waist and tilling the ground, a heavy iron shovel in his hands. Around him the fields were full of other workers, laughing in the morning sunlight as they laboured. As we approached, Arawn stopped digging, shading his eyes and hurrying towards us. To my surprise he caught us both in a huge embrace.

"You did it, you healed the land. Mallt, you truly are a friend to Annwn, and Belis, you have more than earned your reward. I was worried when you didn't return after the shadow fell. I thought maybe you'd been killed in the struggle and would be staying here but you both look well. I was expecting Rhiannon to *rush* you here once she'd recovered herself ..." His voice petered out and I watched as his eyes flittered from Belis to me then at the space where Rhiannon should have been.

"She's gone?" he asked, then nodded before we could answer. "I should have known."

He leaned on his shovel, a faint tremor in his hand, and let out a long whistle. "I'll miss the old woman, she's been here a long time, took the record for it centuries ago. Just wouldn't leave. I'd been telling her to let go for a while. Never thought she'd go without saying goodbye, though."

"She went rather quickly," Belis said. "I'm sure she would have said farewell if she'd had the time."

"Aye, I'm sure she would. Funny to have all that time and then none at the end. I'm happy for her, I am, though there's a vein of sadness, too." He looked up at me. "I've a feeling you'll know a bit about that too, Mallt."

I didn't say anything and the Lord of Annwn sighed. "Very well then. I will make my preparations to release your sister's soul to you. While you wait, I have one final task for you."

"Are you serious?" I asked incredulously. "We've just saved the entirety of the afterworld and you're asking us to do chores!"

Arawn waved a hand. "Come now, this last is an easy one. I simply want you to help me in the fields for the day. At dusk you will be free to go and can follow the sun as it slips back into the mortal world."

Belis slipped her hand into mine.

"One final day in Annwn?" she whispered into my ear. I met her eyes and decided to stop complaining. Arawn tossed a basket towards us and Belis caught it in the air without turning around. I felt a smile tugging at my lips.

"Fine. One more day."

"Excellent." Arawn stuck his shovel into the earth and pointed to a field of trees behind him. "See that orchard? The fruit is ready to harvest. I'll come for you when the birds begin to roost."

I narrowed my eyes at him. "No more brambles."

He smiled. "No blackberries. Just apples and pears. Fill up the barrels at the base of the trees. I promised it was an easy one."

Belis tugged at my hand and we wandered over to the orchard. Wide oak barrels were scattered on the ground, next to neat wooden ladders. The trees groaned with golden apples, rosy pears, each one ripe and ready to eat. Belis picked up a ladder and leaned it against the nearest trunk so that I could climb and reach out for the fruit. I dropped each one down to her and she caught them easily, transferring them to the barrels once she had an armful.

It wasn't hard, climbing up and down the ladder and swinging through the branches, but it was satisfying. I found I enjoyed the rhythm of the work, enjoyed labouring beside Belis. This could be a life that made me happy, I thought, and the realisation made me quick, raining apples and pears down on my beloved until she begged, laughing, for me to slow down.

We had cleared the whole orchard by late afternoon and sat down against a tree, trading bites of an apple.

"We should have an orchard," I said, swallowing my mouthful. "Wherever we end up. We could sell the fruit or pickle it for winter."

"I don't think you can pickle fruit," Belis said. "You have to dry it or store it in a cellar." I waved a hand at her.

"Whatever it is. I'm sure you can work it out. You and Cati."

"What will you be doing while I'm drying fruit?" I heard the smile in her voice.

"I'll be clearing the land or minding the flocks. I trained the hounds, I can train some sheepdogs easily enough."

"You have a very romantic view of farm labour, my love," Belis said, snatching the apple back from my waving hand.

"Or we can go and live in a town and keep a shop. I know all the goblin traders. We can sell fae crafts. We'll go north, keep fifty miles between us and the Roman frontiers. There's plenty of redheads up there, you'll blend right in. Everything will work out."

Belis was silent for a moment. I shifted around to look at her. "What is it?"

Her eyes were downcast.

"Do you think Cati will want to stay? After she finds out what I did to her?" I reached out to cup her cheek.

"Would you forgive her if it was the other way round?"

"Of course. She's my sister."

I smiled. "Then I'm sure she will. It might take a while but we have our whole lives ahead of us."

"I can't regret everything I did," Belis said, raising her eyes to meet mine. "After all, it brought me to you."

I kissed her then, until the birds began to sing their evening melodies and I heard the faint crunch of footsteps.

Arawn was striding down towards us, something white gleaming in his hands. He smiled as we scrambled to our feet and nodded at the barrels of packed fruit.

"Good work. I deem your side of the bargain has been completed. Now for mine."

He held out the thing he was holding. It was a white shell, a whelk, the outside all knobbed and pointed, the inside a gleaming coral. It was strung on a long strand of scarlet thread.

"As agreed, your sister's soul. I have trapped her spirit within this shell. It still yearns to come home to Annwn, so you must reach her body before the tenth day dawns. The matrix of the shell will not hold her longer than that. Place the opening in her mouth and blow.

"You may recognise the thread. Spun from flax harvested from land you cleared with your own blood. It will not break nor be removed from your neck unless you wish it and while you wear it no mortal blade shall harm you. A little reminder of your time here."

Belis slipped the pendant over her head, hanging it neatly around her neck, the shell resting above her heart.

Arawn extended a hand to each of us.

"Come, I will *rush* you back to Caer Sidi. It will soon be night here which means the sun is rising on the outer lands."

I gripped his arm and for a final time felt the sickening whoosh of the land moving around us. Arawn stopped at the foot of the castle steps, the grey light of the evening hiding the expression on his face.

"Farewell, Mallt Y Nos," he said, "until we meet again."

He bowed to Belis. "Lady Beliscena." Then he turned and strode back down the road. Alone again, I looked over at Belis. I took her hand and squeezed it.

"Come," I said, "we're finished with the dead."

She glanced down and smiled at me. "The living world is waiting."

The sea was choppy, the whitecaps bright against the bottle-green sea. I stood on the edge of the cliffs and laughed with delight to feel the cold wind on my skin. Belis stepped up next to me and we screamed into the breeze, whooping and jumping up and down with our success.

By some miracle the boat was still there, bobbing in the swell, the rope glittering with salt crystals. Belis climbed down to it and then came back to help me. We bailed out seawater with our hands then cast off, Belis rowing with the oars while I punted us away from the rocks with her spear.

We decided not to head back to the beach we had left from, reasoning there was no one to return the boat to. Instead, we took the direct route and rowed due east. The winds were with us and the current carried us all the way back to the coast. We landed the boat on a stony shore, pulling it up away from the pebbles to hide our passage.

The woods went right down to the edge of the beach so once we had hidden the boat beneath a pile of leaves we began heading east. The trees were bright with birdsong and the brush was alive with rabbits. We made good time and decided to camp early for the night, Belis pulling me to the ground in a small clearing, to make love in a cloud of wildflowers.

She left me there to hunt, returning an hour or so later, a brace of rabbits swinging from her belt. I rose to kiss her but she insisted on dressing her kill and spitting it over a quickly built fire before she would let me distract her. We paused to eat, tearing off strips of roasted meat, drizzling fat down our chins.

I finished my portion and took a swig of fresh water. Beside me Belis was still chomping her way through a rabbit leg. She met my eyes and I felt desire coil in my stomach. She put down the bone and was leaning towards me when a faint but definite pressure at my throat announced the presence of a knife and suddenly the wood was bright with blades.

# Chapter 18

The knife at my throat pressed against my skin, cutting a thin line of burning heat into my flesh. I shrank back, reversing into a mountain of armoured flesh. A hand grabbed at my hair, jerking my chin up to expose my throat. The blade gleamed in the corner of my vision and I felt my mouth go dry.

I flicked my eyes over to where Belis was sitting. A man towered over her, pressing a notched sword into the base of her thigh. Plated armour gleamed on his chest and the coat that swung from his shoulders was tattered and stained but unmistakeably red. Romans. The Romans had found us.

"Steady now," Belis said in Latin, raising her arms slowly. "We're just travellers. We want no trouble."

"You're out of luck today, then," spat a voice behind me, causing the knife at my throat to dig back into the skin. A figure stepped into the centre of the clearing, kicking out the ashes of the fire. He spat in the dirt then lifted his hands to his helmet, undoing the leather strap and taking off the shining steel. I recognised the dark hair, the hawkish nose, the dead eyes. Centurion Croser had found us.

"I know your face. I've dreamed of it every night since word came to the legion of what you'd done to Camulodunum," he said, the harsh Latin syllables of the words digging into my ears like thorns. "You've grown careless, little princess. Did you think we would give up our quarry so easily? The men of the Fourteenth are better than that. We would have tracked you to the ends of the earth."

Belis froze, then flung herself backwards, bowling over the soldier behind her. She scrambled for the knife in her boot but a tall man with a smashed nose got it off her. The knife went spinning into the darkness and Belis lunged after it. Another Roman caught her hand and twisted her arm behind her back 'til she screamed. She managed to get her feet under her and swung out a kick at the man's knee. It crunched horribly and Belis broke free, reaching for the spear that she had left driven into the ground at the edge of the clearing. She snatched it from the earth, twirling it around so fast that the wood was a blur, driving the blunt end into the nearest Roman's stomach with a dull thud.

I lunged forward to go to her but the blade at my neck pressed deeper, and I felt it bite at my skin. Blood trickled down to pool at the base of my collarbones and I slumped back before I could cut my own throat. Belis spun around until she was facing me and I saw her catch sight of the blood. Her face jerked in reflected pain and she yelled out.

"Drop your spear," hissed the centurion. "Drop it now or I'll bleed your friend like a pig."

"Don't listen to him, Belis, run!" I croaked, in Brittonic, unable to force much breath out. Belis froze, her eyes darting back and forth as she counted the paces between us. I knew she wouldn't make it.

She crouched, moving the spear in a steady arc. I felt the knife dig further into my throat.

Belis screamed in frustration then threw down the spear. The pressure receded and I gasped for breath.

"It's been a long time, Beliscena," the centurion said, a ripple of pleasure passing over his expression at Belis's cries. "I should have killed you years ago, should have told the governor to lay waste to your entire family. How bitterly I regret that now."

He leaned close to her, sliding a knife from his belt and tracing it over the skin of her face. "I could cut your throat now, but

Romans are not savages, we are not slaves to our base urges. I am ordered to bring you back alive and I do my duty. Shackle and blindfold her."

The rest of the squad emerged from the woods, over a dozen men. Two of them threw a rough hessian bag over Belis's head and yanked her arms up, binding them tightly with rope. She wriggled back, biting and kicking. One of them punched her head and she flopped forward limply.

"Belis," I yelled, driving myself back onto the knife. The man holding me dragged me back by my hair.

One of the Romans picked up Belis's spear, weighing it in both hands. He raised one knee as if to break the shaft over it.

"Stop that," Croser said, cuffing the man on the ear. "Look at the engraving, the ivory grip. Damn thing's worth more than you are. The legate will be wanting that to send back to Rome. I have to do all the bloody thinking around here. You can carry that back to camp."

"What of this one?" asked the man behind me. His voice was deep, familiar. I remembered hearing it back in the Cotswolds, what felt like a thousand years ago. "She's a bit skinny but I'll warrant she'd fetch a couple hundred denarii at least. Once that's split up it'd make a nice little bonus for the men. It's been a long hunt and there's still a journey back."

Croser glanced at me, his eyes flicking over my face, dismissing me instantly.

"We've no time for distractions, Terrasidius. Kill her quick and leave her body for the foxes. We ride for Londinium immediately."

Terrasidius sighed and removed the knife. He dragged my head back until I could see the stars above the clearing, glittering in the night sky. I was too stunned to fight. All I could think of was that it had been less than a day since we had left Annwn, that I would be seeing Arawn so soon.

Belis shrieked and I could hear her throwing herself around, hear the sound of blows and kicks landing. I felt tears trickling down my cheeks at her pain.

"No, no, do not touch her!" she cried.

I looked back and my eyes met those of the man who would kill me. They were a bright blue and surprisingly soft.

"If you've any last prayers to make, little Briton," he said, "now would be the time."

"Get on with it, Terrasidius," said the centurion, gruffly.

My mind spiralled. I thought of calling the high fae, of cursing the Romans for rabid dogs, of simply screaming at the sky. In the end I could only think of one final word.

"Belis," I whispered. Terrasidius nodded and raised his sword.

"Won't hurt but a moment," he said. I thought to close my eyes, but the world around me was so bright, so colourful, I wanted every last moment of this life.

"Wait!" shouted Belis. "My sister, my sister is alive!"

"Hold," barked the centurion. Terrasidius paused, firelight playing off the blade of his sword.

His hand relaxed and I took a shuddering gasp of air.

"What do you mean? The two of you were seen staggering from the battlefield with your mother. One of the daughters was seen to be grievously injured. You're clearly alive and well and if I know anything about your mother I'd say she took poison rather than risk capture. She may have been a raging barbarian bitch but she never lacked for spirit."

He paused to spit into the dirt again. "But if you're not injured then that means your sister was, and a wound like that, she wouldn't have lasted the night. She's dead. And you're full of shit." The centurion's tone was sharp.

"She lives, I swear it. I swear it by my mother's spear." There was a muffled sound and then Belis spoke again, more clearly now. I craned my neck to see her. They'd taken the bag off but there was a bruise swelling on her cheek. I felt a wave of hate almost choke me – how dare they touch her.

Belis kept speaking, babbling the words out. "She survived the injury but couldn't travel. I left to try and draw you away from her. Sympathisers from the Atrebates are guarding her, south of the Chalk. Only I know where. It's a place that can only be found by our people, and since you've killed almost all of them I'm your only hope."

Croser crouched down, levering her chin up with his knife. "Why are you telling me this now?"

Belis stared back at him, rage burning in her eyes. "I will take you there, if you let my companion live."

Silence filled the clearing. The Romans glanced at each other. I wondered if they would believe the half-truth.

"You would sell your sister, betray the blood of your blood for this?" the centurion asked, stinging contempt audible in his voice.

"I would. But she must live, live and go free. Let her go now and I will lead you to where my sister hides. You would return to the legion with both the Iceni girls, eradicating any last whisper of rebellion for generations."

Croser laughed. "I'm not a total idiot, girl. I let her go now and you'll suddenly lose all memory of this secret place." He snorted. "You're lying. Kill her!"

"No, wait!" Belis wrenched herself forward, blocking him as he turned away. "Keep her for now. Keep her alive and I'll take you there, take us both, then when you find my sister you'll let my friend go free."

Terrasidius's eyes flicked to his commander, the sword hovering in the air above me. I felt the moment hanging between life and death.

"Done," the centurion snapped. "But if you're lying to me . . ."

"I swear I will lead you to where my sister is," Belis said. She stared at Croser, barely blinking. "Swear you will keep your promise. Vow by the Eagle of the Fourteenth."

"I swear by the Eagle and by the legions that if you lead me to the capture of your sister I will release this girl, alive and reasonably unharmed." The centurion paused and ground his teeth. He leaned forward. "But if you betray me, I will flay her alive before your eyes and make a cloak of her skin for you to wear as you are dragged back to Rome."

Terrasidius let go of my hair and I fell forward, scrabbling in the dirt. I looked up and saw Belis, tears streaming down her face. She tried to reach for me but her wrists were too tightly bound. I crawled forward but someone grabbed the back of my tunic and hauled me up onto my feet. I swayed, suddenly weak from the blood loss and feeling the adrenaline drain from my body. Strong hands steadied me and forced a waterskin into my mouth. I drank greedily. My own hands were tied in front of me, the coarse rope twisting into my flesh. I winced at the pain.

"Behave yourself today and perhaps I'll loosen them a little tomorrow," said Terrasidius. "Once you've proved yourself more trustworthy. You understand me, you speak Latin?"

I nodded. He sighed. "You really would have sold for a good price then. Pity that the commander never breaks his word."

He poured water onto a rag and cleaned the worst of the blood from my neck then wiped down his sword before sheathing it.

"Don't want you bleeding all over my cloak," he said, almost to himself.

I twisted around to look for Belis, desperate to meet her eyes if only for a moment. If I could at least see her, to know if she had a plan or if she had just said anything she could think of to help me. The bag had been shoved back onto her head and Centurion Croser was checking her shackles, tightening them until she hissed in pain. He said something I couldn't hear and a soldier bent to tug off her boots, while another searched her for weapons. I saw the legionary tug at the cord around her neck and felt a sudden rush of panic. The thread held and the man shrugged and dropped it, the whelk shell settling back next to her skin.

Terrasidius left me to shout instructions to the other Romans. They scattered back into the woods, returning with horses, sturdy hill ponies. The saddles and tack were plain and I guessed they had bought or commandeered the beasts. The Romans climbed into the saddle. Belis was boosted up behind one of the smaller men on a stamping black gelding, while Terrasidius pushed me onto a shaggy bay mare then swung up in front.

Croser launched himself into the saddle of a gleaming grey horse. He gripped the reins and swung her in a circle, inspecting the line of troops. Many of the legionaries looked uncomfortable on horseback and I wondered how many of them had ridden before. Maybe there was an advantage to be taken. If I could just get my hands loose then I could try to free Belis. I was sure she could outride most of the Romans, especially after they had spent a few days awkwardly in the saddle.

Satisfied with his review, the centurion kicked in his heels and moved to the front of the pack, tucking his knife into a pocket on the saddle.

He whistled and the men stopped grumbling to each other and turned to look at him.

"There's a week's hard riding between us and Londinium. We have lingered in these woods too long and I am sure you are eager to be back in what counts for civilisation on this miserable clod of an island."

There was a general grumble of agreement. Croser paused for them to settle down.

"We'll go swift and steady, changing horses rather than resting them. I'll brook no delays. Anyone who falls behind is left behind, to the tender mercies of the local savages. Either of our prisoners tries to escape I want you to cut them down. I'd rather come back with bloody hands than empty ones. One final push, lads, and we'll be done with this and there'll be a fine bonus waiting at camp along with a round of wine on me!"

A ragged cheer went up through the legionaries and the centurion dug his heels in, leading us into the dark of the trees.

Chapter 19

Raindrops stung my face as we rode through the storm. I huddled closer to the wool-covered bulk of Terrasidius's back, trying to keep as much of him as possible between me and the oncoming sleet. Our horse slipped, hooves sliding into the sucking mud of the field we were riding through. The Roman cursed under his breath, fighting to keep his seat. I clung to his sodden cloak with my hands, the ties stopping me from getting a secure hold. Terrasidius urged the horse forward, breaking into a canter to get free of the mire. I was jostled back and forth, feeling more bruises blooming along my legs.

We had been riding for days, stopping only to sleep. Croser had called a halt three times to change horses, first at a tiny fishing village where the headman had come out to trade, and twice at Roman camps. I suspected the centurion was keeping the identity of his prize hidden. He showed no inclination to talk with the camp guards, thrusting a battered scroll sealed with a gob of red wax at them and sending them running to fetch fresh mounts. The village headman had asked no questions either, taking care not to peer too closely at the legionaries and scurrying back into the houses with the lathered horses we had given him alongside a half-sestertius. I had debated screaming for help but Croser had positioned two guards either side of me during the changeover and their hands never strayed from their sword belts. Probably for the best – even if the villagers had been inclined to help us the Romans would have cut through them like a blade through water. I didn't consider causing trouble at the camps.

When we stopped to rest the centurion positioned half the troops on watch all night, forming an impenetrable wall of swords between us and freedom. The horses were hobbled before we were even lifted from the saddle and dumped on the ground. Sleep was almost impossible the first night, until Terrasidius insisted the men needed a fire to keep them from freezing. I managed to shuffle close enough to the heat to flush some feeling back into my fingers and ears. Better still, I could glimpse Belis through the glowing flames where she lay on the opposite side of the camp. The Romans kept the bag on her head while we were riding but took it off in camp so that she could eat whatever hardtack they threw to us. I curled up to gnaw on the biscuit and stare over at Belis. If we tried to speak one of the legionaries would shut us up with a kick but they couldn't stop us looking at each other.

Her face was still bruised but she was no less beautiful to me. I wanted to reach out and cup her cheek, to hold her so tight the Romans couldn't tear us apart. She lay and smiled back at me, and I felt new strength in my chest. There had to be a way out of here. I knew this would not be the end for us. I wondered what her plan was, or if she had thrown down her sister's name in desperation, just to save my life. I knew whatever the cost to us that we could not lead the Romans to Cati, knew that was Belis's and therefore my first priority. She had told Croser to go around the southern tip of the Chalk. We would be passing near Cati if not stopping. If we had a moment to get free, we had a chance of reaching her.

The horse beneath me stumbled again, this time going down onto its knees in the mud. Terrasidius hissed in frustration and slipped to the ground, leading the animal by the bridle through the sludge. I shuffled forward in the saddle, trying to get into a position where I might take control of the horse. We had been riding near the end of the column; Belis and her guard were ahead of us, close to the centurion. Several legionaries were between us. I measured the distance, wondering if I could lean down to yank a sword from Terrasidius's belt before he realised what was happening and barrel my way through to Belis. It was unlikely that I'd be able to kill him quickly or quietly enough to make it. What else then? Should I ride off into the night, breaking free to come back and make an attack later? That seemed like a better option. I considered it, weighing the choices in my mind. The horse clambered back to its feet and skipped forward, momentarily wrenching the reins from Terrasidius's hands. I dived for the reins, missed, and fell from the saddle into the mud at the legionary's hobnailed boots. He peered down at me.

"I shall assume that was not an escape attempt," he said, in Latin, "because if it was, I'd have to skin you alive and that sounds like a bitch of a job in this rain. But if you do it again then I'll make the effort. Understand me?"

I scowled up at him through the mizzle and splattered my way to my feet. He smirked at me and clicked his tongue to the horse, which wandered back towards us. In a moment we were back in the saddle and had caught up with the rest of the column and the opportunity was gone.

I wanted desperately to speak to Belis. I doubted the soldiers spoke much Brittonic but we were never close enough to talk, much less whisper to each other. Even when I had tried to call out to her in Latin the centurion had ridden back to warn me against it. I had to know if Belis had a plan, if there was anything I needed to do. This was the worst of it, worse than the miserable weather, the bumps and bruises from riding and the constant chafing of the rope against my skin. I was truly helpless.

The miles between us and Watling Street were ticking away faster now as we drew closer to the heart of Roman-occupied Britain, the roads improving every day. I went over the route in my head, calling up memories from my travels as the Nightshade. Our path would not take us near enough to any possible allies, no Greenteeth pond or goblin stronghold to lead the Romans to. I remembered the wight we had stumbled into on the journey to Annwn and cursed it again. Now was just the time an attack from some undead creature would be helpful. A wight or a lich could provide just the distraction we needed and I wouldn't even begrudge it the meal of man flesh, but nothing lurched out of the woods or crawled from the streams as we passed.

We rode on, crossing the Severn at Glevum. It took three trips to carry the whole troop across. I had hoped to end up on the same leg as Belis but Terrasidius and I went across first with another two guards and the horses. By the time Belis was brought over with the last batch we were already mounted and ready to go.

From Glevum we joined the half-built Via Akeman, which curved north of the Chalk. The granite cobbles glistened wetly in the early winter rain. Riding on the road was still more uncomfortable and we were making better time now the horses didn't have to fight for every step. Croser kept the men going without break, eating up the miles.

At dusk on the third day the road had disintegrated into loose cobbles and potholes. We had slowed to a trudge, the horses carefully picking their way through the rubble. I felt like my mind had lost its structure, too. I slumped in the saddle, drifting through thoughts of Annwn. To the right of the road rough limestone cliffs rose up, pale beige in the rain. The horse in front of us stumbled, breaking the mist of my thoughts. For a moment I thought she would go down but she found her footing, shaking her mane back with exhaustion. Her rider patted her neck approvingly then swore under his breath. Terrasidius urged our horse forward, passing the other Romans up to where the centurion led the squad.

"Sir, the horses are failing, the men, too. We should make proper camp for the night," he called.

"We press on, Terrasidius, we have been gone too long from

the legion," Croser replied, not bothering to turn his gaze from the path ahead.

"We've been riding nonstop for three days already, there's three days' hard ride still ahead of us. The women are flagging. If you want a live captive to present to the legate we should get out of the rain."

The centurion ignored him, staring straight ahead. Terrasidius cursed then steered his horse next to the other man's, so close that my leg brushed the red cloak on his back. I saw a knife tucked into his saddle, the hilt just peeping beneath the leather of his seat. I could reach out and take it, if I only dared. I glanced up at the sergeant, who was still talking.

"Brother, how long have we fought together? How far have we marched together? I know your mind is fixed on the arrival but mine must consider the journey." He clapped a hand on the centurion's shoulder. "There may be a fight if the Atrebates guarding the younger girl refuse to give her up. We will do best to arrive rested and ready. Let us stop for a few hours at least. If we should be waylaid now I do not like our chances. There's a cave near here, I remember it from the journey out. We can shelter there. This rain will last the night; we can dry off a little and ride with the dawn."

I saw the centurion's shoulders tense then sag. For a few moments he was distracted by his friend. I seized my chance and moved forward, pretending to huddle closer to the sergeant, and reached out with one hand to the centurion's horse. In one quick movement I grabbed the knife from its sheath and slid it into my boot. I tried to keep my body as relaxed as possible, worried that Terrasidius would feel the tension in me, but my heart was thundering. Croser glanced back and for a moment I thought he had felt my theft, but his eyes were looking over the other Romans.

"Very well," he said hoarsely, "a few hours only."

Terrasidius nodded and bellowed out to the other men. We rode up the road a little further, peering through the gloaming rain. I was so tired, the fatigue somehow even more unbearable now that rest was near. A shout went up from the back of the column and I turned to see a soldier dismounting and hurrying towards the cliffs. The rain had veiled him from my sight within a moment but he hurried back into view and waved. Terrasidius turned his horse back towards him and within a few minutes the promised cave yawned before us.

The centurion remained in the saddle while Terrasidius dismounted and ordered everyone in. A fire was kindled and watches were posted. The cave mouth was only a few yards across so a legionary was placed at each side. I was too stiff to move properly and with my hands still tied I didn't fancy my chances of reaching the ground without falling. Terrasidius looked back around and saw me still sitting in the saddle. He padded over and lifted me down.

"Make a space at the fire, lads, this one's cold as the Styx."

He pushed me gently towards the hearth and the soldiers obligingly moved apart. Opposite me Belis was seated beside the tall man she'd ridden with. I met her eyes, gleaming green and silver in the firelight. She looked as bedraggled as a drowned rat but there was strength in her gaze and it warmed me as much as the fire. I smiled quickly then dropped my head. Under the cover of my cloak I wound my hand down to touch the outline of the blade in my boot.

There was little chatter around the fire that night; the soldiers ate their hardtack and drifted to the sides of the cave to sleep. Croser sat by the entrance, staring out into the night. He hadn't noticed the loss of his dagger yet. He barely had the energy to lift his waterskin to his mouth. I watched out of the corner of my eye as he drooped forward. Terrasidius was already snoring away. I had spent enough nights beside him now that I could tell when he was in deep sleep. I glanced around the cave. The only ones left awake now were the two sentries, sitting just in from the mouth of the cave. I met Belis's eyes again, trying to communicate with her. She frowned back at me and I mouthed the word "soon". She nodded, almost imperceptibly.

I lay down, huddled against the side of the cave, and half slid out the knife. I looped the rope binding my hands over it, grinding the cord against the blade. True to his word Terrasidius had loosened the shackles the first night we had stopped. I had spent every waking moment since then trying to break free. Now with a few cuts I was loose. I stayed still for a moment then tucked the knife back up my sleeve and rolled over, as if in sleep. I breathed deeply, counting twenty inhales and exhales. On the twenty-first breath I fluttered my eyelashes half open, darting a look around the room. Everyone seemed to be as they were, Terrasidius still snoring. Only the centurion had moved, slumped to the floor now.

I considered my next move, whether to attack the sentries or move to untie Belis. Neither seemed to have much chance of success. I didn't like my odds against both sentries at once so I decided to move towards Belis. I shifted myself over until I was flat on my stomach, my hands hidden beneath me. I pulled my toes underneath and kicked myself forwards, moving perhaps an inch. I looked around again. The soldiers were still asleep. Belis had shuffled upright and was looking directly at me. I pushed with my toes again, creeping across the floor. Progress was agonisingly slow, but it was quiet. Not a single legionary so much as twitched.

I finally got close enough for Belis to lean forward and snatch the knife from me. She was faster than me, even with the tightened rope. In a moment she was free, crouching down beside me. We had a silent argument over who got to keep the knife until Belis solved the problem by lifting a sword from the nearest soldier. She mimed us splitting up and sneaking up on the sentries with a vicious swipe of the knife. I rolled my eyes and took the knife from her and shuffled back across the cave. When I had made it back to the opposite wall I met Belis's eyes and we began sliding towards the cave mouth.

I gripped the knife in my hand, feeling the soft leather of the hilt against my palm. The soldier on my side of the cave had taken his helmet off and was sitting with his head tilted back, looking up at the rain as it fell. He looked young, maybe nineteen years old. I thought about the blade sinking into his throat, remembering the feeling of the knife at my neck only a few days ago. I wondered if he had a family back in Rome, if he'd lost friends in the rebellion. What had brought him here to this island at the edge of the world.

Belis caught my eye and held up three fingers. I chewed on my lower lip for a moment then nodded. She lowered one finger, then another. On the third beat I reached around and dragged the dagger across the sentry's throat. The blade cut deep, severing the windpipe before the man could scream. Hot blood, aerated from the lungs, bubbled over my fingers. I caught him as he fell forwards, propping him up against the rock. I felt the life go out of him and arranged his cloak to cover the worst of the injury. I stood up, looking down at the man I had murdered. Thousands of years of looking over the bodies of the dead should have made it easier but the weight of responsibility hung heavy around my neck. For the first time in weeks I wished for my powers back, to send his soul on his way to wherever it needed to go.

Belis laid a hand on my shoulder. I swallowed hard then looked back. Her own sentry was still; only a faint trickle of blood dribbling towards the mud outside the cave gave any indication of his death. Belis stepped out into the rain, placing each foot carefully. The horses had been hobbled under a stand of trees nearby. I cast a final look into the cave and hurried out towards them.

Between us we made short work of the hobbles, sliding off the saddles and slapping the horses' withers until they vanished into the night. They wouldn't wander far but it should slow down our pursuit a little. And there would be a pursuit, I realised. We had just made our capture a personal vendetta against the entire squad.

Two horses were left, one black, one brown. Belis linked her fingers to boost me into the saddle of the bay.

"Can you keep up alone or should we share?" she whispered, the first words we had spoken in almost a week.

"I can manage."

Belis nodded and swung herself onto the black horse. She kicked in her heels and we vanished into the rain and the darkness leaving fourteen men sleeping in the warmth of the cave and two cooling corpses in the mud.

Chapter 20

We rode hard, heading east beside the half-constructed road until it became sound enough to ride on. Belis reined in her horse as we clattered onto the cobbles.

"We'll keep going for another mile, just long enough so it won't be immediately obvious where we leave the road," she called through the rain. "Then we'll cut south and through the woods."

I looked back to where the horses had left a thick trail of muddy hoofprints and nodded. Belis leaned over and cupped my cheeks with rough hands. She kissed me hard and I felt the saddle sores and cold of the rain fade away.

"I'm so sorry, Mallt, I should have been more careful when we landed," she whispered, resting her forehead against mine. Her hand dropped to the cut on my neck, tracing the raised scar. "You could have been killed."

"But I wasn't." I smiled at her. "We've survived worse than Romans together, I wasn't going to let some damn fool legionary take me away from you. Come, let's go, there will be time to talk when we're out of danger." I kissed her again and then gave my horse its head.

As I rode, I felt the blood of the man I had killed congealing beneath my fingernails. I wondered if he had a wife who loved him the way I loved Belis. I wondered if his soul would find its way back, or if it would linger in the cave forever. I realised it was no longer my responsibility to worry about him. I wasn't the Nightshade any more. The duties of my old life were far behind me. The only thing that mattered now was the woman ahead of me, red hair streaming behind her as she rode.

We covered the distance in good time, crossing a stream just over a mile from where we had met the road. Belis turned to the south, leading her horse up the bed of the stream until our path was hidden from the road by thick forest. From there we slowed to a walk, climbing the lower slopes of the Chalk. The night was nearly done and though we couldn't see the sun rising through the thick canopy of leaves, the light was getting paler. I whistled to Belis and she stopped to let me catch up.

"Do you want to keep going through the day?" I asked, keeping my voice low.

"I think we must; the Romans certainly will. I'm worried for the horses, though, they've barely rested for days. If they drop dead we'll have less chance on foot."

She stroked the neck of her mount.

"Every tactical lesson I ever took is telling me to go to ground, vanish into the wilderness while we have the chance." Her hand went to the shell at her throat. "If we only had more time. I must get to Cati as soon as I can, but we might have better odds if we split up."

She looked over at me and I understood the offer she was making. I took no offence at the suggestion but my mind was set.

"Together 'til the end," I said. Her face wobbled and I reached out to squeeze her hand. She raised it to her lips and pressed a quick kiss on my knuckles. Then she was focused again, the warrior taking charge.

"I don't know these lands well. What's the best path to take?"

I considered the question, running through the map inside my head.

"We're less than a day's ride from Cati's glade. Croser knows roughly where we're headed so there's not much point in feinting. Our best hope is to keep as far ahead of them as possible.

With the time it will take to catch their horses and find our track we might make it. Their horses can't be any less tired than ours."

Belis nodded. "If I were Croser I'd split my forces, send one group north, in case we were lying about Cati. If it comes to a fight we'll have a better chance against half the troop."

She gestured ahead of us. "You should lead, you know the way." She grabbed my arm as I went to pass her. "I love you, be careful."

We picked our way on, following the valley of the Bulbourne as it cut through the Chalk. I looked up at the steep sides of the hills on either side, marvelling at how much I had changed since the last time I had been here on the third day of my new human life. I could almost see myself staggering up the hill, feet covered in blisters, sweating and grumbling. I remembered Belis as she had been then, silent and sick at heart. I smiled to myself and urged my mount on.

The horses were blowing hard by the time we turned back to the east, beginning to froth at the mouth. The valley was deserted, and the rain had kept any villagers inside and away from our path. I was glad of it, wanted no eyes to watch our route and betray us to our trackers. Still better, by early afternoon the rain had disintegrated into a fine mist that covered us in a grey blanket of invisibility, making it impossible to see or be seen.

The horses were close to collapse so I slid down from the saddle to lead them by hand. The mud sucked at my boots as I struggled onwards and almost stumbled. Ahead of us was the little shepherd's hut where we had passed our first night together. Belis fetched the bucket from inside and filled it quickly from the well while I held the horses.

"How long from here?" she asked, holding the bucket up to let her horse drink.

"Hard to be precise in this mizzle but I'd say ten more miles at least. We should be faster going back but I don't want the horses to trip on the slope."

Belis sighed, looking around at the fog. "I know we should make the most of this weather but if we keep going much longer the horses won't make it. I don't know how Cati will be once we revive her but I wouldn't bet much she'll be well enough to walk a hundred miles north. We need to keep at least one of the horses alive."

"We'll have to stop and start again after nightfall," I said.

Belis chewed on her lip, torn. I could guess what she was thinking. There was no way to guarantee our success; we could just as easily be caught on the road as resting. Worse than that, if the Romans found us for a third time there would be no mercy. They would slit my throat and break Belis's legs rather than risk her running again. Cati would lie in her glade until her body eventually wasted away.

"We'll stay here for now," she said eventually. "But if the mist rises we'll have to leave."

"Agreed," I said. Belis unsaddled the horses then crawled into the hut. I shuffled next to her, burying my head in the crook of her arm.

"Get a little sleep," she said. "I'll wake you if the rain stops."

I snatched some rest, drifting in and out of consciousness. When Belis finally nudged me awake it was already dark.

"Come on, the horses are rested. It's time to go."

I rubbed sleep from my eyes and stood up. The mist had thinned a little, allowing me to see a dozen or so yards in any direction. Belis was already tacking up the horses, checking the fit on the girths. The beasts looked better. The few hours' rest had been a good decision.

I led my horse over to the well and climbed up onto the rim to use it as a mounting post. The bay whiffled at me hopefully and I showed him my palms.

"No treats, I'm afraid. Once we're out of danger I'll buy you a sackful of carrots, I promise."

The gelding snorted and tossed his head as I swung into the saddle. Belis finished with her horse then paused, turning back to me.

"Mallt," she looked worried, "maybe we should separate. You could ride south, join up with one of your friends. The Romans aren't interested in you and as long as you stay with me you'll be in danger. We could make a plan to meet somewhere, in the north perhaps." Her hand went to the whelk shell that hung around her neck.

"I want to be with you, that's the safest place for me," I said, leaning down to kiss her. Belis returned my kiss but I could feel the tension inside her. "It will be all right, beloved, I promise. We've been through worse."

She sighed. "I'm scared I can't keep both you and Cati safe. Maybe I should give you the shell and go back to the Romans."

I shuddered at the thought and shook her shoulders. "That's a terrible idea. I'm not leaving you, Belis, as long as I live. I've fought for you. I've killed for you. I'm staying. Stop moping and get on your horse. With luck we'll be there by daybreak."

She found a half-smile for me and did as I said. I watched as she swung herself into the saddle, still graceful despite the lack of sleep. I could feel the nerves coming off her and I wanted to say more but we were running out of time.

We made good progress, rounding the eastern point of the Chalk sometime after midnight. From there Belis took the lead, winding her way easily through the gnarled trunks of oaks and elms even in the inky black of the night. When dawn broke I recognised the shape of the land again and a moment later we were there at the edge of the clearing.

Belis jumped down from the saddle, pausing to tie her horse's reins to a tree at the edge of the glade. I followed, then stepped out into the space. Boudica's body had been worried by scavengers. Belis bowed to her mother's corpse, tears glittering on her cheeks. Then she turned to her sister.

Catrisca lay where we had left her, pale and still, long, straight red hair splayed across the grass like blood. Fallen leaves had drifted around her like petals so that she seemed to be the heart of a great flower. At her feet slept a mighty hound, white fur with red ears.

"Dormath," I whispered. He drowsed a little then opened one golden eye. I held out my arms to him and in a moment he was up and running towards me. He was stronger than me now and I toppled backwards, laughing as he covered my face with slobbery kisses, sniffling at the strange smells I carried from the road.

"Dormath, Dormath, shush," I spluttered, trying to hush his yelps and yips of delight. "I missed you too, boy. You've survived all right without me?"

I sat up and felt his sides. He didn't seem to have lost any weight and the clearing was scattered with rabbit bones. I climbed to my feet and he nipped at my hand to protest that I had stopped petting him.

"Ouch! Oh, give your poor mistress a minute."

He snorted in disgust and went to go and pester Belis. She was standing at Cati's side, still as her sister. Her left hand rested on the whelk shell at her neck, fingers twined in the red thread.

"Belis," I called, keeping my voice low. "Are you all right?"

She blinked suddenly and looked over at me, her fingers still twisting at the pendant. Then she shook herself and hurried forward. She crouched next to me and I reached out to take her hand. I could feel the hummingbird thrum of her pulse in her wrist.

"I know you're scared," I said, "but we have to hurry. The Romans are still hunting us. We need to move as quickly as we can."

She nodded and her fingers interlaced with mine.

"Can you help me? I'm shaking so much, I'm worried I'll drop the shell."

I picked up the whelk, lifting it from the soft skin of Belis's neck, and ran my fingers up the thin linen cord, looping it back over her head. Her long braid had become tangled with the necklace, so I held the shell in my hands while she reached back to unravel the knot. It was incongruously light for something that held the weight of a human soul, the weight of everything we'd fought and bled for over months. Dormath snapped at it hopefully and I pushed him away.

Belis finally unwound the cord from her hair and I handed her back the shell. She balanced it between two fingers, one on the siphon, one on the spire, holding it up to the light. When she spoke her voice was stronger. She was back in control.

"Thank you, Mallt. I think I'm ready now. Can you open her mouth? I need to breathe the soul back in."

I moved around to Catrisca's head, placing one hand on her forehead and one under her chin, tilting it back so that her lips opened. Her skin was stone-cold, but there were no signs of decay and her muscles moved easily beneath my fingers.

Belis crawled up beside me and stroked her sister's cheek.

"I'm so sorry, Cati," she whispered, "I'm here to make this right." A few tears slid down her cheek and I reached out to stroke the back of her hand.

"Whatever happens," I said, my voice thick with emotion, "I love you."

She gulped down her tears and angled the mouth of the shell against Cati's lips. She darted a look up at me and I nodded. Belis bent and blew gently into the spire of the whelk shell. My old eyes would have been able to see the strange corona of the soul, to trace it as it wound its way through the shell's maze-like interior into Cati's mouth, then sank into her chest. My human eyes couldn't sense this, could only see the final result when Cati's chest rose, like the first intake of breath when a swimmer breaks the surface.

Belis sat back, moving next to me. I took her hand and we waited together. The clearing was very quiet; even the birds had stopped singing. Belis was holding my hand tight, as a promise.

For a moment there was nothing but stillness in the glade. Then there was a choking sound and the last of the Iceni was the last no more. Cati retched, the force of the movement charging through her and wrenching her upright. Belis let go of my hand and flew across to her sister, enfolding her in her arms.

I hurried over to them. Catrisca was still coughing but the colour was rushing back into her cheeks. Tears were streaming down Belis's face.

"Cati, Cati, I'm so sorry. I'm so, so sorry. I will never be able to forgive myself."

Cati gasped, struggling for breath. I passed Belis a waterskin and she trickled a little water into her sister's mouth. The girl drank greedily, swilling out dust and the taste of death. When she had had enough she raised a shaky hand, looking up at Belis and me. I saw she had the same grey-green eyes as her sister though they were bloodshot and ringed with purple shadows.

"I dreamed I was dead, Belis," she croaked, "I dreamed I was alone, cut off from this world and the next, floating in the nothingness of the void. I called out for you, for mother and father, but you weren't there."

Belis cupped her sister's face. "You're never going to be alone again. I'm here, we're together now." She fished the shell pendant from her pocket, looping it around Cati's neck.

I stepped back, letting them have a moment to reunite. Dormath growled and I glanced down at him. He was staring into the forest, hackles raised.

Something shimmered in the darkness at the edge of the woods. I frowned and moved closer, peering through the gloom.

"Mallt, wait!" called Belis from behind me, her voice sudden and sharp. The shimmer moved forward and I realised my mistake too late. The rising light of the day glinted off the centurion's helmet as he stepped into the glade.

Chapter 21

The centurion moved forward, the sunshine flashing off his helmet illuminating every hair of the snow-white crest. Three soldiers appeared beside him, their shortswords drawn for battle.

"You've led us a merry chase," said the centurion, taking another stride forward, his eyes fixed on Belis. "And I see that you were not lying, if that red-headed chit there is indeed your sister. But it is over now, no more chances. The legate wanted you alive but he'll settle for your heads. After two escape attempts he will understand why I could not let you live." He smiled then, or tried to; grief and pain twisted his face until the expression was nothing more than a baring of teeth.

"I have prayed to the gods for strength to obey my orders, to deliver you alive. Now I see they have granted the prayer of my most secret heart." He drew his sword. "Vengeance. I will cut your hearts out and lay them on the altar of Mars to give thanks to him."

I started forward but one of the soldiers moved to meet me, grabbing my hand and pulling me back. I kicked at him, struggling in his grip, but he was a head taller than me and he held me fast. Dormath had vanished into the trees.

Belis leapt to her feet, her hand lifting the sword we had stolen.

"Mallt!" she called, looking frantically between me and her sister, still sitting on the ground behind her.

The centurion nodded to his men. "Stay where you are, these deaths belong to me. If they try to get past you, turn them back but don't injure them."

I could see the knuckles on his sword hand whiten and he whispered something I couldn't quite hear. I thought it might have been a woman's name. Then he charged.

Belis met the first blow, bringing her sword up to block his as it slashed down at her. She threw him back, turning all her weight behind the riposte. He snarled and stabbed at her again, short, quick motions that sent Belis stumbling backwards as she dodged.

I writhed in the soldier's arms, trying to catch him off guard. I almost got loose but he wound a fist in my hair and dragged me back. The pain made me yelp and Belis flinched, darting a look at me. The centurion moved in, taking advantage of the distraction and sliding his sword right under her arm. She twisted at the last moment but hissed. When she danced free there was blood glittering on the Roman's sword and a slash in the fabric of her tunic.

There was a scream from behind me and I saw Dormath, fur sticky with blood, clamp his jaws around a legionary's throat. There was a crunch and the scream broke off. Dormath growled and leapt for the second man but he was warned now and my dog had to dodge his lance and shield.

"For my family," the centurion shouted, pressing his advantage. Belis stumbled backwards, tripped on something and went down. The centurion crouched on one knee, scraping his sword along hers until the blade bit into the skin of her face. Belis howled in pain and flung him off, using his weight to pull herself up. With another step forward she stabbed her own sword into his side.

The centurion clenched his teeth, bringing his sword back up to block her follow-up attack. Belis stepped back, blood covering the tip of her sword.

Catrisca had managed to clamber to her feet and stagger to Belis's side. She wiped the blood from her sister's face.

"Cati, go, run," Belis said to her, still keeping her eyes on the circling centurion. "Take one of the horses. I'll hold them off."

"I'm not leaving you again, sister, I've spent enough time cowering from these wolves," Cati said, drawing a long knife from her boot. "We stand together now."

The centurion charged. Belis met his sword with hers, leaving Cati to dash under his arm with her long knife.

The sisters fought together as if they were dancing, each seeming to anticipate the other's moves before they had made them. The centurion was driven back, pressed hard against the edge of the glade. Blood loss was beginning to slow him. The soldiers watching were shifting nervously.

"Sir," called one of them when Cati managed another cut to his leg, "should we join you?"

"Stand by, men," snapped the centurion, "I've not soldiered for thirty years to be brought down by a pair of barbarian wildcats."

As if heartened by his own words he straightened and began a blinding series of blows, raining them down against Belis and Cati. He drove a fist deep into the younger girl's stomach, knocking her to the floor. Her ankle gave a sickening crunch. She tried to get up but slid almost immediately back to the ground.

I twisted desperately against the soldier's hands but there was nothing I could do. I watched frantically as Belis tried to fight off the centurion, standing over her sister. I would have given anything to save her, to save them both.

I collapsed, sagging back against the soldier. He was unprepared and I almost slid from his grip. While he was pulling me back up I made a grab for his knife, driving it up through the meat of his forearm. He screamed and let me go. I dashed for the fighters. The centurion was bringing his sword down, Belis had hers raised, but she wasn't going to make it. I saw the path his blade would take, inexorably bound towards Belis's heart, and in that moment I found a little of my old speed. I threw myself forward, diving down beneath the moving sword. I gasped as I felt it pierce my chest, sliding through my ribcage and out the other side.

"No!" screamed Belis, finishing the arc of her own sword thrust in the centurion's throat. He sagged to the floor, clutching at his neck. There was blood everywhere, his and mine, swirling in the mud, soaking the dark earth.

Belis caught me around the waist, pulling me close. I could feel the metal of the blade grating against my ribs. Strangely, it didn't seem to hurt.

Cati grabbed her sister's shoulder.

"Bel, the other legionaries. We have to get to the horses now!" She pulled herself up, knife in one hand, the other leaning on her sister. "Come on!"

Belis cradled my head in her hands. "Mallt, why did you do it? I could have held him off!"

I smiled, feeling the life blood bubble at my lips. "It was only a little time we had together. I would have liked to be human with you a while longer."

Her tears dropped onto my face and her hands dug into my shoulders, willing my heart not to stop beating. I could hear the soldiers approaching. Above us Cati clenched her fist around the knife, ready to give the last of herself to protect her sister. I could hear Dormath snarling; the soldier who had grabbed me was now coming towards us. I kept my eyes open, wanting to see Belis as long as I could, wrapping my hand around the hilt of the centurion's sword.

Then I wrenched it from my chest. Blood poured out from my body, letting the last of my life go with it.

In death I felt my soul rise, detaching from the empty shell that had been my body. I stretched wide, hugging the whole world to my chest. I had not lost my powers, I realised, they had been hidden inside me all along. Belis's spell had trapped me in a human body but now I was free again. I was Mallt Y Nos, Mallt Nightshade, just as I had always been.

I felt myself sink back into my body, the wounds healing,

limbs lengthening and filling with new strength, with old strength. My eyes flickered open as my vision sharpened, bringing the scene into focus. My ears picked up the thrumming of four human heartbeats. I stepped out of my boots and stood proud on the floor of the glade.

I shimmered back into view, standing between the two sisters and the advancing legionaries. I was taller now, towering over them. I called the night wind to me and on it rode my hounds, the Cwn Annwn, baying and barking at the prospect of a chase. Dormath bounded from behind me, almost bowling my coalescing form over as he took his rightful place by my side.

The soldiers stopped short, terror blooming on their faces. I smiled at them, scenting their fear on the air.

"Run!" I hissed at them.

They did not hesitate, spinning like tops and sprinting back into the darkness. I watched them go, swallowed by the night. I watched them go and found I wished them no ill will. The dogs whined beside me but I hushed them. The Nightshade must have no quarrel with the living.

I could sense Belis behind me but found I couldn't bear to look at her just yet. I bent to embrace my dogs, finding a cwtch, a pat and a kind word for each of them. Dormath pushed his way to the front of the pack and I buried my face in his fur, letting go of the last of my human grief. When I could delay no longer, I turned. Belis was still sitting on the ground, hands stained with the blood that was all that remained of the mortal she had loved so tenderly. Cati had crouched beside her. As I stepped forward the younger girl held out her knife to block my path.

"We want no trouble, lady," she said, her voice trembling. I bent, batting her knife away as if it was a feather. I reached out to lift Belis's chin up, meeting those beautiful grey-green eyes.

"So we have finally kept our promises to each other, Princess Beliscena," I said.

"Mallt?" she said, her eyes full of wonder. "But how . . ."

"It seems the only thing keeping me from life was death."

I dropped my hand and straightened up. I still had business

to attend to. I stepped over to where the centurion was lying, choking on his own blood. I could feel the fury within him, and, beneath that, the fear and pain. I understood that better now, carrying the memories of the human feelings with me into my immortal body. I took his hand then laid my palm on his chest. He seemed so very small, just another man dying far from home.

"Time to let go, centurion," I said and I sank my hand into his chest, pulling out his soul.

His body stiffened and was still. The centurion's soul sat in the hollow of my hand, twisted and rent with months of grief. I raised it up to my lips, turning to the east.

"Go home, centurion. Your family waits for you on the banks of the Styx," I whispered, and blew. His soul tumbled away from me, like a leaf on the wind. I watched as it lifted above the trees and was lost from my view.

# Chapter 22

The firelight danced over the dogs' fur as they lay sprawled on the ground. In the centre of the circle of canines lay Belis and Cati, sleeping back-to-back. They had barely been apart since we had left the clearing and it brought joy to my heart to see. Cati was a sweet girl, and though I would have loved her anyway as Belis's sister, I was growing increasingly fond of her in her own right.

We were up on the hills to the east of Lindum, perhaps a day's walk from the little port I was leading them to. The horses had recovered from the desperate ride through the rain to the clearing, but we'd had to go slow, only covering a few miles a day. That had suited the Iceni girls, both battered from the fight, but the dogs were desperate for a good run. I hadn't minded the delay. It had taken me a while to readjust to my old form and I liked to walk beside Belis and Cati as they rode, talking and reminiscing. There had been many tears – Cati was still reckoning with her mother's death – but some laughter as well and I found the sound of Belis's voice just as sweet as I had through mortal ears.

Now that I was myself again I could hunt, so we ate well on roasted rabbit and partridge to supplement Belis's terrible stews. Cati even joined in as I teased her sister, giggling as Belis pretended to take offence. Best of all, restored to my strength, we could travel without fear. I led the way through the secret woods and paths I had learned through a thousand years of wandering. We stopped to bathe in hidden pools, to pray at long-forgotten holy sites and sleep in sacred groves. With the dogs to stand guard, Belis and I could slip away for a few hours while Cati slept. We didn't talk much, just held each other in the cool dark of the night.

I knew what she was thinking, that what had happened in the glade had split us apart forever, but I still held onto a tiny kernel of hope, the words I had whispered to the wind seven days ago. Tonight, with the dogs keeping guard over the two precious humans, it was time to chase that hope.

Belis snorted a little in her sleep and huddled deeper under her cloak. For a moment I wanted nothing more than to join her, curling my body around hers and winding a hand in her hair. I turned away; I had much to do tonight. I waded through the pile of dogs and traced her cheek with one hand, the freckled skin soft under my fingers. Then I leapt forward and set off along the spine of the wolds.

Winter had tightened its grip on the uplands and I knew that the air was bitter cold but I could no longer feel it as I once had. The physical memory of freezing blood, of a chill that dug its way into my bones so that I woke cloudy-breathed and shivering was already fading, leaving only the idea of discomfort. Further still was the remembrance of fatigue. Now reborn, I felt I could run forever, could ride the winds to the end of the island.

I slowed to a walk at the south of the wolds, beside a long, low mound of earth. I had been here when it was raised from the ground, to cover a king whose name I had forgotten centuries ago. Another lord now stood atop the barrow.

"Gwyn," I called out, striding up the slope in a few bounds.

The Lord of the Wild Hunt bowed his great antlered head towards me.

"Well met, Lady Nightshade, I have come alone, as you requested." His dark eyes glittered in the moonlight as he rose again. "It is unlike you to engage in intrigue. I have not seen you for months and you send a message on the wind to meet at this deserted heath. I'll wager there's a good story behind it."

"It is good to see you again. I have missed you."

Gwyn frowned at my words. I was not usually so plainspoken. I had forgotten the art of speaking with the fae, the constant verbal fencing. If the Hunt had been here they would have seen it as weakness to be exploited, but Gwyn was an old enough comrade to give me a little grace.

"Indeed it has been a while," I continued. "But I cannot tell you the tale yet. I come here to ask a favour."

"If it is in my power to grant," Gwyn spread his hands expansively, "and if you can pay for it, then it is yours."

"I want to turn a human into one of the high fae," I said, and as the words left my mouth I wondered if it was even possible. "Immortal, strong. Able to navigate the Wild Roads."

Gwyn's eyes widened and he laughed, the sound echoing around the hillside like distant thunder.

"Well, that is not what I was expecting you to say, Mallt. There is a better story here than I had thought! You've lost your heart to a mortal? I never thought that you of all the folk would do something so wonderfully foolish. Tell me their name."

"Her name is Belis," I whispered, and even her name brought icy tears to my eyes. Gwyn's smile dropped and he moved closer.

"Love's a terrible burden, Mallt," he said, laying a heavy hand on my shoulder. "Even for ones as strong as us. There is little I would not do for it, would burn the world to bloody ashes if I had to."

"Can you help me?" I asked.

Gwyn filtered through the charms and pendants that hung from his neck on chains of gold and silver. He picked one, snapping the chain as if it were a blade of grass, and held it out to me. It was a fishhook, carved from a splinter of bone. He rummaged in a pouch at his side and withdrew a tiny glass bottle before extending one arm.

"Cut my skin with the hook and catch a few drops of blood. If your girl drinks of it then she will become one of my people.

Immortal life, inhuman strength and speed. If she wants a place of her own she can try for the Hunt, or if you would rather keep her to yourself she can wander the wilds with you."

I looked at the bronze skin of his wrist and then back up at him.

"And the price?"

His lip curled. "You would pay anything, why stoop to bargain with me?" He shrugged his shoulders. "For this there is no price, no payment. This is not a favour or a bargain. I give it to you freely, by right of the years we have known each other."

I picked up the hook and he held up one finger.

"This thing, once done, cannot be undone. It will cut her off from the mortal world, both in life and death. The high fae are not humans and neither will she be."

"I understand." I paused. Gwyn looked as if he had more to say, but the words were not coming easily to him. "Anything else?"

"You know my nature, Mallt. You know what happens when one of the fae gives a gift or grants a wish. There is always a sting in the tail, a thorn on the rose. This is not a warning I would give a mortal. It is difficult for me to say, but you are an old comrade and you should know what you are getting."

I nodded and dug the hook into the flesh and pressed the lip of the bottle into the skin to catch the hot blood. When I was done Gwyn raised his wrist to his mouth and licked at the wound, sealing it shut.

"Come and see the Hunt soon, Mallt," he said. "Creiddylad misses you. It does not do well to walk always alone."

Gwyn stamped on the crest of the barrow and the ground split open beneath him. He waved a hand at me and walked into the earth, the scent of the Wild Roads lingering even after the soil had slid back into place.

Belis reined in her horse as we reached the path, the beast's hooves clattering on the cobblestones. Below us the murky brown sea stretched to the eastern horizon, strafed with thin lines of white waves.

"Wait here," she said, dismounting, her boots slapping on the stones of the road. "I'll go and try and find us passage."

"Let me," Cati said eagerly. "Please, it'll be safe enough."

Belis hesitated for a moment then nodded. We watched as her sister rode down the road to the fishing village. I sniffed the air, enjoying the taste of salt on my tongue. The glass bottle sat in my pocket, heavy as a menhir.

"Gods, I hope she doesn't find a captain to take us," said Belis suddenly. "Not today at least. Just one more day, please one more day."

I wrapped an arm around her waist and pulled her close. She leaned back against me, tucking her head under my chin. I thought of all the things we had been to each other, all that we could be. I wondered whether it was fair to ask her to stay with me. I was a goddess again now; we weren't supposed to be selfish. Maybe one last human act would be all right.

"I have an offer for you, Belis," I said, at last. She turned back to me, her hair wild around her shoulders. I tucked a curl behind her ear and tried for a smile.

"That sounds intriguing," Belis said, grinning up at me. I was taller than her now and her face seemed different from above, softer, younger, but it wasn't too late, we could still be as we were.

I drew the vial from my pocket, holding it out to her on the flat of my palm.

"It's from Gwyn ap Nudd."

Belis looked at it then back up at me. She reached out, picking it up between thumb and forefinger so that the blue glass gleamed in the sunlight.

"The fae king?"

"Lord of the Wild Hunt. If you drink it then you'll become one of them. A woman of the high fae."

Belis's eyes widened. "Fae?" There was a little fear in her voice. "Why? Isn't that dangerous?"

"You don't understand. Fae don't age like mortals, they're not bound to a certain lifespan. You could be immortal."

"Like you?"

"Yes." I smiled at her, reaching out to tilt her chin up. "You could live forever, here with me. You wouldn't have to be afraid of the Romans any more. We could still have that farm in the north, we could have a palace, a castle. We could do anything you wanted."

She looked up at me and her eyes were silvery in the grey light. "Horses? Dogs?"

"All you could wish for. We could hunt in the woods. I would still have my work to do but my days would be yours, and as many nights as I could spare." I stroked her cheek, feeling the warm human skin beneath my cool hand. "Do you still want that?"

"Mallt," she pulled my head down and kissed me, soft and sweet, "I don't want anything else." She let go and looked at the glass again. "But what about Cati?"

"I only have enough for one of you, but she could come with us. With us to protect her she could live peacefully in the wilds with us."

Belis turned to gaze back down the hill. "She can't stay in this country. It's not safe. And she would never settle to an isolated life; she thrives on crowds, on company. She's lost everything and everyone in this world but me. I need to find her a community, the chance of a new family."

"The Romans haven't yet passed the Humber. I can take you further north than they'll ever reach. With the dogs, and you, and the help of the low fae, we can keep her protected, even bring her into one of the Pictish villages," I insisted.

"As long as we're on this island she'll be in danger," Belis said, still looking out at the sea. "The Romans know we're alive. If we stay here we'll always be a threat to them. Across the water we'll just be two redheaded girls with a past. The Romans will not advance further than the Rhine, their influence is limited in the north. We have cousins in the tribes that live in the lake country."

I took a breath then nodded. "I understand. Take her there and then come back to me."

Belis looked back at me and I saw the torment in me reflected on her face.

"Come back to me, Belis, don't go!" I cried, my voice cracking with pain, eyes blurring with tears.

"I swore I would stay by her side, that I would spend my whole life making her happy and safe, trying to atone for what I did. More than that, I promised my father when she was born that I would keep her safe, that I would be the oak to shelter her. I cannot break that oath again."

"Then take the vial and guard her as a fae. I'll wait for you." I wiped my face with the back of my hand, fighting for calm.

"This draught," she said, opening her hand, "it's a poison of a different kind. There is more to being fae than never dying. Their nature is different from humans, cruel and inconstant. If I drank this I would no longer be a daughter of the Iceni, would burn away my mortality. Even if I were able to stay true and protect Cati, I would no longer be her sister. I wouldn't be the person you love."

She put her hand in mine and I felt her slip the glass back into my palm. I wanted to argue with her but I knew she was right, had known it even before Gwyn had warned me.

"But that doesn't mean we have to be apart," Belis said, and her voice was urgent now. "Come with us. Leave the world behind and find a new one with me. You were human once, maybe we can find a way to make you human again. We could spend our whole lives together. Come and grow old with me, Mallt."

This time when I kissed Belis I saw her as I would if I said yes. The thousand smiles that would carve lines in our faces, the silver that would thread through our hair. Her hand in mine for however long fate gave us. I knew the value of a mortal life now, of choosing someone to change for and grow with. I no longer wanted the constant eternity of wandering.

Then I saw the wight lurching through the forest, the mangled bodies on the battlefield. Mother and babe so lost in the pain of childbirth they twisted into one terrible being. The peaceful faces of the dead in Annwn, walking back into the lands once blighted by corruption.

"I can't," I said, leaning my forehead against hers. "I have a duty. The people of this island still need a guide. Now that I am myself again I cannot abandon them."

"So you can't come, and I can't stay," she whispered. "If there's a way out of this, oh Mallt, the wise, the beautiful, the great goddess, please tell me for I cannot see it."

I started to reply but no words came out and I pulled her close. We were silent for a moment, just holding each other. I shut my eyes and focused on nothing but the feeling of her in my arms, the smell of her, the taste of her lips.

"Promise me you won't leave it another thousand years to talk to a human," Belis said, pulling away and looking up at me. "Spend time with Arawn, go and visit Vatta. Find other people to love."

"I promise," I said. "And you will, too. Though maybe stay away from any German death gods. They're not all as sweet as me."

She laughed and leaned into me.

"I love you," I murmured, so quietly I wasn't sure she could hear. "If I could have my time over, and I was in that glade again, I'd still reach for you."

There was a whistle and I pulled away, to see Cati, halfway up the hill, waving Belis over. Her face was bright with success.

"She has found passage then," I said, wiping my face with the back of my hand. "This is where I will leave you. Be well, Beliscena, and know that you take my heart with you."

"I'll leave mine with you," Belis said, and her voice cracked and she clung to my hand. "Will I ever see you again?"

I smiled at her, pushing past the pain in my chest.

"Not for a long time. Not 'til your great grandchildren have heard all your war stories, not 'til you have trodden every acre of the land you choose, 'til the sun has set on thirty thousand of your days. Until you have wrung the last drop from this life. Then I will come and find you and carry you home."

Belis looked back at me and I felt what was left of my heart splinter in my chest. She reached up and kissed me one last time, quick and fierce. Then she swung back into the saddle and galloped down the hill, hooves thundering as she went.

I paused for a moment, watching her embrace her sister. Then I turned on my heel. The dogs yipped at me, eager to stretch their legs. The sun was falling below the western horizon. I could feel the souls of the lost out there, waiting for me to guide them. I wiped the last tears from my cheeks, letting the dogs lick the salt from my fingers.

"Come now," I said, "we have a long way to go tonight."

Acknowledgements

Writing this book was hard work and I absolutely could not have done it without the help of a whole raft of brilliant people.

First up are my parents, who have read all my drafts and provided valuable feedback as well as unstinting love and support. Thank you also to my brother Joey – a lifetime of talking about books with you has helped refine my tastes and skills to make me the writer I am today.

Thanks must also go to Ally, for dragging me to the library to work on the book, to Annie, for the brilliant writing sprints (write for fifteen minutes, chat for fifteen, repeat for hours), and to Puva, for being an incredible cheerleader and my perennial coffee companion.

Thank you to my colleagues in the Geotech team, who have put up with my relentless self-promotion in our team meetings and listened to me bang on about edits for months.

I am also deeply grateful to the entire Orbit team, who have been the best publishers an author could ask for. My UK editor Emily Byron is a genius and my US editor Tiana Coven is probably magic!

Thank you to my amazing agent Sam, and to Greyhound Literary Agency in general. I am so lucky to have found such a great rep!

Finally to all the readers who reached out to say they enjoyed my work, you all inspired me to sit back down at my laptop and finish the job. Thanks for the pep talk!

extras

orbit-books.co.uk

about the author

Molly O'Neill was born in the UK and moved to Australia in 2019. She works as a geologist, building roads and rail tracks, and she also runs Book Fair Australia, a literature festival in Sydney.

Find out more about Molly O'Neill and other Orbit authors by registering for the free monthly newsletter at orbit-books.co.uk.

if you enjoyed
NIGHTSHADE AND OAK

look out for

SWORDHEART

by

T. Kingfisher

Halla has unexpectedly inherited the estate of a wealthy uncle. Unfortunately, she is also saddled with money-hungry relatives full of devious plans for how to wrest the inheritance away from her.

While locked in her bedroom, Halla inspects the ancient sword that's been collecting dust on the wall since before she moved in. Out of desperation, she unsheathes it – and suddenly a man appears. His name is Sarkis, he tells her, and he is an immortal warrior trapped in a prison of enchanted steel.

Sarkis is sworn to protect whoever wields the sword, and for Halla – a most unusual wielder – he finds himself fending off not grand armies and deadly assassins but instead everything from kindly-seeming bandits to roving inquisitors to her own in-laws. But as Halla and Sarkis grow closer, they overlook the biggest threat of all – the sword itself.

CHAPTER 1

Halla of Rutger's Howe had just inherited a great deal of money and was therefore spending her evening trying to figure out how to kill herself.

This was not a normal response to inheriting wealth. She was aware of that. Unfortunately, she didn't seem to have many other options. She had been locked in her room for three days and the odds of escape, never good, were growing increasingly slim.

Her relatives were going to be the death of her.

She had always believed that this was true in a metaphorical sense. Her two aunts and her assorted cousins would have tried the patience of a paladin or a saint. It was only in the last two days that she'd realized it was probably true in a literal sense as well.

Halla rested her forehead against the diamond-shaped glass in the window. Uncle Silas had been reasonably wealthy, partly because he never spent a single penny he didn't have to. All the windows were made of many tiny panes, inexpensive to replace if one was broken. He would have used oiled paper if he could have gotten away with it, like the poorest houses in the village, but as he aged, the damp got into his joints. When not even a roaring fire could drive it away, he finally gave up and put glass in the windows.

It was cheap glass, full of bubbles. The reflection it threw back to her was distorted, so she could see only an oval of pale skin, pale hair, and respectably dark mourning clothes.

She wished Silas had spent more on glass and saved less. Or at least had the decency to leave the money to his other family members, and not to her.

The look of shock on Aunt Malva's face when the village clerk had read out the will had been gratifying for an instant. Then the rest of Silas's family had turned to stare at her and it had sunk into Halla's brain that her great-uncle had really and truly left everything to her.

He'd probably thought he was doing her a favor.

Now I have something they want, and they can only get it by going through me.

Married or buried, I suspect it's all the same to them. So long as the marriage comes first.

Cousin Alver had proposed that first evening. She rebuffed him, claiming that she was still much too distraught to think of any such things. The conversation hadn't gone well after that.

"Your husband is long gone," said Aunt Malva, setting her knife down on the table with a click. "You cannot possibly still be in mourning for him!"

Halla narrowed her eyes and set her own fork down. "My great-uncle passed away *yesterday,* madam!"

Aunt Malva flushed. Her skin was whited with powder to an unnatural shade, which matched the whitewash on the walls. It made her flush of anger all the more vivid, coming out in red blotches around her eyes and her ears where the powder hadn't quite gone on correctly.

Great-Uncle Silas had not believed in wasting money on tablecloths, even if it made the kitchen look like a poor crofter's hall, so Malva's hands were very white against the dark wood of the table. She reminded Halla of a ghost or a ghoul.

Mostly a ghoul. Coming along to gnaw the corpse before Silas is even cold.

Hmm, perhaps a ghoul would prefer a warm corpse, now that I think about it. Maybe it's like fresh bread out of the oven, if you're a ghoul.

"Well," said Aunt Malva. "I suppose I am simply surprised that anyone would mourn Silas, that's all."

"Mother," said Cousin Alver quietly.

"I'll speak the truth, Alver! I always do, no matter how it costs me. Silas was a strange, wretched, tightfisted old man, with no proper affection for his kin or clan."

"He is not even in the *ground*," said Halla, abandoning her thoughts about ghoul diet. "And he was very kind to me when I was young."

"And even kinder now that you aren't!"

"Mother."

"In fact—" Malva began, and then a guttural voice interrupted her.

"Into the pit, the pit, the black pit, when the souls scream and the worms coil . . ."

Halla seized on the excuse gratefully and rose to her feet. "You've upset the bird," she said.

The bird in question was a small, finch-like creature that could have perched easily on Halla's smallest finger, had she been foolish enough to stick her finger in its cage, which she wasn't. It had a red beak and red eyes and most of the time it sang a repetitive three-note song that went, "Tweedle-tweedle-twee!" Occasionally, its eyes would flash green and it would begin roaring in an impossibly deep voice about the end of the world and the screams of the damned.

Great-Uncle Silas had been extraordinarily fond of it. Two priests and a paladin had certified that it wasn't possessed by a demon, although they also all said that there was clearly something very wrong with it and had recommended a great deal of fire followed by a great deal of holy water. Silas had instead put it in a cage in the dining room, because he was that sort of person.

"Hush," said Halla, pulling the tray with the bird's food out. It was built so that you never had to put your hand inside the cage. She took a bit of chicken off her plate and put it in the tray, then slid it back in. The bird leapt on it, cackling in a voice like a very old man heard through a drainpipe.

"Nasty creature," said Aunt Malva.

Normally Halla would have agreed with her, but she didn't want to give the woman any satisfaction. "Silas was fond of it," she said.

"Silas was fond of a great many useless things," said Malva, giving her a look that left no doubt who she was referring to.

"If you'll excuse me," said Halla, "I find I have no appetite." She stalked from the room, angry and shaken and secretly relieved that she had a perfectly good excuse to flee from Alver and his mother.

Cousin Alver had caught her on the stairs. She might have felt the smallest twinge of respect for that, except that she had clearly heard, as the door swung shut, Aunt Malva saying, "Well? Go after her!"

You know that she is wrong, but you feel no need to smooth things over unless she orders you to do it.

"Halla," he said from the bottom of the staircase. He curled his hands around the banister. He wore large gold rings set with stones. The servants said he never took them off, not even to bathe or sleep, and Halla knew that the skin around them was always clammy with sweat.

She could imagine, far too easily, those clammy, ringed hands on her skin. Her stomach turned over and she was glad that she hadn't eaten much.

"Halla, my mother doesn't mean the things she says. She just wants what's best for you."

"She means every word," said Halla. "It's just a shock to her that I'm not her nephew's penniless widow any longer."

Cousin Alver gripped the knob at the base of the banister, not looking at her. "You know she's always been fond of you."

"She's got a damned strange way of showing it!"

"Yes, she does." His voice was so dry that for a minute Halla was forced into unwilling sympathy with him. However hard it was to deal with Aunt Malva in small doses, being her son was probably an entirely different circle of hell. Then he destroyed that instant of sympathy by saying, "She'll be better if there are children. She's always been very good with children."

"I have *not* agreed to your proposal!"

"Well." Cousin Alver still didn't meet her eyes. "We'll discuss this tomorrow, when you're less tired."

Halla wanted to be the sort of person who yelled at her cousin and forced him to acknowledge that she had a choice in the matter. Unfortunately, it seemed that she was the sort of person who ran up the stairs to her bedchamber, grateful for the reprieve.

This was a depressing discovery.

But not, I suppose, an unexpected one.

At least I am the sort of person who slams the door. That's worth something.

She collapsed on her bed, the echoes of the slam still ringing through the house.

The money was useless to her. She knew that she would never be allowed to touch it. They would marry her to Alver and take it away so that it stayed in the family and everything would be just as it had been, except worse because Alver was alive and Silas was dead.

Why couldn't it be Alver who was old and had bad lungs? Why couldn't he have died instead?

Well, but if Alver was old then he wouldn't be looking to marry me, and presumably there'd be someone else to fill the Alver-shaped hole in the world, and I'd be right back here except with a different obnoxious person trying to wed me.

Although at least that person might not have clammy hands.

She got up and stared out the window into the dark, thinking about all the ways a woman could die.

Even if her cousins did not actually poison her or push her down the steps, there were many ways to make an unwanted relative's life shorter. Medicines administered for her "health" that left her docile as a milch cow. Wonderworkers whose talents ran to harm.

Childbirth.

Halla shuddered.

Her late husband hadn't awoken any great passions in her, but at least he hadn't made her skin crawl. They had gotten along tolerably well for a few years, until a late spring fever had swept the land and carried him off. His estate had gone to his brother and Halla had found herself nearly penniless after the death duties.

A young widow, she might have remarried if she were wealthy, but there was no market for widows of no particular wealth and no particular beauty. Her mother's family was far too poor to be burdened with another mouth to feed. Her husband's great-uncle, Silas, had taken her in and she had become a middle-aged widow in his house, running the household and seeing that his old age was as comfortable as she could make it.

He had been a strange, erratic, maddening man, but she had always been grateful. He put up with her, and Halla knew that could be difficult.

She knew that he had saved her from the convent, or worse.

There was a click at the door. She knew without turning that someone had bolted the door to her chamber.

It seemed that *worse* had finally caught up with her.

RAISING READERS
Books Build Bright Futures

Dear Reader,

We'd love your attention for one more page to tell you about the crisis in children's reading, and what we can all do.

Studies have shown that reading for fun is the **single biggest predictor of a child's future life chances** – more than family circumstance, parents' educational background or income. It improves academic results, mental health, wealth, communication skills, ambition and happiness.[1]

The number of children reading for fun is in rapid decline. Young people have a lot of competition for their time. In 2024, 1 in 10 children and young people in the UK aged 5 to 18 did not own a single book at home.[2]

Hachette works extensively with schools, libraries and literacy charities, but here are some ways we can all raise more readers:

- Reading to children for just 10 minutes a day makes a difference
- Don't give up if children aren't regular readers – there will be books for them!
- Visit bookshops and libraries to get recommendations
- Encourage them to listen to audiobooks
- Support school libraries
- Give books as gifts

There's a lot more information about how to encourage children to read on our website: **www.RaisingReaders.co.uk**

Thank you for reading.

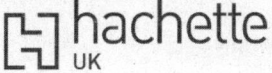

---

[1] OECD, '21st-Century Readers: Developing Literacy Skills in a Digital World', 2021, https://www.oecd.org/en/publications/21st-century-readers_a83d84cb-en.html

[2] National Literacy Trust, 'Book Ownership in 2024', November 2024, https://literacytrust.org.uk/research-services/research-reports/book-ownership-in-2024

Enter the monthly Orbit sweepstakes at www.orbitloot.com

With a different prize every month,
from advance copies of books by
your favourite authors to exclusive
merchandise packs,
**we think you'll find something
you love.**

facebook.com/OrbitBooksUK
@orbitbooks_uk
@OrbitBooks
orbit-books.co.uk